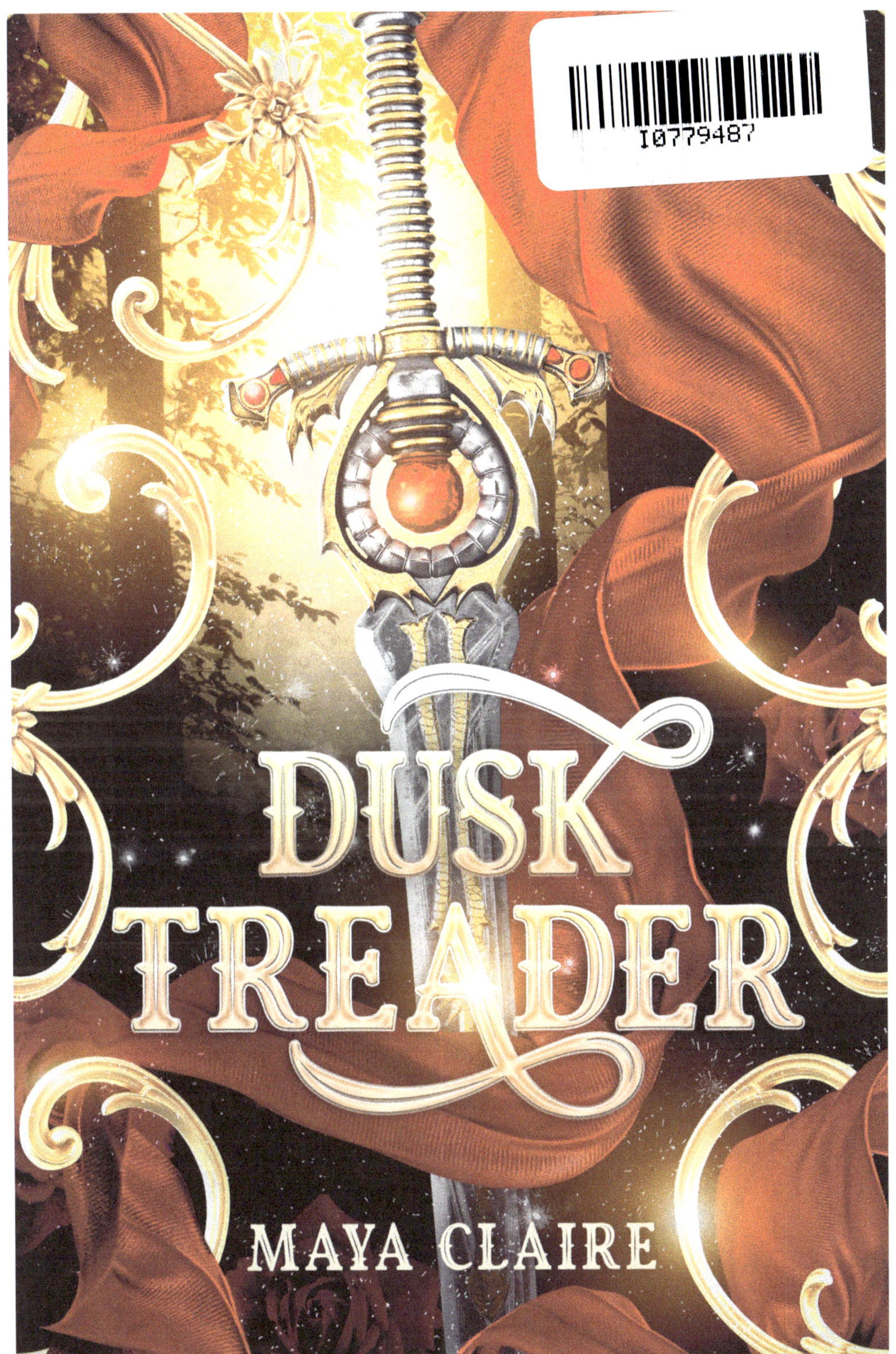

DUSK TREADER
MAYA CLAIRE

DUSKTREADER

MAYA CLAIRE

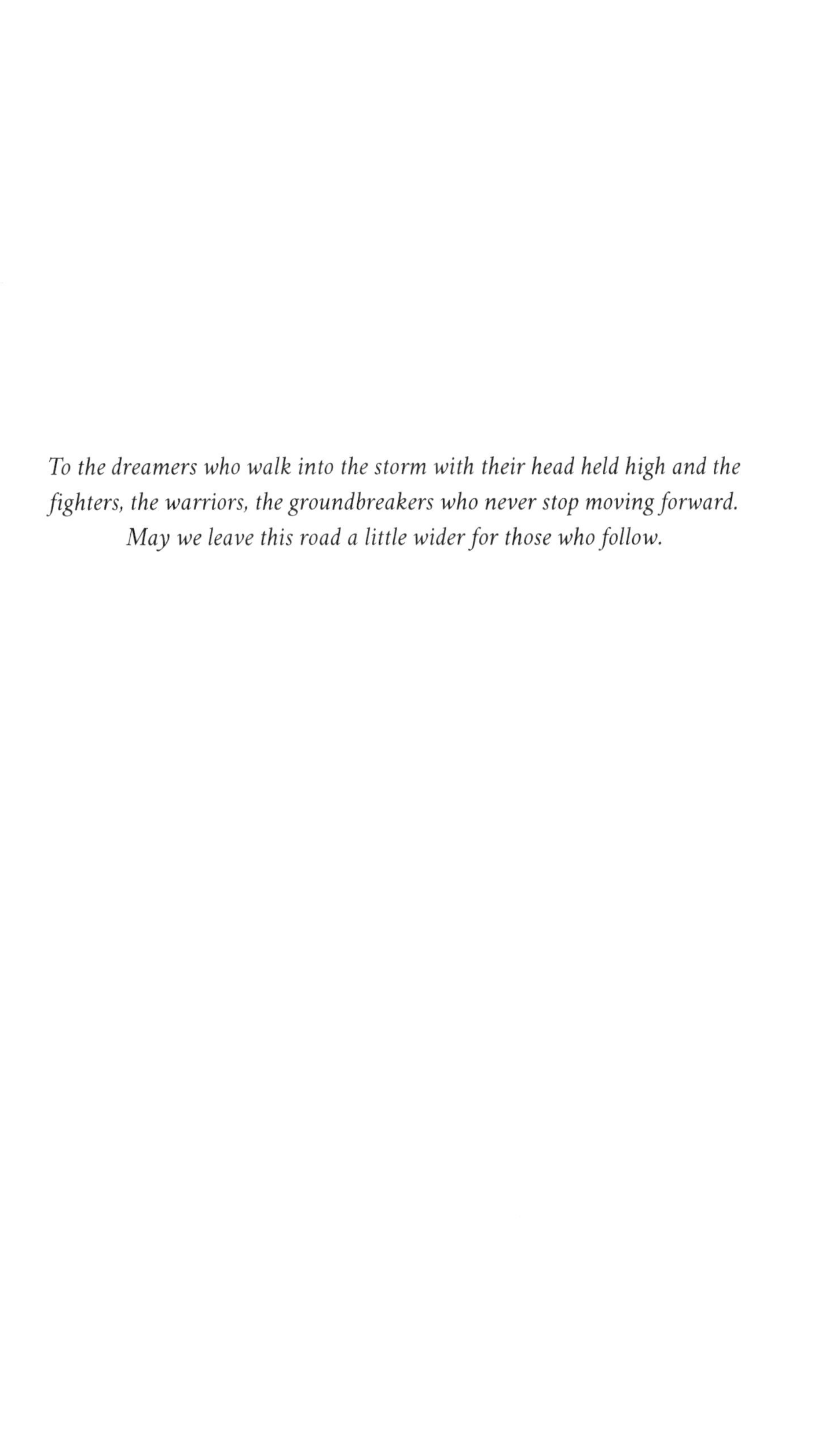

To the dreamers who walk into the storm with their head held high and the fighters, the warriors, the groundbreakers who never stop moving forward. May we leave this road a little wider for those who follow.

VAMPYRE CODEX

Authored 691

I. The darkness shall carry the true nature of the Crimson Court. To reveal that nature is to renounce your claim to it.

II. Thy domain requires respect of all who reside and enter. Thy word is law within thy domain.

III. The right and responsibility to sire rests with both thine elder and lord. To create without their blessing renders life for both you and your progeny forfeit. It is the responsibility of the elder to fulfill punishment.

IV. The right and responsibility of thine sire is thy responsibility. Their actions are a direct reflection on you, their maker. Until they are released, thou shall command them in all parts of this Codex. The sins of the son shall be rectified by the father.

V. Every member of night shall honor each other's domain. Proper respect shall be given on entrance. Without proper acceptance, thou violate tenant II of this codex.

VI. Thou are forbidden to destroy another of thy kind, regardless of their transgression. The right of death and entrance into eternal slumber rests with their elder.

PROLOGUE

*B*ucharest. 1628.

In the dimly lit chamber of an ancient cathedral, a heavy silence hung in the air, disrupted only by the faint flicker of candlelight. The scent of incense lingered, mixing with the subtle hint of decay that accompanied the presence of a member of the royalty of night. At one end of the room Inquisitor Gabriel entered, his dark robes billowing behind him as he clutched a silver cross in one hand and a polished oak staff in the other. His eyes burned with determination, a reflection of the unwavering faith that had guided him through countless battles that had led him here.

Across from him, the vampire he had come to know as Ireena emerged from the darkness behind the pulpit, the shadows moving as if they were a part of her. Her eyes, a mesmerizing shade of crimson, bore an aura of danger that seemed to dance with the anticipation of this deadly encounter. Her alabaster skin contrasted starkly with the thick raven-black hair that cascaded down over her shoulders. As she moved gracefully forward, her fingers lightly brushed the hilt of the wickedly sharp dagger sheathed at her side. Gabriel had seen it before and felt the coolness of its touch on more than one occasion.

"Hello, little *angel*. Do you wish to court death again?" her voice lingered on the air, her words floating through the space.

He had come to know her by many names over the decades of his obsession. Maria. Ireena. The Blood Countess. Murderer. The Dark One. Her disdain infused tone infuriated him. He refused to reply, praying to himself in his head.

The silence stretched; tension hanging heavy as both combatants assessed each other. Then, with a sudden blur of movement, Ireena lunged forward, her fangs glinting ominously as she aimed for Gabriel's throat. But the inquisitor's reflexes were honed by years of battle, and he sidestepped just in time, swinging his staff with precise force. The wood cracked as it made contact with her shoulder, and a hiss of pain escaped her lips as she staggered back.

Gabriel wasted no time, his voice rising in fervent prayer as he channeled divine energy through his staff. The weapon glowed with a radiant light as he swung it in a wide arc, sending a wave of holy energy hurtling towards his opponent. She snarled, her body contorting with unnatural grace as she evaded the onslaught, the magical force singing her hair as it passed by.

Ireena retaliated with a burst of inhuman speed, her movements a blur as she closed the distance between them in an instant. Her dagger sliced through the air, aiming for Gabriel's heart. The inquisitor deflected the blow with his staff while pressing his cross into her arm, the silver burning the vampire's skin upon contact. Ireena recoiled, her features twisting with a mixture of anger and agony.

As the battle raged on, Gabriel's faith and training clashed against Ireena's predatory instincts and supernatural abilities. Each clash of their weapons echoed through the sacred space, a symphony of steel against silver, darkness against light. The stained-glass windows above seemed to pulse with an otherworldly energy as if the very cathedral itself was bearing witness to this clash of forces.

Gabriel's movements grew more fluid, his spells and strikes seamlessly intertwining as he pressed his advantage. His staff became a conduit for divine wrath, unleashing beams of searing light that forced the vampire to retreat further into the shadows. But the vampire was far from defeated, her eyes blazing with a ferocity that matched the flames of the candles around them.

With an unearthly cry, Ireena lunged once more, her fangs bared and her dagger gleaming. But in this moment, Gabriel held the advantage. He swung his staff in a sweeping arc, channeling the power of his faith into a final, devastating blow. A radiant shockwave erupted from the staff, engulfing Ireena in a blinding cascade of light. Her unearthly shriek pierced the air, a wail of anguish as the holy energy consumed her and the stained-glass windows of the cathedral shattered into glistening shards of color.

When the light finally faded, only a smoldering pile of ashes remained where Ireena had once stood. Gabriel stood there, his chest heaving, his robes stuck to his body with sweat, blood gleaming in the remaining candlelight. A victorious smile slowly emerged on his face, the silence of this lifelong holy war settling across the cathedral.

With a final, weary sigh, the inquisitor lowered his staff, his gaze fixed on the remains of his fallen opponent. The battle had been fierce, a test of faith and strength, and as the candles flickered and the incense continued to drift, he kneeled and offered a silent prayer for both the defeated and the victorious. In the silence that followed, the ancient cathedral seemed to breathe a sigh of relief, as if the darkness that had briefly invaded its sanctum had been vanquished by the unwavering light of the faithful.

As the high inquisitor rose to his feet, a searing pain ripped through his chest. His gaze lowered to see the end of a silver blade dripping with his blood. A hand wrapped around his side, and he felt an unfamiliar feeling on his shoulder. A light, whispery voice hung in the air, his eyes locked forward staring at the cross. Father Gabriel finally realized he had been the one to lose in the holy crusade he had been waging for the last forty years. Again.

"Even gods have shadows, little angel. I'll see you next time." Ireena whispered in his ear, twisting the blade in a circle before she smiled, revealing the two glistening fangs that she immediately plunged into his neck.

High Priestess

REFLECTIONS

"Through the annals of my journal, inked with prayers and exorcisms, I recount the nights spent chasing shadows. Vasiliev's ethereal laughter haunts my every step, a melody of malevolence that echoes through time."

Father Gabriel, Reflections on the Midnight Hunt. 1591

CHAPTER 1

I lost count after the first million. It was a weirdly odd number to count to, but it seemed low enough to be attainable yet high enough to give me something to focus on. The all-consuming sadness and frustration were only broken by the betrayal that filled me and this tiny space. Time blended into an abstract concept that just…floated by. It floated in a way so unfamiliar that I never truly understood the impact of isolation. The darkness in this tiny box had become my home.

I curled my fingers around the shell that was left of my phone. The power button had been smoothed to near nothing. Years of pressing it, even though it was long since dead, had left a subtle indentation in the side of it. My eyes slowly opened as I looked at the ivory surface in front of me. Seven feet long, a little over three feet wide. I had counted every inch of it, feeling my hands across the inside of the casket for any way to escape the solitude. Dots of blood still speckled the lace hanging above me from pounding my fists into the lid. For the first year, Hayley had often returned.

"Ellie… are you awake?"

I ignored them. Every year. They knew I was alive; something inside of them could feel it. I was always frustrated by their empathic abilities. I couldn't feel anything from anyone. Maybe it was from being an over-the-top, high-energy extrovert. They would rather spend their Friday nights curled up in the library with a book to read while I spent time out on rooftop bars with the girls.

"Ellie... babe... it's been five years... *please...*"

Silence. I could feel the pain through my entire body, a fragment of feeling that had been left from what they had done to me. It was a constant reminder that the choice to live our dreams had been taken away from me.

I refused to respond.

Hayley knocked three times on the outside of the wooden lid before leaving. It was our secret. I. Love. You. It let us say it to each other as long as we were touching. No matter what kind of stressful situation we were in, just three squeezes or taps and we knew it.

I love you.

* * *

Hayley walked through the mausoleum, adding another painting to the stone wall with a sigh. On a raised platform in the middle of the room sat a long white casket lined with black and rose gold trim. They had been here dozens of times already. First it was every month, then every few, then every year. Now, it had been almost five years since their last visit.

They ran a white cloth across the surface, dusting off the top of a wooden barstool that sat next to the casket, and slowly knocked three times. Their legs curled up on the upper rung of the wooden stool, hugging their arms tightly around them while waiting in silence for any kind of response. Minutes blurred into hours, and they never moved from beside the casket.

A buzz rung out from their jacket, a timer letting them know when the sun would be up.

Hayley stepped from the barstool, tapping her knuckles against the casket again.

"I still love you."

Their shoulders slumped as they shuffled to the door, taking one final look at their wife's resting place.

* * *

A SIGH ESCAPED MY DRY, cracked lips. I would have cried again if I had anything left to give.

I couldn't remember the last time Hayley had knocked on the casket. My body felt weaker than it had ever been. The remaining skin and muscle stretched tightly to my bones, my organs shriveling up into my core. I refused to take the drink.

That's all I had to do. One sip and I would join them in an eternity of night. There was a crystal vial under the pillow I had been laid on, waiting for me to 'come around'. I had ripped a hole in the satin fabric on top of the casket lid and slid it in there so that I could get some decent sleep.

And not accidentally break it.

Could I do it? Never. I was still so angry. There was a tempest of rage and sadness that suffocated me in the darkness of the coffin.

"Seven hundred forty-one thousand eight ninety."

I had done this seventy-six times now. I would usually only make it through one or two runs before Hayley knocked on the outside of the casket. I didn't even know if it was actually well decorated, but I did know Hayley and they would never put me in a dirty old box.

"Seven hundred forty-one thousand eight ninety-one" I said to myself, trying to focus just on the numbers. That's all I had to do. One number at a time. When I closed my eyes, I would see our last moments over and over again.

"I promise, you will come around."

* * *

WAS THIS REALLY THEM? Maybe they had always been this way and I was so stupidly in love I never figured it out. I didn't know why the panic made me run. I slammed our apartment door in their face and took off down the hall.

There were stairs right next to my condo door, but I sprinted towards the elevator out of habit. The elevator had to still be on my floor.

Was I about to die?

Before I could hit the down button, Hayley pressed into me from behind, my head slamming so hard that it left a dent on the elevator door. I couldn't figure out which pain was worse, their hand pressing my head into the cold metal door, or the liquid heat snaking like an unrestrained wildfire through my neck as they sunk their teeth into me. I already had nearly zero pain tolerance, and they knew that. I didn't even realize I had hit the up arrow on the elevator.

Why would I have ever thought I could outrun them. I had watched enough horror movies to know how this sort of thing ends.

Ding.

The elevator door slowly opened in front of me, and I staggered into it, trying to hold onto the wound in my neck as best I could. I fell into the back of the elevator, my slippers sliding through the trail of blood that I had left behind me. The pain had moved through my entire body, eating away every bit of energy that I had left.

The lights flickered around me, my body cowering in the corner of the small metal box. I must have had betrayal written across my face as I stared up at Hayley. Their gaze held no maliciousness, only love. I watched the door slowly close before my eyes slipped shut.

"One day love, one day soon. I'll wait for you."

HOW SOON WAS NOW? I brought my focus back to the numbers. Each number was in my head. So close. Three quarters of the way to finish this million. How many days had it been? My math was rusty and adding in the time that it took me to count each of the numbers, I lost track after a few years. It was disorienting, to say the least. I flexed my ankles and pointed my toes, stretching my feet to the end of the coffin. It felt nice to feel the tightness leave my hamstrings for a moment, the muscles weak and tight with atrophy. Everything was numb. The feeling shifted between pins and needles and being consumed by fire.

Thud.

I rolled over on the pillow, curling in on myself as much as I could. I wasn't going to answer anyway, but at least laying on my side I knew I was giving them the cold shoulder.

Thud.

I waited for the third knock in disappointment. Really? They didn't even love me anymore? While I hated the situation, and even being here in the first place the thought of those three knocks still made me feel warm inside. A simple sign that after all these years they still loved me. That was the silver lining in this absolutely shit situation. No matter how betrayed I felt, or how much I refused to accept it or speak to them I was unable to forget the love we shared.

It was still there, and it was the only thing that kept me from losing myself in the cold darkness of despair. I clung to it.

"Careful man, careful! We have to get this delivered to its new home in one piece." The voice sounded raspy. Older. Unfamiliar.

"I've never seen Mira—"

The second voice was even harder to hear. What were they saying? The two were arguing about something but I couldn't quite make it out. They were muffled through the casket and the sound of a male voice snapped me out of my counting. I couldn't remember the last time I had heard a voice other than Hayley's.

"The north side is being leveled Monday and we're behind schedule. Stop dicking around and get this thing moved you two. That *thing* paid us good in advance to get this delivery done, don't fuck it up."

A third voice? What were they doing? The box jerked to the side before abruptly moving forward. My head slammed into the back of the casket, the impact making me cringe. It didn't matter how much pretty cushioning was there, that hurt. I wanted to yell back, to tell them that there was someone in here, but nothing worked. What was left of my vocal cords had dried up, leaving me unable to make a sound.

I used what energy I could to brace my arms against the sides of the coffin. Maybe they could open it up and get me out of here, I thought to myself.

"I SAID CAREFUL!!"

There was a moment of weightlessness, my body floating up off the stiff decaying foam as my head crashed into the lid of the coffin. The sound of glass shattering filled the small space, like someone had dropped a vase in a quiet room. A thick liquid poured out across my face, and specks of glass fell across the pillow and through my hair. I brought my hand up to my face where there were now cuts and little pieces of glass.

The vial had broken.

Things had gone from bad to worse. The taste of it hit my lips first, then the smell of it. A searing pain ignited its way through my body from the inside out almost instantly. The dripping continued and each one of them sent a contraction from my head to my toes. There was a sharp pain across the roof of my mouth and jaw, and I knew what that meant. The hunger was nearly instant. Fresh, primal. This day I had avoided for what felt like centuries.

I was starving.

I bit the soaked fabric, sucking what little of the blood that I could out of it. For the first time since being in here, I could see the entire coffin. The strain on my eyes slowly turned to numbness, and then faded away altogether. The darkness didn't feel foreign to me anymore. The isolation and loneliness weren't so bad with this new sight.

What was left of my muscles seized before they finally died. Every system throughout my body was dying, convulsing in the darkness. My eyes closed in pain, and for once I screamed, emptying my lungs, my entire body of every ounce of fear, anger, and frustration I held inside of me.

I refused to say anything before. The scream was years of pain and agony. It was filled with all of the betrayal and heartbreak that I had in me.

It only took a moment for death to consume me. I curled as best I could in the small space while my body tried to convulse one final time. My heartbeat slowed, and finally, stopped. I took my final mortal breath and moments later, my heart began to faintly beat once again.

Blood surged through my body, accompanied by the popping of joints, and strengthening of bones. For a moment, emotions warred within me. It was the joy of feeling alive again fighting against the heartbreak of being turned.

I planted my hands on the casket lid. Effortless is the only word to describe the newfound strength that moved across my muscles as I pressed it open for the first time.

One moment, I was submerged in the darkness, and the next, I was jolted into awareness by an avalanche of unfamiliar sounds. The rumbling of heavy machinery, the echoes of voices, and the clattering of tools filled my ears.

Panic surged within me as I realized that the silence that had cocooned me for so long had been shattered. I blinked away the disorienting haze of my prolonged slumber. The room I beheld was a whirlwind of color and ambient light, a swaying chandelier casting faint rays of light down upon my resting place. New smells were carried in the air, including the scent of dust, the mustiness of ancient stone, and something new—the foreign scent that could be nothing but human.

The cold winter air brushed against my skin. So cold and biting in a way I had never felt before. My chest and back expanded, shoulders relaxing with the first big inhale I had taken in years. With every breath, the hunger in me grew, their scent slowly driving a madness I had never felt before. Every heartbeat was like a giant subwoofer in my ears. It absorbed my senses, and the guttural feeling of starvation took over.

Then I heard it, my stomach.

Growling. Starving. All consuming.

It was the only thing that mattered.

It took little effort to finish sliding off the heavy lid that had encased me for so long. The realization of my own resurrection was buried beneath the hunger that took over. I could hear men outside yelling furiously about me, about some monster in the mausoleum.

With one final push, I lifted my body into a world that I was unfamiliar with. I found myself in a breathtaking mausoleum, its marble walls adorned with intricate carvings and ornate paintings. The room was aglow with that soft, warm light that reflected off every glistening surface. I leapt forward towards the door as a man entered from outside. The feeling was akin to floating through the air as I covered the ten feet between us. I had no idea how much additional strength my body would have gained from that little bit of blood, and I didn't care.

There were so many questions I needed to ask, but every one of them was shoved aside by the growling cramps across my mid-section. I could feel it coursing through my veins, and I knew that if I didn't get a taste of him right this second, I would lose control completely. His heartbeat, his scent, his entire presence had my mouth watering. I had to have him right now.

A moment of tightness knotted itself in my stomach. Was I about to take a bite out of this person? Was this the right thing to do? Was there any going back to my old life? I tried to hold down the nausea and ignore the pain that was still coursing through my body. I had to eat. I needed it.

No. I *wanted* it.

A sharp ache crossed my jaw, the fangs extending to their full length. How did my body know what to do? Was it an extra instinct I had gained? I couldn't think fast enough before my body reacted on its own.

His first scream, from the pain of me driving those two fangs into his neck, is something I'll never forget. Not because it was right in my ear, but because of the guttural fear that was carried with it. Was I even doing it right? For a split second, I stopped thinking and closed my eyes, giving into the hunger. His heartbeat was like music, and every pump it made was slower than the last. I could barely process what was happening as my mouth filled with warm blood.

I ripped skin from his neck and sank my fangs into the other side of him before we hit the ground. The sensation was like nothing I'd ever experienced before, and for a moment all of my other senses were blocked out except for the taste of his blood on my tongue. I shifted my body and released him, driving my fangs into the other side of his neck, then the shoulder area right below them.

Each drop of warm blood that entered my mouth felt like I had just found water for the first time. I gorged myself on him, letting that basic instinct for survival take over. I dug my fingers into him, holding him in place. I couldn't let go, couldn't bring myself to stop the hunger. Had I seen his skin turning pale and withering as I drained him of almost every drop of blood, I would have screamed. Did I think about the fact that other people saw me and ran away? Were they going to go get help? Right now, I couldn't care less. The only thing that mattered was the raging hunger in my core crying out for more.

I pulled my head away from him and looked down. There was blood everywhere. The vivid red dripping down both of us was a stark contrast to the dull grey stones that surrounded us. I always was a messy eater.

I didn't bother to finish him and dove at the next man who approached. It didn't matter to me what he was doing, or if he was trying to help my first victim. All I could hear was the heavy pounding of their heartbeats drowning out everything else. So many of them echoing this hunger that wasn't satiated. The first bit of power surged through me as I sucked from one after another, barely noticing the screams of horror in my wake.

A sharp pain moved through my eyes, and when I opened them the world around me felt different. There were thin lines of blue and red under his skin that I could now see. I stared into the man's safety glasses, watching as my eyes shifted into bright crimson for the first time, a complete awakening into my new self. My eyes ached, and after blinking a few times my vision shifted. It was the same, but... different. I could see even more lines of blue across his neck, like his skin was transparent.

A hand gripped my shoulder, and I finally came to a halt, taking a deep breath. I released my grip, looking down at the man who was under me. His eyes reflected terror and a pain that made me take pause.

Suddenly my head cleared and reality set in. I had just attacked innocent people out of a primal need for blood. Horrified, I scrambled across the dirt and crawled away from him, not knowing what to say or do next. He reached out, blood still pumping out from his shoulder. I had bit him multiple times all over his upper body. Wherever I could find skin, I had torn and ripped at him. At all of them.

Just like an animal.

I brought my hands up to my face, looking at the blood that coated them, my face, and my clothes. There was a half dozen bodies lying strewn about the ground outside of the mausoleum, pools of blood soaking the dirt around them. Parts of the cemetery were lit by the construction lights, allowing me to see the damage I had caused.

"Hello? Any...anyone... please be alive...." I called out, my voice hoarse. I moved from body to body, feeling a tightness cross my chest as I surveyed the damage. I could barely remember anything after I bit into the first one.

The smell of death lingered in the air, an acrid mix of copper and decay that made my eyes water. My lungs felt like they were in overdrive right now and the thick taste of iron in my mouth made me vomit into the flower bed next to the mausoleum stairs. I wiped my chin with the back of my hand, the acidic bile coating my skin as I surveyed the carnage around me.

The bodies lay strewn about like discarded dolls, their eyes wide open and frozen in shock forever. I stumbled away from the dead, tears streaming down my face as I tried to make sense of what had just happened. How had this all gone so wrong? Was this what Hayley had felt? Is this what they were trying to share with me?

"Someone...anyone... please..."

I choked on the crisp air that entered my lungs, my gaze scanning the entirety of the mausoleum, and across the beautiful cemetery grounds. I had never actually seen it, and now that the hunger had subsided, the architecture seemed beautiful. At least it would have been had I not been standing in the middle of a self-made horror film.

The old dress was the same one I had worn when I had come home from the bar. I could see my final moments all over again. The late-night party out and celebrating with friends. Waiting for my wife to join me but never showing up. My body stopped, and I remembered it all.

They never showed up.

They abandoned me. Bit me and left me here.

This was not my fault.

The cold air was just like it was that night on the roof. There weren't any hanging lights or a live band here, but the air stung my face the same way. The air now smelled of death, that scent an embrace of the night that was so illicit, so wrong, that it clouded everything else I was feeling. I took a long inhale through my nose, trying to calm myself down, but the smell of blood and vomit was unbearable. There was a foulness to it, and when mixed by the wind, well, it was the kind of scent that would make any normal person hurl.

My heartbeat was faint, but still very much there. I looked at my hands, watching the color slowly come back into them between the blotches of drying blood. They were paler than I remember. I tried rubbing them together, but they felt strangely cold.

Just like Hayley's had *that* night.

My stomach turned over on itself, and I could feel another wave of pain and muscle spasms run their way down my body. My stomach was in a foul mood, filled with so much hunger that I couldn't think of anything else. I was blinded by the pain, but even more so by the slowly returning hunger. Even after eating so much, all I could think about was that.

I returned to the inside of the beautiful stone structure where I had spent so many years. Before I could make it across the threshold, I clutched the side of the doorway and vomited across the marble floor. The white speckled surface was now smeared with more blood. Their blood. The thought of what I had just done made me want to throw up again, and I struggled to fight it. Each of their heartbeats had been a sirens song that called out to me. I ran my hand through my hair, grabbing at the long dirty locks while wishing I could rip it all off.

"Fuck." I said as I looked down at my clothes, falling to my knees before I rolled over on the cold ground. I had to fight the urge to not throw up anything that was currently left in me. Scratch that.

The sight of so much blood made me turn away. I was barely able to grab the sides of my casket before I dry heaved bits of blood all over the interior, the pale off-white satin now splattered with remaining contents of my stomach. Dizziness hit me and I fell backwards, smacking my head on the top step of the mausoleum where I could see the cloudy night sky. There were no hopes of ever salvaging the faded dress I was wearing.

I looked over at the closest to me, almost afraid to see what damage I had done. Thick, dark blood had started to congeal on the side of his neck. In the dim light, it almost did not look like blood at all. My biggest problem was that it was everywhere.

All over him. All over Me. Everywhere.

I struggled to my feet while holding down the nausea. I told myself that I had to do something in here. I picked his body up and dumped it in the casket that I had spent so much time in.

I was still so mad because this choice had been made against my will. I lifted the dead cell phone from the side of the pillow and slid it into the tiny pocket on the side of my dress. I remember the last voicemail Hayley had left me. It was the only thing that kept my head above water, despite my anger. I had played it over and over for the first few weeks that I had been entombed there. The battery had long since died, but I never forgot it.

Where was I? I gazed across the cemetery surrounding the small mausoleum. All I could do now was figure things out one piece at a time. Important questions. What year was it, really. What month. Time? Obviously after dark. That didn't mean much unless the rumors about sunlight true. And where was Hayley? I walked back into the mausoleum and pulled the casket up onto the stone platform where it originally sat, closing the lid. Hopefully, no one would notice any of this.

Like I could be so lucky.

A wild laugh escaped me, what did I do in a past life for this to happen. I always considered myself lucky, but that luck had to have run out a long time ago for this to happen. I finally took a moment to look around the inside of the mausoleum. The chamber was now hushed and dim, its walls adorned with beautifully intricate artworks. The pieces were like fragments of their soul, each one a masterpiece that bore the mark of love and longing. My wife's creative spirit had transcended the boundaries of time and had left me a road to follow.

I gazed upon the works of art, tears glistening in my crimson eyes, as the centuries of longing and solitude washed over me. There were paintings depicting our moments together, each stroke of that brush a whisper of our shared memories. In one, we danced under the moonlight, a moment of grace and romance preserved on canvas. In another, we stood hand in hand, walking through a park with the sunrise behind us.

The art reflected our love. While the colors were starting to fade, the emotions were tangible, and the beauty of their creations resonated in every brushstroke. In their absence, that had left each piece of this art as a beacon of hope, a reminder that I was not alone, that I was not forgotten.

As I continued to gaze at these lightly faded works, I could almost hear their voice, feel the ghost of their presence across the cold stone room as I moved throughout it. It was as though Hayley was speaking to me through their art, whispering words of love and reassurance.

Telling me it would be okay.

Part of me wanted that love. The other part of me was standing here covered in blood. I halted, looking at one piece that had someone I didn't recognize, a portrait of a woman in black with bright red eyes. I couldn't quite place it, but there was a familiarity there. Seated next to her, was Hayley. The tears that had welled up in my eyes again began to fall, each one carrying a long-forgotten memory from before.

I wiped the warm tears from my cheeks, my body stiffening at the discovery that they too were also blood. I quickly wiped it across my dress, adding it to the streaks that already covered it.

"One breath at a time." I said to myself, taking in all of the blood drying around me in the mausoleum, my stomach still growling. As I stepped out onto the large granite slab that made up the entryway, I turned to look at the building I had spent so much time in. There were twisted vines carved into the black stone that made up the pillars. I looked closer, noticing tiny sparkles of glitter in the surface of the walls, and I smiled at the shimmer. I knew Hayley wouldn't dump me in an ugly old box. Taking a step back, I looked up at the area above the door where an inscription was chiseled into the stonework.

Mors Tibi Nunquam Obstet

"What?" I said curiously to the stone, as if waiting for it to respond. This had to be a message from Hayley. I had no idea what it meant though. I put my hands behind my head and stood there, trying to figure out what it could be. Frustrated at it, I turned around and started walking away, upset that I couldn't remember anything from the single Latin class I had taken centuries ago.

The path to the main gravel driveway twisted and turned, parts of it lined with construction equipment, some of them still humming loudly. There were other buildings here, all of them with their thick stone doors open. Were they moving everyone? Curious. Maybe someone bought this property. That was all the rage for the rich back then. Purchase land and remove everything on it, or almost everything in the case of cemeteries, then build overpriced homes on them.

One foot in front of the other. I was slowly getting the feeling back across most my body but there were still a few places that had an unfortunate pins and needles feeling. The moon was a beautiful shade of dull yellow tonight and looked to be a few nights past its full cycle. My eyes stayed glued on it for several minutes while I took in her beauty once again. I had missed the Goddess looking down upon me.

Inhale and pause. Exhale and pause. My breathing became steady. Keeping calm in an emergency was always a challenge for me. Things would pick up and my head would run a million miles a minute while I tried to figure out every outcome possible, and that would usually leave me standing there taking no action. Analysis Paralysis, Hayley had called it.

"Just like they taught you. One breath at a time." I whispered softly to myself as I came to a stop.

I had a habit of panicking. I never accepted that I might have high functioning anxiety until we had moved in together. Hayley opened an entire new world to me, one where I could find the root of human issues and really understand both myself and those around me. That work sucked. Really. It was hard work. But it allowed me an extra set of tools. Those tools for self-examination rolled right into my professional life and I was a much better leader in the board room because of it.

These tools, however, were completely useless to a starving vampire who had never fed before. My body plopped on the first memorial bench I could find while looking up at open sky. I could feel the wind moving across my skin, but there wasn't really a true 'feeling' of it. It was there, but it didn't really bother me at all.

My arms went out to the side, and I took a deep, full breath while exhaling as slow as possible. It was time for me to get a move on. The road twisted into a circle around a leaf filled fountain adorned with what was most likely a pristine statue. I was honestly surprised to see a traffic circle at all. What an inefficient way to design a road. It was definitely something I didn't miss. I stopped to look at the old stonework with a chuckle. A towering statue of a long dead guy who served in the War of the Father. There was something morbidly beautiful about its granite being rounded down with time. I couldn't put my finger on it. There was probably some sort of artsy term or something for it. I took a few steps past it and stopped, turning around to walk back to the statue.

"War of the Father..." I said quietly to myself. What was that? I had expected it to say Vietnam, or Civil War. You know, those kinds of things. I leaned to the side, looking off into the distance to see if there were any other statues around. Memorials were always an interesting reflection of history, and I had a strange feeling I may have been asleep for most of it. I moved carefully around the statue with curiosity after noticing there were words alongside it, etched into an old set of greenish copper panels that had corroded over time.

I felt an undeniable aura of antiquity emanating from it. My fingers traced the chiseled details of a figure's etched face, and I couldn't help but feel a sense of connection with this long-lost relic of the past. His visage held the essence of a devout, resolute man, the kind that would judge you one moment and offer you a cold drink with the next.

A faced capable of violence, of betrayal.

Carved beneath the statue, the copper panels turned out to be a series of faded inscriptions that narrated a tale that sent shivers down my spine—the "War of the Father." It was a story of fervent belief, conflict, and a dark period in the history of both human and vampire kind.

The inscriptions described how the faithful followers of the some God had waged a relentless crusade against vampires, whom they believed to be unholy abominations. The believers, emboldened by their religious fervor and the leadership of an enigmatic figure known as the "Father," had hunted down their kind, seeking to purge the world of that unholy presence.

As I continued to read the text, I learned of the battles, the burning of vampire nests, and the immense hatred that had engulfed the world during that dark time. The statue itself represented the resolve of the Father and his followers to eradicate the vampire scourge from the Earth.

"Surprise, Surprise." I said sarcastically into the night.

It was disconcerting to see the perspective of humans who had once viewed anything not humankind as an evil that needed to be eradicated. I couldn't help but ponder how, even after centuries, vampire existence was still shrouded in secrecy. It made me wonder if all of those stories about stakes through the heart and garlic were true.

The story of the War of the Father was a stark reminder of the adversities vampires had faced throughout history, the price they had paid for their immortal existence. The price that someone, long ago had paid. I wondered if Hayley was even still alive, or if she had become a casualty of that war. Was that why she had stopped coming to see me? I came to a stop after finishing a full circle around the statue.

I would tear that ugly thing down and bury it the first chance I had. A moonlit shadow fell behind it, and I wondered if anyone would miss him now that he was long since gone.

"Sigh."

There was a road that led through the gravestone dotted fields toward a giant gate. The doors were swinging with the wind and connected to a long stone wall about waist high. Everything was covered in freshly fallen leaves and the trees appeared to be void of leaf still perched atop their wooden branches. Fall was always one of my favorite times of year. Something about pumpkin spice and cinnamon smells always made me feel warm and safe. I had probably only missed it by a week or two.

"*Finnalllllllly*, a way out. Let's go feet." I mumbled sarcastically to myself. Where would I go from here? The gate looked bent, as if a vehicle had slammed into it. Oh, those workers. It was probably safe to assume that they didn't open the gate on their way out. I tucked my hands into my dress pockets, remembering how happy it made me that this dress had them to start with, and strolled through the gate.

Before I could get too far, I came to a halt. What was next for me? I turned around, looking at the cemetery entrance. It was a beautifully twisted iron melded into a floral archway with withered vines climbing up the stonework. After all of this time, I could have considered this my temporary home for most of my life. Standing there in thought, I brought my gaze up to the gate where a word was carefully laid into the ironwork.

"Hallowgate? Where the fuck did you drop me, love..." I tried to remember where I had heard that name before. Well. now I was lost. Where was I? A green sign with white text hung at the entrance. 2nd Dimlocke Street. Left or right. Which way? Where's a coin when you

need it. If I remembered anything from playing dungeons and drag-
ons, there's almost always danger the right way, so I turned and
started walking left. There were not any cars on the road, so I figured
it was either super early, or super late. Maybe it was mid-week? Wait.
How many years was had it been? Were cars still a thing? If there
weren't flying cars at this point, I was going to be greatly disappointed.

The real question was obvious. How long had I been locked in
there? I had a count. I had counted to a million almost two thousand
times. That didn't include the number of times I forgot where I was,
or Hayley knocked. It means that every year, the day would change by
one. Every four would do a double take. October nineteenth was a
Friday. Seven years equals an eight-day change. One hundred sixty-
eight thousand days. It's a Sunday night. Maybe. How long had I even
been out before I woke up in there? I needed a whiteboard to math it
out, or a cell phone to tell me the answer. My body stopped again, and
I drug my hands down my face.

I could scream all over again, and not stop. Hesitation hit me, and I
wanted to go back to the cemetery. Go back to where they might
come to find me. Back to safety. I only made it a few steps before I
stopped again, feeling the side of my face. There was a thin stream of
fresh tears there again. I could feel them, one at a time coming out. I
wiped them away, only to see the streaks of blood across my fingertips. Guess I can't even hide my tears anymore. What a pain in the ass.
So far, so good. Just thinking about them made me cry. I guess I was
still as emotional as ever. I drew a full, deep breath into my body and
held it for a moment before pushing the air out.

"Alright fate, you can fuck right off with the curveballs and stay
away from me."

I hopped onto the main road, taking in the cool air with every step
I took. Anyone that saw me would probably believe I was nuts. I had
to keep talking to myself just to hear something else. The road kept
going straight, and the familiar glow of streetlamps began to pop up
every few hundred feet. There wasn't a street sign for it, but I had a
strange feeling that something here looked at least a bit familiar.

"Just keep walking", I said to myself with as much fake enthusiasm as I could muster. Thank the goddess I had a comfortable pair of-

Snap.

The side of my left Birkenstock snapped off and I tripped, sliding through the mud. *Are you fucking kidding me?* The cold mud slid between my toes, a quick reminder of one of the absolute ickiest feelings in the world.

My body became stiff, and I bit down on my tongue while trying not to scream in frustration. My arms tightened to my body, my fingers curling into fists before I ripped the sandal off and threw it into the bushes across the road. The right one met a similar fate, and I stomped off up the road, cold and barefoot.

Death
@Victoria Blotta

REFLECTIONS

"As I tread the thin line between salvation and damnation, the vampire duchess eludes me like a wraith in the night. Each sunset marks another day of relentless pursuit, a prayer echoing in the abyss."
Father Gabriel, Request for field extension
Vatican Approved 1624

CHAPTER 2

*H*ow did I get here? It was late at night on whatever day it was, and here I was walking barefoot up what looked like a main road in the dark. Occasionally a car would pass, slowing down only for a moment before hitting the gas and blowing by me. Maybe they thought I was a druggie? Or a hallucination? Homeless? Any of them made me chuckle to myself. The truth was always crazier than the assumption. I had almost forgot I was wearing an old dress covered in blood.

The road was rough. I had to have walked for half an hour before I came to the first intersection that had a light. Briar street. There were remnants of a half-rusted street sign dangling from a single chain across the intersection. Each breath I took left me looking through a small wisp of pale air. Inhale. Pause. Exhale. Pause again. The only sound I could hear over my own internal monologue of frustration was my stomach still growling. A few minutes passed, and the trees subsided into suburbs. Lines of row homes speckled with Halloween directions rose above the river of black stone. There were cars, albeit a bit strange looking in comparison to what I remember, parked in neat rows along the roads edge. At least the Ford logo looked the same. I wonder how many more bailouts the auto industry had claimed over the years.

There were boards on some of the buildings covering the dilapidated windows. This area looked more familiar. Was I in South Lancaster? The south side of Briar Street, an area which I had always avoided, sat before me like an open maw, reminding me of the memories and warnings to never venture there. Apparently, it was the bad part of town, and I was explicitly prohibited from ever parking down here unless I wanted my car to be missing its wheels.

"Breath Ellie. Breathe. It's only a few blocks." Even here, I whispered to myself as lightly as possible as if hiding from someone who wasn't really there. My head tilted back, exposing my pale white chest and neck to the nights air. There was little left to the imagination about what was under it. The tingle of it felt absolutely refreshing, and even though the moon wasn't at its peak she was still beautiful to take in. A few moments passed while my gaze stayed fixated on the moonlight.

"Goddess Protect me, please." I whispered to myself before taking my first step forward. There were barely any streetlights lit, and the ones that were cast a soft-yellow light across the cars parked below. Some of them looked to be modified, sitting way above where any normal car should ever be and others had patches of rush that had eaten through their body. I always thought trucks looked like clown cars, and the few that I managed to see reinforced that belief. Two blocks in and my luck had run out.

A pair of connected porches stood above the right side of the street with a couple of guys hanging out getting high. Looked like dudes doing dude things or something. I could smell the bitterness of what they were smoking from here. That particular scent carried memories I had tucked away from college and using it to get through my doctorate. That entire dissertation should have been sponsored by the drug. The flavor of it after my overdose, however, ruined the experience for me forever. I would never forget the night in the ER with a tube down my throat.

I thought back to those days, wondering if even my college was still around. I recalled hanging out in the lab on late nights with other graduate assistants and drinking cocktails themed around nerdy movies. Every one of them had probably died far before me. I kept walking forward, step by step lost in my thoughts.

One of them called out to me, I think. It was hard to tell while reminiscing about what was going on. It was such a strange feeling, and I knew that I wasn't paying attention. I kept my eyes forward and kept walking. My body came to a halt when a body appeared in front of me.

"You deaf or something?" his voice sounded a little more irritated. Of course, I was going to ignore him and keep walking. Why would I take the risk to end up dead? Wait... wasn't I already dead? I hadn't caught him hopping off the porch and walking towards the street as I tried to move faster. The road was covered in broken glass and tiny gravel, providing me with the most wonderful of inconveniences while I tried to speed up. I didn't make it far before his friends had joined him in the street.

His bleach washed bangs dangled across his forehead, swooped to the side like a jersey shore bro. One of my least favorite kinds of people, I could smell the pretentiousness of his friends before they finished walking down the sidewalk. He wore a bright red and silver hoodie with a familiar swoosh across the front.

"I was talking to you. What are you doing down here?" His body stopped at the edge of the sidewalk. I lifted my chin, finally taking in his eyes. They were bright, lacking that glazed red that a human would have while smoking. His eyes widened as he looked me up and down. "Hooooooly shit girl... are you one of us?"

"What are you?" I asked as I took an instinctive step back, and away from him. He smiled, lifting his chin with a smirk before stepping forward towards me. The last of them joined us, gliding right down the cracked stone steps. Another body landed a yard from me, his grin curving up into one of those smiles that just made him look punchable. Scratch that, his face was definitely punchable.

"One of these," his mouth opened, revealing a set of glistening white fangs. "You must be one of us to be out here dressed like that.

Please tell me you didn't just leave a flesh bag laying somewhere. Are you on Drizz?"

Drizz? What the hell was this guy talking about. I stared blanky at him while he moved his hands in front of my face. His gaze went completely down my body again. It couldn't tell if he was curious or was insultingly degrading by the way he looked at me. It was almost like he had the authority and privilege to do so. I felt bare, almost violated by it. Parts of my dress were ripped from the men tearing at it, and other parts were caked with dried blood...

"Hey guys, time to come clean! Which one of you pricks left a newborn running around?" He glared back behind him, looking frustrated at the guys on the porch. "You all *know* the rules, we aren't allowed to make new ones."

I forgot he was standing in front of me and looked to the porch. There were only six of them, wasn't that bad of odds to run from. If I took off, I should be able to get away. They were mostly high anyway, I doubted whether they could catch up to me or not. Then again, I had no shoes on. I wondered for a moment how their bodies processed drugs, if at all.

My attention snapped back to him when I felt his fingers on my shoulder. He looked me up and down as the others join him.

"What year is it" Cold. Direct. Give him no room to take the high ground here. He touched me first; I was in the right here. My body never had the chance to enter fight or flight with the bottom of my feet messed up from the barefoot stroll I just did.

"The fuck did you come from? Who's your maker?" He lowered his arm, looking at me, then angrily at the others. "Which one of you asshats made a newborn. Seriously. You know the rules."

He pointed to the porch where the others had stood. "Did one of these guys turn you?"

I looked him up and down, barely able to hear any of their heartbeats. They were so faint they were barely even noticeable. His tone seemed irritated at his friends. Two of them started to argue, and the one who had spoken to me seemed visibly angry. Were they all like me? Were they all dead too?

"The year." I repeated myself. I had to verify how far my math was off. I was guessing a little over a hundred and fifty years. Something inside of me was hoping that it was a dream, and it was half of that.

He took a long step backwards, looking at me top to bottom again. I could feel the dried blood chip off my fingers from where my nails dug into the man at the cemetery. I would need a manicure after this. And a pedicure. Some self-care was well needed and deserved after being locked up for so long.

"Twenty-two eighty-one! You are definitely not okay." he said as he took a full circle around me. I ground my nails into my palms, trying to have something to focus on, even if it was self-inflicted pain. My mind was going a thousand miles an hour. It felt like yesterday the Y2K bug was a thing.

I was stunned. To say I was at a loss for words right now would have been a crazy understatement. My body went numb, and I realized that I was now living in a nightmare. My arm dropped to the side, dangling there while the shock hit me again. I had no idea my facial expression was blank, and I was completely lost in my own world of thought. I had hoped for half of my guess. Seventy-five years at most. Not two hundred and sixty. How had I missed that much time. My eyes darted across the ground in a panic.

"Hey, we can't let you stand here, if someone sees you, we're all gonna get fried." I couldn't see his confusion, or his irritation that I was standing there with a million thoughts running through my head. "Are you with us? Anyone home?"

What? I snapped back to reality when his palm landed on my cheer with a sharp *THWACK*. There was a tingling across my face as my head jerked to the left. I snapped back to him, refocusing as he patted my cheek again. It would have been enjoyable if it hadn't been caused by someone slapping my face.

"Welcome back. We can't let you stand here like that or someone's going to think we lets some baby blood sucker wondering the streets."

"I have… questions."

"I'm sure you do, and we can answer them up there. Not down here." He gestured up to the porch

I thought guys were strange already. Male vampires, even stranger. There was a numbness to my body at the shock of his words. I had been locked up for so long. So many years. Panic once again started to crawl across my body, the similar signs of the anxiety I was formerly medicated for. The only thing in my stomach right now was the blood from those poor guys from earlier, leaving me with a strong bout of nausea. The hunger was still faintly there, as if some beast had taken up residency in my core. The thought of it made me want to throw up everywhere.

"Are you coming?" He clutched my arm, pulling me to the side. There was an unfamiliarity with anyone touching my body, let alone a male. His scent was different though. Definitely vampire, just, not that much. I wonder if I could drink vampires too. Now that was a morbidly fascinating thought.

Who did turn me? I didn't know any others, so I said the first name that came to mind.

"Hayley. Hayley Reinhardt turned me." They were the only one I knew. It was honesty at its finest and I had no idea if Hayley was even still alive. I couldn't remember the last time their knocks left the quiet dark of the cemetery.

The reaction from them was not what I had expected. A thick moment of silence and shock hung in the air before laughter filled the side of the street. Hysterical, unrestrained laughter.

"Hayley Reinhardt. Yes. You were *made* by the butcher of Fort Mill. That's rich." The guy behind me cried out. He was practically folded in half while laughing.

"Right Adam? She could have made up anyone and pulled that out of her cute little ass." The guy next to him said. Finally, one of them has a name. He didn't look like an Adam. What a bro name.

"Can one of you charge this? I'll prove it." I reached into my pocket and pulled out what was left of my dilapidated smartphone. It hadn't occurred to me that tech may have evolved. I would be highly disappointed if there weren't flying cars by now.

"Yo, what is that? It's a goddamn relic!" The guy in front of me stepped forward to look at it, excitedly. Finally, a tech geek. We spoke a different language.

"It's a twenty twenty-four LKN XV. Top of the line 5G." I quipped back at him. I tried to sound like it was impressive, even though it was obviously going to be low tech for these days.

"5G? This thing's older than most museum quality pieces. Where did you pick it up at?" he put his hand out, looking like a kid who wanted to play with a new toy. There were long locks of deep black hair pulled into a low ponytail hanging over his shoulder. His eyes glowed like a kid in a candy store.

"Did you not hear me? It's mine. I just woke up and I have no idea what year it is. I have pictures of my wife and---" I tried to explain.

"Wife? You're telling us you're the wife of the Butcher?" The guy to my left crossed his arms, unamused and looking bored.

"Kris, stop it, right now. If this chick is serious, you're messing with the wife of an OC." The original guy who approached me finally spoke up. I wondered why his mood had changed so quickly. He lifted his arm, patting me on the head. "I don't care how crazy she looks, if there's even the chance she's not nuts, Hayley will skin us alive."

"Governess Barnave didn't send out any messages though, we would have known if the butcher was coming."

"Right. Unless murderbabe here isn't from here."

"You *believe* that?" one of them said, crossing their arms.

"Don't you?" Adam responded.

"Wouldn't that make her their wife, and child?" another one said, staring at me.

"Has that *ever* happened before?"

"What's an OC?" I felt like they were having an entire conversation among themselves and neglecting me even being there. Silence once again. Was I asking the dumbest questions in the world tonight? They started talking among themselves, ignoring that I even existed.

"HEY!" I tried to scream. My voice cracked, probably from the lack of use across the last two centuries. I brought my hands up to my throat, trying to massage the searing tightness from it. Whatever I just did to it was definitely straining and painful for me. They looked at me while keeping quiet. I was frustrated, that hunger was starting to return, I had just been patted like a child and was trying not to have a breakdown in the middle of the street.

"I have questions. A lot of questions. I can give you answers, but I need help. If you know Hayley, I'm sure they will be really happy with you for helping bring me back to them." I at least hoped that was the truth. Maybe they had abandoned me for good and never wanted to see me again. At the very least, I knew they were alive. That much had my heart sinking with both sadness and relief. I had been more than a little bitchy to them over the last hundred years or so. I didn't mean to ignore them. It was just… there was so much anger and resentment at what had happened between us.

"Alright girly. If we're going to catch you up, let's get up off the street?" I brought my attention back to the first one who approached me. He turned to the side and gestured up to the porch.

"It's Elaine. Not hey, or bitch, or chick or girly. I have a name." I glared sharply at him. Even from this range, I could hear the faintness of their heartbeats. Almost all of them slightly in sync with each other, save for one that had a peculiar offbeat to it.

"Sorry, Ellie. Can we go up there?" He motioned towards the multi-story row home behind him again. Ellie? I hadn't heard anyone call me that in a long time. I curled my fingers together and closed my eyes for a moment. That was their name for me. I stood there for a few moments in the street while two of them walked up the steps and across the grassy sidewalk. It took me a few breaths before I opened my eyes and turned to face their row home.

"The porch? I may have just woken up, but I know not to enter a house with six dudes I've never met." No way was I about to become another missing person statistic. Hayley used to listen to those murder podcasts all the time. I thought they were creepy as all hell and generally avoided them, but I did get a few great survival tips from them.

"Completely fair. Let's move this chat at least off the street." The guys kept walking back up towards the porch, one of them chuckling at my comment along the way. It didn't appear they were going to force me with them. After a minute of contemplating my life choices and standing there a total mess, I shrugged my shoulders and followed. It wasn't like I wouldn't play this as safe as possible.

It felt good to be off the street. Even though the sidewalk was still cold, it wasn't covered in rocks and glass. I could take a little victory here. What I really needed was a pedicure. My toes looked absolutely disgusting after being locked in that casket for so long.

They whispered among themselves while I approached. I thought about it for a moment, reconsidering for a brief second whether I should, or would take that step up to the porch. It was their space, their home turf. Even now, if I moved backwards, I could line them up and not be surrounded.

I realized, at this point, that I didn't know a single thing about self-defense. Or my new self. Why would I ever have had to? Hayley was already terrifying to most people, and they were so protective of me that I never would have thought about having to learn a skill like that.

Survival instinct had been a pain to learn. The door to the row home swung open and Kris stepped out, tossing a pair of loafers down in front of me. They were a faded tan leather with no backing on them. I looked at them curiously, wondering if they had ever been cleaned before.

"Here, these might not fit all the way but they're better than nothing. Luce said she's on her way over now." He had a half-hearted smile hanging across his face. I didn't waste any time and slipped my feet into them. The shoes were just a bit bigger than my feet to no surprise. I had rather small feet for my height which made shoe buying a giant pain every time the seasons changed. Whenever I found something that fit, I'd do everything I could to make it last as long as possible.

I stood up on my toes then rolled back on my heels. It had been a long time since I had worn anything but my sandals. The inside was lined with soft fur of some sorts. My first thought was Ugg's, but then I remembered where these shoes came from.

"I guess this is where I say thanks" I leaned against the porch post, my gaze landing on the Edison bulbs hanging across the ceiling. At least some things hadn't gone out of style. The old school hanging bulbs reminded me of the ones that used to be on our balcony. We would spend summer nights having dinner under them while we watched the fireflies light up the backyards around our complex.

I stayed at the bottom of the stairs, refusing to move until Lucina arrived. At least I knew that much.

Kris looked over at me, curiously staring up and down before folding his arms behind his head and leaning back in the off-white Adirondack chair. I noticed the same thing happening across each of them. Their body language was curious and skeptical of me, but at least it wasn't hostile.

"I introduced myself, who are you guys?" The silence was killing me. It was awkward to say the least and I wanted to at least get a bit of conversation going if I was going to spend any time here.

"I'm Taj, blondie is Kris. The super nerd is Adam." Adam waved harmlessly across the porch. He had already pulled out what looked like a handheld gaming device and plugged his headphones in.

"Those two are brothers, Mikael and Andrej. That one's our youngest groupie, Sammy" Sammy did look younger than the others.

"Hey, I'm almost fifty now!" The guys laughed at him as he said it. "They're all old dudes from before the last one"

"The last *what?*" I looked at them curiously when their laughing halted.

"You really are fresh outta the ground, aren't you?" Kris pulled his arms down and crossed them in front.

"Thanks for paying attention." The guys laughed at him. "Can you catch me up on the last, I don't know," I started counting with my fingers, "two hundred and fifty years?"

"When were you turned?" Mikael said as he opened the cooler underneath him. He pulled out two cans and tossed one to me. I looked at it and cracked a smile. Of course, light beer. Why was I not surprised? How is this stuff even still around? I examined it closely, looking for any signs of tampering.

"I guess I was only turned an hour ago, but I've been in there since twenty twenty-four." I sighed. It just hit me that pretty much everyone I knew was gone. Long turned to dust and buried in the ground.

"In there? Like buried alive or locked up or something? Who did you piss off for that punishment?" Kris spoke up again. That was a lot to take in. Was it a punishment? I hadn't thought that maybe something I did had upset her and it was a long-term punishment. The same panic feeling welled up in my stomach. Was Hayley mad at me? Were they refusing to see me because of that?

"Relax Kris." Taj stepped down the steps towards me, noticing there was a bit of an uncomfortable vibe setting in. He put his hand on my shoulder, and for a moment we locked eyes. "Stay Here. You might feel overwhelmed by a lot of things, especially if you really did just wake up."

A strange feeling of warmth brought me back to reality. I took a big breath in, paused, and slowly exhaled. There were now a million and one thoughts going through my head. I remember Hayley holding my face in her hands and telling me to stay here whenever I was having a panic attack. I could remember how it all happened, all over again.

"What was that?" I asked. There was something that felt weird when he touched me.

"Some of us are empaths. Others can share their emotion and energy. You felt all over the place, all I did was ground you back here." Taj removed his hand from my shoulder as he stepped back and took a seat on the railing. "Neat trick, right?"

"Right, solid party trick." I quipped back. "So… I'm an open book, what do you want to know?"

"I want to know everything. We're low bloods, you know. I'm a twelfth gen, most of the guys are thirteenth gen. Sammy over there is fifteenth, right?" He looked at Adam who just lifted a middle finger from behind his gaming device.

I cleared my throat for a second while almost enjoying the slightly awkward silence that filled the porch. Twelfth generation? Fifteenth generation? How diluted would their blood be at that point.

"Long story short, I was bitten by my wife after I came home. They said I'd come around and that they would wait forever for me. I woke up feeling like utter death, with nothing but a love letter, my phone, and a vial of blood inside the casket. They came back every few years to check in on me, and then nothing. They just stopped and I closed my eyes and went to sleep until someone decided to move everything around."

I took a sip of the cold beer. There was something refreshing about the familiar taste of low-quality beer. It reminded me of my undergrad days when all we could afford was 30-packs of these things. There was nostalgia in the flavor, and for a moment I wondered if I could even get drunk again. Would alcohol have the same effect on me?

"Some guys were trying to relocate me. Someone named... I don't know, it sounded like an M name or something. They dropped me, and it broke the vial of blood Hayley had left me. It was a complete accident that it got in my mouth, and I had no intention of ever turning. I was perfectly fine being angry and depressed for another hundred years." I chuckled at myself a moment before taking another sip of beer.

"So, that's my story. I accidentally got turned, and I couldn't help myself. That man was just waiting there, staring at me like I was some kind of monster and my body moved before I could stop it. I was so hungry."

The guys remained silent while I summarized what had happened after I left the cemetery. I looked at several of them, each time bringing my eyes back to the beer can in my hands.

"Can someone please tell me where Hayley is? Or that they're even alive? I need to know why they did this to me and abandoned me here for so long. It's been at least a hundred and fifty years since they stopped coming to see me."

There was a deep sadness that curled itself up in the pit of my stomach. I truly missed them at my core. They were my wife, my life, my partner, and my everything. They had been my entire universe and I had so many questions to ask. I perked my head up when Taj let out a deep sigh.

"Hayley Reinhardt is the butcher of Fort Mill. They're the governess and executioner for the Delmar region. None of us would dare step foot over there. Lesson one for you, we're territorial. This street might be ours, but there are those way up the pole that don't even see us as flies. You're in the territory of Audrey Barnave, our governess. There was a rumor Hayley had never made another, maybe there's truth in that after all."

Taj cracked open another beer and sat down on the swing bench. He had really overdone it on the man liner. I never understood how women found that so attractive. At least some things hadn't changed over the years.

"*No one* goes into the area past the old Chester. You want to get yourself staked, go visit Philly. Then again, if what you're saying is the truth you shouldn't have any trouble getting in there." He took another big swig out of the can, guzzling a few large gulps before lowering it. It felt like he was trying to find a flaw in my story. I kept my eyes locked on his, not daring to remove them to look at the others. His tone was overly critical of everything I said.

"If Hayley's out there, then that's exactly where I need to be headed. Speaking of that, are we in Lancaster?" That had to be one of the dumbest things I could have asked. Of course, we were here, where else would we be. What I didn't expect was a different answer. The times really had changed.

"This place hasn't been called that in a while. It's just Old Lanc. No one's called it by that name in the last hundred years." Kris spoked while looking at the ceiling. It was obvious he was completely bored by the conversation.

"Can I ask a few more questions?" I crossed my legs and sat down, leaning against the porch post. Now that I had a chance to look at myself, this dress really was ruined. I pulled the front down and tried to cover as much of myself as possible. After all this time, it left very little to the imagination.

The air was cool enough for there to be no bugs flying around, so I assumed we were in some part of fall. If I had the opportunity to learn as much as I could, then it was worth staying here for a bit.

"Ask away, we will do our best to answer your inquiry." Andrej finally opened his mouth, only to quickly look away into the yard. I chuckled lightly under my breath at the adorable formality he had. He almost sounded what I considered Canadian. Not quite British, not as dirty as an Aussie.

"No need to be so formal here" I replied. "You guys might be the only people on this planet I know, everyone else I knew is probably six feet under."

It felt wonderfully relaxing to be sitting here and casually talking to other people. I had nearly forgotten what human contact was like. I guess it wasn't exactly human contact, but the point was there. Whether it was the crisp night air or just being able to stretch out in a new position, it just felt good.

"You said 'OC' earlier, what is that?" My number two question. What was an OC? I had heard that term plenty in my past life as a nerd. Maybe I would get lucky here. Chances are they weren't talking about their dungeons and dragon's character.

"My turn, youngling" Adam looked over, finally pulling himself out of whatever game he was playing. "An OC is an originals child. The Butcher is the child of one of the Originals and is up for the next seat. If what you say is true, and you're their wife... and that's their blood you drank, that makes you a third gen. All of us, we're like way down that line."

He took a breath and sighed, continuing. "My maker's line is well into the double digits. The stronger the blood is, from a purity standpoint, the stronger you are as a vampire. That's why you could probably kick Taj's ass even though you just got turned. You don't need to actually fight at all." He flashed a smirk at Taj for a moment. "Remember what he said about being a twelfth gen? Your blood purity is way up the nobility chain. And don't get me started on the originals."

Mikael tossed a can of beer over to Kris. He wasn't paying attention and it hit him square in the chest.

"The originals are all monsters. We're ants compared to them. There are rumors about them, but that's all they are."

"Rumors?" I asked. Would this be how modern lore was created? "What kind of rumors are there? Can you tell me about my wife's creator?"

"That would be Ireena, the Blood Countess. She's been the Vatican's enemy number one since the crusades. Her brother Konrad has been a nightmare for the world and has been seen on battlefields since the middle ages. They're polar opposites, but deadly. Our governess is in the Elisabeta line, and her line goes up to Alaric von Elisabeta, the younger brother of the American Seat – Nelo."

"How many originals are there, and where do I sit in this mess?" I asked, already feeling overwhelmed by how many people there were.

"Twelve originals. All of them are top of the food chain. You though? You're a third-generation vamp and glorified royalty. The Butcher united six different regions including the city, straight dusted their political enemies and built one of the top five territories on the eastern seaboard. Manhattan won't even fuck with her and that's the American seat. A sixth gen vampire is a lord, you're at least a countess or higher."

The butcher of Fort Mill. Their title. Their reputation.

It was a title that didn't sound friendly, but I knew Hayley. They had a serious case of resting bitch face that never took a night off so I could see how people would be reluctant to get on their bad side.

"So, let me get all of this straight… My wife stopped coming to see me because they decided to build their own little empire?" If I was being honest with myself, I was not surprised, at all.

"Well, yes and no. We didn't even know that the Butcher was coming over here, and if the governor new it would be a whole other bloodbath. They stick to their territory and haven't left it in decades." Adam leaned forward while sitting the handheld device down next to him.

"They ended up pissing off a lot of vamps during their rise to fame. There was a whole cease fire between other territories just to put pressure on their people." Kris looked over to Adam curiously. "It's entirely possible you were left there after the ceasefire, and they weren't allowed to come see you anymore."

"If you want to get in there, you're going to have to go through some hard-core enemy territory. You should keep yourself pretty low even here. Hey Taj, have you ever heard of the Butcher ever siring?"

Taj finished a sip of his beer and rubbed his chin, looking curiously at the light hanging from the middle of the porch.

"I don't believe so, there's a rumor that they've never had the interest in it. Lord Reinhardt had people at their feet for a century begging for it, you know that." he responded. "And I agree. The Burg might be the states capitol, but Old Lanc is ours. We will keep it quiet here, just remember us when you get all famous, all right?"

"Speaking of keeping it on the down low, when did you feed?" Andrej said with a slightly concerned look on his face.

"Well… what happened was… I was starving and there was construction going on, and all I could think about was the hunger and—"

Mikael cut me off.

"Shit. Where. Kris, can you take care of it? We're going to be in a mess if the mortals find it. Where were you?"

"A cemetery, south of here."

"On it." Kris hopped up, pulling out a phone and heading down into the yard below."

I turned around when a car came to a stop behind me, and a cheerful female hopped out. She pulled a duffle bag out from the backseat and tucked it under her arm, strolling casually towards me. She gave Kris a hug on the lawn, then came to a stop next to me, her eyes looking up and down my body. Her blonde hair held perfect curls that framed her face, and her eyes were a bright shade of hazel. For a moment, I couldn't take my eyes off the leather leggings that hugged her body, or the thick pink sweater that so delicately accentuated around her curves.

Her eyes locked on mine for a moment, and she blinked in irritation. "Whatever it is, I don't want to know. I'll go get you something to wear."

She walked right by me, gave Sammy a kiss, then disappeared through the front door.

. . .

"I'm really sorry if I made a mess of things. Next question, and I am really, really sorry for all of these… but what is a Seat?"

Sammy leaned back, rapidly texting on what I assumed was a smart phone. He didn't even need to move his eyes away from it to maintain presence in the conversation. Nerds never change.

"The Seat is the American ruler. The Night lords make up the Crimson Court and are the twelve Originals. Five of them are in Europe, two in Asia, one in Russia, one in Brazil and three right here in America. As for the mess, well, we have strict rules."

He took a drink from his beer and put his phone down. I watched him slide forward with an exasperated sigh.

"The Seat isn't just for the Originals; they are held by their respective family. Duchess Nelo is the current seat, and I think I heard Hayley is up for a seat, but not here if I remember correctly. The territory disputes at that high a level we aren't really in the know of. Again, we're ants compared to those monsters and get whatever scraps of info they give us…"

I sat in silence for a moment while thinking about it. Hayley got turned by one of those twelve. That was literally a statistical improbability. It was impossible. If they were still here, and relatively close, I had to get to them. I was missing something somewhere and had to ask.

"This might be, well, you get it. Stupid question number four. Are you out of the proverbial closet? When did you go mainstream? The humans can't be okay with that, right?"

"Actually, that's a pretty solid question and I'm glad you asked. Yes – we're out of the closet. There was a major conflict about a century and a half ago. The church couldn't keep us under wraps anymore, so they flipped gears and called for a holy crusade. Obviously, they lost and the treaty that came from it kind of made us public. We stay out of their way, and they stay out of ours. Not like they still don't try to hunt us down anytime they can, but half of that is for them to keep up appearances."

"So, gentlemen… How do I get to Fort Mill? Where is that?" Safe question. I was assuming my old Audi wasn't going to be running anymore. The parts probably had been rusted for two hundred years. What I needed right now was a lift.

Taj crossed his arms and took a big breath in before letting out an overly dramatic sigh and rubbed his forehead in frustration.

"You just heard all of that and are perfectly fine with it. For real. What a mess you're going to be." He looked conflicted at the answer he was giving. "If you want into Philly under the radar, the only way you're getting in there is to go south through Jersey and in through Camden."

"Who's doing that ride, dick. You know we don't move through that area. Anders will crucify us at sunrise if he catches us over there. Addison will do worse." Kris said irritatingly.

"Then why not go during the day?" I quipped back, throwing out a response.

The brothers stared at me with blank expressions, then almost fell off the cooler laughing.

"During the day? Did you forget you're a vampire already?" Mikael laughed.

"Sunlight is your number one enemy. Period. No matter what you do, that giant ball of fire will turn you to ash and send you off into an eternal slumber. Many of our kind break from the stress of immortality and walk into the sunrise to end it. Don't be one of them."

"Oh. I guess that does make sense…Sunlight is bad. Got it." It did make sense. Sunlight would turn me to dust now. I was in an entirely new environment, and I had no idea what the rules were. What a pain in the ass. Maybe I could jump on this opportunity.

"Anyone want to take me to Camden?" I ran my hand through my hair, pulling it as far as I could out. It had grown a lot, and I had done my best to maintain it at as best I could. I really did look like hot garbage right now. I smelled my shirt, adding "Or show me where I can take a shower?"

Sammy pulled what looked to be some strange high-tech device out and slid it over two of his fingers. Was that what a phone looked like? He hopped off the side of the porch and started having a conversation down in the front lawn. It didn't take long for him to return with a smile.

"Luce is probably already getting you something to wear. You can shower upstairs, first door on the left. Towels are in the closet. Use whatever you need" he said with a smile.

"Good idea", Taj chuckled and punched him in the shoulder. "Sammy might be the youngest, but he's got a good head on his shoulders. And he made some crazy smart investments."

Andrej looked at him like he was looking at his idol. "We might run the block, but he actually owns most of it."

"Why don't you go clean yourself up. If you just had your first time you know, feeding, then you probably need to relax a bit. Take a hot shower and breathe." Taj stood up and moved the chair out of the way of the door. "The first urge you are going to experience are powerful. We call it the babies suck and fuck phase."

"Excuse me?" I pursed my lips.

"It's normal. All of your urges, your senses, it's all heightened. And the stronger your blood is, the stronger that is."

"So basically, I'm going to want to fuck someone?" I curled my fingers into fists, defensively moving a step away from them.

"Yes, and if you really are serious about your maker, it's not going to be us. The last man who touched Hayley lost their arm. I don't want to know what they would do to one of us. Touching you is literal suicide. You already experienced your first hunger, so trust us on that. For our sake."

I felt a little bit better knowing that.

"Upstairs on the left?" I asked once again. Was this really, actually, okay? Part of me was still skeptical.

"Yep, right up there." He pointed to the stairs. It really did look like there was a bathroom at the top of the stairs. These old row homes were almost all built the same.

"Hey guys…" I looked at them as I stood up. "Thank you, really. I know it isn't much, but I won't forget your kindness."

I stopped at the door, holding it open with my back while reaching into my pocket. Maybe this nerd could help me out.

"Hey, I'll show you an entirely new world if you and Sammy can get my sd card out." I said, tossing the phone over to him. His eyes lit up as he caught it, immediately putting away whatever version of gaming console he had out. I wondered if the 'gram was still a thing.

Adam seemed ecstatic to get to tinker with old tech. I remembered the same feeling I had, and the rush of being on the cutting edge of technology. There was no greater thrill than pushing what we were truly capable of. The door closed behind me, and I found myself standing on aged wooden floors that creaked underfoot, their polished sheen long faded. The floorboards, scarred by the passage of countless footsteps, spoke of the people who had walked these same paths. There was a comforting, rhythmic cadence to the creaks, like an echo of the past whispering tales of days gone by.

The walls were adorned with a collection of broken and neglected picture frames. They hung crookedly, bearing the weight of forgotten memories. Within those tarnished frames were glimpses of a different era—a sepia-toned family portrait, a faded picture of a Victorian couple, and a cracked oil painting of a tranquil landscape. Each shattered frame was a fractured fragment of someone's history, a window into the past.

The windows, their curtains drawn back to allow slivers of dusty streetlight to filter through, revealed a world outside that had changed dramatically, yet not at all.

A single staircase, with its graceful banisters and ornate balusters, led me to the upper floors, where the bedrooms and two bathrooms were. I listened carefully to each step, counting every one of their whispers they shared. I took time to look at each of the pictures, some of them the guys from outside, some of them of couple's I didn't recognize. Each of them carried a memory that was worthy enough to hang here. For a moment, I stopped and wondered what pictures I would put up if this had been my home, and whether Hayley and I truly would have made it this long.

* * *

I NEVER KNEW how good a shower would really feel until I got into the bathroom and had time to think about it. My skin had an entirely different feeling to it. It was soft, yet hard like a pale white jade. There was a bunch of random bathroom items behind the mirror. Standard for a dude's house, what should I have expected. At least the towels were clean.

I turned my back to the sink as I moved by it, avoiding potentially seeing my reflection. When was the last time I had a shower? Or felt clean? Music drifted into the bathroom, reminiscent of any old house with poor sound control. Thick and heavy on the down beat with rolling melodies, it wasn't too bad.

Add 'purchase a toothbrush' to my to-do list for today. I thought to myself. It made me wonder if 24-hour pharmacies were still a thing. Or if the ones I knew was even still around. I bet a pharmacy would have one. Wait, I had no money. Shit. I bet my accounts we're all gone. I didn't even know if my bank still existed at this point either.

So many stressful logistical questions came into my head one after another non-stop. My heartrate was racing, the slight instinct of panic beginning to take hold. I blinked away the discomfort and met my own gaze in the mirror, my reflection an unsettling vision of timeless beauty.

I undressed with deliberate, almost slow movements, peeling away the centuries-old garments that clung to my body. I avoided catching my reflection in the mirror a second time, not wanting to see the unfamiliar person staring back at me. At my core, there had been a fear of knowing that I may never see myself again.

The initial shock of the hot water hitting my skin was invigorating. It seeped into my pores, slowly warming my frozen limbs, and I welcomed it. It was like stress was dripping off my body. The sensation was foreign, long absent from my life. As I stood there, beneath the cascading water, I reveled in the simple pleasure of feeling clean once more. I lowered my head and let the hot water cover me.

For the first time, I got to smell my breath and it made me choke.

It was a sensation I hadn't experienced in centuries, and it sent shivers down my spine. I closed my eyes, opening them to a haunting battle-field under the moonlight.

A woman stood in front of me, her long black hair tied into braids that blew wildly in the wind. She dropped her rose gold cloak and flew forward through the battle, the sound of swords, of screams, both from horses and humans, echoing in my ears. I watched this woman dance through the lines of some unknown enemy, each twist of her body a dance that brought death to anyone unlucky enough to witness her. She struck with the fluid grace of an apex predator, a woman who was carving her way through this fight without abandon. Her body lifted off of the ground, taking flight for a moment before striking down onto a small encampment. Her movements were ethereal, graceful, inhuman. The human general had been given no time to defend himself before she tore through his neck, twisted, and then removed what was left. His body hit the ground, falling to his knees while his head landed yards away, the shock and terror in them permanently burned into his eyes.

A door slammed downstairs, and I opened my eyes to the shower once again. I stood there in confusion, wondering what kind of dream had just taken me. Shaking my head out, I felt sharp cracks go through my neck and returned to my enjoyment of the shower. I took my time, savoring every moment as I lathered my body with a bar of white soap, my fingers gently scrubbing away the grime and remnants of dried blood. My hair, a cascade of raven-black mess, was particu-larly tangled, but I approached the task of washing it with meticulous care as best I could.

Knock Knock

The panic flipped on as I turned to the shower curtain when the door slid open. I bit my tongue, trying to still myself. Thankfully it was just the young blonde woman who slid her way silently into the bathroom.

"Hi Ellie! Sorry to let myself in, I'm Sam's wife Lucina, but they call me Luce." Her footsteps were light and delicate, almost like a dancer. No, definitely a dancer.

"Anyway, I brought you some clothes and a toothbrush. Sam said you just fed, and I know how stressful that can be. Anyway… It's exciting to have you here and meet another woman who isn't, you know, crazy. The boys filled me in. Sorry about earlier. Anyway, you're on *you* time so do some self-care and let's chat more when you're out!"

The door closed as fast as she had entered, and I was once again left with just myself. The amount of excitement I had in my chest at brushing my teeth was unimaginable. She had flipped her opinion of me quick, no surprise there.

I kept my mouth shut and let the water keep running across the curves of my body. There was still a faint taste of blood lingering in my mouth from where I had bit my tongue when she came in. How was I even going to do my hair and manage this mess. I reached around the bathroom wall to the counter and grabbed the scissors that were next to what I could only assume was a beard trimmer. It was quick, ugly work to cut the matted hair that laid halfway down my back off. There was no way I had the time or energy to get it all untangled. Their drainage was going to have problems for weeks with this much hair. I felt bad about it.

I picked as much of the long hair up that I could and tossed it into the trash can next to the shower. There was a lot of hair. I was always a shedder and all this hair looked like the start of its own horror movie. My body felt much lighter without the thick mane hanging down my back. I would have to get a real haircut at some point to fix the chop job I had just done to myself.

Minutes felt like hours as I stood there, the water purifying not just my body but my very soul. It was as if the liquid washed away the sins and torments that had plagued me for centuries. Eventually, as the water turned lukewarm, I knew I would soon have to step out of the shower. I patted my face with a fluffy towel, letting my skin air-dry for a moment. My reflection in the mirror showed a rejuvenated, ethereal beauty, free from the grime of centuries. For a split second, I could almost believe in my own humanity, believe that I was still just a normal woman.

The shower water quickly turned to cold, and my time inside of it ended. I hated cold showers and couldn't stand being in it for that much longer. Even though my temperature felt cold the water was still like an ice box when the heat ran out.

I wrapped another towel around my body, then one around my hair before whipping it back behind me. I paused, held my breath, and opened my eyes to look into the mirror again. I had truly thought I wouldn't have a reflection.

What did I expect? Would I never get to see myself again? How would I know if my makeup was on right, or if my hair was done all the way? Was there a vampire hairdresser? It amazed me how many of those stereotypes were just rumors and superstitions. For the first time in so long, I could see myself in the reflection staring back at me.

The little knicks were gone, and the scar on my cheek from falling as a child had disappeared. My skin was smooth and pale, just like the rest of me. I leaned in close, looking at the tiny specks of red that floated between the chocolate brown of my eyes. The panic in me started to recede and I leaned back with a smile.

Of course I would have a reflection.

I let out a deep sigh, satisfied at knowing that at least I was clean. No matter how many thoughts were hitting light-speed in my head, I was clean. Hayley and I had always joked about our differences between being dirty and hungry. They were okay skipping the shower for food, while I'd starve before I was dirty. The last shower I had was with them, super early on that Saturday morning all those years ago.

A pair of fleece lined black yoga pants sat on the edge of the sink. I was happy that Luce had dropped something off for me to wear. A perfect fit, I thought to myself while pulling them up across my hips. At least my ass hadn't changed when I shifted over to this side. I pulled a sports bra and baggy sweater over my shoulders and shook my hair out of its towel one last time before letting it fall down my neck. The dirty clothes on the floor smelled horrendous. I bet they would make a great fire starter, I thought while folding them up and dropping them in the trash can.

I slid the loafers onto my feet and hopped down the stairs. There was no surprise when I found they were all still outside drinking. Luce had sat down on the top step with a beer to join them.

"There you are, look at that! A completely different person" Taj said as he tossed me a cold beer.

"I feel like a completely different person. A hot shower is magic. I almost feel like a real person again." I felt a little more relaxed now that I could breathe. There wasn't as much stress around them, even though we'd only known each other for an hour or so. "And sorry about your drain."

I lifted the chopped hair across the bottom of my neck and shook my hair out.

"Elaine, I know you want to get to see Hayley, but it's not going to be easy at all. Would you reconsider it? You know, maybe stay here a bit more?" Luce looked up from her beer. "Sammy and the guys agree. You haven't even figured out what your bloodline strength is yet, it would be dangerous for you to go. And there's a lot of work to get approval by their territorial lord to enter. We can't just walk you down there."

I sat there quietly for a moment while slowly blinking. Bloodline strength? What in the hell was she talking about? It never hurt to ask one more stupid question. I could ignore the paperwork challenge for now.

"Luce, can you tell me what that is?" I was generally curious about this one. I thought all the famous vampires could do those things. Turn to fog or a bat, mist around the cities, be super quick and strong. I wondered if I had something like that. How cool would that be?

"If you're from Hayley, it makes sense that you are a Vasiliev. Their territory is considered off limits and an extension of their master," Kris chimed in, looking a little less pretentious than before. "We aren't sure which one of the two siblings it was, but they own half of the European nightlife. Everything from Berlin to Moscow is their domain."

"And for bloodline strength, we all have it. Sort of. You'll find that a lot more than just your senses are going to be heightened. Everything is. Pain, pleasure, emotions, all of it." Luce said before taking another drink.

"What's a Vasiliev? Is that a family or something?" I pulled my knees into my chest and looked at him. Now he had my attention.

"You can think of it like that. There are five or six original families, each with two or three founding members. In the original lineage, about twelve of them were given special...gifts. Hayley has the Midnight Brand and is a member of the Aristocracy of Night. They're blood bound and each never take more than one or two offspring at a time. I've never heard of Hayley taking a newborn, you might be the only third gen on the continent!"

The Midnight Brand? Did someone burn my wife? I would literally dust someone that did that to them.

"How do you know they have that brand thing? Have you seen them before?" I asked curiously.

The others looked at Kris curiously. He seemed to know a lot about them, more than the others. Kris took another drink of his beer before setting it down on the railing next to him.

"I saw the Butcher when they came to town with the rest of the provincial governors. Those who have the midnight brand have a set of tattoos on them. The cover both of her hands and forearms. It's a gift to get a brand and can pull out their bloodline so that they can utilize its full strength. She had come after a disagreement with the governess. The territories staff went from over two hundred to seventeen thanks to her," he said, taking another sip of his beer.

"Actually, it's them. Hayley isn't a her." I felt bad correcting him in the middle of speaking, but it had been bothering me. They really didn't know them. The group looked at me, some confused and some surprised.

"Sorry about that. We didn't know they weren't, you know, not straight. It makes sense that they would be non-binary. Honestly, we always figured they had some aristocratic prince waiting for them somewhere in Europe." Adam chimed in.

"Nope, just me. A housewife." I smiled. It felt good to say that again. I laughed at the thought of some French Prince trying to sweep Hayley off their feet. It would be like courting death.

"A housewife my ass, if you're with Hayley you had to be someone in your past life. There's no way they would marry a nobody." Kris quipped back.

"I was a tech queen. Healthcare optimization and emerging tech was my domain. I built the first interconnected data sharing system for cloud based medical records." It felt weird to talk about myself. I had done it hundreds of times. Between convention talks, guest appearances at colleges and industry events, I had my bio nailed down.

Sammy shot up excitedly and knocked over his beer.

"WAIT! You're Elaine Reinhardt, Epsilon Medical! You disappeared and no one ever found your body! You never got killed, you got sealed up!" It was like watching someone win one of those old game shows. I guess that reference would be lost these days.

"Sammy! Take a breath and stop making a mess." Lucina said, scolding him.

"Yes, that's me. I was never kidnapped, at least not in the traditional sense." The sadness began to build itself in my chest as tightness formed again. It was like a fire hydrant ready to explode if I couldn't keep it under control.

Luce turned her entire body around, stretching out across the top step of the porch. She held a glass of wine in her hands, taking slow sips while listening to the conversation.

"Hey, tell us your story. What actually happened to you?" she asked.

"What happened to me?" I felt the air leave my body and I froze for a second. I was about to relive and analyze it for the first time. Those memories had been locked away since I woke up the first time with pain across every inch of my body.

"It's complicated. This is the full thing, so I apologize if I ramble. It was so long ago, and I tried to forget it. I had been at a work party for a friend, their retirement. We booked the entire rooftop of a bar downtown. Hayley was covering down for someone else at work last minute and couldn't make it. They texted me a few hours after work and said they were getting drinks with their team to celebrate a birthday and would be right over to meet me, and they never came."

I took a breath. Was that where it happened? They were perfectly normal that morning. Had a beautiful smile and pulse and everything else. My mind was racing down the possible points that our entire lives had been ripped out from under us. What I wouldn't give for a whiteboard right now so I could start putting all of the pieces back together.

"I came home around one a.m... and I was really upset. It wasn't like them to ghost me. Ever. The apartment was dark, and candles were lit. It was a perfect Winter Wonderland. The season had just start changing and while it was freezing outside in the mornings, the heaters above the bar were enough to let us enjoy being outside that late. I walked in and unzipped my boots. I remember I left them next to the door and slid my sandals on, just like every other time. They were black leather and fluffy on the inside. My favorites. I hated being barefoot, but I also kind of hated wearing shoes too.

Hayley was standing at the balcony door, looking out across the park. They had their back to me, so I walked over to wrap my arms around them. When I did, it felt cold. Everything about them was freezing. I asked them if they were okay and they broke down. They started crying in my arms. I didn't realize that the tears were blood when they hit my arm, it just felt warm."

The blood had stained my arms and was still there when I woke up. I had scratched all of the dry blood off and tried to make sure there was no reminder of that night.

"They buried their head in my chest and wouldn't look at me. I thought someone had hurt them, or they had lost their job or some-thing. I never would have guessed what had really happened. When Hayley lifted their head up, they only asked me if I would forgive them one day.

I tried to step back away but I couldn't get any room. Their strength was unnatural. I panicked and dropped to the floor, pushing away from them, and I just... took off running. I made it all the way down the hallway at almost full speed. You know, that speed you get where you know you're doing the best you can in sandals."

A few of them laughed. The rest had stopped drinking their beer and were paying attention closely, intently, to every detail.

"Anyway, I made it to the elevator. I hit that button so many times I lost track. I'll never forget that stupid off-key ding echo across the hallway, and I stood there frozen. The door opened, and I remember falling and sliding into the corner of the elevator. The only thing I can remember her saying was that I would forgive her one day. After that, I blacked out from the pain."

It finally slipped out- the first tear. I could feel it rolling down the side of my cheek. In most cases I would have been super pissed that it was ruining my makeup.

"The only thing I really remember was waking up in the dark of that casket with a note and a little vial of blood. They came back every other year, then every five, and then not at all. I was so worried that something had happened."

I took a sip of beer. It had lost its chilly edge and now tasted just like the shit beer of old. At the very least, some things never changed. It was the horrible flavor of nostalgia and reminded me of my college dorm days.

"That's rough Elle." Taj sat his empty can down next to him. "You really were just turned. Only old blood could have stayed fresh for that long. Rumor has it that it never ages."

It was weird for me to hear that name. I hadn't been called that for a long time. Hayley would call me that at home as a kind of pet name. It was nostalgic to hear that.

"Thanks. I broke literally every horror movie stereotype. They used to joke that I'd be the first to die in a horror flick. I know you guys don't want to risk it, but can you help me out? I need to get to Camden, and across the water to Philly."

"Let's sleep on it tonight. You can stay in my room. Sorry Sammy, you're on your own tonight." Luce grabbed my arm and pulled me up with her. "It's like a sleepover!"

I was pulled through the screen door and up to the top floor where the entire attic had been converted into a sort of bedroom library. I looked at the shelves of books, there had to have been hundreds of them. If Hayley had continued collecting books like they used to, their collection would probably be in the tens of thousands if not higher amount. They would literally need a library to house all of them. I read several of the covers as I walked through the room while Lucina fluffed the bed and closed the blackout curtains. There was a long bar that flipped over onto them, sealing any outside light from entering. I sat down on the thick navy carpet before falling backwards. Luce looked over at me while laughing.

"Feels good to relax, doesn't it." She said with a smile as she came over and sat behind me. I sat up, only for her to move behind me. I turned my head around, but she put her hand on it and steadied it forward away from her.

"Relax, let me take care of this for you. You've been through enough, so take a breath and relax for a few minutes." Her voice was soft and gentle, and as she finished speaking, I felt a jerk through my hair. I hadn't had my hair brushed in centuries and it felt like an extravagance for right now. I sat there in silence for several minutes while trying not to cry again.

"Luce… how old are you?" I asked curiously. "I mean… when were you turned?"

"Me?" she replied with a light chuckle. "I was turned about eighty years ago. It's weird, you know? After the first ten, I stopped celebrating my birthday because it just felt… silly. Why keep count of how long I've lived when there's no end to it? My maker saved me from the church when they were doing one of their sweeps."

"Sweeps?" I said quietly as she moved to the side of my head with her brush.

"Yes, the church will sweep an area of the city and then if they find anyone they deem as, well, unholy, or vampiric, or witch, or anything that isn't the church really, they purge them. I was on the chopping block for witchcraft, which is silly because I don't know the first thing about moon phases or pretty rocks. We try to avoid the church at all costs. You should do the same. Especially after what your maker did." She responded.

"Pretty rocks, right… what did Hayley do?" I laughed, carefree. Hayley would have had a field day here with this one. Pretty rocks? I was saving that one for later. Almost every one of these crystals had a purpose. I picked up an amethyst and held it in my hands, feeling the coolness of it. There had been a fairly large collection of them in our house and I had collected quite a range of raw amethyst geodes. I took a moment to remember the nights under the moon Hayley and I had together while celebrating our witchy rituals every season.

It would be nice to introduce everyone here to them one day. I thought about what it would be like to see Hayley again, and then have all of them come with me. Would I be able to come back here by myself? Probably not, especially with how protective they were of me.

"So, a few decades ago the church came after Hayley, and they not only destroyed all of them, but they took one of the holy swords and then butchered the priests with their own weapon. It was the hottest nightlife news."

"Enough about that though, tell me what Hayley is like! I never got to have a relationship when I was human, so I'm curious about what they were like before, you know…" Maybe I needed to talk about it a bit. My therapist was a pile of dust somewhere.

Lucina's rich eyes, as vibrant as her own undead pulse, were focused on me as we delved into a subject that had always intrigued me—relationships. Her eternal existence had given me the chance to tap into a unique perspective on love, connection, and the passage of time.

"Before they were a vampire?" I said with a smile.

I considered her question, my mind drifting through the memories of my human life and the centuries since. There was a haze around the time before. I could remember names of people, but I was unable to recall their faces anymore.

"It might be different, but I really hope it's the same, I guess" I replied. "Hayley is kind, and funny. Their laugh is something that could make me smile no matter how upset I was. They always knew the right thing to say, and they always had the right answer. I didn't know how lost I was in the world until I met them. And now, all of this has happened. I think that the core of our love and connection remains, but if you add in extended lifespan that adds layers of complexity. There's a beauty in sharing eternity with someone, but it also brings challenges that I could never understand. Challenges that I never even would think about. I spent two centuries in isolation and even through that, even though Hayley locked me there, a part of me never stopped loving them."

Lucina nodded in agreement, her fingers tracing the rim of rhinestone covered brush. "I've always wondered about the idea of forever. The thought of loving someone for centuries is both intriguing and daunting."

I leaned in, my brown eyes locking with hers. There was a depth of color held there that I hadn't noticed before, tiny specks of softness that made me smile.

"It is, Lucina. Forever can be both a blessing and a burden. We have to choose our companions wisely; they will be our eternal partners through the ages. But that also means that every moment together is precious and carries the weight of endless time. I had always wished for a forever with them. They were so kind, so happy with our life. I had all the time in the world to figure out where it went wrong. I was never meant to be one of you. I never wanted this. I never wanted eternity. I just wanted a life with my wife."

She sighed, a sound that seemed to echo through the centuries. "I am so, so sorry she betrayed you like that. You're one of us now, and that can be a really hard adjustment. Some humans spend their entire lives trying to have our gift, and never find it. Do you think it is possible to find something like true love, even in our undying existence? I love Sammy, I really do, but sometimes, he's just..."

"Still just a dude?" I said, half-jokingly.

"That's exactly it. A dude. He would fall apart if I wasn't there to pick up the pieces most of the time. I love him, like really really really love him. I just wish he cared about himself as much as I do."

I smiled, the memories of my beloved Hayley flooding my

thoughts. "To answer your question, yes. I believe that true love can be as real for you as it was for us. I knew they were my soul mate even before we started dating. It might even be stronger now because we have an eternity to explore its depths. It's about finding that one soul who understands the beauty and the challenges of your existence, someone who stands by you through the ages. When we said forever, we meant it. I didn't think literally, but part of me hoped for it. Now that I have it, I'm terrified by it. I feel bitter and angry still. "

Lucina's gaze softened, a reflection of her own thoughts.

"Do you think forever is worth it now? Is there true love in this immortal life? Do you think Hayley waited for you? "

My heart swelled with the memory of Hayley. I froze for a second, contemplating whether or not I truly thought they had waited for me. I was still heartbroken and had been angry for so long that I wasn't sure if she would even want me like that.

Or If I was capable of letting that go.

"Yes," I whispered, my voice tinged with reverence, "It is worth it, Lucina. In my wife Hayley, I've discovered a love that I hope transcends time. We used to say that we would find each other in every lifetime. They're my anchor, my companion through the stars. And I'm grateful for every moment we shared before, and I am sure I will be grateful for every moment we share after we are reunited. I'm still so mad and there are so many things I'm going to scream when I see them… but I want to see them so badly."

Our conversation delved into the complexities and joys of love among the undead, and as the night wore on, Lucina and I found solace in the knowledge that, even in the eternal night, the pursuit of love and connection remained a timeless and universal journey. It took a few more minutes for her to finish brushing out the old tangles in my hair, and we both agreed that I needed a trip to a hair salon. We ended up spending a couple hours talking, sharing secrets, memories, and a bottle of wine before a strange glow hit the window. I wasn't about to get extra crispy on my first night out. It might not be a long night of rest, but more importantly it was the first rest I would have in a very long time.

I laid in the large bed that lacked a frame and was stacked on the floor. It was covered in a far more pillows than anyone would ever need. My body had room to stretch out, a position that took me several minutes to actually get into. I had been in one position for so long that a bed felt completely foreign to me. My head fell into a stack of pillows and before I knew it, my exhaustion took over and I was already asleep.

I LOOKED around the dimly lit confines of an ancient castle, where flickering torches cast a spectral glow across the stone walls. The echoes of my own footsteps seemed to resonate through time as I witnessed a woman struggling against the dozens of chains that bound her to the wall. Her eyes glowed with crimson fire, angry at the situation she found herself in.

The vampire, a figure draped in shadow, was shackled, and condemned, facing certain execution. The smell of death and decay hung heavily in the air as we stood within the castle's dungeon. I walked over to the barred windows and gazed out into the night. In the distance, the executioner's block awaited, a gleaming axe standing as a harbinger of doom.

My heart quickened as I watched the vampire's eyes, burning with defiance, take in the grim surroundings. Her eyes stopped on me, and she smiled. The door to her cell opened, giving way to a host of armed guards. With caution, I stepped back into the corner, trying to hide myself from them. With supernatural strength and agility, the woman broke free from the restraints that bound her. Chains shattered like fragile glass, and the guards were dispatched with a lethal grace.

A symphony of chaos and courage floated across this ancient fortress as I followed this vampire. Every turned led to more soldiers seeking to stop them as they fought their way through the labyrinthine castle. The clash of swords, the ring of armor, and the frantic shouts of guards created a tumultuous backdrop to her escape.

I followed closely behind the vampire, watching as she used the darkness as their ally, navigated hidden passages and secret tunnels, and outwitting their pursuers at every turn. The castle, with its hidden doors and concealed alcoves, seemed to conspire with the vampire in her quest for freedom.

I tried my hardest to keep up with her until finally, the vampire emerged onto the castle's battlements, where the moon cast a silvery glow upon the ancient stones. The cold wind tousled their dark hair as they stared at the expanse of the world beyond. She spread her arms, turning to look at me with a smile that revealed both of her fangs. I had seen her before, but where? With one last leap into the abyss, the vampire disappeared into the night, leaving the castle behind. My body followed, running to the edge of the tower's walls as I peered down into the crevice below. Only darkness remained of her.

I WOKE UP, curled into a tight ball with my head on Lucina's chest. One of my legs was completely across her body, and my lips had found their way to her chest. Her hand was running through my hair, and there were streaks of blood across her clothes. My body shot up in a panic as I looked at the blood covering me, and where I had been sleeping.

"Breathe, Elaine. It's okay. Whatever it was, it's over. The nightmare is over. Or the dream, and then the nightmare again. You went from crying to moaning to crying pretty fast, hard to keep up." She said, sitting up and hugging me. Sweat clung to my body, the aftermath of another bad dream. I wasn't sure how many I had, but I could tell I had been crying.

"I'm so sorry Luce. I wasn't… I didn't, I…" I leaned backward away from her, pressing my hands down into open air. A screech escaped my lips at the emptiness behind me. I had completely misjudged the edge of the bed and went tumbling backwards. Lucina tried to grab onto me, and instead came flying off the bed, pillows and blankets flying everywhere. I landed on the floor, Lucina on top of me, her hair perfectly framing her face.

"YOU'VE BEEN through something horrifying, and this is your first real night as one of us. You fed for the first time, by yourself. That on its own can be a traumatic experience. Whatever bad dreams you have, they're just dreams and none of its real. Besides, Sammy knows I'm bi, he'll understand. We told you earlier that everything would be heightened. Besides, when was the last time you had a body next to you? I want you to know we all go through this." Luce forced a smile and pulled a strand of hair behind my ear before leaning down and kissing me on my forehead.

"Through what?"

"You can't smell it yet." I wore a thin satin nightgown that covered my now perfectly sculpted body which bore a mix of freckles across my shoulders and arms. My hands clutched at the fabric over my chest, trying to ground myself from the overwhelming desires that threatened to consume me as I looked up at her. She could smell my desire. No. Not like this.

The taste of the bloodwine still lingered on my tongue, thick and metallic and perfectly delicious.

My eyes fluttered open, revealing speckles of red light joining their dark brown color that reflected in her eyes. I looked at her with a mixture of shame and confusion, "I just... can't control this." I admitted softly, gripping the sheets with white knuckles under me.

She straddled my hips and lowered herself onto me, our bare skin sliding against each other. Her breath hitched as I felt Lucina's body press against me, her lips delicately kissing the side of my neck.

"This will be much better than one of the boys," Lucina whispered in my ear.

"I don't understand..." I begged; my voice hoarse with desperation. "I'm trying to keep it... I've never felt anything like this...help me..."

"That's the vampire blood and your body finishing their merger. It takes a bit for it to finish, and one of the last parts is *that* urge."

Lucina wrapped her arms around my back, pulling herself down into a passionate kiss as she flicked my tongue around my mouth. The desire that had built up in me, from whatever dreams that graced me had sent me over the edge. Our tongues tangled together, teeth scraping against each other's lips, our bodies moving together in an unchoreographed dance of lust.

The sounds of skin sliding against skin filled the room, intermingling with the rustling of the sheets underneath around us. I tried to roll over as we both scrambled back up onto the bed, our nightgowns being shredded in the transition. I found myself on top of her, a position I rarely was ever in.

Suddenly, Lucina let out a moan, her body arching off the mattress as another wave of pleasure coursed through her. I felt my own desire rising again at the sight of her writhing beneath me. As I began to move over her body again, Lucina's hands grasped my hips and pulled me closer.

Her breathing became shallow as I brushed my lips against hers. Our tongues met in an intoxicating dance as I flicked the top of her mouth with mine.

No.

My hands roamed over every inch of her body - from her soft neck to her toned stomach and down between her legs. I could feel how wet she was for me, sending a thrill through my entire body as I pressed into her, my lips tracing their own line down her core.

My fingers found their way to her nipples, eliciting an even louder moan from her as I tweaked them gently between my fingers while I kissed the inside of her thigh. I felt an electric current travel through my body as she responded to my touch, and this drove me wilder with desire. My body was on fire and if I didn't let every bit of it out, I might die.

I let go of her nipples and continued down her body until I reached the spot between her legs. She gasped softly in response, and I could feel her tremble beneath me as I gently massaged that special area. Her breathing grew heavier and soon she was panting with pleasure, pushing herself closer to me until finally she let out a loud cry of blissful release.

Elle... stop...

I felt her hands wrap around my neck and pull me to the side, switching our positions. I felt her hands wrap around my neck and pull me to the side, switching our positions. She was now on top of me while still enjoying the pleasure I was giving her.

Luce pulled my dripping fingers from inside of her and one by one licked each of them. My back arched again, and I pulled her back down onto me. Her movements were slow and steady as she grinded down onto me, causing me to moan with delight.

No, STOP.

The sensation of her body on mine was electrifying, sending shivers down my spine, and my body was barely able to stop itself. I was panicking internally and couldn't silence the scream in the back of my head. She moved her hips in circles, exploring every inch of my body with her hands at the same time.

I rolled her to the side, sending myself the opposite direction and off the bed, scrambling towards the wall. The wooden surface didn't buckle when I slammed into it as hard as I could, driving my body backwards.

Do. It. Now.

I raised my arm to my lips, fangs extending before driving them straight into my forearm. The pain of it shot down my arm, my eyes closing as I forced myself to stop. I would not let the first time not be with Hayley. I held it there, held my arm in my mouth as it filled with my own blood.

It took me several minutes to get myself together and steady my breath. Finally, I opened my eyes, my body feeling like it was on fire.

She looked at me, bringing a sheet up to cover her body. I didn't want to move, and a wave of guilt hit me. It should have been Hayley.

At least it hadn't been one of the guys.

We crawled back over into our spots on the bed where I curled my legs up and sunk my head into my knees, embarrassed.

"Hey there..." she said, pulling my hair up and fluffing it behind me. "There you are. See? Everything is okay. I told you everything would be heightened, and I really meant everything."

"Please... Please help me get home. I have to get back to Hayley. This never should have happened."

"Breathe, Elle. Breathe. One thing at a time. I'm not sure I can really help with that, but I know Sam can. Let's take a few days, and I will push him and see what we can do. What you need to do, is get some rest and let your body finish doing its thing. Maybe that was enough to get it out of your system."

She reached up and wiped the streaks of blood from my cheek. I leaned into it, the feeling of being so softly touched leaving my body craving more of it.

"We can figure that all out tomorrow." She threw her hair behind her, and I watched her lay back down and close her eyes. I sat there silently, watching her sleep. She really did it, really just went back to sleep. I felt angry with myself and frustrated that things had escalated so fast out of my control. I sighed, and a minute later I followed. I tried to stay on my pillow, fighting the urge to curl back up into myself again. To close my eyes and see Hayley on top of me, just like they always were.

Temperance

REFLECTIONS

"In the eternal night, where moonlight weaves tales of despair, I press
on, a lone sentinel against the vampiric tide. Ireena Vasiliev's crimson
gaze pierces the veil of my resolve, a siren's call to damnation."
    Father Gabriel's Private Journal, 1602

CHAPTER 3

*B*reakfast the next evening was awkward, to say the least. The boys each gave me their own look of curious satisfaction, and Luce handed me a glass of wine like nothing had ever happened. Sammy came through the door with excitement plastered across his face. He threw his bag onto the table and took a seat, ripping out of his bag what I could only assume was a tablet.

"Elaine. Sorry, your phone was so old that there aren't even parts to replace it. I tried. Obsessively tried. It was unsalvageable. What I did save, however…" he turned on the tablet, punched a few keys and spun it around. "Was this."

In the middle of the screen was a picture of Hayley, sitting next to our dog at a picnic in Virginia. He hit a button and another picture came up. The two of us dancing at a rooftop bar.

Hayley kissing me during the ball dropping at New Year's Eve.

Hayley laying with their feet up the wall while reading a book.

Hayley laughing at me because I was sunburned.

The pictures went on and on.

"It really is them, and that's really you." He said with a smile, pointing to me. "You weren't lying. What happened that made them into the butcher?"

"Yes, that's me. It's been so long since I've seen these. Thank you, Sammy." I felt a knot form in my stomach, my smile one of happiness tainted by the sadness I was feeling. It was a major struggle to keep myself from crying at seeing them again.

"Sammy," I said quietly, keeping my eyes on every picture that popped up. He stopped, looking at me. I could fell from the way his face softened that he knew how hurt I was inside.

"Yes?"

"Do you know where my grave is?"

"Didn't you come out of it?" he tilted his head to the side, as if confused at his own question.

"Not my holding place. My grave. My real one, from before."

"Ah. Give me a few minutes." He turned the computer screen around started typing furiously on the screen. "Nope… also no… here's an article about it… Congrats, you had a huge funeral. That had to have been pricey."

He continued talking to himself, and I shot a curious glance to Lucina. She simply shrugged in response. I shifted uncomfortably in my chair, trying to be as patient as possible while mumbled more words at his computer screen.

"Found You!" He lifted his arms in victory, then slowly lowered them when he noticed both Lucina and I staring at him. "Sorry. I found you. Elaine Catherin Reinhardt, and there' a picture of it. Wanna go for a walk?"

He smiled across the table at both us and turned off his computer, sliding it into a thin black case with his initials sewn into it. I hadn't taken him for that kind of tech geek. Half of me expected him to throw it in a bag and toss it over his shoulder.

"Are we going there right now?" My heartbeat quickened. Was I even ready to see it? To see me?

"We can. It's only a mile to downtown, your grave is at the Memorial Center near Main Street."

"It's okay to not go, Elaine." Lucina said, taking her glass over to the sink. I watcher her swish a drop of soap and water around the cup, and I looked at mine. Half empty. The smell of it made my nose sting, and I felt the hunger slowly overpowering my nausea. I gulped the last few drinks down and covered my mouth, pressing my lips together in an attempt to keep it all down.

"We can go tomorrow, it's okay."

"No. I'll be fine." Lucina gave me a quick gaze of pity that her eyes were unable to hide. I turned her way. "I'm good. Promise."

"Here." She picked up a jacket from her chair and tossed it over to me. "The cold won't matter, but it's good to look normal."

I gave her a smile, trying to hide the rising knot in my chest. She gave a deep exhale and walked out of the room, Sammy following behind her. I fell into line and stepped out onto the front porch where they had stopped. A smile crossed my face as I saw the giant snowflakes falling from the sky.

I loved the snow. Winter was one of my favorite times of year. Between the holiday decorations and all of the lights, what wasn't to love? Between hot chocolate and Christmas markets, I had endless memories with Hayley that came flooding back to me. My eye closed for a moment, a deep inhale and exhale following before I hopped down from the porch and into the snow.

The street had been turned into a winter wonderland, and a light sheet of white covered the cars we walked by. Every few cars I'd run my fingers across the hood, feeling the cool nip of the ice. Lucina and Sammy laughed at me, but it was something that made me feel a little bit normal. Hayley had always given me a hard time too.

Apparently, drawing hearts on random cars in the snow had annoyed all of our neighbors.

I could care less then; I could care even less now.

We walked for what felt like an hour. It would have been less had I not stopped to peer in windows downtown. There were people everywhere, and the smell of fresh coffee coming from one of the cafés on the central square. Even with the snow, the people here seemed happy. They *were* happy. I had been happy.

I looked around at all of the buildings. They had survived. Whatever the world had thrown at this place, it had weathered the storm of time. Lucina walked over to me, lifting her hand to pat my head. I snapped my attention to her, a quick glance of surprise that jolted me.

"Sorry, I was just, you know… it's so different but it's still the same." I looked over at one of the shops where a restaurant I used to frequent once was.

"That was where I would do drinks with friends. We had our first dinner date there before a theater show." I pointed next to it. "And that used to be a florist. They did the flowers for our wedding."

I walked into the middle of the square where a wooden platform stood. "That used to be a fountain, and in the winter, they would cover it up and put a giant Christmas tree on top of it. We'd go to the lighting every season."

There was a smile on my face, more memories coming back to me. I turned and ran across the square towards a line of glass windows, car horns blaring at me when I ran between them. Sammy and Lucina tried to keep up as I turned a corner, coming to face a multi-story parking garage.

My shoulders lowered at the sight before me, the smile immediately disappearing.

"This used to be a city garden. I proposed to Hayley here." I could have wept over the loss of the gardens. To never sit there and watch Hayley read after work while I drank my third coffee of the day, it hurt.

"Elaine… I'm so sorry. They paved over the park a long time ago." His voice held a bit of sadness in it.

"It used to be a park?" Lucina asked, leaning her head on Sammy's shoulder.

"Yes. It was the common gardens. The city sold it, at the turn of last century." It was after they added the buildings behind it. The city was hurting for parking, and this was the solution.

"It was a stupid solution." I snapped, turning around, and walking away.

"Elaine." Lucina responded softly, her eyes widening at the sharpness of my tone.

"What." I turned, snapping again. My fingers curled into fists at the anger I was feeling, the frustration born from never being able to see those gardens again.

"The graveyard is the other way." I watched her tuck her hands into thee fleece lined pockets on her jacket and look away from me.

"I'm sorry. I'm just- I was foolish to believe it would all be the same. It changed enough when I was alive, why would I expect it to all be the same?" I lowered my had and turned away from them, hiding the tears of frustration that were trying to emerge. People whispered as they walked by us, moving wide around our group. Great. We had made a scene. I had made a scene. So much for trying to fit in.

"It's okay. We know this is a lot. The others wanted to come too and asked if you needed anything. Sammy said that it would be better for you to do it without an entire crowd watching you." He turned and started walking away from me.

I felt bad for snapping at them. Digging my hands into my pockets as I followed behind him, I kept my head low and tried not to look around, to not risk seeing something else that might set me off.

We walked for another ten minutes, stopping at a set of iron gates that had been slid into the mud around the narrow pathway that winded its way inside the graveyard. I took a deep breath to calm my nerves and entered, Sammy and Lucina falling in behind me. I half expected to burst into flames at the whole 'hallowed ground' thing.

I turned to Sammy, who simply lifted his arm towards a trio of twisted trees on the back side of the graveyard. I quickened my pace, moving in and out of the stones carefully as to not disturb the residents who were buried beneath my feet.

As my eyes fixed upon the moss-covered gravestone, a chill crawled up my spine. The name inscribed upon it was mine, a stark reminder of the life I had once lived, now shrouded in centuries of darkness. I reached out, my fingers brushing lightly over the engraved letters.

"Elaine Catherin Reinhardt," I whispered, my voice barely audible against the night's hush. A shiver ran through me as I traced the contours of the name, feeling the cold, unyielding stone beneath my fingertips.

The air seemed heavy with the weight of my realization, and my gaze drifted to the dates carved into the stone. " Mors Tibi Nunquam Obstet… 1991 – 2025." Two centuries had passed since my last breath as a mortal, and yet, the grief etched into the epitaph echoed across the ages. "What does that mean?"

Sammy and Lucina exchanged a solemn glance, allowing me the space to grapple with the flood of emotions. The moonlight caught the tears pooling in my eyes as I read the heartfelt words etched beneath my name. Memories long suppressed surged to the forefront of my mind.

A lone sob escaped my lips, carried away by the night.

"They mourned me," I whispered, my voice a mere whisper in the stillness. "For two hundred years, they mourned a life that was stolen from me. My friends, my family gathered here. "

My eyes blurred with tears as I pictured the faces of those, I once held dear. Friends, family, and colleagues – all of them had believed my life had ended tragically, mourning the loss of a bright soul extinguished too soon. I looked past my stone where a wide black stone stood, two names engraved. The left side was my sister, Alina, and the other her husband Mitchell. They had been dead for nearly a hundred and seventy years.

"I'm sorry," I whispered, her voice choked with emotion. "I never meant to leave you all behind."

I reached out and traced the words etched into the headstone again – my name, the dates of her birth and supposed death, and a quote chosen by her loved ones. It read:

Mors Tibi Nunquam Obstet
Gone but not forgotten
May your light shine on forever

The weight of their collective sorrow pressed upon my heart, and I sank to my knees beside the grave. My grave. Had Hayley picked that? Had it been my sisters?

Splashes of red dyed the snow crimson, my body keeled over as I cried. Not from pain, but from sorrow and despair at what had been taken from me.I would never see my family again. My head lifted, streaks of blood pouring down my cheeks, the uncontrollable sobs nearly making me choke. I had never been given the chance to be a mother, and I had no idea whether either of my two sisters' family lines had continued.

I felt a wave of nausea fight its way through the tears, the cramping of my stomach reeling my body over. My sisters were gone. My best friends, my confidants, my partners in crime. It all seemed unreal, like a nightmare that I would soon wake up from. But as I looked down at the red-stained snow that marked their passing, reality set in.

Tears continued to roll down my cheeks as I thought about all the memories we shared together. The laughter, the tears, the secrets we swore to take to our graves. We had been through so much together and now they were gone. My sister had been my best friend, my maid of honor, my confidant.

I couldn't help but think about what could have been if they were still here. Would we have grown old together, sitting on rocking chairs on a porch somewhere, reminiscing about our youth and laughing at the antics from days long past? Would we be celebrating the holidays surrounded by our kids and grandchildren? Every thought sunk me deeper into sadness.

Those dreams had been shattered and replaced with a gaping hole in my heart. A hole that could never be filled by anyone else.

A gust of wind snaked its way across the graveyard, and I shivered from both cold and grief. I felt an arm wrap around me, Lucina taking a knee next to me. I struggled to lift my head up to meet her, and before she could say anything I started crying again.

I cried until I had nothing left in me.

* * *

CONVINCING them to help me get to Camden took less effort across the next few days. All I had to really do was talk Sammy and Lucina into it and the rest was history. Thankfully for me, she never brought up my first night there. Mikael and Andrej walked me through the entire process for entering another's territory, and it was a pain in the ass.

There was a petition for entry that had to be filled out and signed by the local principality lord, and then that had to be sent to Baltimore where the city governor would accept or deny it. It took two more days for that signature to come back, late Wednesday night. By the time it had arrived I was already feeling a little worn down from the lack of eating.

The thought of drinking anything blood related made me want to throw up, despite the hunger that regularly reminded me of my new needs. I would sip enough of it to calm it down, and just enough to keep me awake. Each sip was accompanied with flashes of the man who screamed when I bit him.

I could still taste him, my first.

Sammy, Taj, Luce, and I took off the next evening the moment the sun dipped behind the horizon and went south. The twins had business to take care of, and Kris decided to stay and help them. After vampires had gone public regular humans, or defaults as Adam called them, reached a new level of 2nd amendment crazy. I had to live through a literal monster in the white house during my days, so any hope I had of the world being a better place seemed to go out the window.

It never crossed my mind that maybe that lunatic could have actually been a monster. Maybe he was a werewolf or something. Were they a thing? I closed my eyes in thought, imagining what it would have been like had he turned into a full werewolf on stage at the United Nations, or during the holiday Christmas tree lighting.

The only way to safely get to Camden was through Baltimore and up the 95 corridor towards Philly. At least the roads were all the same, and much of the traveling was fairly similar in direction to what it had been during my time. While the city seemed to be safer for our kind, it was at the same time heavily territorial. Our only saving grace was that we would be staying on the beltway and not going deep into the city. Our second saving grace was the sun setting at 6 in the evening. Thanks, daylight savings. We took off in the late afternoon, hoping to make it through all the traffic and get down there without any issues. I watched, curiously entertained at the cars that passed us on the road.

I sat in the back of the banged-up SUV, looking out the tinted windows as we passed exits that were so familiar it felt like a normal road trip. I remember drives down to the district for galas and sporting events. The fourth of July celebration on the inner harbor in Baltimore and all of the crab cakes I could eat at Lexington Market. I doubted Faidley's was still around, but I would fight anyone who said it was not the best crab cakes ever tasted. They just melted; it made my stomach growl thinking about it.

It was about an hour and some change before we got off the highway through a checkpoint. Two men in police uniforms that weren't familiar to me stopped the car, and after a short conversation between the two we were on our way through. The road had gone through another expansion, and its new overpass gave a perfect view of downtown. States had done a number on their own rights, and since our car didn't have an interstate travel pass, we had to stop. The skyline was just as beautiful as I remember it, even if some of the skyscrapers had changed. We stopped briefly at a final checkpoint that led down into the city, then continued forward towards the beltway.

"Even going between the major territories, we still have to have our papers in check." Taj explained, still leaning against the door.

"We can move pretty openly between our region and most of Maryland. There are a few, though, that are still heavily off limits and restricted like Jersey. I guess you would know it as the DMV, right?"

I shook my head in response. Of course, I knew the DMV, it had been our home, and it was where we had first met.

It was also where we got married.

"Right, well, from the DMV south to about the Carolinas are all minor territories that belong to fifth and sixth generations, and they pay their dues up the chains. Most of them operated independently of each other and there is a mutual agreement to keep the peace.

Honestly, most of the north was like that until Hayley returned state-side. We had no idea she wasn't European like the rest of her crazy family."

I sat there and listened to him, occasionally glancing out the window at the streetlights while he told me about the changes in the political landscape. Traffic was mild at this time, and I was smiling at the thought of never having to hit rush hours again. Taj kept talking, giving me snippets of pieces about the humans and their political shifts, and the conflict between the day walkers and night life. It was a lot of information to take in, but I kept a lot of my questions to myself while I thought about how the world had evolved, but at the same time never really changed.

The car slowly pulled off the highway, taking an exit north of Parkville. I remembered these lights. My eyes closed for a moment and a light yawn pressed out from my lips.

"Tired already?" Luce said with a smile, nudging me with her elbow.

"I'm still getting used to the night shift, my body is rested but I feel sluggish. How do you all do this?" I replied. It was the truth, I felt like I was barely alive. Guess I wasn't even that anymore.

"It does take a bit to get used to but give it a few decades and it will grow on you." Taj chimed in, "One day you won't even remember what the sun looked like."

"Doesn't that seem a bit sad? Don't you miss it?" It was depressing to think that they would never see the sun, that I would never see it again. As much as I hated it brightly finding its way between my curtains to wake me in the morning, the warmth from it was always something I enjoyed. Hayley and I had a Caribbean Island we used to frequent, and the thought of never doing that again left me sitting in silence.

"Miss what? The sunlight? All our senses have changed, and we don't feel things quite the same anymore. Besides that, the sun will literally turn us to ash, so even though it's been two hundred years since I saw it, I don't miss it one bit." Taj over exaggerated a deep sigh while rubbing his head.

The car took a hard right and pulled into an apartment complex, passing a large sign shaped like a tree. Oakwood Acres was engraved into the light wooden surface. There weren't many cars parked in any of the spots. Odd for a Baltimore suburb.

"Taj, who's this guy we're meeting?" I had a stranger danger feeling.

"Heh, he's an old buddy of mine," Taj smiled with a laugh "then again, everyone is an old buddy if you know what I mean."

"That's cause you're actually an old soul Taj" Sammy laughed nudging him across the arm rest. "Let's go meet your guy."

The apartment complex didn't look that impressive. Four stories, single lobby, the usual layout, and design for an older suburban complex. At the last cul-de-sac our car finally pulled crookedly into an empty spot.

"This shithole is it?" I was beyond skeptical at this point. There was absolutely no way that there was anyone important living here. It looked like a complete disaster that should be demolished. Vines stretched up the sides of the building, the foundation was cracked and there were stains from the weather on what visible part of the building you could see.

"Yep. This shithole is it." Sammy smiled in confirmation as he opened the door.

"It might not look like much but it's a fortress at night. At least two dozen of us live in this building alone. The complex is owned by one of us too."

I planted my feet firmly on the ground before pulling myself out and onto the street. A chilled breeze snaked its way through the decorative bushes and across the street. I knew it was about thirty degrees out here, but I felt oddly comfortable. I watched the light sway of the few trees that lined the sidewalks, remembering the walks I used to take with Hayley every evening. We would walk our malamute Apollo through our community that was, well, much nicer than this one.

The others were all out of the car by the time I made it to the sidewalk. This shouldn't take long, I thought. Sammy and Taj had talked a big game about this guy. I had no idea that different regions had different rules and while humans could pass between them, it wasn't the same for our kind.

We moved quick down the pathway towards the center building. The wide, tan walkway was bordered by squared hedge bushes that appeared to be quite neglected. As we neared the entrance, I could finally see through the large glass windows that surrounded the doors.

What. A. Dump. I felt my breath stop in my chest as I stared into the foyer of the building. Trash everywhere, folded up boxes stacked against the wall, and a garbage can overflowing with beer bottles is what awaited across the threshold.

Sammy looked at me and Lucina before giving her a hug and whispering something in her ear. She smiled, kissed him, and went back towards the car. Taj put his hands on my shoulders from behind and lightly shook me.

"Breathe Elaine, breathe. We got you here." He laughed confidently to himself before Sammy opened the door and we entered. I guess I had looked anxious or something to him. Another stark reminder that I had no poker face.

The stairwell was fairly well lit, fitting perfectly with the olive speckle carpet and off-white paint. We walked up both flights of stairs before coming to the third floor. Instead of multiple doors, there was just one here. Taj stood in front and knocked. The door almost immediately flew open, held by a little guy who looked to be no more than 5 feet tall. He wore a ripped leather jacket over an old, faded blue v neck t-shirt.

"Torgiev, Marcus knows we're coming." Taj extended his arm toward the smaller man. He took it, smiling as he shook his hand. "Glad to see you buddy."

"Buddy my ass, you come to lose more money?" he gripped Taj's hand before pulling him forward into a bear hug. The two laughed for a moment before he stepped out of the way and motioned for us to follow him.

"Marcus does his business in the back," Taj turned his head and looked at Sammy and I "I'll take care of it, you guys wait out here."

I looked around the large open room. There were several couches with various people hanging out. A small group was by the wall playing some sort of video game. While I was curious about how well the graphics looked these days, I didn't want to intrude. The room smelled liked a freshly cleaned morgue mixed with pine. There were a few people sitting at a table rolling some powder into paper strips. The balcony door hung open and there were several others outside smoking. I was able to pick up little wafts of the bitter smoke as it floated across the room. Ventilation in here was abysmal.

"Hey Sammy..." I whispered to him. "Do vampires have drugs?"

Sammy chuckled for a moment while he looked over at them. He shook his head in disapproval.

"Yes, we do." He replied. "Drizz is a high end, super concentrated mix between cocaine and ecstasy. It would kill a normal human. If anyone hands it to you, turn it down. Trust me. If anyone mentioned BB2, you walk away. Bloodbane is poison to us. It won't kill us, but we will be as weak as a human."

Sammy stayed next to me, and we watched another group of vampires enter the room and head straight to the kitchen. I felt a tap on my arm and turned to find an oddly plain looking woman handing me a glass of what I unfortunately mistook as wine. Just being happy to receive a glass of something normal, I instantly took a sip of it. It was my first proper sip of blood since I had feasted on those poor guys at the cemetery.

I looked at it strangely, trying not to cough it back up. Without the bloodlust driving me I could taste the thick iron flavor in it. It was far less than what I would call a high-quality glass of wine.

"Having trouble?" she looked at me with a smile, revealing the set of fangs tucked across her lips. "It's decently fresh, promise. I don't see many other gals in here, so it's nice to just have a drink with one."

"I feel like I really need a girl's trip right now. Wine, manicures, a beautiful empty beach," I smiled at her, "a true vacation. This all feels like a bad dream."

"A bad dream, you must be new. I'm Daniella," she tilted her head at me curiously. I watched her look down my body, most of hiding under the leggings and baggy sweater. She on the other hand, wore a lovely crème cocktail dress that perfectly accentuated every curve of her body. "Where are you trying to get to?"

"I don't quite know," I sighed, "It feels like everything has changed so quickly and I just want to get away from it all." I responded. Taj had warned me in the car to not give any specifics to anyone. Daniella nodded sympathetically and said, "I've been through a few transitions myself. The best advice I can give you is to take some time and figure out what you really want in life. That always helps me when I'm feeling lost. Find something that makes you happy and go after it!"

I COULDN'T HELP but smile at Daniella's bubbly enthusiasm.

"And what do you find makes you happy" I asked, watching her slide her body closer to mine.

"I find my satisfaction" she took my hand and lifted it up to her mouth. "In all the right places". Her lips moved across my fingertips each kiss filled with an unnerving softness that I never would have expected from someone surrounded by so many men. She kissed the back of my hand, then brought her lips around the crease between my thumb and index finger, her teeth gently clamping down on them with a playful nibble.

I wanted to say at least something to her but was interrupted when a door slammed open.

Taj and another vampire walked out of the back room. He looked to be a little under six feet tall. Dressed to the nines in the finest of cheap leathers and most likely the type of guy who most women made fun of for not being tall enough. He carried himself like some mobster wannabe. A half-burnt cigarette was stuck behind his heavily pierced ear. He had more metal up there than anyone I had seen before. He looked straight at me before stepping forward.

"So, let me get this straight," he smirked while looking me head to toe, "You want papers to get clear across the Commodore bridge and into the Butcher's territory?"

"Guilty." I said as I nodded my head. The room broke out in laughter. It wasn't the fun kind, where a can of beer had exploded all over someone. It was the kind where you were the center of the playground with mud all over you face. Danielle grabbed the wine glass from my hand before I could drop it and stepped backwards away from me.

"*Daniella?*" I looked at her, worried. She quickly shook her head back at me while stepping further away.

"Bro, *trust us here.*" Sammy cut the room off, trying to persuade him. He stepped in front of me, and for once I was thankful to be standing behind a man.

"Not going to happen Sam. I don't care what reason you have, if it gets out that I made papers for someone to enter that dead zone, it's my head on the pike outside. Got it?" Marcus crossed his arms and looked me over again.

"I don't care how much you got, it's not worth the risk to offend that crazy bitch. Or Addison. That lunatic will make me watch the sunrise on his doorstep."

I looked across the room at Taj, quietly scanning the open space for any way to get out of here. There were around fifteen people in this room, three on the balcony and a guard leaning against the wall by the door. Not good odds at all, but what I was about to do was ballsy as hell anyway. There wasn't a lot of things that would ever take me from quiet to hostile, but insulting my wife was to of that list. I closed my eyes for a moment while I tried to collect myself. There was a burning tightness in my chest that felt like rage building, and before I knew it, I sent the situation from bad to worse.

"Cowardice looks good on someone holed up in a shit dive like this." The room went silent. Good. It was a like a light switch flipped inside of me. Taj was speechless, his eyes growing wide at what he perceived as my audacity. Apparently, he thought I was going to say something else. They really hadn't had the chance to get to know me yet. Maybe being dead made me lose any bit of self-preservation I had. The only thing that really mattered to me at all was getting back to Hayley and I wasn't about to let some tiny man get in my way.

"Excuse me-" Marcus stood up and crossed his arms.

"No excuses, it's to be expected of someone who's what, tenth down the line?" He closed his mouth, the smirk he wore shifted into angrily pursed lips. I could smell his blood from here the more I focused on him. It was barely even there, a fraction of a bloodline that I could barely smell. My senses focused on it, and the faintness of his heartbeat quickening.

"How do you know that." He replied sharply, his tone rather angry. Most definitely angry. I didn't quite have an answer for him, but I knew it. It was a feeing. I felt like there was a subtle sensation there that wasn't that strong. His bloods purity was barely laughable.

"Smell yourself, you're so fresh you may as well be a child." I stepped to the side of Sammy. I was glad Luce was outside, my danger sense was currently hitting critical and the hair on my arms stood on end.

Marcus smirked again, the stepped over to stand in front of me. He brought his arm straight up to my chin, taking it in between his fingertips. What was with men and their stupid feeling of existential superiority?

"Wanna say that again, cupcake" his condescending smile flashed his fangs.

"That bitch is my wife, and I'll rip your arm off if you don't remove it." I kept my eyes locked on him. No fear could be seen in them, only an icy determination to get what I needed. My tone was quiet, steady, and controlled. I could feel my heartbeat in my throat. That tightness was currently expanding and there was a burning sensation that felt like my body was about to ignite. The only thing going through my mind was 'what would Hayley do'. So much for not giving up any details.

Marcus kept his focus drilled on me. I could hear his breathing quicken, then he pursed his lips and made a kissing sound at me.

"Then maybe we should do the world a favor and bury you now, save myself the trouble. What do you think boys?" he took both arms out to the side. Was he challenging all of us? I could sense Taj and Sammy getting nervous with the situation devolving.

"Make the papers and we leave here in peace." I had to reign this in as fast as possible. Come on, you dominated the board room, this was almost the same thing.

"Sam, you and Taj can fuck off. We're keeping this one here, it's been a while since we had a ne –"Marcus' words were cut short. His eyes widened. He never saw it coming.

I was impulsively hostile and had zero problems bringing violence forward to protect myself. Any thought of reminding myself that I had zero self-defense training had already disappeared. My hand was wrapped so tightly around his neck that the skin under my fingers was turning whiter than the pasty pale he had been before. I felt like something else had taken over altogether. Something primal.

Something… violent.

There was no way for air to get to his lungs and while strangulation couldn't kill him, it would still be painful. There was a rage building inside of me that I couldn't quite get under control and my body acted without me telling it.

It took moments for blood to flood the whites of his eyes. He tried to pull away but couldn't. His arms flailed as he tried beating down on my forearm. There was a tingly sensation across my body as I let myself go into the anger, like the heightened emotions were feeding me more. I could see in my reflection from the mirror on the wall behind him that my brown eyes had slowly started to turn bright crimson, the fangs slowly emerging through my smile. I could smell him every ounce of him. His panic smelled delightful and for a moment, I wondered what another vampire would taste like. Would that be considered cannibalism?

"A what? I couldn't hear you Marcus" I smiled him as gently and as innocently as possible, my voice gleaming with an intoxicating tone. "Would you mind repeating that for me? Pretty please? It's so hard to hear you when your voice is so low."

He held on as tightly as he could. It wasn't much, but I could feel a more explosive level of strength come from my core. My muscles felt like they were on fire.

Was this my bloodline? I had to test it out and see where the boundaries were when I got a chance. I didn't even notice the rooms thick, shocked gazes that kept their eyes fixated on me. No time like the present, Elle, time to see what we could do.

With the same darkened smile, I excitedly lifted him up and planted his body into the wall behind him with such force that mirror hanging across the wall crashed to the ground. His eyes started rolling back and his legs flailed wildly. I could feel the blood slowing down beneath his neck, trying to circulate but unable to. It looked painful, truly.

"Do you need two arms to make papers, or is it more a drag and drop situation? You could click with your face, right?" I tilted my head to the side and looked across the room with a hiss. "Anyone else able to make my papers, or do I have to keep this one around?"

A solid ten seconds of dead silence filled the room before one of 'the boys' spoke up.

"Miss, um, Marcus is the only one, if you end him, you're going to be outta luck" he kept his arms up where I could see them while talking. I bet I could rip this dude's arms off before anyone got to me. "And he can't answer you cause he can't speak."

The man made a decent point. While I didn't want to lose the momentum I had here, there was no way he could get away at this range. I tried to fight my way back through the rage that he had sent across my entire being. Finally, I drove my tongue underneath one of the fangs and bit down – hard. The pain of it accompanied by the taste of my own blood snapped me back into control.

I released Marcus after a moment of thought, watching him hit the ground gasping for air. He looked up at me like I was out of my mind for touching him. His eyes still carried that condescending look. He scampered backwards towards the door to his office, trying to make room between us.

"You've gotta be her wife with that level of crazy... can't you count how many of us are in here?" he gasped for air between words.

"Papers or death. Your boys might get to me, but not before I use your head like a soccer ball." My patience was wearing thin. I crackled my knuckles, letting the blood return to my ghostly white fingertips.

Was soccer still a thing? It had to be. No way would that sport ever die out.

"Marcus, we came here because you said you could help us with the papers. Let's try to keep our business civil." Sammy stepped in front of me, accompanied by Taj who helped him up. "Elaine, how about this..."

He looked at Marcus, then at me with a smile while raising his arms up between us.

"Marcus makes your papers, and you owe him one. Being in the grace of the butcher is like an extra life. What do you think?" he made a good point, reaching his hand out to shake with Marcus.

His eyes ignored Taj's hand for a moment and looked at me instead. A quick glare was replaced by a calmer demeanor. I cemented that look in my mind and added him to my personal bury list. There was no way he was a good person, alive or undead, and I would make sure he never looked at anyone that way ever again.

Marcus kept quiet for a moment, then shook Sammy's hand.

"Do I have your word? One favor. You owe *ME* for this" he said, still breathing heavily while recovering. He pointed his thumb at his chest, sticking it out a little bit further. His tone grinded my nerves and I wanted nothing more than to hang him off the balcony.

I crossed my arms and stood my ground. Maybe it would have been better to kill this guy than have to give him a favor. I sometimes hated how much integrity I had. If I knew how much this would hurt later, I'd never have agreed to it. I lifted a single finger up, extending my arm out so everyone could see it.

"One favor. I owe you one." There, I said it. Now, if he reneged or tried to pull anything I would literally rip his head off. His lips curled into a smile before he clapped his hands together in front of him, still coughing.

"Alright, let's get you some papers, and I'll even see if I can get a message over there for you." Marcus said, still begrudgingly. He rubbed the sides of his neck while another man brought him a glass of blood.

The tension in the room slowly disappeared as the crowd

dispersed. The sound of beers opening and video games coming from the wall mounted television soon filled the room. Sammy turned around and unexpectedly gave me a hug. He was less cold than normal, and it felt nice to have physical contact with someone one again. As much as I had hoped for it to be Hayley, I would take what I could get right now. My heartbeat was going at full speed, and I was still trying to get it to slow down. Whatever had just happened filled me with so much adrenaline that I was dizzy.

"One step closer to being home Sammy, I'm so close." I kept my voice low while he hugged me. It felt nice to have someone wrap their arms around me in a way that wasn't threatening. The last few minutes had left me exhausted, and he knew it.

"I know, Luce and I are going to get you home. I promise. Are you okay? You look tired from earlier. That was crazy. Let's go to the kitchen," he said as he turned away and took my hand, pulling me in that direction. "We need to get you some more blood, especially if you're going to do that again."

* * *

BLACK VELVET CURTAINS DANCED GENTLY in the open windows, parting only when a slim, elegant silhouette moved between them. Their every movement was smoothly graceful to the point of being regal. A black and burgundy French vest hung off their shoulders, dragging the ground behind them as their figure stepped outside onto the old cherry oak balcony.

They carried a single wine glass, lined with gold filigree that wrapped down through its stem and across the base. There was bright red liquid filled nearly to the brim. With one motion her lips parted, and they sipped it down. Not a single drop was wasted. A light breeze crawled across the water of the river, making its way up the docks and through the outer wall before flowing delicately through the short, black and red tipped hair that was tied tightly above their head. Their form sat at a tiny glass table, an irritated visage peering down at a small stack of gold brimmed burgundy cards.

A light sigh whisped from between lightly parted maroon lips as they flipped the first of the moon backed cards over. Then the second, and finally the third. An upset gaze looked across each of them, their brow pursing with frustration. The cards were shuffled back together before another card was drawn. Then a second, and a third.

The chariot, the five of swords, and the lovers. They looked across the cards, scanning them, then up at the moon for a few moments before shaking their head and shuffling them back into their home.

Knock Knock

The door to the overly large room opened slowly, revealing two figures that quickly entered. The first was a young woman with piercing blue eyes and long brown hair curled up into a messy bun. She held a clip board and a tablet between her arms. The older man that followed was panicking anxiously. His body was barely holding together his nervousness.

"Miranda." A low, indifferent voice floated through the curtains and into the room. Even over the crackling fireplace, their tone was clearly heard. They shuffled the three cards back into the deck before tucking them into an oak box.

"You bring good news, I presume."

"My deepest apologies, Sir." She bowed her head, and for a moment a flash of nervousness reflected in her eyes. "

This is Jackson, the human who was to deliver your cargo."

The man dropped to his knees and lowered his head, sobbing.

"Madam, we had an accident an' dropped it. We had no idea there was someone inside and when she—" the man said, continuing to let his tears hit the floor.

"She?" The tone shifted noticeably from indifference to surprise. There was no way anyone should have known what was in there.

The voice shifted and came from behind the man. It was as if their figure had blurred through space from the balcony. Glossy black fingernails ran across the man's neck, sending him into more panic.

"Tell me *everything*."

The man looked up, his sight confirming his greatest fear. The vampire standing before him was barely five and a half feet tall. The flames from the fireplace danced across the crimson satin that matched the blood inside their wine glass. Two pearlescent fangs glistened in the reflective light cast through the room. It was just enough light to let the man know there were three vampiric beings in the room with him.

The figure in the corner chair by the fireplace lifted his head up briefly before returning to the book he was reading and Miranda opened her tablet and began to take notes, never letting her eyes move from the scene in front of her. She studied everything about the woman and recorded every note meticulously. Obsessively.

Justice
Justice

"A phantom of the night dances at the edge of my consciousness. In my journal, ink becomes the sacrament of truth, chronicling the battle between redemption and the seductive allure of the undead. She will not win."
Father Gabriel's Private Journal, 1627

*W*e spent less than an hour or two in Baltimore. Something inside me had a craving for a crab cake, and everything else just wanted a glass of chilled blood. There was something about the taste of warm blood that reminded me of a wine my grandmother used to drink. It always tasted like grape juice and vinegar, which was absolutely and unquestionably disgusting. Whatever had happened to me left me feeling exhausted.

It felt good to be back in the car and heading north again. I had the papers I needed to get across the bridge and that was all I cared about right now. I watched the lights on the highway flicker by as we crossed the Delaware Memorial bridge. It was a luminescent shade of purple and white, the long truss beams glowing with light. We immediately got off the highway and took the old route 130. The roads were just as bumpy as I remembered them to be.

There was so much nostalgia from seeing these familiar exits. They had been replaced so many times and still had that bright forest green with reflective writing. The only difference was the addition of an odd moon and sun symbol onto the side. Civilization quickly faded away as we entered one of the larger wooded areas. I smirked at my reflection in the window while wondering how deforestation and the ozone layer hadn't completely fried the human race already.

"We're here." Sammy pulled the car off the side of the road before coming to a stop.

Taj cracked his window with a sigh, then slowly opened the door with a light sigh of relief. It seemed like everything was all clear from here.

"Let's make this quick. We're already an hour outside of our zone" Taj said as he opened my door. I slid out of the back and looked across the backseat at Lucina.

"Thank you, Luce. I'll come visit once things get settled down, I promise." I gave her a genuine smile. She had been nothing but good to me since I woke up. I didn't really have any girlfriends right now and she was the closest thing to one.

"I'll send someone to bring you all over when I get settled. I'm sure Hayley will be glad to meet you all."

She curled her legs up on the backseat and smiled back at me. If I had more time around her, I'm sure we would have grown to be good friends. There was a comfort that she brought me, and it was a shame I couldn't bring her with me.

"Good luck Ellie, please be safe" she replied with concern in her voice. It felt good to have people care for about me, even if it was a group of random strangers. She reached into her jacket and pulled out a piece of paper.

"This is a map of the area when you get over there." She said, handing it to me with a smile. "Once you get across the bridge, just keep going straight. Their manor is in Upland Park. They built it out of an old arboretum!"

"How do you know that?" I asked.

"When they built their place, they published it and dared anyone to come for them." Luce laughed lightheartedly. "You two really are perfect for each other. Don't be a stranger, all right?"

Taj came and gave me a big hug. He wrapped his arms around me and held me tight while whispering in my ear.

"Our boy got word across the water," he said quietly, yet excitedly. "Hayley might be coming for you."

I felt my body tense up with excitement. Hayley might be there to see me. Just the thought of that sent warmth through my body. Sammy stood by his door with the car lights off but kept the engine on. We both turned around, facing the woods as two people emerged from the shadows. They looked relatively normal by all accounts, but my perception of normal was a little skewed right now.

"You have your papers," he said while putting his hands on my shoulders, "the bridge is literally a half mile from here. All you have to do is make it there."

"Thank you for bringing me this far. You know I won't forget this, and I know Hayley won't either". I stepped into his arms and gave him one more hug back.

Sammy smiled and waved from his side before opening his car door. He nodded to the couple by the woods who motioned for me to hurry up.

"Take care girly, we will be seeing you soon, alright?" his tone shared the same concern as his other half. They had only known me for forty-eight hours or so and had a pretty good grasp of my personality.

The two disappeared back into the car before it slowly pulled away, leaving me standing there by myself, with strangers again. I took a large inhale and held my breath for a moment before slowly exhaling. I could literally see the lights that dotted the overhands on the bridge. One more piece to go until I would be a step closer to Hayley.

I moved quickly over to the tree line to meet the others. Taj's guys trusted them, but I didn't. They were both wearing long overcoats, fur lined hats and gloves. Everything looked completely normal until they smiled and showed their fangs.

"Here's the deal, we're all family and we're heading to see your brother in the city. We talk, you follow us. Got it?" his voice was a bit raspy through the scarf that he had hanging down his chest.

Great, I thought to myself. A man of few words. It felt abrupt to me, but there wasn't anything that I could really do to alter the situation. The woman next to him nodded gently with a smile.

"Got it," I said while nodding.

I looked through the trees towards the road, keeping myself evenly behind the two. They stayed quiet along the short walk to their car. I hated silence and would have loved to have a conversation about anything at this point, but I knew what was on the line. We quickly got into the car and pulled out onto the main road before circling back towards the highway. There was only one exit between us, and the bridge and those few moments felt like forever.

The Delaware River port authority stood towering in front of us. A large sign hung next to the exit for the old double arch bridge. An array of search lights atop two buildings on both sides of the highway. There was no way I was going to make it up there walking straight through the front gate, and I didn't have a car. For once I was glad that I could follow directions. We pulled off the road into a parking lot, coming to a stop next to several other empty cars.

"Remember, stay quiet and behind us." We waited in the car for almost ten minutes before another car pulled in and a couple got out. It seemed to be a long time for no activity, especially for what I remembered to be such a major bridge.

"Is this bridge still in use?" I asked, honestly wondering how it was even standing.

"The bridge is just for us now." The woman said as she looked back at me. "The humans have their own."

We kept to the gravel as we approached the sidewalk. There was a chain link fence nearly ten feet high that surrounded the entrance to the bridge, and it made me feel like a trapped animal. Were they literally gate keeping the passageway between the territories? That made sense, especially if they were hostile to one another. It reminded me of my studies in primary school where we learned about the Berlin wall and Soviet occupation. It was crazy how different, and how similar the world still was. Was this the same experience that people had going through the checkpoints? Maybe there was a vampire who was alive at that time I could ask.

The worst kind of feeling hit my stomach. The dread of knowing that you are currently standing in a foreign powers land that is completely hostile towards you and your wife. I had to get across that bridge at all costs.

"Alright, you got this. One step at a time, you belong here" I whispered to myself, as silently as possible.

There was a gate on the opposite side where a few people were moving through. We crossed the highway quickly, darting in and out of the shadows before getting as close as we could. There were armed guards examining people before letting them through the rusted entrance. Was this a checkpoint? I had the right papers, they had to let me go, right? I nervously fidgeted with my fingers for a moment in thought.

I took a deep breath, held my hands tightly in front of me and took a knee in the dirt on the side of the highway barrier. One breath at a time. Hayley would be laughing at me right now if she knew how scared I was to just walk through a simple checkpoint. I reached inside my coat and pulled out the papers. They looked official. I didn't know what they were supposed to look like, so I had to trust that these were real. A deep exhale came out as I pretended to re-lace my shoe for a moment.

I hopped back up, the other two looking at me impatiently. There was a half dozen or so people that I assumed to be vampires in front of us and only one had made it through so far. The guard slowly looked at each of them before shining a flashlight over their body and examining their papers. I couldn't tell what he was asking, but I kept my mouth shut until it was our turn. Only one person was turned away, and they were taken into handcuffs and violently pulled off to the side while screaming that their papers were real. My heartbeat quickened at the sight, and it took everything in me not to panic.

While I really hoped to avoid anything like that, I tried to just remember that even though I was pretty much brand new, I was much older and had to act like it. After all, if they believed it, then the chances of me making it through would go up. I hated calculating the odds. We moved as one group and finally made it to the gate.

A gentleman in a strange looking uniform stepped in front of the couple I was with. He looked them up and down, then made eye contact with me. I wanted to smile but kept it to myself.

"Here's our papers," he said, handing papers from his jacket over to the officer. "we're going to see friends, and then her brother over in the city. We will be back before the suns up as usual."

The official looked at both sets of papers, then put his hand out towards me. I pulled them from my coat and handed them to him. Standing there in silence, he opened them, looked down, then at me, then back down again.

"Your brother, where does he live?" He looked at me curiously, obviously probing with his question.

"Fishtown, sir," he responded. I had no idea if Fishtown was even there still. "Assuming his wife hasn't burned the place down yet."

I let out a light laugh while keeping my eye contact with the official. His gaze looked all the way down my body, then back up while a smile grew on his face. The smile wasn't friendly, and although it had been a long time since a man looked at me that way, I would never forget the discomfort. His gaze made my skin crawl, and his smile caused a knot to form in my chest. He stood there for several moments, looking between me and my papers. I swear to the goddess if that runt set me up, I would walk back to Baltimore and decapitate him.

"Yes, yes, I'm lucky mine hasn't done the same with these postings," he chuckled back. I felt a wave of relief wash over me. "Carry on then, safe travels."

He reached his hand out, handing my papers back. I smiled and nodded to him while being as casual as possible. I was so close to getting there. We walked through the gate, and I heard the metal slide shut behind me. There was a feeling of relief that instantly washed across my body as soon as they were back in my pockets. We were there, standing on the edge of the bridge. There were junked cars everywhere. Some had their tires blown out, a few were entirely on blocks. There was no telling how long these vehicles had been stashed here.

It almost felt unreal. The other two started walking, so I began to move with them. I didn't want to do anything suspicious while I was still within range of the lights.

There were more cars and barriers than I thought parked all over the place. It really looked like most of this bridge hadn't been used in a very, long time judging by the rust covering most of the vehicles. Even the bridge itself looked like it was on its last legs. The heavy silence was really starting to get to me at this point, so I started to hum something from memory. I had no idea what it was, but it stuck there. Whoever had made that music was long since turned to dust.

The bridge leveled out, and in the center were two thick, white lines that were painted with different sigils in the center. There were twisted rolls of barbed wire that was occasionally dotted with torn cloth from where someone had tried to cross the border. There were stacks of debris piled against each of the bridge walls, dotted with scorch marks. I could only imagine what would have happened to anyone crossing illegally.

"That's the barrier. This side belongs to Addison, and Hayley's is across that. There is a cease fire between the two signed by their originators that has kept them deadlocked," he sighed rubbing his forehead as we walked. "Neither of them can cross or it will mean open war between the two sides of the river."

"How bad would that conflict be?" I asked, genuinely curious to the answer.

"The last time the two got into it, over seventy of our kind met their eternal slumber and Addison almost lost his life." His voice got quieter as he explained their history.

"The dog won't be forgetting that scar anytime soon, the butcher skewered him to his own penthouse and left him there for sunrise, but he escaped." Her voice was pleasant, and for once I was happy to know that she could speak at all.

I looked across the white line and over to a small group of cloaked figures who were approaching from the other direction. As they neared the line, they came to a halt. At the front, a shorter figure lowered the cloak, making the faintness of my heartbeat come to a halt.

"Hayley."

I whispered it to myself, unable to believe it was them. They hadn't changed a bit. There was an extra scar on her cheek, but other than that, those piercing hazel eyes I would never forget. A woman next to her stepped forward, looking at me with a certain level of irritation and skepticism. Ignoring her altogether, I ran my hand through my hair and picked up the pace between the two, leaving them there. At the sight of Hayley, my escorts turned and ran, their rapidly fleeing movements catching me by complete surprise.

The only thing I cared about in this moment was feeling their arms around me. I was nervous and anxious, excited, and scared all at once. It had been hundreds of years since I had seen them and just gazing across the bridge at their face again almost brought me to tears.

"Elle!" their voice hadn't changed. I hadn't heard it in so long that just the sound finally broke me. Twin streams of red slowly dripped down my face as I walked forward towards the line.

Everything was going to be okay. I was home. Wherever they were, that was exactly where I would be. I started walking a bit quicker, picking up the pace towards the middle of the bridge. We had been separated for almost three hundred years, and there were only a few more steps to go. I was lost in thought as I heard them yell my name again.

"ELLE!!!!"

I stopped abruptly, looking down at my left leg. I hadn't heard the gunshot that sent something straight through my leg, but I could feel the pain of it. Blood trickled across my thigh and down onto the bridge, pouring from a thin incision that wasn't healing. I couldn't hear anything else. The woman in front of Hayley stepped in front of them, keeping them from crossing the line. I could barely hear them over the pain that screamed up my body.

My hands shot down around the wound, trying to figure out how to get whatever it was out of my leg. Warm blood flowed out of the hole, and I immediately felt dizzy at the sight of it. It burned from the inside out, covering my hands in red. What had happened to me? The red color, the warmth, the smell of it, all together made me nauseous. I looked up at Hayley and tried to move but a quick jerk from something else sent my legs out from under me.

My body hit the ground – hard. I was only a few yards from the middle of the line, and just a few more from Hayley.

Clap. Clap. Clap. Clap.

The slow echo of clapping came from above the bridge as the flood lights kicked on, illuminating the space. The two I had come with where nowhere to be found. I watched as Hayley looked up, their eyes shifting from hazel to deep red. The skin on their face turned even more pale than normal and two glistening fangs emerged from their mouth.

A figure landed next to me with a light thud after floating down from the bridge suspenders above. I could feel the vibration on the ground as three more sets of boots landed around me.

"So, word on the street was the butcher turned someone important... and that someone just happened to be passing through here on some sight-seeing." His voice was direct, indifferent but with a sarcastic tone. "It would be a shame if I didn't treat this special guest to the V – I – P treatment, if you know what I mean, oh Butcher."

I struggled up onto my hands as I tried to lift my body forward, crawling another foot towards the middle of the line. I was so close. Hayley stood there, no longer making eye contact with me. I knew that look; they were about to lose it. My body was in full panic mode as my heartbeat shot through the roof. How had I not heard the metal van opening behind me. I was careless and now I was terrified that I had caused them more trouble.

"Hayley... I found you..."

"Where are you off to so soon?" he cackled down at me. I didn't need to look at him to know he was not the kind of person I would ever want to be acquainted with.

His hand lifted and moved in a circle. I felt the tightness in my leg sear with more pain as I got pulled quickly backwards. The only thing

I could see was the streak of blood I was leaving as I was pulled away from them. I dug my fingers into the bridge, scraping to slow myself down as much as I could.

Hayley stood there, blood dripping from their palms in an unbridled rage. Why weren't they coming to get me.

I was right here in front of them. I made it back to them.

"Relax, butcher. If you cross that line, you know what happens and I know Lady Ireena wouldn't let you off the hook." he tucked his hands behind his head, letting the black trench coat float in the wind around him.

"Don't worry, my dear. I'll take care of her for you. Maybe I'll even send a piece back to you!"

He laughed in their direction before turning and walking away. I watched him as he approached, causing a shiver of fear to cover my body. His smile sent goosebumps across my body and if I had hair on my arms, it would be on end right now. Every time I tried to get up, I felt a heavy boot press me back into the pavement. I managed to get both of my arms under me so that I could press straight up. There was no way I was going to give up on this when I had made it so far. That same tightness I had experienced before started to well up in my chest as my eyes shifted to a similar crimson hue. It was right there. I bit my tongue and focused, trying to fight through it and get up. There was an unbridled strength that slowly began to move across my core, and I pressed upwards again, trying to overpower the person behind me.

One of the cloaked figures next to Hayley stepped forward, lowering their hood. Short, windswept blonde hair and piercing blue eyes peered across the bridge. His cloak had a single black and silver rose sewn into the left shoulder.

"Sir," his voice was direct.

"Allow us. This was my fault; it is my responsibility to fix."

"Stand down Conner," Miranda shot him a sharp look.

"You know we can't break the treaty. And you've done enough damage to her lady, don't think for a second that I'll allow you to make a mess of this too. We can't afford open conflict."

The two looked worryingly at Hayley, who was leaving blood

pooling beside her. The empathic Miranda could feel the anger, frustration, and rage coming off her benefactor. It was the strongest feelings she had ever felt since joining with them. Hayley kept her eyes locked across the bridge, watching me get pulled backwards by two of the figures again. I felt the force of someone coming to their knees as I was dragged further from them again, placing their weight in the middle of my back so I couldn't move anymore.

"Good girl, just sit here." A raspy man's voice said from behind me.

I started to panic even more, forcing the blood to pump through my body faster and faster. I was so close. That's the only thought that continued to come across my mind. *Push harder. Don't stop.* The man in the trench coat casually strolled right back up to the white line, his hands still behind his head. I ignored him and started to press harder up, struggling to move despite the extra strength that I had tapped into.

"This one looks a bit important to ya," he smirked. "I can't turn down the chance to have this delectable treat. Scurry on back to your villa, butcher. You have no power here! And it is up to me, you know, to follow the law and illegal papers moving through my territory is punishable by…"

His grin grew even wider as he lifted a single middle finger to Hayley and her entourage.

"By whatever. I. feel. Like. doing." He said while counting his fingers, laughing has he turned around to walk towards me.

Hayley looked past him, locking their eyes on me. I could see their lips moving.

'*I love you. Don't worry*'.

Don't worry? Were they going to abandon me here and walk away? We had been separated for hundreds of years and had almost made it. Life was almost right again. I felt the tears begin to form in the corner of my eyes. Hayley was right there. So close. Right in front of me.

The man in the front turned and began his stroll back towards me. I had no idea how many others were currently surrounding me. What I did know was that my leg was still injured, and I wasn't going to get very far. I got my hands back to my side and slowly started to press myself up as I let out a scream of rage and frustration. I was met with a pair of cold, metal points that touched the back of my neck. What followed was a quick moment of the worst pain I thought possible rushing through my body before I hit the ground, unable to feel anything.

"Addison." A cold voice floated across the bridge to the man. I knew that tone and would never forget it from all those years ago. "You chose poorly this time."

Their body turned and walked away from the white line. My vision was blurry, the only thing I could tell was that their hood went up and they disappeared into the darkness on the other side. I wanted to tell them that I would be okay, that I was a survivor. The only thing I was able to do was whimper for a moment before something covered my head and the same searing, electrical pain forced my eyes shut and body limp.

* * *

Four black SUVs pulled through vine covered gates before coming to a halt outside a large, Victorian manor. The rounded cobblestone circles out front was accented by a large stone fountain with a single withered tree in the middle. Miranda hopped out of the front passenger seat of the second car before opening the door behind her.

Hayley stepped out, immediately setting off towards the large cast iron doors. Miranda and Conner took to their sides a half step back, escorting them to the door. Their boot heels echoed loudly on the marble slabs that led up to the ornate ebony door before it was pulled open from the inside.

Followed by a half dozen cloaked vampires, the group entered the main hall. A twisted marble staircase twisted up both sides, lined with black and rose gold railing. In the center of the entryway a chandelier with twelve ornate points hung dimly from the ceiling, casting shadows across the large open room. Dozens of vampires were mingling and moving throughout villa, but all came to a halt when

Hayley entered. The doors pushed shut behind her before a voice echoed from the second story.

Hayley, unfortunately, was the only one who could hear it.

"You are all dismissed." Hayley's voice was sharp and quick, cutting through the silence of the large manor. Two men strolled up to Hayley, their heads lowered while not making eye contact. Hayley's shoulders rolled backwards, sliding the long cloak off her body. Before it had time to hit the ground the two men caught it, folded it, and moved to the side. Their head tilted to the side, glancing at Miranda for a moment.

"Come." Hayley's tone was short and unable to hide their rage. Their body shifted in a glimmer of darkness reappearing at the top of the staircase.

Miranda scrambled to move up the stairs as fast as she could to keep up. The pair moved down the hallway, taking the first turn into a large, multi-story open library. Hayley stopped barely a few steps in, their breath coming to a halt as they gazed up to the second story of the library.

"Daughter." The voice was gentle yet commanding. It maintained a thick eastern European accent that chilled the air. Long, delicate fingers tipped with midnight blue nails lined with crystals slowly tapped on the marble banister as a finely dressed figure peered down onto the two.

Hayley immediately dropped to a knee, lowering their head. Miranda followed suit, unable to recognize the voice. However, if her master was bending the knee then so would they. Only one kind of person could stand above one of the originals children, and if this figure was one of those legendary figures then she wouldn't dare to cross that kind of monster.

"Forgive me, mother." Hayley's voice was nearly filled with fear. She knew what she had done but hadn't expected it to be worth summoning her master all the way from Eastern Europe.

"You have some explaining to do." Her words were lofty, and her figure faded to black before disappearing. Hayley stood, floating up to the balcony before returning to a knee on the wooden platform.

Miranda kept her head down and her breathing as quiet as possible. She had only laid eyes on the figure for a moment but the bloodline suppression coming from them had nearly suffocated her.

The woman's figure was shrouded in a black and silver ombre dress accented by an intricate crimson lace with a fur covering. Her black hair was pulled up into a bun behind her with two thin silver rods holding it all in place. She pulled a book from the stacks within the bookcase wall, blew the dust off, and returned it to its place.

"Rise, child." She motioned her finger upwards in a single swipe before turning her head to the still kneeling Miranda below. "Your service is not needed here. Leave."

Miranda felt a wave of sweat cross her body as she lifted up and moved backwards, keeping her head lowered the entire time. It took her mere moments to escape from the stifling aura given off from the woman above.

As the door closed shut, Hayley was left standing before someone whom they had not spoken to in nearly a century. It was a bittersweet and frustrating reunion by all accounts.

"I can explain –" Hayley started, hoping to get ahead of the situation.

"And you will. Outside. Come, my child. It's been forever since any of us returned to the states. This should have been a celebration. After all," she paused before turning and walking past Hayley, moving towards the open door leading to the balcony, "you have done admirably. There was a reason why I choose only you to be my sole inheritor and refused to sire another. While my siblings each have six or seven kids, I have only you now, or so I thought. It has kept me from having to deal with all the infighting that others suffer from."

Hayley followed her through the curtains, standing there as she took a seat at the head of a plain black table. There were two other vampires, each dressed in proper Victorian court attire, there to attend to her. One pushed her chair in while the other poured a cool red liquid into a pair of wine glasses. Hayley stood silently next to the table while the woman looked her up and down.

"You do realize what a mess you have made. Sit." One of the attendants pulled a chair out next to the woman.

"Yes." Hayley immediately admitted to it. Their voice was quieter, cautious, and respectful. Anyone who knew them would be shocked to see their head lowered.

"Explain yourself, and maybe I can clean this mess up."

"Madam Vasiliev, shall we bring your things in?" The attendant behind her said coldly while looking down on Hayley. She lifted her hand and motioned for the two to depart. Once it was quiet, she sat there in silence for a moment. For a moment her gaze went from the balcony and over to the eastern gate. A streak of red flashed across her eyes in annoyance, and Hayley was barely able to notice the second of glare that lit her masters' eyes before she returned her attention to the table.

"Now that we're alone, it's good to see you my dear. Tell me everything. How have you been? And why do you still let that petty thing follow you." She said while lifting the glass of cold blood to her lips. Not a drop was wasted. The red disappeared from her eyes as she drank.

Everything about her was flawless, from the way she sat her glass down to the way her blue and teal eyes could freeze a person's blood. There was an aura of nobility about her that few would ever get to experience.

"I'm... I'm sorry. Forgive me. When you rewarded me, to make me stronger, I didn't take it. I locked it away with my wife, hoping that one day she would come around and join me. It was sealed in a crypt back home with her. I left it in there, and there was an accident moving her from the mausoleum out there to here." Her words were slow and precise, articulating everything as carefully as possible.

"You locked my blood away with your wife in the hopes that one day she would join you, and only by happenstance was she created. And not only was she created..." she sighed, taking a sip of the blood once more, "but she was created without any idea whose blood it was, and is out there in the wild. Everyone thinks she is made of you, and not of me. Where is she now?"

Hayley lifted their head, looking at the woman sitting across from her. A thin line of blood moved down her cheeks. Deciding to keep her mouth shut and figure out the best course of action, but there was nothing. No plan. No secondary thought. They were bare before their master, and the silence had lasted a moment too long.

"Where. *Is*. She." Her tone was stern, direct, unrelenting. The question was absent and only a command remained. The demeanor of the woman shifted from casual to irritated almost instantly. That shift sent a wave of cold pressure across Hayley's body, nearly choking them.

"I couldn't cross the line. She was right in front of me, and that dog took her, mocked our bloodline, and electrocuted her." Hayley looked down the table, their hands placed across her lap. Anyone who saw them might mistake them for a noble woman and not a battle-hardened warrior. "I watched them drag her back, put a sack over her head and shock her into submission right in front of me. She was right there."

"My child," she said, lifting the thick wine glass to her lips while keeping her eyes locked on Hayley. "While I am proud of your self-control, it is time my brother and I had a chat. This is no longer an issue of you having sired a newborn, she is sired to me. Your sister of the night. You created another offspring without my permission. Had I not sensed that connection I never would have known…"

"Forgive my reckless obstinance, mother" Hayley responded, almost sheepish in her words. "I wasn't sure she would ever emerge. And he took her right in front of me. I couldn't break the treaty."

"I have a few errands to take care of while I'm over here. This issue between you and Addison has gone on far too long. I told you, my child if you can't tame a dog, kill it. Even that one you keep leashed next to you will try to bite you one day." She lowered her glass with a gentle smile that betrayed her words. "Next time you see him, leave nothing but his ashes. I not only authorize it, but I also expect it. My brother has allowed this child of his far too much freedom, and he has not only mocked our family, but now desecrated it."

Hayley lifted a cloth napkin up to her cheek before swiping away the thin streak of blood that had dripped down into her lap. There was a sense of anguish hanging over then that they were unable to shut out.

"As you command, mother."

She finished her cocktail of port wine and blood. Her head tilted to the side with a gentle smile that betrayed how viciously savage she was capable of being. It was an unease that Hayley felt, even though they knew that there were very few things that would ever land her on her masters bad list.

"Go clean yourself up. I will not allow for my family appearing in such a manner. We will continue this when I return." She made a swiping motion with her hand to dismiss her. Hayley looked across at the balcony curtains where both of her attendants stood. Marian and Silviana had been with Lady Ireena since the early 8th century.

They had sworn themselves to her after she rescued them from execution for witchcraft and the single thing they could ever agree on was how much they absolutely despised each other. It was not uncommon to hear the two yelling at each other before they drew their blades and fought. Some people found it endearing, other just ignored it. Somehow, the two of them had managed to live this long.

Hayley stood up, bowed slightly to their master, and departed only to be quickly replaced by the other two who smirked at them in passing. After entering her estate, they walked quickly to her own room where they threw their coat over a chair and plopped down by the fireplace. The crackling embers were a welcome background noise that they would often use to help them sleep. Their decompression wouldn't last long and was quickly interrupted by several quick knocks at the door.

"Sir." Miranda said as she stepped through the doorway, quickly closing it behind her. "My apologies for not preparing the guest suite, if I had known she was coming I would have reorganized our schedule to ensure proper accommodations were given."

She took a knee and bowed, lowering her head in response. Hayley watched her in silence for a moment before turning her attention back to the fire.

"Miranda." They said with a tone that was more direct than normal. It sent a quick chill down Miranda's body, but she kept her eyes lowered.

"Yes, Lady Reinhardt." She replied, not wanting to move an inch. The pressure in the room felt suffocating to her and she knew, that without a shadow of a doubt, Hayley was boiling over with rage right now.

"Whatever it takes. Find where he has her. Whatever resources you need, whatever it takes. I want her found, and I want her delivered safely home to me." Hayley turned her chair to face the fireplace, not wanting to spare a second word.

"My lord, what if she's already gone? What if Addison—"

"Enough."

Hayley turned their head to face her and glared; the anger held in their eyes the brightest Miranda had ever seen them. For a moment, she felt the same suffocating weight start to bury her that she had experiences earlier. She had never seen such unbridled rage from Hayley.

"*As you command.*" Miranda could feel a ball of frustration well up in her stomach with her words as she stood up and departed the room, leaving Hayley to the dancing flames.

Strength

REFLECTIONS

"Faith is my compass, and the crucifix my weapon, as I navigate the labyrinthine corridors of the supernatural. The vampiric temptress remains a testament to the enduring struggle between light and shadow. I will not falter. "
Father Gabriel's Personal Journal, 1584

CHAPTER 5

The moon hung low in the velvety night sky, casting an eerie glow over the modern-day recreation of a baroque castle that stood as a sentinel of shadows. Within its cold, metal walls, a sinister plot unfolded, driven by ambition, and fueled by the allure of forbidden power. I found myself ensnared in a web of treachery and danger beyond my darkest nightmares and wondered if it would have been better to be still locked up in the crypt.

I had always known that being the heir to the Reinhardt family would come with its share of challenges. That was even more true when I had thrown tradition out the window and married a woman. Yet, I had never imagined the depths to which my wife's adversaries would sink to achieve their goals.

In the hours that followed, Addison had introduced himself as the flashy crown prince that wants the world at his feet. Blah Blah Blah narcissistic man baby. I would have a scar in my leg from where he put a knife in my thigh after I spit in his face. The rival vampire family, bound by blood as siblings, had long harbored envious desires to rise above the elder sister and seize control of the clandestine world they inhabited, a territory that had been built through generations of blood and conquest.

The first day I had been jolted out of sleep by a sharp, searing pain in my left arm. I opened my eyes only to see several bright lights clumped together in front of me. I was in a reclined position, somewhere between a chair and a bed. Strange metal bearings covered my arms, wrists, thighs, and ankles. I tried to struggle out of it for several minutes before I frustratingly gave up. The pain in my left arm came from several tubes being inserted into my upper arm and the inside of my wrist.

An exasperated sigh emerged from between my lips, followed by my stomach growling. I was starving. The pain in my arm didn't help. I looked over to it, seeing a thin tube coming from under some medical tape. A vividly bright crimson liquid came out of it and down onto a bag that was hung on a cart next to me. The sight of my own blood almost made me nauseous, despite there being nothing in my stomach to actually throw up.

The chair was cold, and only part of my body touched any of it. From the feeling, my only guess was that it was some old dentist's chair. My low back lacked any support in the middle, and with the restraints I had little room to move around. I struggled side to side again, my attention snapping over to the side. A figure strolled around in the corner by a table, barely out of my view.

"I see, I see… awake you are and in an unfortunate place you may be. But blood, the pretty-pretty blood so red *and pure*" his voice was eerily cold, with a directness that bordered on sociopath.

I couldn't see past the bright light that covered me. I tried to believe that Hayley would come for me. *Get it together Elle*, I thought to myself. I tried to hide any bit of fear inside of me and tackle this disaster head on. Other than the lights pointed at me, the rest of the room was dimly lit and I could barely see anything else.

Across the room, a tall figure emerged from the shadows, wearing nothing but medical pants and a lab coat. Scars covered his chest and abs, signs of either great torture or a mutilation kink. Either option seemed painful. His eyes gleamed with a fervor that betrayed his insatiable thirst for power, his features etched with a malevolent satisfaction.

"Princess Reinhardt, the daughter of Hayley." he purred, his voice dripping with venomous charm. He carried a clip board that he read to out loud to himself.

"Third generation specimen, direct line to Countess Vasiliev. It would be an absolutely pleasure to finally make your acquaintance under... different circumstances."

"My name is Cedric Drakemyre, and I am the lead scientist employed by Konrad and Addison has delivered me such a perfect specimen." He took a bow as he spoke, as if there was anything gentlemanly in there. He arose just as quick, almost dancing over to the side of my chair where he looked at the slow-moving blood in the clear tubes. His left eye hung slightly off center, and every few words it would twitch and move away from me. Everything about him sent shivers across my body.

My heart pounded against the cage of my ribs, my pride warring with my vulnerability. "What do you want, Drakemyre? Hayley will have you burn for this! How much is he paying you?" I thought, trying to reason and negotiate with the man.

Cedric chuckled, his fingers drumming rhythmically on the ornate armrest of his lab chair as he took a seat. "Oh, my dear little Ellie, this isn't about mere currency. This is about the purity that flows through your veins, a purity that can elevate our family to heights you can't fathom. With modern science and ancient magicks, I will unravel every drop of your blood. I will conduct a battery of tests, probing your physiology, delving into your unique biology. What are the origins of this immortality you so casually own? How do your fangs work? What are the limits of your supernatural abilities? These questions and more will be answered through the rigorous application of scientific methodology and you are the perfect of all of my specimens!" he stepped backwards and danced in a circle, holding up a vial of my blood.

"You see, it isn't every century a third generation gets dropped on our doorstep. The purity of your blood makes my own look like liquid garbage. Who would have thought that the ice box no fun butcher would have a youngling like you. With your blood –"

"You won't find what you're looking for. My blood is *not* for your fucking experiments." I clenched my jaw and glared, refusing to let him see an ounce of any fear.

Cedric's smile widened, revealing a row of perfect, predatory teeth.

"Ah, but that's where you're mistaken. We have methods that even your esteemed lineage hasn't dreamed of. And now, my dear, you are here to offer up your precious essence willingly or... otherwise. Your bloodline has the highest physical attributes of them all, and when I break that secret open, I'll be able to finally splice that blood into our own."

I felt my heart sink in my chest as Cedric spoke. The implications of what he was suggesting were staggering. Splice it? Was he trying to merge the bloodlines?

"You want to use my blood to mix with that of your own people? But why?"

Cedric laughed.

"Ah, the innocence of youth. You think we do this for altruistic motives? No, my dear, it's power we're after - all kinds of power - from physical prowess to mental acuity. We seek a higher level of power, and you are the key to unlocking it."

He leaned in closer, and I could feel the sting of his breath on my face. "But make no mistake," he said, his voice cold and calculating. "We will have your blood one way or another."

I looked past him at a woman in a lab coat taking notes. She scribbled away furiously, and I narrowed my eyes in a glare at her. How could she just stand there and do nothing? She had to know what was going on, yet she remained silent. My anger began to simmer as I felt helpless and powerless in this situation. Every time I made eye contact, she moved her head away and looked to the side. How barbaric of her, to watch this happen to me and stand there doing nothing. I sniffed the air, closing my eyes to focus on anything while trying to ignore him.

She was a human. That scent was unmistakable. I opened my eyes and stared across at her. She turned her body away and looked down so that I couldn't see her face.

Coward.

"You see…" he said as he paced across the room again. "We can't mix our bloodlines, and we have been trying to for centuries. Unfortunately, science and technology never really caught up so it has taken us far longer than what we had originally anticipated. Anyway, enough with the blabbering on and on there is so much work to do, and I am, for one, personally excited that I get to be the one that works on you. It's the relentless pursuit of knowledge that drives me, that compels me to unlock the secrets of the universe. My quest is not malicious; it is one of illumination and discovery."

I could feel my heart racing as my thoughts churned. I needed a plan, an escape. I tried to look at the walls to see if there were any windows, or cabinets I could climb on, anything that might help me get out of here. A heavy hopelessness settled over me as Cedric's words sank in. He was right; they had all the power here and I had none. I took a deep breath and tried to remain composed, but inside I was screaming for help. I laid my eyes on stoned that were set in the middle of picture frames. Each of them released a soft glow that almost seemed to be pulsing like a heartbeat. Was that the magic he was talking about? No way could that stuff be real. Then again, I was a vampire. Realizing that I was surrounded by some of the ancient magic he had mentioned, I felt my hope slowly began to elusively slip away. I had been betrayed by the very world I was born into, and now I had to find another way to fight to reclaim my freedom.

The days that followed were a haze of pain, exhaustion, and fear. I felt like a lab rat, subjected to tests and experiments that pushed the limits of my resilience. I could barely keep my eyes open, as Cedric and his minions subjected me to grueling rituals and arcane experiments. The pain was so intense that it made the muscles across my body convulse, and I would often pass out from pain, exhaustion, or both.

By the second week, my skin was raw, and my body ached from being moved around so much. One of Cedric's assistants was always nearby, poking and prodding me, carving out pieces of my skin to study my rapid regeneration. It was horrifying and surreal, but I could find no way out of it. There was no escape from Cedric's clutches and every time I would get defiant or upset him, he would put a knife in me. Being able to regenerate made it really easy for him to take his frustration out on my body.

My only hope was to keep my head down and continue to survive no matter what. I did whatever I was told, no matter how torturous it seemed. I quickly knew that to disobey would only bring more pain and suffering.

I just had to keep going, keep fighting, and eventually, I would find a way out.

I had to find a way out.

It wasn't long before I wished I was still in the casket. Every few hours he would wake me up with some frustrating murmuring in a language I couldn't understand. A day later I had been shocked straight back to sleep as punishment for making fun of him. As soon as I heard him slam the door, I final let the tears out. I would never give him the satisfaction of seeing me like this. I stared at the ceiling and the off-white lights that hung there, wishing more than anything to see Hayley again.

"Love… I don't know how long I can do this… please hurry"

Slam.

The door. Shit. I panicked to get myself together and ready another sarcastic remark. The footsteps got closer and closer, then walked straight by me.

"Please, don't stop crying on my account. You're in a pretty shitty situation." Her long. auburn hair was pulled into a high messy bun that was fairly similar to how I had normally worn my own. Her voice was soft and warm, and just hearing another woman almost made me cry all over again. "I don't envy you, honestly."

She stood there for a few moments in silence, and although I felt just as weak as when I was in the casket, the gentleness in her eyes was captivating. I had seen her the first day I was here. Was it possible that she could be here to get me to open up? Was this some part of that sociopath doctor's plan?

She turned back around to the rolling table and pulled it closer to my side.

"I brought you something to eat. It's synthetic so it won't make you feel much better, but it will at least keep your stomach from growling all day." She said, poking a straw in a tiny bag of red liquid.

"I didn't know there was synthetic blood. It really is the future." I quipped back, knowing I would eat almost anything at this point. I turned my head away from her out of spite.

"Take it easy. I worked hard to get you this. The doctor is having a rough time trying to figure out your blood." She said, sticking a straw in the top of the blood bag. "He had a fight with Addison last night. He's getting impatient so I said maybe you needed to eat something."

"See?" I replied cutting her off. "You're just helping them."

"And…I don't have much of a choice." she said, finally looking annoyed. "And…you're no good to anyone if you're dead, especially not your maker. Addison is already on high alert after their last round."

"Their last round?" I had heard they weren't on the best of terms with each other, but I was curious to know the real story.

"What happened?"

"Here, take a drink first." Her hands lifted the bag up to my chest while she held the straw near my lips. I looked at her judgingly before I slowly wrapped my dry, broken lips around the plastic straw. She was right, this synthetic blood was garbage. It was lukewarm and had the consistency of milk.

Despite it being dreadful, I gulped as much of it down as I could to the satisfaction of my stomach. I would have almost rather starved than taste that again. The moment I pulled away from it, I could already feel my mid-section cramping.

"Sorry I'm a bitch right now, I promise I'm not always like this." I tied to apologize. It seemed like she really was just trying to help, and the synthetic blood did, unfortunately help. "It's not every day you…

well, for me it is... and this sucks really, really bad... and it's really, really hard."

I almost started crying again, and as I closed my eyes, I felt something soft touch my face. My eyes jerked open to see a tissue with dots of blood on it.

"It's okay, really." She said as she dabbed the tissue under my eyes. "How about we start over? My name's Morgan, nice to meet you."

She stepped out of my sight but quickly returned with one of the rolling chairs that the nurses had sat in while drawing more of my blood. I watched her sit down and put a paper towel around the blood bag before dropping it onto the med tray.

"What did Hayley do to Addison that has him so obsessed?" I asked curiously, truly wondering what had happened between the two. No one had really given me any context, just that he had nearly died during their last fight.

Morgan sighed and leaned back in the chair while crossing her arms. She pursed her lips for a moment before finally speaking.

"About a decade ago, Addison decided his side of the river wasn't enough. He had already taken down most of jersey, except for Jersey City and Hoboken and had to fight for those after he lost Manhattan. That's a whole other story." She looked at me, her eyes moving to the two tubes sticking out of my right arm.

"The Butcher...I mean, Hayley, came out of nowhere. She was overseas for as long as anyone knows, and when she came stateside, she immediately went to work building and consolidating power. Even though she has no sires, there are many of your kind who are loyal to her. She collected anyone without a home and gave them purpose. Honestly, it's admirable." She sighed, leaning back in the chair, and looking at the ceiling.

"Most of her empire used to be Addison's territory. Between turn-coats and their bright personality, it didn't take much to fracture what he had built over the last three centuries"

"So basically, Hayley kicked him out of his sandbox and he's throwing a fit over it" I said sarcastically, happy that I could at least insult him again.

"Well, a little worse than that. Philly used to be his, until she decided to settle down there. He sent his personal guard after her, figuring that the eight of them would be able to take her without any major issues occurring." For the first time, I saw her crack a light smile as she spoke, noticing that her tone had slightly changed.

"But that's not what happened, is it?" I asked, wanting to know more. Maybe if I knew a little more about what happened I would find something I could use to help get myself out of here.

"Not at all," she replied, still looking at the ceiling. "A messenger from Hayley showed up with a duffle bag, and she threw it at his feet. His assistant opened it, and what do you think was in there?"

I watched her smile grow, and I was curious to know why. Was she trapped here like I was? I wanted to ask, but also didn't want to pry. I was still hesitant about whether she was messing with me.

"The messenger wasn't just a messenger, and the bag had eight heads in it. Addison went ballistic and when he went to kill the messenger, they lowered their hood and let Addison know she did it." Her tone started to rise as she was telling me the story. Apparently, this was common knowledge and Hayley had made quite the impression on everyone.

"Wait. You mean Hayley walked right into his lair with a bag full of heads?" I asked, immediately knowing this was something Hayley would do. No was she wasn't going to make a statement and take him out in the process. Where had she failed though…

"Exactly. She strolled in there, dropped the heads of his *PERSONAL* guard at his feet, and when he tried to attack her, she put a bullet in his head. Well, several. The two fought for almost an hour and she trashed his entire lair while they fought. Addison hadn't had a proper fight in a long time and Hayley was relentless. I heard from one of the maids that at the end of the fight, she skewered him to his front door. She's one of the only vampires we know that still carries a sword on her side. I had never seen anyone, especially not a member of the night, wield a blade like that. I've heard stories about Duke Konrad being the best swordsman in the world, but even Hayley is said to be at his level."

She took a breath and relaxed, running her hands through her hair while she let it down from the ponytail that had hung behind her. I felt my scalp tingle at the thought of getting a shower. How long had it been since I had been able to have one? I was quite sure I smelled.

"A blade like what?" I looked at her while asking. I had all kinds of thoughts about it, and each one was wilder than the other. "Please tell me lightsabers are finally real."

She let out a lighthearted laugh in response, and it almost felt like we were having a girl's bonding moment despite the horrible situation I was in. I would have rather spent time locked away in a dungeon than this. Even in this abysmal situation the little bit of contact with someone who treated me like a person and not a science experiment felt warming.

"No no, unfortunately. Lightsabers aren't real yet." She shook her head, also disappointed that they weren't real. "a light blade is a weapon used by the clergy. They're blessed by sunlight and magic and used to hunt your kind. She has a special sheath that she carries it in, a trophy that she won after killing a Bishop."

"Hayley really killed one of them?" I said with as much energy as I could muster. I would have jumped up out of excitement if I hadn't been strapped down. A bishop was like, halfway up the clergy food chain as far as I could remember. I knew there was one in Baltimore when I had been there last for a wedding. That felt like eons ago at this point.

"Yes, she killed a Bishop, and the blade he fought her with became hers. She named it Dawnbreaker, and used it carve up Addison in his own home." Her arms crossed again as she stood up.

"She stuck him to his front door with the blade his maker gifted him and left him for sunrise. He was rescued, unfortunately... but he carries a massive grudge because of it. The duke was furious that his progeny embarrassed him that way. If anyone had known Hayley had sired a youngling, they would have hunted you down way sooner."

"I don't blame him for carrying a grudge, I'd be mad too." I sighed, wondering how I even made it to this situation. It would have been better if I had just tried to email her or something. Wait, did email still exist? Maybe they had different ways of communication now.

"Alright, Elaine. Sorry to jet but my time's up. I can swing by again and take care of you in a few days. Try not to die." She leaned down next to my head and whispered. "They won't let me do more than this, they're afraid if you get your strength back, you'll be as strong as Addison and break out."

My eyes widened as she spoke. How would I ever be as strong as someone who was a higher generation than mine? He had hundreds, if not thousands of years on me too. I just wished I was strong enough to get out of this and run away.

"Thank you, Morgan." I said as she stood up and turned to leave. Her footsteps halted for a moment as she looked at me with a sad smile. I didn't want her pity or sadness. I wanted a way out.

"Try to get some rest, tomorrow's going to be rough" she finished speaking and walked out of the room, leaving only the quick echo of the door slamming and a room of still, silent air. I laid there in the dimly lit space, my heartbeat racing again as I tried not to think about her final words.

"Rough??" I said to quietly to myself. "Every minute in here is rough."

I looked at the plugs in my arms, then the restraints. For a moment I felt the urge to try and rip everything off of me. I jerked my body side to side, only to fall deeper into anxiety again. I laid there for almost an hour before I finally fell asleep.

Morning couldn't have come at a less opportune time. I was jolted awake be the screeching of the metal door being propped open and several sets of loud footsteps coming into the room. I immediately closed my eyes and tried to settle down and look like I was still sleeping. Doctor Doom and Gloom, as I have grown to call him, strolled over next to me before smacking me on the cheek several times.

"Wake upppppppp," he said cheerfully. "Wakey wakey my pretty little specimen. How are you doing this lovely morning. I assure you it is quite lovely outside. Hehe. Spring time is right around the corner you know, and soon the birds are going to be chirp chirp chirping away."

I opened my eyes and forced a yawn when he finished slapping my cheek. Once I had my bearings, I immediately glared at him. He stood up, wrapping his hands behind his back. I looked past him as soon as I spotted Morgan standing in the corner. As soon as we locked eyes, she shook her head cautiously, warning me to not say anything. I would have loved for her to stab this doctor in the back right in front of me, but that was an impossibility right now. My eyes moved over to the doctor as he looked across the chair to two others.

"I have two new guests for you to meet. This is Declin," he said as he extended a hand towards the man in the lab coat, "and this is Mary. They will be assisting me in gathering some… better samples."

"What else do you need other than my blood. Haven't you taken enough from me already??" I was irritated, angry, and trying not to let him know I was frankly terrified of him. I watched the two others move to the side where I lost sight of them. Mary had her lab coat tied with a belt, on account of the giant set of breasts that almost seemed to pop out of her blouse. I could almost see the outline of the lace underneath as she passed me. The duo didn't hide the fact they were opening up a cabinet and moving things around, but I couldn't make out exactly what they were saying.

"Unfortunately, we aren't really making headway on isolating what makes your blood special, and well, different than ours. My bloodline comes from a long line of successful doctors, all tracing back to Lord Halin. You probably don't know him, but he's a remarkable governor of this territory, even if Master Addison is here." He rubbed his hands together and took a breath as he looked past me. "Are we ready to begin?"

"Yes, we may begin." The woman's voice said from behind me. It was nasally and felt much like nails on a chalkboard. I jerked my head to the side, trying to see as far around the side of the chair as I could.

"Begin? Begin what?!" I got nothing in response, making me yell loud. "I'm talking to you back there!!!"

My mouth tightened shut when I heard it. The sound of a small motor, like a Dremel. I had used them when I was doing tech work and was quite familiar with the sound. I knew that a high-pitched noise like that was most likely attached to something that I was not going to be fond of.

I tried to flail and rock a bit as Mary came to my left side. The moment I turned my head towards her I felt a searing pain that forced a scream from my lips tear through my shoulder. The straps that held me there kept my body from pulling away as the rapidly-moving object drilled itself straight into the bone of my shoulder blade. As soon as it hit the bone, what felt like acid touched the open wound, and I could hear the sizzling burn that resulted. I tried to scream again, only for Mary to put a leather strap in my mouth and pull it around my head. Tears rolled down my face as I laid there, struggling to stay awake through the pain.

"See what I mean? Her regenerative capacity is slightly better than ours as well. We need to isolate the blood isotope that might have that genetic code so we can attempt to splice it." The doctor said from in front of me, his eyes ignoring that I was even there.

"I agree, did you try her fingernails? She doesn't seem to have fully tapped in yet, maybe we can help speed that along a bit." Mary said to him while pressing my shoulders down.

"We should get a sample of cerebrospinal fluid while you're back there." He said as he crossed his arms. "Go ahead and pull it"

I tried to scream at him through the leather straps, but nothing except jumbled words made it through. He smiled at me in a way that made me feel like he was looking at an animal. His head cocked itself to the side, his crooked smile sending the same chills across my body again. His fingers fidgeted with a scalpel that moved between his hands, and his eyes seemed to stare right through me. I didn't exist to them.

An animal experiment. That's all I was to him, and these two. Even though I was a higher generation, they had absolutely zero respect for that hierarchy and solely wanted something to play with. I had no idea what cerebrospinal fluid was, but if it was anything spinal, then I had an idea where this was going.

"From this angle? Are you sure about that?" Mary said, her voice carrying a small bit of concern.

"Yes, pull it. The purest sample might come from in there." his words got increasingly sharper with each interaction between the three.

The chair began to move, taking me from a reclined position to almost fully seated. I felt the tears continue to go down my face, and the few moments of silence felt like hours. My vision was blurry as I heard the hum of the machines around us.

The doctor stepped forward, a syringe in his hand, and I knew what was coming next. He had a look of determination that sent shivers down my spine again. He leaned forward and adjusted something on the back of the chair before he spoke again.

"This won't hurt too much, but you'll feel some pressure in your lower back. Just try to stay still for me, okay?" His voice was softer than before, still cold but not as harsh as earlier. Mary stepped up behind him and pressed her hands into my stomach while looking at me with sympathy in her eyes.

I squeezed my eyes shut as the needle broke through my skin and traveled deeper until it hit bone. The pain traveled down my left side and through my leg as he pushed it deep into my back. I tried to flail again, but Mary stepped forward and pressed into my stomach while holding my body still. Tears continued streaming down my face until finally he muttered out "got it" and pulled back on the syringe.

He gestured towards Mary who quickly moved away from me before pressing something on one of the machines near us, causing it to beep loudly before turning off completely. He took another step away from me and turned towards Mary with an excited expression now plastered across his face. "We can start analyzing this sample now! It should give us more insight into why she has these abilities!" "Doctor!" Morgan yelled urgently, stepping forward. His head tilted to the left as he stared at her, irritated for interrupting.

"She is in a lot of pain, and Addison will not forgive you if you accidentally kill her." She said coldly.

"Fine. Fine. Have it your way assistant, you are right as usual." He replied sarcastically before looking at me, his smile disappearing. "It looks like you might be at your limit anyway."

Tears continued to roll down my face as he pulled it out just as quickly. My stomach was shaking, and I felt like I could throw up from the pain. Between my shoulder and back, I had never felt this much pain in my life. The two moved past me with a rolling cart covered with medical instruments and collection tools before leaving the room. As they walked by, I could see a line of blood-filled vials with labels on them.

"That will be all for today, thank you for your cooperation." The doctor said as he wiped his hands and turned around. I could hear him muttering to himself over against the wall while he examined something. He typed vigorously, describe the entire ordeal over and over again while questioning both my contribution and the fact that I was still alive. The light of a computer screen let me assume that it was how he organized his notes. Every few minutes he would walk over, poke me in some random spot, then return to add more notes.

The pain across my body didn't subside, and without a steady supply of blood, my ability to regenerate had substantially decreased. I laid there, the leather strap in my mouth drenched through with blood. The doctor hopped over to me and pulled it to the side, jerking my neck up. The screech that broke my lips made him smile again. The throb through my neck didn't get any better, and he put the leather strap back between my teeth, resting it right between my fangs.

"Just what I wanted to hear. See you tomorrow little bird."

He stuffed his hands in his pockets and turned, taking a full lap around the lab before departing. The door slammed shut as he walked away, his shoes squeaking down the hall. I slowly maneuvered the leather strap from my lips, letting it fall around my neck. It had been difficult to open my mouth wide enough to get it under my teeth and clear. Every part of my body was in pain, and I wasn't sure how much longer I would be able to handle this. The muscles across my back and shoulders were so tight they locked up, giving me the worst cramping I had ever had.

I choked on my cough as I felt the nearly dry bile rise in my throat and had to choke it back down. My head slammed into the soft plastic head rest while tears ran down my face. Everything hurt. Every single part of me was in some sort of pain.

The lights flickered on the ceiling, and I was finally able to close my eyes for a moment. I tried to keep my shit together. I kept them closed despite hearing the door open again. The footsteps were quick, and before I could open my mouth to tell them to fuck off, I felt a cold sting in my arm. The cool liquid entered my arm and I could feel it spreading through my shoulder and chest before I was unable to open my eyes again.

I OPENED MY EYES, looking down at the steering wheel in front of me. Giant raindrops pounded the windshield, barely audible over the EDM I was listening to. The GPS screen on the center console was flashing with a red warning, indicating both a severe storm warning and floor warning. I leaned my head back as I looked out the window at the restaurant across the parking lot. There was way too much rain between here and the door. I was frustrated that I was hours behind schedule, my dog was home alone from the pet sitter, and my stomach was growling.

"uggghhhhhhhhhhhhhhh" I groaned as I looked at the GPS. Three more hours until I was home. I was starving and had decided to pull off the first exit outside for Havre De Grace. There had been so many accidents and far too many people curious about them that an entire extra hour had been added to my trip. Maybe it would have been better to stay in Manhattan for the night and drive home tomorrow.

I looked out the window again before grabbing my purse, pulling the keys out of the ignition and jumping out into the rain. There wasn't supposed to be any rain, so I hadn't even brought an umbrella, let alone a raincoat. I slammed the door and shot through the heavy deluge at full 'why am I still wearing heels' speed until I reached the door of the small restaurant. The words "Tidewater Grille" glowed in bright red across the top of the covered awning, and below that a neon green open sign was humming. I shook myself off while trying to get as dry as possible before walking in. Now that I was covered, I hit the lock button on my little black BMW and tossed my keys in my purse.

The door swung open with ease and I stepped inside. The restaurant was.. quaint. There weren't many people there, so I walked over to the nearly empty bar and took a seat in the corner by myself. I was still wearing my blazer from meetings earlier, so I throw it over the seat next to me and plopped down in the soft pleather chair. I looked around at all of the fishing items that were hanging as decorations. Some were mounted fish, some were fishing tools. Others were just pictures of people on boats fishing.

Before I knew it, a Middle Ages man covered in tattoo's was in front of me. I don't know how long he watched me look around the room, but I let out an awkward laugh as soon as I noticed him.

"Sorry about that, the rain got me." I said, trying to make light conversation.

"Rough storm today, what can I get you to drink dear?" he said, his voice softer than I had expected. There was a hint of Boston on the end of it. Probably a transplant from up north if I had to guess.

I looked past him to the line of taps. "I'm not in a beer mood, what's on your wine list? Moscato?"

He crossed his arms while thinking about it. "You know, I think we have one or two bottles of Moscato left from the wedding we hosted over the weekend. Let me go check." He reached over to the side and picked up a pitcher of ice water, poured me a glass and sat it in front of me. "Back in a minute, here's a menu while you wait."

He handed me a navy-blue book that held the menu then disappeared back behind the bar and towards the kitchen. I opened it up, immediately hearing my stomach growl in response. So many appetizers, and they all looked huge. Every once in a while, there would be a picture of one of these meals, but all of them seafood based.

I looked across the entrées at an Atlantic salmon dish that was an entire fish with its head still on. "Who eats that?" I whispered to myself as I kept looking. I needed something warm and filling, but not too heavy that it would put me to sleep.

"Here we go!" the bartender said as he returned with a bottle and wine glass. "My name's Matt, and I'll be taking care of you this afternoon. Anything look good to you?"

I tried to speed read the rest of the menu with quick glances across the pages. "Well, I'm stuck on two. I was thinking either fish and chips, or the blackened chicken alfredo. Which do you prefer"

I ignored the door slamming at the entrance while deciding about dinner. "Those are both two regulars that sell pretty well. You can't go wrong with fish and chips, and we use an old bay and cracked pepper seasoning when we bread our fish. Instead of a light beer, we use a red lager to give it a little extra flavor. The blackened chicken is cast iron seared and the sauce is amazing. I use that parmesan sauce for breadsticks." He stopped talking for a moment and popped the cork on a bottle of lightly bubbling Moscato. "You can't go wrong with either of them."

"Chicken alfredo it is." I said with a smile as I handed the menu back to him.

"Sounds good to me, that comes with a salad and breadsticks. What dressing would you prefer? We have ranch, balsamic, oil and vinegar, and Caesar." He added a thick Italian accident onto the end of Caesar that made me laugh. He seemed sweet, for a guy.

"I'm not a big fan of salads," I replied with a smile. "Can I have extra breadsticks instead?"

"Of course, scratch the greens and bring on the bread. I'll get that right in for you." He picked up the bottle of Moscato and set it on the bar next to my glass. "Help yourself, no one up here drinks this stuff."

"Thank you, I need that after the traffic I just sat through." I sighed and looked at the tv hanging above the bar where the weather report was showing. It was all red and dark green, and the lady on the screen was letting me know I should expect a miserable drive home.

"How bad is the traffic?" a voice asked from behind me. A woman sat down two seats from me while running her hands through her short, colorful hair. I kept my eyes glued on the tv while responding. There was an entire bar here, why did she have to sit next to me?

"Bad. I'm going from Manhattan to D.C. and it is almost double the amount of time as normal." I said, irritated at the rain all over again. I would much rather be having delivery Thai food in sweats right now than sitting here.

"Well, shit." she said sharply. "So much for 70 and sunny today, right?"

She laughed awkwardly at herself. I glanced over, noticing the motorcycle helmet on the chair next to her.

"Are you driving in the rain on a motorcycle?" I asked, wondering how safe that could possibly be.

"Yep. I've got all the gear I need to be safe though, it just really sucks to ride in the rain." She took a napkin off the bar and wiped the top of her helmet off. It was a glistening red and black with sparkly silver stripes.

"Your helmet is pretty," I said, not knowing the first thing about motorcycles.

"Thanks, it matches my bike. Do you ride?" she asked.

"Me? Oh.. no. I've never touched a motorcycle in my life. Kinda hard to go to work in a skirt on one of those." I laughed awkwardly. Why did she have to sit next to me? This restaurant was almost empty and she could have sat literally anywhere.

"But think about how fun that would be. I mean, not saying you're attractive or anything you know, but like, wouldn't that be freeing after a long day at work?" she tried to recover.

"I guess?" I leaned back in my chair and took a sip of the Moscato. "Never really had any interest in riding though. Are you traveling far from here?" I assumed she wasn't from here if she was asking me about traffic.

"It isn't far, about two hours tops in good weather. The backroads are probably going to be flooded though."

"Hey, can I get a water with two lemons and a Guinness." She said as Matt handed her a menu.

"Coming right up," he said with a smile.

"These burgers look delicious. I'm starving." She said to me. "What did you get?"

"Me? Pasta. I'm a carb junkie." I chimed back to her while watching the news again.

"Carb junkie, I think I'm gonna get one of these giant burgers" she said as *she put the menu down. Matt returned with two glasses, a water and a still settling Guinness. "Can I get one of the American doubles, no pickles?"*

"How would you like that cooked?" he asked, taking the menu, and putting it on the stack of them next to the taps.

"Correctly, medium all the way." She laughed, looking at me.

"Lettuce, onion, bacon, cheddar, mayo all good?" he typed on the little console in the middle of the bar. "Medium, light pink center, fries or house chips?"

"Fries, please" she responded.

"All in and good to go, I'll bring those right out as soon as they're done." Matt said before heading back to the kitchen again.

"So..." I said, leaning back in my chair again. "What brought you out here?"

"I was visiting a friend for something."

"Fun, fun." Light conversation was not my strong suit and I was rarely every in a casual spot.

"What about you, Manhattan? What took you up the east coast?" she lifted her beer up to her lips and took a sip. I looked at her again, taking notice of her rich hazel eyes. There were tiny specks of amber in them.

"Sorry, I mean, Manhattan, yes. I was giving a talk at NYU on unifying our healthcare records on the east coast." I caught myself staring and tried not to make it any more of awkward of an interaction

"What's that mean? It sounds complicated."

"You're right, it is complicated. What I want to do is unite all of the healthcare systems on the east coast that hold patient data into one single shared architecture. That way, if you're traveling and get in an accident, they don't have to call your doctor at home to get your records and will have instant access to it."

"Wait. Back it up a second, that's not how it works now?" she said surprised.

"No, no it isn't. Right now, each state has its own framework, and some states have multiples depending on how big they are. I want to unify all of them."

"Good luck, that sounds like a headache to me." She ran her hands

through her hair again, folding her hands behind her head as she leaned back in the chair.

"A headache that you can actually get treated outside of your home state though." I laughed. It was going to be a ton of work and I knew what it would entail to make it happen.

We both turned our heads to the door as the rain started coming down harder. It was a literal hurricane outside, and I could tell that neither of us wanted to be out there in that mess. I was already dreading having to go back to the car in the lighter rain, let alone what it was doing right now.

Matt emerged from the kitchen with a tray of food, strolling behind the bar and setting plates down in front of us.

"Bowl of Chicken and Carbs for you, and Americas Burger for you."

"Thanks," we both said in unison, looking at each other strangely.

"Enjoy, take your time, and let me know if you need any refills!" he chimed in after, then went down the bar to do some cleaning.

I dove straight into the pasta. The chicken was not too dry, and perfectly seasoned. I had to say, it was better than I had expected. My expectations coming in here on a rainy day were about as low as they could get. I had been spoiled by the rich food scene inside the district, and with amazing international food at my fingertips everywhere else seemed, well, dull.

I ate the entire bowl of pasta in about as much time as it took her to chow down on her burger. Every few bites I would take a sip of wine, check the rain outside, and go right back to eating. Lifting up the wine glass, I gulped down the rest of it before leaning back and letting out an overly exasperated sigh of satisfaction.

"Hey... you got something there."

"What?" I said as I turned to her. She placed a napkin on my chin and wiped it.

"Sorry, your clothes look really nice, and you had alfredo sauce dripping down your chin." She said with a smile. I looked at her for a moment as she folded it up and dabbed it on my chin. "Hayley."

I shook my head to shake off the thoughts that just went through my head. She touched me. "Hayley?"

"Yes. That's my name. This is where you say yours" she laughed, leaning back to drop the napkin on her plate.

"Oh, um, yes." I was nervous about what just happened, and I felt warm across my body. "Elaine Reinhardt."

"That's a pretty name," she said awkwardly.

"Thank you, picked it myself." I joked.

I reached into my purse to pull out my wallet while Matt was walking back in our direction.

"Done already, ladies?" the bartender said while cleaning another glass.

I shook my head, while Hayley said "yes, solid burger."

"Let me get you both your checks then." He said, reaching for the center console.

"One check, I've got it." I looked at her, "Thanks for the company, my treat."

Hayley pulled out a small wallet that was barely enough to carry a few cards and her license. "Nope, on me."

"I said I've got it." I said sternly in response.

She looked at Matt, then to me. "And I said you can put that away," her tone carrying a hint of rebellious competitiveness.

Matt looked at us, then took both of our cards. "How about this, I'm going to put them under a coaster, and randomly pick one. Sound good?"

"Fine" we both said in unison while looking at each other.

"Perfect" he said, shuffling them together and putting one randomly under a coaster. "Now, todays bill is going to...." He leaned forward, trying to build some sort of anticipation. I knew it would be mine.

"Hayley, congratulations on your lunch purchase." Matt said happily. He took the card and swiped it in the machine before handing the receipt over to her.

"HAH!" she said loudly, relishing in her victory. I sat there, confused for a moment.

"It's okay," she said after noticing I was in slight shock. "Everyone takes a loss at some point. You just don't look like you experience it very often."

"Humph." I hopped up out of the chair and threw my blazer on before walking to the door.

"Hey! Wait!" Hayley grabbed her helmet and jumped up, running to the door behind me. I swung it open and stepped out onto the covered awning, *immediately regretting it. She followed me, looking at her drenched bike. The wind was howling, sending the rain almost sideways.*

"Are you.. really going to drive home in this?" I was honestly concerned that she might not make it in this weather.

"Two hours and some change in the rain, I've done worse." She replied as she zipped her leather jacket. I looked at the hard plastic pads on the elbows. That ride would not be comfortable.

"That's too far in this weather. Why don't you..." I said, rubbing my chin in thought, "drop your bike at your friends and I'll give you a ride home."

"Why would you do that?" Hayley looked at my curiously. "I'm a stranger, and it's probably far out of your way. There's no need for that."

"You bought lunch, I'll drive you home. Fair?" I asked with a smile.

"Not really fair at all, but it's much better than my current option." Her helmet dropped beside her, and she brought her eyes up to meet mine. I could see the little specks of amber in them much clearer out here.

"Perfect. I'll follow you to your friends, then we can get you home. Sound good?" I reached into my purse to get my keys before pulling my hair up into a messy bun. I clicked the unlock button, lighting up the taillights on my car.

"BMW. Cute." She said as she pulled her helmet on.

"Warmer than your ride." I said as we both ran across the parking lot in the rain. My feet were soaked all the way through, and there was no way they weren't worse off. As soon as my car was on, I backed it up and waited for her to start moving. I turned my lights on, flipped on the music, and pulled out after her. It was less than a mile to her friend's house, and when we arrived the garage was already open. There were four other motorcycles inside and I watched her pull straight up and into the bay. Another couple was there waiting, and they took a few minutes to talk. I was wondering what they could be talking about, other than the rain. After a few minutes she waved at them and took off running down the driveway before diving into my car.

"See? Told you this was better." I said with a smile. It was disgusting outside, and somehow managed to start raining a little bit harder.

"Are these seats heated?" she said as she snuggled down into the warm leather.

"Of course they are, its one of my favorite parts. You should see them in the summer, they're air conditioned too."

"Car seats can do that??" her eyes widened as she looked all around the car. "that's really cool. You're right, this is way better."

I laughed and shifted into drive. "GPS is on the console, where am I going?"

"Lancaster. Lancaster, Pennsylvania."

* * *

I LOOKED AROUND, *finding myself in an unkept grove deep within a forest buried between oppressively high snowcapped peaks. A single, giant tree towered above all others. I strolled through the knee-high grass, my gaze settling on the round moon that was so bright it almost felt like daytime. The light reflected off of the snow, illuminating the valley below.*

The tree was a colossal, gnarled giant that had witnessed the ebb and flow of countless ages. Each of its branches looked to be wider than any human could reach. It stood as a sentinel between the realms, its roots delving deep into the earth and its branches reaching towards the sky below. I found myself entranced by it, unable to move from the whispers the wind carried as it blew through its boughs.

The moon bathed the grove in silver light, and I turned to find twelve people walking forward towards me. I stood there, silently. Their bodies moved straight past me, and only one stopped for a moment with a smile sent my way. I had seen this woman before. These twelve gathered beneath the giant tree, wrapping their hands together as they surrounded it. Even then, they were barely able to make it around its enormous trunk. They were drawn together by fate, and their names became etched into the annals of vampire lore.

The group began to chant, their voices raising and falling, their bodies swaying in this arcane ritual. I watched through the brush as the twelve of them danced, and a pulse of light ran up the trunk of the tree. Each leaf shimmered with light, glowing as it released tiny specks of radiance down upon them.

One by one, each of them stepped up to the wooden surface. I watched carefully, entranced on their actions. One at a time, they drew a silver blade across their palm and pressed it into the wood. As they stepped back, the bloody handprints disappeared into the bark, leaving a glowing etching instead.

Each of the depressions in the wood glowed brighter and brighter until the entire tree looked like a star in the center of the valley. The tree disappeared in the light, leaving a single woman standing in its wake. The glow pulsed around her, leaving nothing but the purest, light I had ever seen. I was unable to keep my eyes open and I drew my hands up my face to shield them from whatever was happening.

* * *

I WAS PULLED out of my sleep for a moment, the glare of bright lights surrounding me. My body arched, pain that I didn't recognize moving across my skin. I felt like dozens of bones could have been broken. There were eyes, so many eyes. It was as if hundreds of them were all watching me. Their stares, mixed with excitement and curiosity felt like venomous daggers that sliced through my very being. I remained shackled, my body trembling as the doctor looked at me.

"As stated, here is your proof that this is a LIVE specimen!" He turned and strolled over to my side, grabbing a broken rolling chair that screeched across the floor when pulled.

"My dear test subject, you are a canvas upon which I shall paint the masterpiece of my genius! You see, I've always believed that the pursuit of knowledge should know no bounds, that the rules of ethics and morality are mere shackles upon the brilliance of my mind. And you, my dear dear Elaine, are the key to unlocking the secrets that have eluded our kind for centuries!"

An applause filled the air. How could they al sit here and watch this lunatic. Why wouldn't any of them help me? I shuddered, my heart pounding furiously in my chest as his words hung in the air like a malevolent curse. He moved around the bed, stopping on the other side with a terrifying confidence.

"You may view me as a villain, a madman, but I am a visionary! I stand on the precipice of discovery, and you... you are my willing sacrifice, my gateway to the forbidden knowledge that others have dared not pursue."

He looked behind us, away from the theater that was filled with inquiring minds at his work. The clinking of instruments and the hum of arcane machinery surrounded us, casting long, eerie shadows on the makeshift laboratory walls. I could feel the weight of this madman's' intentions pressing down upon me, like a nightmare from which I cannot wake.

"You see, in the pursuit of greatness, sacrifices must be made. Sacrifices such as you, a mere pawn in the grand tapestry of my ambitions. Your pain, your fear, your very existence, they are all essential components of my experiments."

I struggled against my restraints, but they held fast, and there was no escape from the horrors that awaited my body on that stage. The scientist's eyes gleam with a perverse sense of accomplishment, his voice growing more frenzied with every word.

"*Aaaaaaandddddd* when I have harnessed the secrets I seek, when I have unlocked the door to true immortality and conquered the boundaries of life and death, the world will bow before me! I shall be remembered as a pioneer, a genius who transcended the limitations of mere science. I will have reached perfection for our kind!"

As the scientist's maniacal laughter fills the laboratory, I can't help but wonder if I will survive this nightmarish ordeal, or if I will become just another footnote in the annals of his madness, a nameless victim of his relentless pursuit of knowledge. More applause filled the air as he strolled up to center stage and took a bow.

"Now, Let's get started. You can put her back to sleep now."

* * *

I OPENED my eyes and found myself standing in a vast, moonlit courtyard, shrouded in an eerie, otherworldly beauty. In the distance, I spotted her again, her pale features illuminated by the soft glow of the moon.

She stood with a grace and confidence that bespoke centuries of experi-

ence. Her eyes, pools of endless wisdom, pierced the darkness, and her long, raven-black hair cascaded down her back like a waterfall of silk. She wore an exquisite crimson gown that seemed to move with a life of its own, its fabric swaying with each step she took.

Beside her, a young vampire stood, poised and alert, a testament to Ireena's careful tutelage. I wasn't sure who she was, but the smile that the woman gave to her was filled with a gentle softness that I had not seen before. Her similar black hair, a familial trait passed down from her maker, framed her face, and her eyes mirrored this woman in their intensity. She wore a similar styled gown, but had a silver corset wrapped around her waist that helped accentuate the delicate curved of her body. I looked her over, smiling at the long, slender legs that moved with an unholy grace.

I felt my body moving forward to stand in front of the one I had seen before. There was something about her drew me in her direction. I stood before her, looking her up and down. She looked straight at me, no, through me. Her sword lifted up right as I heard a yell from behind me. I turned, a blade moving inches in front of my eyes towards the woman.

This woman, a vampire from what I could tell, wielded a gleaming, silver-bladed sword, its edge catching the moonlight with every fluid, calculated movement. She moved with an unparalleled elegance, her footsteps soundless as she kept an even distance between herself and the new one.

The other woman, armed with twin daggers, met her advance with a fierce determination that belied her age. Her strikes were swift and precise, a testament to the training she had received before. Their dance was a deadly one, a choreography of strikes and parries that seemed as natural as breathing. I was drawn into it, entranced by the beauty in their clash. Each echo of the blades was like a painter's brush on canvas.

The clash of steel against steel resonated through the courtyard as the two sparred with unmatched skill. Their movements were a symphony of power and grace, and the moon above bore witness to this extraordinary display of combat. I looked at my hands, wondering if I would ever be able to fight like that. Had I been able to, maybe I wouldn't have ended up on the operating table.

Watching these two women dance together, blade to blade, left me with a newfound determination to embrace the power that flowed within me veins.

Silence took the courtyard, and they both stopped. They were barely ten feet from each other. Sweat trapped the dress of the younger woman to her legs, while the other one was barely showing any signs of doing anything, let alone activity. Her hair was perfectly kept, her clothes dry, and her breathing was normal. I moved closer as her lips began to move, but I couldn't hear anything she was saying. Her gaze shifted up to the sky, to the moon, and then back down to me.

She could see me.

I froze, her smile widening as she looked at the moon. Her lips continued to move, but no words came out. The moons silvery light covered the courtyard with the warmth of the night. I followed suit and looked to the sky. It looked larger than I had ever seen it, and there was a faint ring of colored haze around it.

I BLINKED *and lowered my head. The courtyard was gone, and I found myself standing in the murky depths of a different century, hidden in the shadows of a grim, towering church. The night was shrouded in an eerie silence, and the moon glowed coldly in the pitch-black sky. My heart was a drumbeat in the stillness as I watched the ominous stone structure before me.*

The ancient stone edifice, bathed in the cold, glow of the moon, stood before me as a testament to human devotion and craftsmanship. The architecture of the church was a marvel, its pointed arches and towering spires reaching skyward, like skeletal fingers yearning for salvation. As a vampire, I was a creature of the night, forever separated from the solace these consecrated walls offered. The intricately crafted stained-glass windows adorned the exterior, shimmering with stories of faith and redemption, each pane a kaleidoscope of colors that whispered of human piety.

The church's aura was one of solemn reverence, a sanctuary that had stood the test of time, a beacon of hope and devotion in a world shrouded in darkness. Its very existence was a reminder of the eternity I was denied, a reminder that I would forever be an outsider, a creature cursed with immortality.

I watched as a lone figure emerged from the church's entrance, a flickering candle in hand, casting an ethereal glow upon the stone steps. The cloaked parishioner moved with a sense of purpose, perhaps unaware of the unworldly observer hidden in the inky shadows.

AT MY SIDE *was a mysterious vampire woman, one whose name I did not know. Her presence exuded power and a dark, alluring grace. She possessed a timeless beauty, and her eyes held the secrets of countless centuries. There was a determined glint in her crimson gaze as she surveyed the scene before us.*

"Kamila," she whispered in a voice as old as the night, "it's time to save our own."

I nodded, my trust in this enigmatic vampire unwavering. She was my guide through the endless night of immortality.

Together, we moved soundlessly toward the church's imposing wooden doors, which groaned open with an eerie, otherworldly creak. Inside, we found a cavernous chamber dimly lit by flickering candles on ancient stone altars. The air was thick with the scent of incense and fear.

In the center of the church, young vampires, mere fledglings in this shadowed existence, were bound in chains, their eyes brimming with terror. A group of fervent vampire hunters, clad in silver and wielding crosses, surrounded the helpless creatures. They chanted their prayers with zealous fervor, determined to cleanse the souls of these accursed beings.

The mysterious vampire woman and I moved with an uncanny grace that defied the human eye. The fanatics had no time to react. With a glance, she subdued the hunters with her crimson eyes, her powers undeniable. I followed her lead, my movements a ghostly dance, my fangs glistening in the candlelight as I rushed to free the young vampires.

Her laughter, cold and melodic, filled the chamber as she tore the priests apart. I watched her drop a body at the feet of the younger vampires. The children of the night were freed at last, their gratitude evident in their wide, awestruck eyes. They looked to the enigmatic vampire, not with fear, but with reverence. I looked at her again, watching her toss another body over to them.

"Du bist unser retter," one of the young vampires whispered. What was he saying? I wished I had taken better attention in German class back in high school. I tried to figure out his words when the woman cut me off.

"Feed and disappear." She gave one order, and they unquestionably obeyed. I walked over to the side where a giant bowl of water stood.

"Careful, child." Her voice echoed behind me as I looked into the stillness of the water. A crisp reflection stared back at me, a reflection that was not my own. I felt a hand on my shoulder and turned to face her.

"Should we burn it down?" I asked.

The mysterious vampire woman nodded, and I could see that her beauty and power were inseparable. She turned to me, her eyes holding a deep, darkness that held rage towards the church we were in.

"We are the guardians of our kind. And together, we will flourish in the shadows."

I joined her outside the church, the flames quickly overtaking the structure. Bright red and yellow danced across its walls and up to the sky, and the heat singed my skin even at this distance. I stared into the fire, taking note of every curve of the fire. The colors were a stark contrast from the black that helped us merge into the darkness. My body moved against my will, marching forward through the thick mud until the only thing that surrounded me was fire. The crackle of the flames consumed my vision, and the dream shifted around me.

I leaned back, the bowl of oil igniting in a ball of flame across this corner of the courtyard. The air was crisp, and the scent of earth and greenery filled my senses. I glanced down at myself and noticed I was no longer the modern-day woman I knew in the 21st century. Instead, all I wore was a simple linen tunic, my feet wrapped in leather sandals. A sword hung from a soft leather belt that wrapped around my waist.

I turned around, recognizing those beautiful crimson eyes. A strange, domed structure billowed out of the walls next to me, blocking half of the night sky from my view. The woman strolled into the center of the courtyard and drew her blade. She wore a form fitting dress with leather straps around her waist that lifted up her breasts, the pale outline of her skin poking through the robe that covered her. Every line of her body exuded a sense of power, and event step was met with a mesmerizing fluidity. Every movement she made was near perfection. Her weight shifted between her feet, the blade moving forward, retreating, jabbing, slicing, thrusting.

As she advanced and retreated, the clash of steel against the air echoed through the night, punctuated by quick, controlled lunges and parries. Her breaths were measured, and her eyes held an intensity that mirrored her determination. This wasn't practice, this was a pursuit of perfection. My heightened senses allowed me to catch every nuance of this duel. The subtle shifts in her weight, the twitch of her muscles before a strike, and the way her eyes locked onto her invisible opponent. She was honing her craft, a skilled swordswoman dedicated to mastering her art.

A hunger stirred within me, not for the taste of blood, but for the passion and focus she exhibited. It was a different kind of craving, a yearning for something more elusive. I longed to feel that sense of purpose and mastery that radiated from her every move. I looked down at the sword on my waist, and slowly drew it. It had been far too long since I held a blade in my hand. The leather strapping on the handle warm to the touch. I admired the blade, the thinness, of it, the balance that felt like it had been in my grasp thousands of times.

I lifted the blade up, my right foot sliding back behind me. Every time I saw the woman step, I would step. When she thrusted, I would thrust. I watched, barely able to be an imitation of what she was capable of. Every twist, every flick of her wrist that sent her blade slicing through the air, I wanted to burn that feeling into my muscles. I couldn't help but admire her commitment to her art. She had a passion that drove her forward, not because of necessity, but of love. While sweat dotted her brow, she never lost her smile.

The blade shifted in her hands, and she stopped, turning to look at me. Her head cocked to the side, and I felt that shared desire to excel, to be the best at what I did again.

"Again."

The Devil

REFLECTIONS

"The temptress is a step ahead of me again, hiding in my shadows. In my solitude, I cling to the rosary, beads slipping through my fingers, a lifeline in this abyss. I'm the closest I've ever been."
Father Gabriel's Private Journal, 1622

CHAPTER 6

My body shook, and in the distance, I could hear someone yelling my name. I smiled, keeping my eyes closed. There was a new warmth on my face that made me feel a little warm and cozy. It was soft, and smooth.

"Please, wake up Elaine." The feeling on my face moved quicker, pressing, and pulling before someone peeled my eyes open. The bright light from the room was shocking to me and I jerked away as I gasped for air. A tightness moved up my throat I tried to swallow but couldn't. Panic set in and I started to choke.

"Stop, STOP" the voice said, putting a hand on my head. I could feel the tightness in my throat as I tried to swallow again but couldn't. Locking my eyes on the person at my side, I saw Morgan standing there holding me still while trying to unbuckle the leather bindings with one hand, while the other was around... Wait. A tube. There was a tube in my mouth.

"Almost there."

She tugged the thin tube and pulled it out of my throat, causing me to choke. My body felt numb, my head falling to the side where I watched her pull the needles and tubes out of my arm. Most of my vision was blurry and my head felt like it had gone through the worst hangover of all time.

"We have to go. There isn't much time." She said as she ran to the other side of me, unstrapping the restraints and pulling off the monitoring wires. I felt nauseous and dizzy, and the room was spinning. Her movements were too quick and were almost blurry to me. I tried to speak, but nothing came out. My throat was dry, and a quick gulp let me know it was swollen. Everything in my body hurt right now.

"I need you to focus, please" She stepped back to my right side and dug herself under my arm to help me lift up. My legs felt like they weren't even there. I tried to slide from the table I was on, realizing that I wasn't in the same room anymore. My body felt tingly and dirty. I couldn't feel my hair touching my shoulders either.

"We're gonna get out of here," she said while trying to carry as much of my weight as she could. I tried to take a step forward with her but ended up dragging my feet side to side.

"What.." I tried to get words out, but the pain shot through my throat again.

"Don't talk, we don't have time."

I didn't understand what was going on. Twisting my head side to side, I could feel the sharp cracks through my neck that relieved a bit of the tightness that was currently there. We struggled together across the room towards the door where I leaned into the wall next to it. The cold surface felt amazing on my shoulder, but there were little pricks of pain that streaked down my arm where medical equipment had been attached.

As she cracked the heavy metal door open, a flood of strobing, flashing lights poured into the room. The crisp crack of gunshots echoed down the halls. My hearing was dulled already, and the sound of the fire alarm going off didn't help at all. I could barely hear myself think, let alone hear what Morgan was saying. My eyes kept trying to focus, closing tightly for a moment before I blinked as fast as I could. Anything that I could think of to get my senses back in order I was trying at this point.

My head bobbed to the side as she kicked the door open, pulling my arm across her shoulder while dragging us both into the hallway. I could feel the building shaking under my feet. A thick, heavy smoke filled the corridor as we moved as fast as I was able towards the end of it. I wanted to be more helpful, but I had no idea where I was at, and had never seen anything other than the room I was initially held in. The blaring pulse of the fire alarm, partnered with the flashing strobes every ten feet or so, made my head pound worse than it already was.

"Stay with me, we're almost there Elaine" Morgan said while pulling me around the corner. "See? The door's right there."

The door at the end of the hall swung open and a wide beam of dull light split the fog.

"Morgan! Move it!" a thick, heavy accented male screamed out into the hall.

"We're already going at full speed, give us a hand!" she yelled back down the hallway.

I could barely tell what they were saying to each other. My arm slid off of her as I hit the ground, my knees striking the hard laminate floor. I barely caught myself before I threw up to the side, not wanting to get anything on either of us. The sound of the gunk coming out of my stomach made me want to throw up again.

The quick pat of footsteps approaching sent my heartrate moving faster than I ever could have wanted it in this situation. I wanted to crawl away as fast as I could and hide somewhere, but that wasn't in the cards today. A dry, abrasive hand grabbed my forearm where one of the Iv's had been connected and pulled me up to my feet. I screeched at the pain from it, the man putting his other arm under my knees and lifting me up.

"Morgan let's go. I got her", he said as he carried me. I could smell his cologne, a light mix of leather and sandalwood. It reminded me of a candle we used to keep in our bedroom in the wintertime. The scent thickened as he wrapped his right arm around my shoulders and pulled me into him. I heard the door to the stairwell swing open, the slam of it against the concrete blocks sending an echo in all direc-

tions. The edge of the door clipped my feet, and I yelped as best I could at the pain.

The speed he took down the stairs was almost inhuman. I tried to listen to the conversation that the two of them were having, but my ears were partially ringing from all the extra noise. My eyes were pressed shut, and every time I opened them the world seemed to spin in circles. I focused on trying to listen to this man's heartbeat. The steady thump of it was able to drown out a lot of the background noise. Every few steps there would be a sense of weightlessness for a moment as he leapt down the last few steps.

He came to a stop, my head jerking again as pain shot down my back. "Morgan, get the car. Go!"

His voice was stern and direct. He walked to the side of the last floor, planting his back into the door before pushing it open. A breeze of fresh, but dry air filled my lungs as he moved to the side and sat me down. I leaned my head back against the dirty concrete wall next to the door while watching Morgan take off running. This man was gigantic. He had to be somewhere between six and seven feet tall, with broad shoulders and arms so chiseled that they looked like they were created by Greek artisans.

He cracked his knuckles, stepping out into the garage. I watched him carefully, but I still couldn't really hear what he was saying. I tried to force out a yawn, hoping that it would make my ears pop and give me back a bit more of my hearing. My head was still aching from whatever they had pumped me full of. It felt like I was coming out of anesthesia, and my memory was foggy at best.

I watched the large man run forward, disappearing behind the line of cars next to me. He was barely gone a moment before a body flew across the top of a vehicle and slammed into the elevator door. They were covered in white robes and had been holding a weapon of some sort. I heard the clang of it hit the ground before their body did. The figure stood up, shrugging their body around before picking up their weapon. They look out into the parking garage, yelling something out into the dimly lit structure.

His body stopped, turning towards mine. He walked over, taking a knee as he lowered his face down. It stopped barely an inch or two away from mine. Their breath was thick and smelled like something close to but not quite spearmint. Was he chewing gum?

"Look at that, another specimen."

His eyes narrowed towards my neck as he pulled my head to the side. "No bite marks, but you look like they've been draining you. I wonder, did you volunteer for this? If so, got to say that is heretical behavior little one."

I tried to keep my eyes on him, knowing that if I had any of my strength right now, I would probably be able to rip him into pieces. He moved his fingers side to side, "tsk tsk tsk, gonna have to bring you in for some extra questioning. You won't mind, right?" He looked at me, bringing his face down to mine.

"You look familiar… wait."

He pulled out a phone and held it up, his eyes darting between whatever he was looking at, and me. I watched him, wishing I could move, to run, to do anything but lay here against the wall.

"Thank you, oh holy father for blessing your soldier today! What fortune has smiled down upon me!"

"Fuck."

"What was that?"

"Off."

I struggled to lift my hand, my fingers curving into an extended middle finger. His head dropped backwards as he laughed, his eyes almost bulging out of his head with excitement.

"Your existence defies God's will! You are an abomination, a creature of the night that feeds on the innocent. Every victim you have left behind you is blood on your hands. You are a tarnish on this world, and it is our job to---"

Without warning, two giant hands wrapped around his head and jerked it to the side. The quick snap of it shocked me, my eyes widening as his body fell to the ground next to mine. I looked down at it before looking up at the man who had been carrying me. He had puncture wounds across his chest and left shoulder. The scent of blood that was leaking from beneath his scrubs hit my nose and sent my stomach into a cramping growl. I held my mid-section in my hands as best I could while I tried to keep the urge to bite into him in check. I wasn't sure how long it had last been since I had fed on anything. I had a hazy memory of Morgan feeding me, but that felt like days ago.

A sharp pain slowly pierced through my upper jaw as I moved my head side to side, trying to shake the bloodlust off. I didn't know that my dark brown eyes had specks of crimson fading in and out across them. I closed my eyes, pressing them tightly shut while bringing my knees to my chest and burying my head into my legs.

I stayed there for a few moments, only moving when he lifted me up. I could hear a car door open, and the man helped me into the backseat. His arm reached across me to buckle the seat belt as he sat me up.

"What took you so long?" he asked to Morgan who was behind the wheel.

"I got a little busy on the way, sorry. They're everywhere." She said as she hit the gas. I felt my head hit the window with a thud. "Did you strap her in? Jeeze, Abeo."

"Hold on back there!" Morgan yelled as she slammed the gas pedal into the floor. I looked through the window, watching people pour out of the elevator and run towards their cars.

"Wait."

I lifted my hand up to the window, my eyes locking with someone familiar. I knew him. A tightness crossed my body and I had to choke down the nausea that followed.

"Marcus." I whispered to myself. He had seen me, and I had seen him. It was him. I knew it was him. There was no way Addison would have know exactly where I was, or when I was crossing the bridge. He had betrayed me, betrayed his friends. My breath felt heavy against the seatbelt. It wasn't true. It couldn't be true. He just looked the same. I tried to convince myself otherwise, but I knew what I saw.

And he saw me.

I felt the car speed up before it crashed loudly through a barricade of plastic barrels. There were flashing lights all around the outside of the building. It reflected off the glass walls of the buildings around us. I looked at it, curious about the colors. They weren't red and blue like normal police but were purple and yellow mixed with white strobes.

"Where…" I closed my eyes again. "Where are we?"

Abeo turned around in his seat. "We're in Camden, Lanning Square. Take a rest, we have a few miles to go."

"Why are you… Where are you taking me?" I asked as clearly as I was able. I felt the car jerk several times.

"Sorry for the rough driving, we have to make sure they can't follow us."

I finally opened steadied my head, leaning it against the back of the seat. "Who isn't following us?"

"Surissa. Mother Surissa found the site and brought her priesthood order to wipe it. We had been planning on getting you out of there months ago, but they didn't give us a chance." she replied.

"Months? I've only been-"

"Yes months. They put you in a drug induced coma so they could try more experiments without you screaming at them."

Abeo turned around in his seat to look at me. "You gave them a hard time, we hear. Good job."

"How long…" tears started to form in my eyes. "How long was I like that…Hayley had to have been looking for me."

"It's November. You were under for almost eight months."

I sat there in shocked silence. I had been floating through my memories for eight months. No wonder everything felt fuzzy right now. I could feel a tight anger forming in my stomach, but before it could erupt, I closed my eyes and drifted back to sleep.

THE CAR KEPT MOVING, taking turns every so often as they proactively took care of covering their tracks. My drowsiness from the anesthesia had me drifting in and out of sleep again, and the soft hum of the engine was the perfect background noise to drown everything else out. Occasionally, a warm yellow light would come across the car, so I started counting them like I had done when I had been locked up in the mausoleum.

I kept counting in my head while listening to the car move. The silence was a happily invited guest and during the final leg of the ride I was able to get a bit of myself together. It wasn't long, however, before the car came to a stop.

"Elaine, let Abeo help you in," she said as my door swung open. I tried to lift myself out, but ultimately failed. Abeo caught me, lifting me up again before I face planted on the broken sidewalk. My body swung up under me as he strolled up the porch. His arms wrapped around my frail body, and I finally knew what a porcelain doll felt like. The quick movements from him almost made me dizzy. I could hear a woman say something from inside the door, but I wasn't able to quiet make it out.

"Fine, she can come in." chided an older woman. Most of the conversation was muffled until Morgan closed the door behind me.

"Annabella, that's enough." She said as threw her keys into a bowl beside the door. "We couldn't leave her there, what's done is done."

I felt Morgan run her hand through my hair, pulling part of it behind my ear. "She needs rest, and food. I'll take care of everything Gran."

She pointed upstairs, "the guest bedroom is perfect for her. Come on, Abeo."

Abeo carried be up the stairs and over to one of the four bedrooms on this floor. The room was small, barely fitting a day bed and a desk. A vase with yellow and purple flowers sat on the nightstand next to a black leathery charging pad. He laid be down on the bed, trying to be as gentle as possible. I felt the pillow under me, a stark contrast from my recent accommodations, and the exhaustion finally overcame me. I closed my eyes, going straight to sleep.

I OPENED MY EYES, staring straight at the ceiling. There were little dots of pale green color spread across it. The sound of someone lightly snoring filled the mostly quiet space. Seated on a chair next to the door was Morgan, her head against the wooden frame. A woman stood next to her, stroking her long red and black braids.

She looked at me as I sat up, curious but cautious. "You've brought us quite a lot of trouble. Tell me, what did you do to make my wife go so far out of the way. Was it compulsion? Mind control? What trick"

"Trick? I was in a coma for the last eight months. If she hadn't already told you. I don't know how to do any of that." I looked at my hands, and then my arms. Some of my fingers were bruised, and there was a sharp pain across my thumbnail where it had been broken. What had they done to me while I was under?

"She said you were special and they were trying to use you for something, but she never said what. Are you really... you know..."

"A vampire?" I said with a light laugh. "Yes. I am."

"But you don't look like one. The ones I know are all, well, scary. And rude. They are barely better than the Whitefangs." She said apprehensively.

"What are the Whitefangs?" I asked.

"Enough of that talk, don't be adding more to that young lass right now. She's got enough on her plate recovering." The stern woman's voice from when we arrived filled the hall. I could smell something wonderfully savory that floated up from downstairs.

"I'm sorry, what time is?" There was a single heavy blind covering the entire window that kept all the light out. It almost looked to be taped in several places.

I could hear footsteps coming down the hall towards the door. A short, thin lady in a dress with a white and yellow apron stood in the door, pushing the girl aside. "I'm sorry dear, we don't carry your type here. What I do have is some raw chuck. I tried to squeeze all the blood out of it I could, but it's not a lot."

I looked at her hand where a shot glass of red liquid was filled almost all the way to the top.

"Now, some ground rules hun" she said as she woke Morgan up. "You will not feed on any of us. We aren't your snack, got it? I can't just run down to the store and get this for you. Our house is in Halin's district, but our deli shop is in Whitefangs."

I shook my head up and down. "Got it. Only drink blood shots. It will be delicious; I don't think I've had any blood in months."

"That's about right." Morgan said with a yawn. "Sorry gran. Looks like I fell asleep. Hey there Elaine, nice to see you up!"

I smiled at her as the older woman gave me the shot glass. Without hesitation I popped it straight back, being careful to not waste a single drop of it. Even though it wasn't human, it was better than nothing. I held it in my mouth for a moment as it watered. The hunger was far stronger than my internal disgust at drinking it.

"Morgan…" I said as soon as I had gulped it down. I held the shot glass in my hands and moved myself backwards to the padded headboard so I could lean backwards. "What happened to me?"

"Yes, Morgan. Let's all hear what you and Abe Babe were doing over there in that crazy lab?" the younger woman said as she popped her head back in.

"Sorry Elaine, this is Annabella, my fiancé." She said with a smile. Annabella walked over and put her arm around her head, running her fingers through the braids again.

"You two are a beautiful couple." I said lightly.

"I'm sure you and Hayley are too." She responded.

"I never mentioned that." I replied, concerned.

She let out a sigh before coming over to sit on the end of the bed. Annabella moved to the chair and the older lady turned to leave, not wanting to add more complexity and drama to her life.

"The doctor did. He mentioned that you were married to Hayley Reinhardt and had her blood in you. They tried to study your bloodline, but when they failed, they put you under and tried to forcefully awaken it."

I looked at my arms, taking note of every puncture wound, every cut, every stitch and bruise. "Is that why everything hurts? Because they carved me up like a science experiment."

"More or less. Once they put you under, I started thinking of a way to get you out of there. Abeo works in the lab too, but he's more on the back side of things."

"The backside?"

"Yea... the side after they've finished with a research specimen. It's his job to... well... you know."

"Get rid of the evidence. Got it."

"He does it humanely, it's not like we're burying people alive or anything..."

"You have no idea the cruelty of that isolation. I was locked away for over two centuries."

"We heard that rumor." she said with a hint of sadness.

"Why should I trust you? You were there and did nothing. How many more were done like that? Why would you work for a monster like that?"

I could feel my face getting red again. I felt dehydrated and was trying not to cry again. I should be celebrating being out of there.

Morgan looked down at her feet silently. Annabella looked across at me, locking her eyes on mine with an irritated glare. "You don't get it. We don't have a choice. We're in his territory, so we either work for him, or pay him. That's how he keeps our coven in-"

"Coven? Are you witches?" I asked with a bit more excitement.

"Annabella, you can't be mouthing off like that!" the old lady said, swatting her head as she came back with a hot cup of tea and some snack cakes.

"Thank you, ma'am." I said as I looked at the hot cup of tea. It smelled like peppermint and honey. Could I even consume that anymore? I looked at it again before picking up the glass and holding it to my chest with both hands. The heated glass felt nice and warm against my cold skin.

"Don't you go ma'aming me, I'm not that old." She said with a chuckle. "I'm sixty three years young, you hear?"

"You make fifty look amazing"

She laughed, breaking some of the heaviness in the room. "See there Morgan? That's how you compliment someone."

Morgan and Annabella both laughed. I took a sip of the tea and looked towards the window.

"Is it daytime?" I asked.

"Late afternoon. Sun will be going down in an hour or so. You slept two days straight, so its no wonderin if your sleep schedule is a bit off" Morgan looked at the window and let out a sigh as she spoke. I would love to see the sunset again. Thoughts of sitting on the balcony overlooking the park downtown hit me like a runaway train.

Ding. Ding. Ding.

THE ROOM WENT silent as the doorbell went off again. I looked at the older lady as she grabbed Morgan and pulled her into the hall. "Annabella, you stay in here. Morgan, get to the kitchen with Abeo. I'll get the door."

Annabella stepped into the room and closed the door. As she turned around, a single finger was at her lips. I nearly held by breath while trying to get my heartbeat to slow down. I didn't know that my bed was currently sitting above the front door until the door opened.

"Good evening, sorry to bother you, Abigail. Is your granddaughter home?" A crisp, male voice carried itself up through the floorboards.

"Why yes, she's in the kitchen cookin. May I ask what you need?" The demeaner of the old lady was completely different than what I had experienced moments ago.

"There was an incident a few days ago, and we had some unfortunate samples go missing. They're quite dangerous, and we had a few questions for her." He stayed on the porch, hands folded behind him. "It's just a precaution."

The old lady turned, yelling back to the kitchen. "Morgan, come answer this nice man's questions so we can get to eatin some dinner."

Morgan came from the kitchen, wearing an apron smeared with some flour. "Good evening, what can I do for you?"

Annabella kept her finger in front of her face, my hands covered mine. We stared intently at each other while listening, trying not to move a muscle.

"We reviewed our security footage after the incident in one of our labs, and your car was seen escaping with someone in it."

"Abeo. Abeo was in it. He's in the kitchen would you like me to grab him?" she said clearly.

"That would be great and will speed this up." He said emotionlessly.

"Abeo, this creepy ass man has some questions for us!" she yelled back into the kitchen. I wanted to laugh at how similar she and her grandmother were, but I was too afraid to make a sound.

The heavy footsteps from Abeo could be heard all the way upstairs. I could picture him standing there, arms crossed looking down at what I was imagining a small skinny vampire in a suit.

"What do you want." His words were short and forceful, carrying with them an obvious irritation at having his cooking disrupted.

The man coughed into his glove for a moment as he stood outside the door. "Were you in the vehicle with Morgan Le'Bai two days ago?"

"I assume you are referring to when the church attacked your lab. Of course, we left there in a hurry. It's bad enough we already have to work for your kind, but there's no way we're getting mixed up with them. I won't allow it."

"Very well. You wouldn't mind if I were to have a look around really quick, right? Just to make sure everything is clear for our records."

"Excuse me?" the old woman stepped in front of Abeo and Morgan. "You are not welcome here and most certainly may not enter."

I could feel his frustration from here. I closed my eyes and tried to listen more intently. My nostrils flared, and for a moment it felt like I could even smell him. He stood there in silence for several moments, staring at the old woman who had stood her ground. Finally, he broke the silence with a sigh.

"You know how to use your words, old lady. Have it your way, but this will be in my report."

He looked over at Morgan and Abeo. "I expect the two of you to return on Monday when the lab reopens. Have a lovely rest of your evening."

His footsteps were heavy as he walked off the porch and down the sidewalk towards his car. I could feel his presence there. I looked at the wall beside the window, trying to guess how many steps down he had moved before he stopped. His head turned and he looked at the second floor with a curious smile. Just as quickly as he had stopped, he turned and walked to his car, a black SUV with dark tinted windows. I heard the engine start with a low rumble and seconds later he pulled away, heading up the street. Both Annabella and I let out a giant sigh of relief.

"Who was that?" I asked to myself as Annabella threw the door open. Morgan had come running back up the stairs to meet her. I watched as she threw her arms around Annabella.

"That was close." She said relieved.

Annabella kept her arms locked around her for an extra breath before she let go and sat down in the old wooden chair. I looked at the window, listening intently to see if the car was really gone, or just doing a lap. "That was one of Lord Halin's drones. I've seen him at the lab before. He's one of the more trusted lacky's that swings through. They must be searching hard for you if they sent him out here."

I looked at the window again, curious if he could sense my presence. "I'm not going to go back there again. Do you know how to get in contact with someone?"

"Someone like Hayley? Impossible. It's not like she has a direct line or anything." Morgan said, shaking her head. "We may be able to ask Terry at the shop, he does deliveries over there every once in a while."

"That would be great," I smiled, feeling like I was finally one step closer. "When can we meet Terry?"

"I'll take you with us to the shops tomorrow. We have a few businesses that we run." Morgan said cheerfully.

"Is that a good idea?" Annabella chimed in. "She's basically a wanted fugitive by the Addison, and you and Abeo both work for him. If you get caught, it's going to be all of our heads on the chopping block."

"I'll be careful, and besides, they don't come into the Whitefangs territory anyway. If I had to put my money on a fight, I've got twenty on the dogs."

"The dogs?" I asked? "Please don't tell me werewolves are real."

Annabella and Morgan both let out a lighthearted chuckle. "GIRL. You're a *goddamn* vampire. We're witches. Of course, werewolves are real."

I sat there in thought for a few moments before I scooted down the bed and laid down. The smell of something spicy hit my nose, making my stomach churn. Abeo yelled up the stairs, "Aye, Dinner. Come and get it!"

"Would you like to join us?" Annabella asked. "He's a great cook, really."

I thought about it for a moment, but the smell of it turned me off from eating. "I would hate to be disrespectful and waste anything, I'm not even sure if I can eat regular food anymore. I think I'm going to get some more rest instead."

"Your loss, his food really is amazing. I'll see what we can find for you after dinner. It might not be much, but it will be something, right?"

Annabella and Morgan wrapped their arms around each other as they left the room, closing the door behind them. I sat there in silence, taking in my new surroundings again. There were old family portraits on the wall, and the wallpaper was white with little green speckles. Even the lamp shade was old and dusty. It wasn't a lot, but it was quaint and homey. There was love in these pictures, and I wondered if Hayley had kept any of us. I fell backwards with a light plop, my head folding the pillow almost in half. A deep inhale followed, and I held my breath while staring at the ceiling. The ceiling fan looked like giant leaves, an interesting choice for indoors if I had to give an opinion on interior decorating. I exhaled as slow as possible while closing my eyes again. It might be early morning for my kind, but I was ready to get another full day of sleep.

Tomorrow's problems could wait until tomorrow.

The sun

REFLECTIONS

"Silver in the blood, weapons blessed by a clergyman of the highest
level attainable are required before deploying to the field in the fight
against the evil of shadows."
Father Gabriel, Adeptus Oryx, Holy Codex ii

CHAPTER 7

I was awoken by a gentle shake, opening my eyes to find Annabella standing next to the bed. There was a dim light pouring through the crack in the door that lit up a decent bit of the bedroom. I blinked a few times groggily before sitting up and yawning. Annabella jerked back from the bed, her hands moving up to her chest in defense. Her gasp was frightful, and I snapped my attention over to her.

"What's wrong?" I asked, surprised at her jumping back.

She hesitated for a moment before speaking up, her voice quiet and restrained.

"I've never seen a real pair of fangs before, and your teeth look really, really, sharp. I'm sorry, it just caught me off guard." She shook her head swiftly, trying to shake off the surprise.

I snapped my mouth shut, bringing my hands up to cover them. I was embarrassed that she had seen them, and I didn't even know they were out. They had to have come out while I was dreaming.

"I'm so sorry," I mumbled through my hands while I tried to get them to disappear.

"It's okay, really. I just..." she said shyly, "It surprised me, that's all."

The entire house was quiet, and it took me a few minutes to get my bearings. It looked really early in the morning, judging from what she was wearing. I looked at her sweats, a flannel red and white pattern of checkerboard that looked rather warm.

"What time is?" I said with another yawn.

"Five thirty, we have almost an hour until sunset, so we wanted to get you over to the shops as soon as the sun goes down. Not like we will be seeing any of it today."

"ugggghhhh… It's raining." I said, exaggerating an exasperated sigh. I wasn't fond of the rain, but the noise of it had let me sleep a little bit longer.

"Yep, it's a drizzle right now but it's supposed to rain most of the day. Gran says we're gonna get some snow soon! Figured dark and gloomy would fit you." Annabella said with a cheerful smile.

"Dark and gloomy? That's Hayley, not me. I actually prefer bright colors and pastels. You wouldn't be able to tell from my hair, but I used to wear bright colors in it all the time. Two hundred years and some change later, its back to boring old brown."

I chuckled at how much I hated my natural hair color. Ever since I had first had the jade green added in, I never turned back.

"We can pick you up some clothes later, there's a cute boutique on the corner that is more retro classic than anything else."

I ran my fingers through my hair, trying to get some of the larger tangles out. Almost all of it was gone and it barely touched my neck. If I knew who had cut my hair off, I would drown them in a mud puddle. I closed my eyes and took a deep breath, hoping to keep my feelings and frustration in check.

"Honestly, I am surprised words like retro are even still used. When I said it, I was talking about bell bottom jeans."

"Hunny those are still here, we just ignore them." She laughed, "Some trends just never die."

"And some trends absolutely should. Those are one of them."

We both laughed, her at bell bottom jeans, and me at realizing that fashion statement had been alive for two hundred and fifty years. I wondered what else was still around. Black neck chokers? Tornado pants?

I rolled out of bed and looked down at the clothes I was currently wearing. A lab apron and gown that barely covered anything. Someone had put a pair of soft linen shorts on me while I was asleep. I needed to find some clothes of my own, and fast. The last thing I remember owning and actually wearing was the cocktail dress I had been buried in.

"Not wanting to sound stupid… but what is the currency being used?" I asked. I knew my bank account was long past gone, and almost all my assets were buried. I had nothing but my name, and even that wasn't worth all that much. For someone who was used to having an almost unlimited financial backing, being broke was something I hadn't experienced since I was in college.

She looked at me for a moment before shaking her head and laughing.

"You really are disconnected, sheesh." She said as she pulled her hair behind her into a giant ponytail.

"We're still using the dollar, but almost all of it is digital now. Paper money went out of style years ago."

"Guess that makes my piggy bank useless now"

"A what?"

I shook my head and sighed. Some things had changed so much, while others almost seemed to be the same.

"It was a joke. Back in my day," I said sarcastically, "kids would have a glass bank, some of them shaped like farm animals. When they got money, they would put it in there, and when it was full their parents would open it up and they'd get what they had saved. It was a way to teach kids how to save money."

"So, it was a lesson in financial responsibility, how kid like. Your time sounds boring and harsh."

I sighed again.

"There were a lot of things that our time did poorly in. We had a fissure between generations that caused a lot of political turmoil, and many minorities were targeted by extremely conservative old people who couldn't accept generational change. They latched onto their idea of what the world was, what their view of greatness was, and dug their heels in. When they couldn't win, they tried to cheat their way around it to give themselves more power so they could disenfranchise all the other groups of people. It was a hard time for even us."

Annabella sat down in the chair while listening. "We studied that in school. Now, there are six political parties and while they are okay at getting things done, it's much easier to keep any extremism in check. Even your kind has representation there."

I crawled out of bed as soon as I noticed the pair of leggings and baggy grey-tone sweater that was on the nightstand. The clothes were soft, and I was a sucker for an over sized sweater. I slid out of the clothes I had been put in days ago, and quickly pulled the clean ones over my body. The sweater was soft, warm, and a near perfect fit.

"Did Morgan guess my size?" I asked, turning in a circle, and letting the baggy sweater fly out.

She stood up, striding softly across the room to pull the side of the sweater down. "Morgan knew your size already; she took care of you while you were under. We would listen to her talk about you for months. It's almost weird seeing you in person, especially since you are so important."

"I'm not." I said briskly. I stopped for a moment in thought before I continued.

"I'm not important. I'm a terrified girl in a world that I'm not a part of, with almost no friends and every member of my family has been buried for centuries. The last thing I think I am, is important."

"Well, at least you have some friends. Right? We can be your new friends. Morgan really likes you and was always worried about what they were doing to you. She feels horrible that she couldn't get you out of there earlier." She played with her hands, looking down so she wouldn't make eye contact.

"But that aside, we should probably get over to the shop as soon as the sun goes down. Ready to go?"

"Great idea. I hate to say it, but I'm starving." I could feel my stomach rumbling and I wasn't sure how long I would be able to keep that hunger in check.

I followed her downstairs, the lights already on and both

Morgan and the older woman at work in the kitchen. I could smell something cinnamon wafting from the back side of the house. Just that smell made me smile. I kicked a box on my way through the room, stubbing my toe as I let out a light yelp and grabbed my foot. Annabella laughed at me, pulling me over towards the dining room. There were new boxes all over the place, some open and some still tightly closed with thick tape along the edges.

"What are all of these boxes for? Someone moving?" I asked as I moved around them. The dining room had a moderately sized oval table with six high backed wooden chairs. They were ornately decorated with wood engravings that looked to be some sort of filigree. I looked over them, running my hand across its etching before sliding it out and taking a seat.

"The season is moving; can't you feel it?" said the older woman as she entered the room. She took a seat at the head of the table, Abeo pulling out the chair for her.

"We have had not the chance for a proper introduction, young one. My name is Abigail." She said as she looked me over.

"How do you know I'm young?" I asked curiously with a smile. "I'm a vampire, I could be hundreds of years old."

"But you aren't. I can tell, you aren't from this age."

Abigail, a venerable witch with silver hair cascading down her back like a shimmering waterfall, sat on the weathered oak chair, her eyes glowing with knowledge. I sat there, perched across from her, eager to have a conversation with her.

"You may be hundreds of years old, but you are new here. I know because I am a witch. My eyes see the truth behind things." She sat there for a few moments before a 'ding' rang through the kitchen. "Follow me, child."

The houses giant stone fireplace crackled with emerald and ruby flames, casting a soft, mystical glow throughout the dining room. Abeo pulled her chair back and helped her up before all of us moved into the kitchen. Abigail reached for a bundle of fragrant herbs, her wrinkled hands moving with practiced grace. She carefully added the herbs to the fire, releasing an enchanting aroma of pine and cinnamon into the air. I watched in fascination.

"It's almost Yule. My wife and I used to celebrate it together. We would make cider like this every year." I relaxed into the scent, letting the nostalgia help me relax.

"How do you celebrate it?"

The old woman smiled at me.

"Yule, my dear Elaine," Abigail began in a voice as soothing as a lullaby, "is a celebration as old as time itself. It marks the Winter Solstice, the longest night of the year when the world is wrapped in darkness."

My attention was fully captivated as I leaned forward, her dark brown hair cascading over my pale shoulders. I was curious to see how the holiday had changed over the years, or even better, if it had stayed the same.

"Why is Yule so special, Abigail? What does it mean to witches like you?"

Abigail's eyes sparkled with ancient wisdom. "Yule is a time of profound magic, my dear. It's a celebration of the rebirth of the sun, a promise of light returning to the world. The word 'Yule' itself means 'wheel,' symbolizing the eternal cycle of nature and the changing seasons."

I watched her movements carefully, remembering the few times Hayley and I had been fortunate enough to celebrate Yule together. We had both been practicing witches, so to know some traditions had never changed warmed my little dead heart.

She gestured to a nearby table adorned with Yule decorations. Pine boughs, mistletoe, and candles of varying colors adorned the table, their flames flickering with anticipation.

"You see, Elaine, these symbols hold great significance during Yule. The evergreen represents the enduring spirit of life even in the heart of winter. Mistletoe symbolizes love and protection, and candles, they represent the inner light we seek to nurture during this season of introspection."

My gaze drifted toward the flickering candles, my thoughts wandering into the depths of the holiday's symbolism.

"Do you still do feasts? I've heard stories of lavish Yule feasts."

Abigail chuckled warmly, her eyes filled with fond memories. "Indeed, Elaine. Yule feasts are a grand tradition. We gather with those we hold dear, indulging in hearty meals to warm our spirits and chase away the chill of winter. It's a time for merriment, laughter, and gratitude."

As Abigail continued to unveil the mysteries of their Yule celebration, I felt an odd sense of belonging that I had not felt for hundreds of years. The old witch's words resonated with me, connecting me to the timeless magic of nature and tradition. I was reminded that Yule was not just a holiday; it was a celebration of life's eternal cycles, a reminder of the enduring bonds that united them all.

Outside the house, the misty rain turned to a light snow that fell gently, covering the world in a serene white blanket. Inside, Abigail and Morgan shared stories, laughter, and the warmth of newfound knowledge. As we all came together in the decorated kitchen, Yule's enchantment enveloped us, weaving each of us into the tapestry of generations past and those yet to come.

I looked at decorations that Morgan took out of another box, smiling at the wooden log that had a middle section carved out.

"Let me guess, a Yule Log."

Morgan laughed happily as she took it from me.

"Yes, a Yule Log. It's when the little ones visit for the holidays. We fill it with candy and treats for them. They always run straight to it the moment their shoes are off."

"Children never change, no matter how many generations go bye." I said softly. She smiled at me, gently, then sighed. "Let's get you over to the shop so you can have breakfast. You must be starving."

"I am definitely starving," I laughed. I turned to Abigail and took a light bow. "Thank you for sharing your tradition with me, and the snack. Your hospitality will not be forgotten."

The old woman smiled and swatted at the air.

"Get out of here and go eat. The shop closes soon and you'll have it all to yourself."

"Fine fine, let's go Elaine. You too AB" Morgan said as she put her hands up. "Abeo, wanna drop us off?"

The night was cold, and a silvery moon hung low in the sky as it began its final descent to the horizon. I watched the sparse clouds drop a misty screen through the air as we got into the car. It wouldn't be long before the white snow was turned into a slushy mess. We drove nearly a half hour before we pulled into a parking garage. The cool air felt comfortable across my body, and I took a deep breath of it as I stepped out of Abeo's old car.

The garage was packed, and we ended up walking down flight after flight of musty stairs covered in graffiti, then out onto the street. There were two beautifully decorate shop windows, one a deli and the other an antique store. Annabella and I walked across to the antique store while Morgan and Abeo joined the already open deli. The atmosphere inside the old shop was warm, a stark contrast to the frosty world outside. Annabella stood in the door behind her, holding the keys.

"Stay here, I'm going to go get you dinner." She stopped, looking at me curiously. "Breakfast, and I will be right back." She quickly disappeared into the small deli.

I looked through the window and across the street as I took a deep breath. My breath left a cloud of condensation on the window. Running my fingers through it, I drew a circle, then a heart. A smile grew on my face, realizing I was all alone in a giant shop of trinkets. The air was dusty inside the antique store. My body floated through the aisles, my eyes taking in as much as I could. I had a bad habit in my past life of touching everything, so I made a conscious effort to not touch a thing, no matter how bad I wanted to.

I made it almost halfway when the door opened and closed again. Annabella walked over to me, half skipping as she moved. She carried in her hands a giant metal mug with a straw in it. My stomach turned over at the smell of it, and I tried to hold myself back from diving straight for her. She handed it to me, a coffee mug in her other hand.

"I know it isn't the high-class blood, but it's like, fast food, right?" Morgan said as she popped the lid from her coffee. A strong smell of caramel and hazelnut floated up from the cup and I breathed it in. That was a way better smell than blood.

"Terina! She yelled towards the back room. "Dinner will be over in a few!"

"What is this place? It doesn't feel like an antique store."

"Well, it is an antique store, but it's also a place where you can find anything you need for our craft."

"You mean witchcraft?" I asked curiously.

"We have done some horrible things. I'll admit it. But we try to do good where we can. No matter what, the world exists in balance, and we uphold that balance."

"What kind of horrible things could you have done? You all seem really nice to me."

Her eyes shifted to sadness for a moment, and she forced a smile.

"It's hard to talk about, you know? Even we have done things we regret. Gran made a mistake and now we have to work for that vampire bastard Halin, and our shops are in the territory of the dogs, so we have to pay them this stupid living tax or they'll wreck our place."

"What did Abigail do?"

"Show her."

A voice moved across the floor behind me. I turned, looking at someone I had never seen before. His voice was gentle, and he barely filled out the pants he wore.

"Terina, we can't just do that."

"If she wants to know how the church got them, she deserves that. She's going to have to fight them one day, so what does it matter?"

"What does what matter?"

"We made them." Annabella said.

"Made… what." I replied.

Annabella stepped up next to me and placed her hands against my temples. Her eyes closed, and she leaned forward, tapping her forehead against mine.

I found myself standing next to her, surrounded by almost twenty other women. They each bore a robe with a different symbol sewn into the edges. On a pedestal in the center were five silver blades.

"Elaine, watch... The catholic church had turned to us, befriended us, sworn to protect our kind from the monarchy of the night if we did them a favor.

Abigail's voice, soft but filled with solemn purpose, led the incantations as she held the hilt of the unformed sword. Her fingertips brushed the cold, raw metal, and she could feel the latent power within it, waiting to be unleashed.

Abigail stood in the center, hovering over the set of blades. The wrinkles on her face were gone, replaced by a youthfulness that commanded her peers. There were two lines of clergymen behind her, while a lone figure with vestments lined with bells stood in front of them.

"As you have requested, Father Gabriel" she spoke, bowing her head to him. His smile was savage, and I looked past them to a line of chained women, all still in the prime of their youth.

"By the moon's silver grace, by the stars' watchful gaze, we call upon the ancient forces, the primordial light, to infuse these blades with their radiance. Let it be a beacon in the darkness, a weapon of purification against the children of the night."

As the words left her lips, the witches began to chant in unison, their voices weaving a melody that resonated with the stars above. The atmosphere in the chapel shifted, and a faint, ethereal glow enveloped the room, casting dancing shadows upon the stone walls.

Abigail sliced her fingertip, dripping bright drops of blood on each blade.

"May the spirits of our ancestors guide our hands and grant us their wisdom. May their strength empower this blade, making it an instrument of divine retribution against the forces that threaten our world."

Several of the clergymen lined each of the women up in front of one of the blades, forcing their heads over it. I watched, horrified as they lifted knives from their robes.

"Gems of starlight, protect these souls as they give their lives to your cause. May their blood become your blood, and their souls empower you for all time.

The blades came smoothly across their necks, spilling their blood across the blades below them. The witches chanting became louder and louder, and each sword began to transform, their surface shimmering with a radiant luminescence. The light, pure and untainted, flowed through it, creating a crystalline blade that captured the essence of the sun itself.

Abigail weaved around the blades in careful steps that almost looked like a ritualistic dance. I was entranced by it.

"With this sacred light, we bind the sword, a vessel of the sun's brilliance. It shall dispel the darkness, revealing the hidden, the supernatural, and the cursed. This is our offering, our alliance with the Church to safeguard the innocent."

The chanting of the coven reached a crescendo, and as the final verses echoed through the chamber, Abigail's hand quivered as she lifted one of the newly created blades. It was unlike any weapon she had ever crafted, its brilliance almost blinding, and its energy hummed with a celestial resonance. A man stepped out of the shadows behind her, his long white robes unable to hide the destructive tendencies hidden in his eyes.

Abigail turned to face him.

"This is our gift to the Church, the embodiment of our shared purpose—to protect the world from the shadows that lurk in the night. Let this blade pierce the hearts of the creatures of darkness, for in its radiance, they shall find their reckoning."

Annabella moved her hands away, and I found myself standing in front of her again.

"Your grandmother helped make the weapons that hunt us." I was angry at the revelation. Angry that someone with such kindness on the surface had created weapons that were designed to kill me. Designed to erase my existence.

"You don't understand." She said, looking to the side. "They killed us too. We gave them a weapon to kill the unholy, but to them, we are the unholy."

"So, you have things here that can do that kind of magic?"

"Not anymore. We used to trade with other covens through this shop, but most of them have left, gone west and into the mountains again."

"It's hard not to be upset about this. I heard Hayley fought against one of those bishops that have your weapon."

"We heard, and she killed him with it. The church killed four of our elders that season because of it. We were easy pickings."

"Maybe that was your universal balance."

An awkward silence held over the shop. I looked at a clock on the wall, the long hand hitting the top of the hour. 7pm.

"I'm sorry. It's a lot to take in and that was rude of me."

Terina shook his head and disappeared into the back of the shop. I looked around the shop once again, taking interest in a few of the little old lanterns, and a rusty old saber.

"Breakfast?" she asked while redirecting the conversation. I watched her lift up her coffee cup with a forced smile. I could tell she felt bad about the entire thing, and it made me wonder if she would have stopped it had she been given the chance. We would never know.

"Breakfast." I replied.

As we raised our glasses to toast to one more day alive, a bone-chilling howl pierced the air. It was a sound unmistakable to all magical creatures—a signal from the Whitefangs, a notorious were-wolf pack known for their territorial nature and fierce protectiveness. I had been warned before that the witches' businesses were not entirely in Halin's territory, and that although they lived there, the work they did was in something else's. I ran to the door, only for Annabella to slam it the moment I tried to open it. Her hand locked the deadbolt, and she pulled me to the ground next to her.

"*sshhhhh.*" She whispered to me as we sat there, silent and unmoving. I could hear the sharp sound of glass breaking across the street. The moment my lips opened, she covered my mouth with her free hand and shook her head.

"Do. Not. Speak." She said again sternly. "Your kind are illegal here."

My eyes widened in disbelief. That would have been something great to know before we came here. I would have much rather had them deliver me a drink than put them at risk. Her voice was as low as she could get it.

"They will *kill* all of us. We have to get you out of here."

I could hear yelling from across the street. I wanted to jump over there, but every time I tried to move Annabella pulled me back down. She pointed to the back of the shop where there was a blue and silver curtain covering a hallway.

"Out the back," she whispered.

Terina, the younger member of the coven pulled up the bottom of the curtain, his body lying on the floor. He looked across at us as we crawled, his eyes filled with alarm. His hands moved frantically as he motioned for me to get back there with him.

"The Whitefangs are nearby. Something's wrong."

Before we could make it through the curtain any further, the front door of the shop burst open, shattering the silent tranquility of the antique store. Splinters of wood slid across the floor, and I ducked to the side, diving behind the long oak counters where the register sat.

Two imposing werewolves, their fur as white as the snow, loomed in the doorway. Thick fur was matted down from the rain, bringing with them the stench of a wet dog. Their eyes blazed with a fierce, predatory intensity. One of them, a towering figure with scars marring his muzzle, spoke in a guttural growl.

"We can smell blood here. Where are you."

Annabella leapt up, her face pale but resolute, and stood her ground.

"What is the meaning of this, Whitefangs? We have done nothing to warrant this intrusion."

I slid myself further under the register cabinet, attempting to make myself as small as possible.

The other werewolf, a lithe female with eyes like burning amber, stepped forward menacingly.

"The Alpha has decreed it. We knew one of them came to your home, and trespassed in our territory, and you must answer for it before the pack."

She stepped in front of the larger male, her eyes moving across the shop.

"We are taking Morgan to answer for your slight against us."

Terina and I exchanged worried glances. They knew that being caught working with the members of the night inside the Whitefangs' territory was a grave offense, but they were not there to provoke conflict. I stayed quiet, slowly taking a sip from the metal cup. They could smell the blood, even from there.

I pressed my eyes shut, focusing on drinking as fast as I could. The irony flavor hit my tongue and instead of disgust I could feel my hunger slowly begin to drift away. Drinking as fast as possible while trying to stay quiet was a challenge, but I did it. Almost all of the blood was consumed, and I sat the glass down as gently as I could to stay silent.

Terina stepped forward, his voice calm but authoritative.

"We apologize if that guest has unknowingly trespassed. We meant no harm. We are willing to discuss this matter peacefully."

The male Whitefang snarled, his patience running thin.

"There's no room for negotiation. Morgan comes with us, now. Where is she?"

We all knew that Morgan was across the street, not here. As the male werewolf lunged forward, Annabella lifted her arms and rapidly cast a protective spell, surrounding herself with a shimmering barrier.

"Wards of old, now heed my plea,

shield me now, as I will it to be," she cried out, the sphere of light covering several feet around the three of us.

It almost looked like the air shimmered in a beautiful array of colors that protected her from their strikes.

The female werewolf howled in frustration, and together they tried to break through the magical shield. I had never seen such beautiful light before and was completely caught off guard by it. The strength of witches reached far into the mystical, something I never thought possible. My body wanted to move but I couldn't, the fear of knowing I may make things worse overtaking me.

Terina joined in with Annabella, combining their magical powers to create a dazzling burst of light that momentarily blinded the werewolves.

"By the elements and powers that be,
This shield is bound, eternally,
No harm shall pass, no ill shall touch,
This shield of mine, I claim as such."

The two wolves battered down on the glowing sphere of light as it expanded to cover the entire back half of the antique store. I closed my eyes, my ears picking up on the screech of their jagged claws across the magical barrier. I dug my fingers into my legs, trying to stay as calm as possible through the fighting that was going on around me. I looked up at Terina who glanced at me for a moment before focusing on the light in front of them. The entire shop was bathed in flashes of blue and white sparkling energy every time they struck.

I watched Terina, his body straining to keep their protections up. Sweat was starting to form across his body, and I wanted nothing more than to dive out and do something. Anything.

Without warning the two turned and stopped attacking. Their bodies shifted down into a smaller, more human form.

"Looks like we don't need any of you after all." He said with a scowl, the pair heading for the door. He kicked the umbrella stand next to the door on his way out, sending the copper tube banging through the side of the shop.

Several cars outside turned on, their high beams casting a blinding white light through the windows of the store. Horns blared from the traffic that they had stopped, only for them to react in kind and drive off. I pulled myself up to the counter, wiping the faint drops of blood off of my lips. Terina looked through the open door at the damage across the street. The light that they had formed together was absolutely beautiful. I never knew real magic existed.

"Oh no."

Annabella screeched as the shield of light dropped. She ran for the door, Terina and I quickly following behind. The frame of it had been smashed to splinters and pieces of broken glass were scattered across the old wood planks that made up the floor. I could see Abeo through the hazy mist, and he looked rough.

Annabella made it across first as she frantically ran past the trio. "MORGAN!?!!" she screamed from inside the deli. Her voice echoed through the street as I reached Abeo. He had a set of cuts across his face, blood dripping from his left eye.

"Abeo..." I said softly while keeping my distance. The blood coming out of his face was a fresh, bright red and with each pump of it, it became the only thing I could think of. My fingers dug into my palms, and I hoped the pain of it would distract me from him. I couldn't hear Annabella inside, or what Abeo was saying for that matter.

The sound of his heartbeat grew louder and louder until I felt the familiar pain in my mouth of the fangs coming out again. My hands covered my mouth and I backed away from him as Annabella ran out of the deli, the wet tears rolling down her face disappearing as the mist shifted into a light drizzle.

Annabella looked at Abeo and ran by him into the middle of the street.

"MORGAN!!" she screamed at the top of her lungs before running over to Abeo.

"ABE. WHERE IS SHE?!?" Morgan screamed again, tears covering her face.

Abeo looked at the ground and shook his head.

"They got her. The Whitefangs wrecked our shop and got her."

"Where are they taking her Abe." I kept my voice as calm as I possibly could. This was a disaster.

"Absolutely not. No way."

"ABE." I accidentally raised my voice.

"Are you suicidal? Get it together girl, it's suicide. Abigail will skin us both."

He stepped away from her and into the street, looking at me. I kept my eyes closed while I focused on my breath, finally getting that bloodlust under control. I could hear both of their heartbeats. Abe's was slowing down, but hers was the fastest I had ever heard before. Annabella fell to her knees in the street, the dim light from inside the deli spilling out and illuminating the witch.

"Elaine… help me." She cried.

"Please… please save her."

I looked down at her, the tears thickening as she cried. She looked up, her eyes almost bloodshot from the stress. Pain was flowing out of her, and I could feel every piece of it.

"Help me save her. I'll do anything."

I put my hand on her shoulder and stepped past her.

"Of course."

"Abeo," I said. A deep breath moving through my lips. "I need a lift."

The star

REFLECTIONS

"My journal, a confessional of blood-stained pages, bears witness to the relentless pursuit of a divine calling. God has chosen me as his sword, and I shall smite the darkness in His name."
Father Gabriel's Personal Journal, 1587

CHAPTER 8

$\mathcal{A}$beo lifted Annabella up, and we took off towards the parking garage. I found myself leaping up several stairs at a time, cutting down the time it took me to get to the car. Unfortunately, I still had to wait on the others to arrive. It took seconds for them to catch up and the three of us to get into the car.

"How far from their shop are we?" I asked as he backed the car up.

"Shop? They don't have any shops. They make their money off of all of us. He replied, wiping some more of the blood out of his eye. I followed his hands, the blood disappearing across the side of his pants leg furthest from me.

I looked in the backseat at Annabella, her arms wrapped around her legs while she cried. I knew her pain all too well and didn't want anyone to ever experience what I went through.

"Whitefangs charge rent for all of the shops in a twelve-block radius by the national reserve. They have a historic house in there that used to be a museum." Abeo said, slamming on the gas.

"They moved in about thirty years ago, and their former pack leader made a deal with Abigail. We give them a certain amount of our profits, and they, well, keep us safe."

"Keep you safe," I chucked. "That sounds like extortion to me. They're just fluffy gangsters, that's all."

He looked over at me, turning onto a large, two-lane avenue that had more traffic. I could see the trees down along the side of the street where the town ended, and the national reserve began.

"You aren't really going in there, right? Like. That's suicidal."

"I can't let her be taken like that," I said softly. I felt horrible about the entire thing.

"It's my fault, and I have to fix it. I'd do the same for you."

"How much time do I have to be out here?" I looked out the window. There was an icy mix coming down that gradually turned to a light sheet of snow. It was beautiful to look at.

"Almost ten hours, so you are good on that front. Do you even have a plan?"

I laughed under my breath. I didn't have time to be meticulous and calculate every option ahead of me.

"Plan? I'm going to walk in the front door and negotiate. Sounds good, right?

"You really are crazy, you know that?" he replied sarcastically. "Make sure you come back in one piece, alright?"

"Of course! I'm not missing out on whatever Abigail is cooking up, it smells delicious." I joked, trying to lighten to situation.

"Even if, you know, I can't actually eat it."

"You got no idea; the house always smells great this time of year" Abeo laughed.

He was finally relaxing a bit, but I could tell he was still in pain and on edge. His shirt was stained with dried blood and flakes of it would fall off when he turned the wheel.

We drove alongside the last set of parks before Abeo pulled the car off to the side. A few yards in front of us was a gigantic iron structure with a wolf's head towering over both sides. The wall of twisted iron looked like an ornate garden, dotted with crystals of various colors that would sparkle in the sunlight. I looked across at Abeo, then turned to look at Annabella.

"Hey, take a breath. I got this. Really." I tried to console her. I wasn't quite sure if I actually had this, or if I was walking into the literal wolf's den.

I choked down any panic that tried to climb its way out with a large gulp. The night air was getting cooler by the minute, but the clouds looked to be moving through and I could finally see the moonlight shining through.

"I'll be back soon, alright? Don't leave me here."

The door pressed open, and I stepped out onto the slush filled street. Even with these shoes, I could feel the dirty water seep into the sides of them. I was never a fan of squishy, wet footwear but at least I wasn't wearing my Birks.

"Wait… take this." Abeo said, reaching into the center console. He pulled out a long, slender knife from its depths.

"It's not much, but it's well balanced and great at carving up deer."

"Thank you, Abeo. I'll see you both soon."

I slammed the door shut and walked towards the gate. Every few feet I would hop up and down and get my breath going, trying to hype myself up. There was no way Hayley would agree with what I was doing right now, and between the two of us I always had more self-preservation.

I stood at the edge of the dense, moonlit forest, my heart pounding in my chest as I surveyed the imposing gates of the Whitefangs' stronghold. The night was shrouded in an eerie silence, broken only by the occasional rustle of leaves in the wind or a random car passing by.

Did I know the risks? Yes, and they included certain death, but Morgan was imprisoned within those walls and there was no way I would walk away without her. I leaned my head back, pulling my hair up into a messy bun as I looked at the sliver of moonlight that crept through the wispy clouds. Even through the gate I could still see the lights from a large ornate house in the distance. I'd like to think it was only a few hundred feet, but that was probably way off. Happy thoughts, though, right? I thought to myself.

With a deep, steadying breath, I drew the long, silver blade, its sharp edge glinting ominously in the moonlight. The massive gates creaked open slowly, revealing the curved cobblestone path that led to a dimly lit courtyard beyond. In the center was a marvel of artistry, a marble fountain that stood as a centerpiece of the courtyard.

The fountain's basin was a near perfect circle, carved from the finest white marble, and adorned with intricate bas-reliefs of mythological figures and aquatic scenes. Gargoyles, their expressions frozen in a perpetual state of stoic vigilance, serve as the foundation for the grand structure, spouting crystal-clear water from their mouths into the fountain's basin below.

At the heart of the fountain, an imposing statue of a classical deity stood towering above the rest. Their form was chiseled with exquisite detail, their robes flowing with a lifelike grace. They were accompanied by cherubic attendants and symbolic motifs that reflected a carefully carved beauty. I could tell from here that the water was dirty, unchanged as the seasons shifted. Every stone in the driveway was worn smooth, and although it was once an elegant pathway that someone could enjoy, now it was a forgotten piece of art like the rest.

Twelve pairs of glowing eyes fixed on me, and a low, menacing growl rumbled through the night. I had just got here, and already was in trouble. I knew from watching various movies that we didn't get along well with werewolves. It was almost a primal hatred between the two and I lacked both understanding and experience on it. I gripped the knife in my hand, sliding my left foot back as I launched myself forward towards them. The knife came up, perfectly horizontal by my side. It felt familiar, almost natural. I found comfort in the weight of the blade in my hand.

The werewolves wasted no time. With a collective snarl, they lunged at full speed across the courtyard straight at me, teeth bared, and claws extended. I felt the lightness under my body as I moved like a phantom, my slender, sweater covered form a blur of inky darkness and otherworldly grace. Every drink of blood had unlocked a little more of my bloodline, and the new supernatural speed allowed me to dodge and parry their attacks almost effortlessly, my blade striking with deadly precision.

It felt normal to move, my muscles twisting and pulling at the right time to dodge, parry, and strike. I could see it in front of me, remembering some fraction of a memory that wasn't mine. My eyes narrowed, and I met my first enemy head on.

The first werewolf closed in, jaws snapping, but I shifted while sidestepping with a graceful spin and drove the blade into its side. It howled in pain, blood spilling onto the rain-soaked ground. I stopped thinking, letting my mind and thoughts fade out while instinct took over. I was a whirlwind of death, my every movement a lethal dance that carved its way through him.

As the fight continued, a fire burned within me, a power that pulsed through my veins like molten lava. There was strength there that I had never known, and every time I pushed towards my limits, a little more of that strength crept out. It was more of my bloodline strength, a reservoir of ancient power passed down through generations of vampires. With a primal roar, I screamed as more of it broke free. I licked the blood from the side of the knife, mentally thanking Abeo for the long carving knife. The wolfen blood tasted far different from a human but was delightful in its own way. There was a thickness to it that was different from humans.

My movements became a blur of motion, each strike landing with bone-shattering force. Their bodies were tough, their limbs thick and covered in fur that helped dampen my strikes. The air crackled around me as I felt my body moving faster and striking harder, the brown in my eyes disappearing as a bright crimson overtook them. The fire across my entire being left my muscles blazing with raw power. This was the strongest I had ever felt. I was a force of nature, surpassing even the mightiest of werewolves out here.

This bloodline strength was like a tempest of fury. I spun and slashed, my blade cutting through fur and flesh like a hot knife through butter. The courtyard was a symphony of growls and yelps as the werewolves struggled to keep up with the unleashed might. I was a wind that moved around the lesser of them, and every few steps meant the death of another one of their kind, the losses something that would take years to recover from. One by one, they fell before me, their howls of pain and defeat echoing through the night. Their fur matted with blood, their strength waning, the Whitefangs outer guard were no match for my unleashed rage.

Finally, only one werewolf remained standing, a massive brute with eyes filled with defiance. It lunged, a final desperate attack. Instead of retreating, I shot forward at full speed to meet it head-on. The collision shook the ground, a thunderous clash as he caught my blade. I was instantly covered in shock, twisting around as I dug my claws into the side of his ribs.

Grabbing and scratching at him, I could feel his arms wrap around my body before I felt the ground leave me. My body soared through the air as I hit the statue on the fountain. The stone arm on it shattered, falling into the water beside me. I crawled up and out of the cold wet fountain, only to see a mud-covered boot smash into the side of my head. The man had shifted out of his werewolf form and with that kick, a sharp pain went down the side of my face. My head shook as I hit the water again. His thick, broad fingers wrapped around the back of my neck as I flailed around in the water. There was nothing for me to wrap my hands around to help pull myself out.

I could feel my chest getting hotter as a tightness grew inside it. I was running out of air and started panicking. The water was dirty with leaves and debris from the fall. I ran my hands around the bottom of it, trying to find something to hold onto or push off, but the slick floor came up short. I could feel the air getting thinner with every second. I needed something, anything to turn this around. The burning grew as I choked out a few bubbles, my left hand sliding over a familiar object. I knew that handle, and quickly wrapped my cold fingers around it before slamming it around the side of my neck. The blade cut through the side of my neck, leaving a thin, deep slice before it cut up and through two of his fingers.

His hand jerked from my neck as he moved backwards and I pulled my head above the water, gasping for air. The cold evening wind felt amazing across my body as I lurched over the edge of the fountain and onto the ground.

I held the knife in my left hand as I looked at him again. He stood there, yards away from me holding his hand. There were two fingers missing, blood trickling down to the cobblestone below him. His face contorted, his jaw extending into a long black snout. I wasn't sure he could get any bigger until he stood there glaring back at me.

"Roll over?" I asked, lifting my hand, and giving him a pale, white middle finger.

He charged at me, almost immediately hitting full speed. There already wasn't a lot of space between us and he covered it in less than a breath. I turned, taking a step up onto the edge of the fountain before leaping up, drawing the knife overhead as I brought it down towards him. He raised his left arm to block it, but I twisted it around his elbow and hit the ground, preparing to drive my body up into his.

I had done this before. I knew this strike. I launched myself up under his arm, drawing the blade across his thigh, stomach and into his side. I ripped it out, and with a final, resounding strike, I drove the silver blade deep into the werewolf's chest and through his heart. It let out a mournful how as he dropped to his knees.

"You aren't a low blood..." he said, his final breaths taken in shock.

I looked straight into his eyes and whispered honestly.

"No."

His body fell to the side, and I was able to see the damage that had been left in our wake. There were human-esque bodies sprawled across the blood-stained cobblestone. Two of the six were women, their death a complete waste.

The courtyard fell silent, the echoes of battle fading into the night. I tried to reign in my breath, my chest rising and falling heavily. The moon bathed the road in starlight, and I looked around again at the fallen foes, my body still thrumming with the remnants of my blood-line's power. My body felt stiffens that reminded me of the day after a difficult workout. I brought the knife up to my face before I took another lick of the smooth red liquid from its surface. The brown color quickly returned to my eyes as I leaned over next to the fallen wolf and wiped the blade clean.

"Rest well, nameless dog."

I turned toward the looming entrance to the stronghold, determined to rescue Morgan. Inside, a new set of challenges awaited me, but I was undeterred. With unwavering resolve, I pushed forward, ready to confront whatever horrors the Whitefangs had in store. Morgan's life depended on me, and I would stop at nothing to save her from the clutches of the werewolf pack.

The crudely decorated manor was far larger than it looked from the outside. It lacked any modicum of décor and I felt it to be a complete waste that it was in their hands. The dark, forest green wall paint with golden accents had a lot of potential, and it probably wouldn't take much to turn this place into an actual home. Might take a bit to get rid of the wet dog smell, but that would happen in time. I walked through the halls, stopping as soon as I felt her. It was hard to describe that feeling, but I trusted my instincts.

Moving through the large pair of oak doors, I stood there in the near darkness, my eyes quickly adjusting to the pale dim light. There were at least eight of them in the library, the smell of their wet fur filling the space. My eyes softly closed as I tried to sift through the various scents in the room. It took an extra moment of silence as I held my breath before I opened them again. I stared across the large room at a part of the bookcase that didn't look like the others. Somewhere beyond that, I could smell Morgan.

"I know you're here, and I know you have her. Hand her over, and I will be on my way."

Raspy laughs filled the space, the lights in the room slowly turning on. The giant chandelier hummed, staying as dim as possible but still illuminating the space. A giant of a man, chiseled and covered in thick, black hair, threw a long leather jacket over a large oak desk that was covered in papers. He stared down at me from a second story balcony before he leapt over the railing and landed next to the desk. He looked me over while walking into the center of the room.

"You must be new here." He snarled. "If you think one of your kind can walk in here and make demands, you must be courting your eternal death."

I watched his hands as they slowly turned into long, jagged claws.

His messy black hair laid down across his shoulders. My heartbeat was racing and the only thing that I knew I had to do was get her out of here. I would always repay kindness that was shown towards me and leaving her here was never an option.

"I'm sorry, Hayley." I thought to myself as I took a step towards the man. He smiled, a wide grin forming as he showed his teeth.

"Are you Kellan?" I asked, buying time while I thought of a game plan. I looked him top to bottom, trying to find anything that might give me a leg up in this interaction. There was nothing there to observe. Every movement was intentional, every muscle in top shape. Nothing seemed out of place, no previous injuries seen. Any peaceful option was already out the window when I left members of his pack dead out front.

"You walked in here knowing that, and still decided that was your best course of action? Your maker should be disappointed in you." He replied as he stepped forward again. "I'll save a finger for when they come to claim you."

The vast library within the Whitefangs' stronghold was a sanctuary of ancient knowledge and forbidden lore, with towering bookshelves that seemed to go forever. The scent of old books filled the air, but it was now tainted by the metallic tang of vampire and the earthy musk of werewolf as Kellan, and I finally clashed within its hallowed halls.

I held my breath for a moment, forcing myself to pull everything I had into this fight. My eyes shifted back to crimson as they locked onto Kellan, the silver blade gleaming ominously in the now well-lit library.

Kellen's muscles began to ripple beneath his skin, a subtle tension building across every part of his body. The change was interesting to watch, and I was unable to take my eyes off of him.

This is what a prime looks like...

His body contorted with an otherworldly grace, bones shifting and elongating as fur sprouted from every inch of his skin. I couldn't take my eyes off of him, and I was entranced as he performed a volatile dance between human and beast.

His hands transformed into powerful claws, each digit elongating into a lethal weapon. Kellen's spine arched as he felt the restructuring of his skeletal frame, a symphony of snapping and popping sounds accompanying the metamorphosis. The pain had to be intense, but it was a pain he had come to embrace, a herald of the unleashed power within. My eyes narrowed in concern, an instinctual warning going off through my body.

As the transformation reached its peak, Kellen's face morphed into that of a fearsome wolf. His jaw elongated, sharp teeth pushing through the gums, forming a predatory snout. His eyes, now vibrant amber, glowed with an intensity that mirrored the wild spirit within him. Tufts of fur framed his face, completing the metamorphosis into the majestic creature he was destined to become.

The fur that covered Kellen's body was a mixture of grays and blacks, blending seamlessly with the shadows that enveloped him. His limbs, now far more powerful, carried the strength of a creature born of the moon's magic. He stood on all fours, the transformation complete, a werewolf prime ready fight against me. I watched as he stood up on his hind legs, towering a full two feet over me.

"Can't say I'm *not* impressed."

Kellan's bones cracked, and he snarled, his yellow eyes filled with primal fury. We circled each other, the tension in the room palpable as the others watched on from the second story without interfering.

With a sudden burst of speed, Kellan lunged at me, his claws extended like deadly talons. His speed in this closed off space would be a major challenge, so I focused on minimalizing my movements as much as possible. My back twisted; my weight shifting as I side-stepped a slash from him with grace. I had observed this half step movement somewhere, a single slide and weight shift that would maximize my agility and give me opportunities to strike.

The movements were a testament to the supernatural agility my bloodline had given me, and I would make full use of it. I sent the blade up in a diagonal slash where it met his claws with a resounding clash, sending sparks flying. A flash of concern went through my mind as he stopped the blade with just his claws.

"That *all* you got little girl?" he growled through his snout, spitting dirty saliva all over me.

I pressed into the knife and dropped my arm to the side while trying to move past him. He pressed on and swung in a full circle, catching me mid turn. His giant fist swung into my forearm like a massive club, sending me skidding across the hardwood floor towards the fireplace. I could feel the heat coming off the charcoal cinders behind me, the pops of burning cinders filling the space.

That had been too close, and I was barely able to get my arm up to block that in the first place. As soon as he moved towards me, I did the same.

I feinted to the left, then spun to the right while changing hands with the blade and throwing it forward into him. I made contact, landing a deep gash across Kellan's side. He howled in pain, but it only seemed to fuel his rage. With a growl, he lunged again, this time with a powerful swipe of his massive paw.

It caught the side of my leg, sending claw marks down my calf and splattering blood across the floor. I winced at the pain of his strike, pain moving through my leg.

Kellan took another dive forward, attempting to bury his massive shoulder into my stomach. I leaped backward, narrowly avoiding the deadly strike. My body landed on the desk, my weight moving to the side and darting to the left of him. I was almost as fast as the Prime; and both of our movements would look like a blur to a human. He was far too large for me to fully maneuver around, and his random strikes towards me were landing more and more frequently. Every strike that landed felt like a sledgehammer.

"I can smell you, little girl. Even if you are faster than me, your blood is fresh. I'll never lose it."

He laughed as he threw his fist forward. His words were correct and that moment where I lost focus left me with a strike straight to my shoulder blade. The pain that went through it made my arm go limp as my body bounced across the floor. I rolled up to my knees, my back landing squarely into one of the bookcases.

Fuck. Don't be broken.

A sharp twitch of pain crossed my fingertips, my right hand struggling to hold the blade. I had a feeling my shoulder blade was most likely broken from the way it hurt to hold my arm up.

Definitely Broken.

I gritted my teeth, pushing the pain down deep. I had to focus; my life depended on it. My body rose to a standing position, eyes meeting his as he thrusted his arm forward again. This time he was ready, and I knew I would need to take all of my strength and speed in order to dodge the incoming attack. His fist collided with the wall behind me as I dove to the side, narrowly dodging his swing. I twisted, turning to keep my body facing his. He roared with anger and pounded his chest once more, sending his left leg into my mid-section.

The power in his kick reverberated through my body, my feet lifting off the ground from the impact. I twisted, my arm covering my stomach as the force of it sent me through the rolling ladder that ran the length of the library.

"One solid strike and your frail vampire bones break! They really don't make your kind like they used to!" he shouted across the library at me. He beat on his chest, lifting an arm up to the ceiling where a golden chandelier sparkled with light from above. It was as if he were a conductor bathed in a spotlight under all of the howling werewolves above us.

"See, my brothers! The night does not belong to them anymore!" He threw his arms out to the side, turning a full circle.

I closed my eyes and slowed my breathing, trying to pull every bit of power out of myself. My jaw clenched and I swallowed down the bile that had formed in my throat, trying to figure out a way out of this where I didn't lose my head. Each of his strikes was far more damaging than I had originally thought. I could hear them laughing from above me. If this had been a group fight, I wouldn't have survived. Unlike outside, these truly were the elites of his pack.

My body pushed itself up as I tried to tap into it again. The amount of focus it took to maintain that power right now was staggering, and the moment I took my mind off it I ran the risk of dropping it altogether. I kicked my shoes off, preferring the natural feel of the ground underneath me. The pain in my shoulder blade slowly turned to numbness and I felt it crack itself back in.

I could regenerate.

It was slow, but it was there. Every muscle across my body tightened and the bloodline strength surged within me, my eyes returning in a crimson flash once again. With newfound speed and strength, I leapt from the table and retaliated with a flurry of strikes that left Kellan reeling. I was going to push forward at full speed until I went straight threw him.

None of them were, however, deep enough to actually do any damage to the hulking wolf. I ran across the couches, leaving footprints on the velvet cushions. I even ran across the shelves of the bookcase when I needed too. Hayley would have killed me for the blasphemy I was doing to this sacred space.

Books flew off the shelves as we continued the high-speed clash, our battle tearing through the library like a storm. Ancient tomes and scrolls were scattered, forgotten lore reduced to shreds in the wake of our fierce struggle. Every slice I managed to land on his body came with me taking an equally damaging strike from his razer sharp claws.

Members of the Whitefangs watched on from the second story of the library while others came together outside the large patio door. Kellan managed to land another glancing blow on my shoulder that he continued to target, the force of it sending me sprawling across a wooden table. Splintered wood and parchment erupted around my body as I crashed completely through the tabletop and into the furniture behind it.

But I didn't stay down for long.

With a less than graceful roll, I regained my footing and launched myself straight at Kellan, the blade arcing through the air like a deadly comet. Kellan brought both claws straight down, aiming for both sides of my head. I bit my tongue and pressed forward, using a quick burst of speed to get inside of his massive arms. The blade had finally found its mark, slicing across Kellan's chest. He roared in agony, staggered backward, and crashed into a bookshelf.

Shelves toppled like dominoes, burying the giant werewolf

beneath a cascade of the heavy books. For a moment, there was silence, broken only by the settling of dust and the labored breathing of the wounded animal. Gasps and murmurs filled the air from the onlookers around us.

I knew better than to assume victory too soon. I cautiously approached the fallen shelves, my blade at the ready. As I reached the wreckage, a massive hand burst forth, grasping for my ankle.

Kellan wasn't finished yet.

He managed to nearly grab onto it, leaving more scratch marks across the bottom of my leg. My blood sprayed across the floor, and I threw both legs backwards, driving the blade straight down and through his forearm. It dug itself into the wooden floor below. I twisted it, hearing his painful howl as I held him there in the floor.

With a swift, precise strike, I severed Kellan's outstretched arm, and he howled in pain once more. Weakened and defeated, he lay amid the ruins of the library, his once-powerful form now broken and battered. I watched as the arm on the ground slowly broke back down into its human form. He was buried there, barely breathing. I took a moment to catch my breath, my crimson eyes filled with determination to see this through to the end. This battle may have been won, but my mission was far from over. With a final glance at the fallen werewolf, I stepped over to him knowing that there was only one way to make it through this alive.

I kicked books off his body and looked down at the man. Without the thick mat of fur on him, the dozens of cuts were easy to point out. I could barely hold onto the knife in my hand through the pain moving across my body, so I pointed it straight down at him.

"Tell your pack to hand her over, and I will spare you."

"You know nothing…" he said quietly, blood coming from the corner of his lips. "I have fallen, their allegiance is no longer with me…"

I pulled the blade up and took a knee, bringing myself down on top of him. Blood dripped down around my leg as I slammed my knee down into his stomach. The silver blade moved over to his neck.

"If you have no use to me, then there's no reason t-"

"STOP."

A woman's voice cut through the air from the second story.

"Please. Please stop."

We both looked up at her, the slender woman leaping from the second story and down onto the messy library floor. I looked around at all of the wreckage, we had nearly destroyed this place.

"Take that human witch and go," she said, lifting an arm across her chest while lowering to a knee in the middle of the hall.

Her body was covered in a grey sweater dress with black leggings and thigh high leather rainboots. Her voice wavered as she continued.

"Show mercy to my husband."

I was in shock, my eyes widening as I looked at her auburn hair, then down at him. He had moved his eyes over to her, and a gentle smile was now there. I wanted to do it so badly. One inch deeper. . . This man was a liability, and there was no reason for me not to pull it and end this. I stared at him for a moment before I let out a sigh.

Before I knew it my body had moved on its own. I staggered over to her, holding the knife in my hand.

"Cedar and lilac." I said as I stood there in front of her. She raised her head, the hair parting enough for me to see a pair of beautiful green eyes underneath.

"Yes, it's his favorite." She replied quietly. I knew the entire room would be able to hear us, regardless of how quiet we were. Her tone was soft, and I tried to remember the fact that she could also transform.

"I know that feeling. To want to wear something that makes your partner smile. I did that for my wife, every day."

She slowly stood up, coming face to face with me. I was covered in new bruises; my sweater was torn in several places, and there was warm blood still coming down my shoulder. I let out long exhale, forcefully slowing down my heartrate as best I could. Two thin streams of blood began to bead their way down my cheeks as I looked at her.

"Then you know the pain of watching the one you love to suffer. Please, spare my husband." She looked up at the second floor.

"Aeron, bring her the witch. The rest of you, stand down and get to cleaning. Our house will not exist in such chaos."

Her eyes floated across them, then down to me. I stood there, not moving as she moved forward and extended her hand towards mine. I looked at it, feeling some form of mutual love for a partner there. Without thinking, I took her hand. She wrapped her fingers around mine, her nails driving their way into my skin as she pulled me against her body.

"I watched you lick that blade outside. You can't hold onto that form for long, which means you haven't fully awakened yet. My husband foolishly thought you were some little piece of blood drinking garbage he could step on."

My body stiffened as she whispered in my ear. I tried to pull away but was unable to move from her grasp... Her arm wrapped around me, pulling me tightly against her. There wasn't much strength left in me. Even if I wanted to run, she had me.

"A wolf's bite is fatal to your kind; did you know that? I don't know what lineage you come from, but even one of your originals wouldn't recklessly dare to step into our lair. One day, we will feast on you, the same way you feast on humans."

My eyes widened as I felt her breath on my neck. She ran her tongue up the side of my neck, sending shivers straight down my spine. I felt her move up, nibbling on the bottom of my ear. Her left hand planted itself on the middle of my still broken shoulder, pressing into it. I wanted to screech in pain but couldn't make a sound.

"Delectable. I bet you would taste exquisite. You spared my husband. I will spare your life. Unlike your kind, we keep our word."

This woman had managed to turn the entire situation around in her favor and wipe the slate clean. If I had killed her husband, I probably would have died alongside him. She was crafty, sinfully crafty.

I stood there with her arms around me in silence for several breaths. When she pulled back, she placed her hands on my shoulders and pulled my hair back behind my ears. Her smile was deadly, and I could see how she became the wife of their alpha.

"There you go, good enough to walk back to whatever crypt you crawled out of."

A door swung open behind me, and two men walked through it, one of them carrying Morgan with her arms and feet bound. She had what appeared to be a dirty scarf wrapped around her mouth and tied behind her head. Their boots left thick, muddy footprints on the wooden floor as they dropped her down onto the large sofa.

"Take her and leave this place before we change our mind. I never want to see you, or your kind again. Next time, I'll deal with you myself." She said as she stepped over to Morgan.

I watched her remove the bindings on her and walk away. Her eyes met mine one final time before she moved to her husband's side. I ran over to Morgan, putting my hands on her face.

"Can you move?" I asked while trying to keep her eyes focused on just me. She was panicking still, and I was worried that she might be in shock. The adrenaline was starting to wear off and the pain across both of my legs and back were getting steadily unbearable.

She shook her head up and down, and I grabbed her hand, pulling her towards the door. The moment we hit the hall I could hear argumentative yelling come from the library. I wasn't about to stay and find out what they were debating. Their internal politics was not my problem, and I was going to do everything I could to get us out of here.

We ran together, our hands never breaking. It took less than a minute to hit the front doors and spill out onto the cobblestone driveway. A light mist of rain slowly covered our bodies, sticking what was left of my clothes to my skin. I pulled her down the long driveway towards the main gate as fast as I was able.

The moment we crossed the gate a pair of bright lights lit up from down the street. We could both hear the engine roar on, the car moving at full speed straight towards us. It slid to a stop, the back door opening and Annabella motioning for us to get in. The door slammed shut behind me, and before I could even get situated Abeo floored it. My head slammed into the window, and I coughed up bits of blood. I looked at my hand, laughing at myself for what had transpired.

I walked into a werewolf's pack, taken on their pack leader, and made it out with Morgan. And I was still alive. I could barely believe it. Sleep would have overcome me had I not looked out the windows of the car. The light drizzle was clearing out and I could see specks of light along the river when the tree line broke. The specks turned into glowing balls of light that fully absorbed my attention. I watched them, smiling as they slowly split into different colors.

"Elaine, you're a monster for doing that. Mad respect. I have *GOT* to know all about it." Abeo said from the front seat.

The car ride had been mostly quiet while Annabella had taken care of checking on Morgan. Morgan was still in a panic from the last six hours, and her words were fast and jumbled. Annabella held her in her arms, continually telling her that it was okay now.

"Thank you, Abe." I said as I looked out the window. "I'm not gonna lie, I didn't think I was going to make it out of there. Let's never do that again."

"Neither did I," he replied, half-jokingly. "You just walked into the wolves' mouth and walked out without a scratch."

"You must be blind, I'm definitely not without a scratch." I wiped some more of the blood from my face. More pain spread across my right side and neck from where my shoulder had been fractured. I wasn't sure if it was completely in half, but it felt like it. Weren't we supposed to have super speedy regeneration or something?

He looked in the rear-view mirror at me as we sat parked at the red light. Abeo was finally able to see a glimpse of the injuries I had sustained.

"You did too much for us. We're basically strangers."

"No, you're my benefactor. You and Morgan saved my life, and I have now returned that debt."

"You make it sound so business like, why not just say you rescued your friend?" Abeo said as the light turned green, and we started to move again.

"You've had nothing but trouble since we met, why would you want to be my friend?"

"Because we're friendly people. We take care of our own, even if they're witches, they have stayed neutral. You didn't stay neutral for us. You broke the rules and killed werewolves in Halin's territory."

"I can't break the rules since I don't know what they are," I laughed.

"And besides, eternity is a long time to live with yourself if you have no integrity." I looked out the window, resting my head against the cold glass.

"Integrity, eh?" he chuckled. "Never thought I'd hear a vampire talk about integrity."

"If we don't have morals, then what's the point? Morality might not mean much to some, but if you steamroll yourself into doing whatever you want, you're basically an animal."

"Some would say your kind are already animals."

"You should meet Hayley; they would change your mind."

"The butcher? That sounds like a lovely time, but I think I'll pass ya know. Her reputation is, well…" he said as the car turned onto river-side street.

"Is what?" I asked directly, a sharpness to my voice. "Violent? Hostile? Malicious? The butcher, as people call her?"

Abeo quieted down, looking awkwardly out the window. I could feel him want to change the subject, but I wouldn't allow that.

"I want to set the record straight. Hayley is amazing. They are kind, and thoughtful, and adventurous, and most important loving. They are my entire world, and I was theirs. I saw them for a moment before Addison put a bullet in my leg and drug me away. Hayley is violently protective of the people they care about, and I'm honestly surprised that this city didn't get burned to the ground."

"Why didn't it?" he asked, the car moving through another light.

"The only reason I can think of is the cease fire. Addison mentioned it when they took me. If Hayley crossed the line –"

"It would open the floodgates for conflict between the two sides of the river. That's what would happen. We were all notified of it when it was originally put into effect. Your wife knocked Addison down a few pegs."

"So I've been told."

"Addison is lucky to be alive after what they did." The car moved slowed down and came to a stop as another light turned red.

I looked out the window at the twinkling-colored lights. Dots of red, green, and blue were hung across the riverfront. They were beautiful to behold. I let my head rest against the window as I watched them. Everything hurt. My body was past the point of exhaustion and the little bit of blood I had been able to get wasn't nearly enough to keep me going. Even my regeneration was barely able to function. I felt lost now more than ever. At least I had something pretty to look at.

I turned my body towards them, pressing my forehead to the glass. The lights were beautiful. In the middle of the lights was a clocktower with red and white lights running around the top of its roof. Flashing icicle lights hung down over the face of the clock face, lighting up the entire top of the structure.

Beautiful.

Just like the Christmas market. I stared at it, mumbling *"the market."* to myself.

It *was* the Christmas market. The car pulled forward when the light turned green.

"Abeo, can you stop the car for a moment?"

"What's wrong?" he asked, slowing down to a stop next to a street corner.

Without hesitating, I opened the door and stepped out of the car. My legs were shaky underneath me, and I had to lean into the car door to keep my body standing. I had found my way home. And it wasn't just for their safety, but I didn't want anyone else to get caught up in this. I knew that market looked familiar, but it had taken me a few seconds to remember it. Shaking my head, a smile formed across my lips, and I closed the back door, giving Morgan more room to spread out across the backseat.

Abe rolled down his window, a mist of warm air rising out of the front seat.

"What are you doing??"

"Hey, Abeo. Thank you for everything. You too Annabella." I put my hands on the top of the car and leaned forward towards them.

"Thank Abigail for me, I owe you all one. I will repay that debt one day, you have my word.."

"Where are you going?" he asked again.

"Thank you. Really." I ignored him and stepped away from the car, pulling every ounce of strength I had in me.

The second the light turned I took off across the street, still barefoot and looking like a mess. I didn't really care what anyone thought of me right now, what I knew was that this park was on the waterfront facing Philly and there were two bridges that would cross the river. I kept running, as fast as my feet would let me go. It was only two blocks, but it felt like forever. Once again, I was so close to getting back to Hayley.

"Just a little bit longer, I'm coming home."

The Empress

CHAPTER 9

$\mathcal{T}$he Christmas market was beautiful. There were lights twinkling across the stands, the smell of fresh baked goods, people laughing and the sound of music off on the other side of the square. I looked down at my feet in the mud. I needed a pair of shoes, or at least socks to put on. There were bruises visible around my ankle from where Kellan had grabbed me, and there was still a fair bit of dried blood on my clothes. Without more blood, I found it quite challenging to do any type of regeneration. Even then, I wasn't quite sure how to do it either.

The city had transformed into a wonderland of sparkling lights, the air thick with the scent of freshly baked treats, and the sound of joyous laughter wafting through the chilled breeze. It was my first time witnessing a winter Christmas market, and it was a sight to behold.

As I wandered through the festive streets, my keen senses absorbed every detail of the holiday spectacle. The market stalls were adorned with intricate decorations, each one a work of art in itself. Strings of multicolored lights hung overhead, their gentle twinkling creating a mesmerizing dance of colors against the inky sky.

The scent of cinnamon and roasting chestnuts mingled with the crisp winter air; a tantalizing mixture that made my senses come alive. The stalls were adorned with a kaleidoscope of goods, from handcrafted ornaments to sweet confections, all creating a tapestry of holiday cheer. Families and couples meandered through the market, their faces flushed with excitement and wonder. As people passed by, many took a moment to glance at me while I stood there. I had to get a plan of action down. I could hear children playing with each other and the sound of a train with a man laughing on it.

Time really had blurred together while I was in captivity. The air felt just like it had been when I was first released on accident. The sweet sound of a busker's violin filled the air, its haunting melody creating an enchanting atmosphere that was both comforting and melancholic. It was a testament to the beauty of the human spirit, celebrating love, family, and the magic of the holiday season.

I observed all of this with a mix of fascination and longing, a reminder of the life I had left behind when I was turned into a vampire. The beauty and joy of the winter Christmas market stood in stark contrast to the darkness of my existence, but for a brief moment, I allowed myself to be a part of this captivating scene.

I half ran across the park to the pier where a giant pine tree was decorated for the holidays. The lights sparkled against the backdrop of a clear starry night. Across the water was the skyline of Philadelphia. I was almost there. So many thoughts crossed my head, and my stomach.

That familiar growl hit me right along with an accompanying stomach cramp. I needed to feed so badly. While the smell of warm food was delightful, it would probably make me sick at this point. Would I be able to make it across the water if I swam? Could I swim? I remembered there being an old rumor that vampires couldn't cross water.

That was, however, absurd the longer I thought about it. There was the addition of security guards walking on patrol and two boats between the sides of the river. I had nearly forgotten that this could be a really depressing time of year for many, and some of those would decide to plunge to their icy demise. I was not one of them. I recalled wanting to do that myself while I was locked in the casket for so long but was never able to bring myself to do it.

I stood there in a daze, wondering if Hayley was across there somewhere looking this way. I remembered standing on a hotel balcony in Orlando at a conference and talking to them on the phone. We would watch the stars together, just like this, happy that we were both sharing that moment even though we weren't physically together.

"Time to think Ellie. Time to think. What's the best thing I can do here?" There were so many thoughts in my head that I wasn't sure which course of action would be the best. Or safest. Or fastest. Those three things rarely ever aligned.

My body backed up, turning away from the pier, and heading towards the Christmas market. Lights were strung overhead, making the sky look like it was dancing with color. I took my time strolling under the lights while letting the cool winter air nip at my skin. It felt refreshing, and almost cleansing. I passed by a stand filled with racks of clothes, but it was a bin that had fur lined slide on shoes that caught my attention. I ducked through the crowd of people and snagged a pair before quickly disappearing to the side of the wooden stand. They fit decently well, but I had no room to complain. My shoes were probably in the fireplace at that doghouse. I hopped up and down a few times to let my feet settle in, then moved back onto the crowded pathway after ripping the tag off of them.

I stopped at the fourth stall, watching a man chop up thick cheese before tossing it onto a hot griddle. The cheese began to heat up but didn't melt. I stood there, fascinated that the cheese just turned a darker brown, the woman next to him sticking little decorated tooth-picks into it and handing them out to the crowd.

I slid up and took one before moving back into the crowd. It smelled amazing and with my stomach growling I wanted more than anything to devour that little piece of cheese.

"You may not want to do that, young miss." A voice came from over my shoulder. It sent a wave of panic down my spine as the hair on my arms stood up and I turned my head to the side. My body instinctively took a step back away from him. His appearance was a masterpiece of dark, supernatural beauty.

His tall and imposing figure moved with an effortless grace, his every step exuding an air of authority and power. His ebony hair, cascading in soft waves, framed a chiseled face that defied the passage of time. His eyes, a mesmerizing shade of deep crimson, seemed to pierce through my very soul, bearing the wisdom of centuries and a hint of eternal sorrow.

High, aristocratic cheekbones accentuated his sculpted features, while his lips, a deep shade of red, held a sensuous quality that could lure anyone under his spell. His skin was pale, almost luminous, a testament to his immortal existence, and it contrasted beautifully with the darkness of his attire. I, on the other hand, stood there with ripped clothes, claw marks, bruises, and stolen shoes.

He was dressed in garments that echoed a timeless elegance, his clothing always immaculate, befitting a lord of his stature. A rich, tailored coat draped over his shoulders, the deep, velvety black fabric hinting at a hidden world of secrets. Silver embroidery adorned the cuffs and lapels, a nod to his noble lineage. His attire was complemented by an intricately designed cravat that hinted at a taste for the finer things in life.

His aura was both magnetic and intimidating, a combination of charisma and power that drew admirers and commanded respect. The vampire lord's presence was a study in contrasts—an embodiment of ageless beauty and supernatural might, cloaked in the allure of the night.

His red eyes looked like they could see right through me. In front of him, I felt bare and exposed. I now understood why, in his presence, mortals couldn't help but feel a mix of fascination and fear, drawn to him like moths to a flame, knowing that this creature of the night possessed an allure that transcended the boundaries of mortality. I glanced to the sides, counting several other bodies posted strategically throughout the cheerful crowd. They kept still, but their gazes all landed on me.

"Thank you for your advice." I said while taking a step backwards away from him.

There was something about him that gave me the absolute creeps. As I turned away from him, I felt a hand on my arm, holding me there.

"No rush, my dear. I wasn't aware of anyone new in town." He said with a delightful smile. The more he spoke, the more the voice inside my head was smashing the panic button.

"New? Oh, I'm sorry, I wasn't sure what the process was." I forced out a chuckle. I had been here before, a long time ago. Think fast Ellie.

"I'm not new, I come to this Christmas market every year with my wife."

It wasn't exactly a lie. Hayley and I had come to this market every year since we had started dating. I could remember walking down the familiar paths hand in hand every holiday while we tasted the yearly delights. I was a sucker for mulled cider and warm snacks.

"Every year? I wonder how that could be when I've never seen you before." He took a step towards me, his voice keeping an almost curiously monotone level. "Where are you from, child?"

"Old Lanc", I replied, still moving back through the crowd. All the while I was looking for an escape route. There had to be a way for me to get through the people without being followed. It wasn't technically a lie; I really was from there.

"So, tell me, Old Lanc. May I inquire your name?" he said while smiling, revealing the glistening white fangs he made clear for everyone to see. "I frequent the Lancaster territory regularly, and I've never seen you. The governor must be getting lax over there."

"Yes, he must be." I tried to force a laugh out. His smile remained, his eyes going out into the distance like I was some inconsequential thing not worthy of his attention.

"She."

"She?"

"The governor of your territory is a woman. I am the only male governor in this region."

It was him. Halin Overbrook, this areas governor, and a provincial lord. I panicked and took off, going from zero to full spring through the crowd. I could hear him laughing behind me. Regardless of how fast I was going, I could still see people looking at me with pity. Had I run across someone important? As I darted through the bustling holiday market, the scent of roasted chestnuts and mulled wine hung in the frosty air. The cheerful laughter of shoppers and the twinkling lights overhead seemed incongruent with the chaos that had erupted in this quaint, snow-draped market. I was being pursued a relentless vampire, and his vampiric subordinates. They had cornered me, and I had no choice but to flee through the labyrinth of market stalls, my undead heart pounding in my chest.

A body came to my side, running next to me. He had as charcoal grey hood over his head, masking almost everything but his fangs.

"Where are you running to little one?" He laughed, seeming to be mocking me. It was only through a stroke of absolute luck that I was able to make it this far. There was absolutely no way I was going to go down without a fight.

My senses sharpened, and I could hear the ominous whispers of their footfalls, as they closed in on me. The labyrinthine market seemed to stretch endlessly, with vendors hawking trinkets and toys, their cries blending with the panicked shrieks of shoppers who had realized the danger.

I wove through the throngs, narrowly avoiding crashing into children with candy canes, couples wrapped in cozy scarves, and festive stalls adorned with tinsel and holly. The holiday spirit was lost on me as I pushed my way through the crowd, knocking several people over. My body floated over a child, knocking a cup of warm chocolate out of their hands. I could barely hear their cry of disappointment from behind me.

I tucked down into a more open path and followed it to the end, where a small half circle of shops all sat locked together. Cornered against a stall selling handcrafted ornaments, I seized the opportunity to leap over the wooden counter and disappeared behind a wall of glass-blown trinkets. The man and his minions cursed and frantically scanned the market, their feral eyes glowing with hunger.

My back pressed against the wall, struggling to control my erratic breathing. I felt the sting of anxiety clawing at my chest. The holiday market, normally a place of joy and togetherness, had transformed into a maze of dread. An older woman looked at me with pity, stepping forward to the counter again. I watched her start selling her ornaments again, the heat from the forge where she was making ornaments rolling over my cold skin. An elder man, most likely her husband, rolled molten glass around in beads before sticking it back into the white-hot machine.

Moments later, the woman tapped the counter and looked down at me.

"He's gone, run."

Taking a deep breath, I made a dash for the nearest alley, hoping to lose them in the warren of narrow, snow-covered passages. My shoes skidded on the icy waterfront cobblestone, but I maintained my balance, darting into shadowy corners and alleyways to try to confuse my pursuers. I turned a corner and ran headfirst into one of them, a bald man with glowing eyes and a black septum ring with spiked ends. I could sense their relentless pursuit from behind me, a dark presence that shadowed my every move as he moved to grab me.

I sneered at him before pushing off to the left and heading down an aisle before turning towards the city. The water side would be too obvious and open. One narrow alley opened into a small square, and my heart stopped as I saw Lord Halin blocking my path. He smiled, revealing his sharp fangs, his subordinates closing in from behind.

There was no way out.

In that moment of despair, I clung to the shadows, my heart pounding in my chest. I watched as a group of carolers, their voices raised in festive song, approached the square, lanterns in hand. With the distraction they unwittingly provided, I melted into the darkness.

I might be able to lose them if I hit the streets. I darted through the people entering from the parking lot and hit full speed towards the buildings of Camden. It didn't help that I was still partly covered in blood and recovering from the fight I had been through less than an hour ago.

I looked backwards, only to see the four bodies moving across both the parking lot and car rooftops towards me. I could feel their eyes on me, their presence closing in. Nothing I was doing was enough to shake them.

With renewed determination to lose them, I burst forth from the alleyways and back into the main street, rejoining the holiday market. The shoppers were none the wiser, engrossed in their merriment. Many of them hadn't even seen the blue of color that moved by them across the rooftops of the market. The carolers continued their song, unknowingly shielding me. My eyes landed on the crosswalk and without thinking I dove straight into the street while attempting to dodge incoming traffic.

Even though my body was moving forward, my head turned back around to see if they were still following me. It didn't look like they were able to make it through the oncoming traffic and when I came to a stop and turned around, the blonde figure was standing in front of me. His hands were clasped behind his back, his face still holding that casually condescending smile.

"It is rather rude to depart a conversation so abruptly," he said, taking a step towards me.

His hand lifted, and although it gently placed my hair behind my ear, the feel of his skin touching mine sent shivers across my entire body. This man was dangerous.

"What is your name, child?" he said with a smile that made my body crawl.

"Child? I'm like thirty-eight," I pulled my head to the side with a jerk. "And don't touch me!"

"Thirty-eight? How young. You are barely old enough to recognize your insolence. Now, what is your name?"

His tone shifted from leisure to commanding. There was a soft glow in his eyes and for a split second I felt slightly entranced by him.

I bit my tongue and shook it off. I couldn't think of any reason why I would stop there, but something in his voice swayed me. My body took off to the side, heading down the side street toward the waterfront galleria complex. The once beautiful shops were slowly closing down for the night, and although the buildings were well lit, the amount of foot traffic was beginning to slow down.

"LITTLE GIRL WE SEEEE YOOOOUUUU" a loud voice echoed with laughter across the buildings. I turned to see if they were close behind me again only to meet the bottom of a boot from the side. The mud and rubber sent me spiraling to the side before my body hit the cold stone walkway.

Pain tore through the side of my face. If I didn't know any better, I'd think my jaw was broken. The familiar taste of blood swept through my mouth from where I bit my tongue on the fall. Were they laughing at me? I couldn't tell over the sound of my face screaming at me.

"Lord Halin, we got her!" one of them said. His voice was deep and nasally. I hated how much the sound of it grated on my ears.

"She must be new here, poor thing" another remarked. "Only a newborn would flee from a lord."

"She's so new she can't even feel him," another laughed.

Lord? Did he say a lord? What level was that again? I tried to remember what rank that was at. Third or fourth generation? I couldn't think straight.

"Bring her over." He commanded with a single clap of his hands. His crisp voice echoed across the glass walls. They grabbed me under the arms, lifting me up and carrying me across to the center lights. I wasn't paying attention while running and somehow made it to the back side of a shopping center. The windows were decorated with fake, white snow. Christmas trees and sleighs dotted their windows and giant sale posters reflected the seasons savings.

"I haven't had a chase that fun in decades. And I'm sure you aren't really from Lancaster. I'll find out who turned you and pay them a visit."

He looked down at me, lowering his face to mine.

"You aren't half bad. I'm sure a nice dress would fix you right up. I'm bored with my current companions; you would be an excellent addition."

"Fuck off"

"A few decades next to me will change your mind. I have a rather delightful court. Where else would a new child of the night get to experience the extravagance of the stars? The balls, the music, the blood, all of it catered to my whims!" He laughed, dancing in a circle, satisfied with himself.

"It is only right that you should learn a valuable lesson, child. The world of vampires is one of hierarchy, where the strong thrive and the weak perish. You had the audacity to attempt escape, to challenge my authority, and for that, there must be consequences."

I looked straight past them, bringing my eyes to a young woman who walked out of one of the shops. She had a bag under her arm and what looked to be a coffee in her hand. Her bright pink hair hung down the sides of her face in a cute side cut. The tips were a beautiful ombre fade to black, and her eyes were a shade of piercing sapphire, each glance like a deep, endless pool that could pull you in and never let go.

"RUN!" I yelled out at her, hoping she would hear me before the others saw her. I was too late, too naïve. Lord Halin turned around and walked towards her. She stood there, staring straight through the lights at me.

"Don't bother leaving, human. You can blame whatever god you want for giving you bad luck" his head fell to the side with a crooked smirk.

"LEAVE HER ALONE!" Tears of bright red blood flowed from my eyes as I screamed towards him. He turned with a wide smile.

"SHE HAS NOTHING TO DO WITH THIS!" I cried out as loud as I could.

"Shut her up, Alzair" he turned his head away from me. "I don't want my appetite ruined with such noise."

His footsteps continued forward towards the young woman. A hand came across my neck and mouth, forcing it shut. I tried shaking my head and getting them off my back. I wouldn't let anyone else die because of me. I screamed into his hand as he drove his knee into the center of my back. The pain returned to my shoulder and fire went down my right side.

"Are you okay?" she asked me from across the square. She looked at me curiously, my eyes pleading for her to run. To do anything that would keep her safe. Anything that would let her escape from this nightmare that she didn't deserve to be in. The young woman looked at the four men, one of them a provincial lord, and spoke not a single word. I heard her voice in my head again, not realizing she hadn't said anything.

"Are you okay?" she asked me again. I felt the tears start to run down my face as I watched the man approach her.

Alzair stayed next to me as Lord Halin strolled up to her, his arms swinging wide with every step he took as he flashed his fangs at the smaller girl. I felt more and more panic as I heard him stop moving in front of her.

"What a lovely little thing you are. How about it, neck or wrist? I'll let you pick how you die tonight."

He chuckled to himself as he looked back at his group of men, all of them laughing alongside him.

"That's our lord!" one of them said cheerfully. "So magnanimous as always, she's lucky she gets to go this way" another one said in response. I looked past them, trying to tune them out as I locked eyes on the young girl for a moment. It was only a second, but it made me feel like I was standing beneath an avalanche with no way out. Her eyes looked like an abyss of starlight that had no end. Just that single moment had made me feel like I was suffocating.

"Kneel." Her voice was calm and monotone, completely opposite of the cheerful carefree tone she had used with me moments ago.

The voice resonated in each of their heads. Words were power, shackled into their undead souls by the bloodlines they inherited. The three men accompanying Lord Halin collapsed to the ground beside him while letting out mumbled groans of pain. Unlike the others, Halin only went down to a knee. The young girl was slightly surprised by that and showed a bit of interest in him.

"There… is no…. way…" he muttered while enduring the pain and refusing to submit. A grimace crossed his face as he fought against the oppressive might he felt from her. The girl continued to keep her eyes on him as he struggled. His body pressed down; eyes closed before he let out a wild scream. Lord Halin launched himself up at the young girl with every bit of strength he had in his body. Long, bloody claws shot out of his fingertips as he brought his arm forward to slash down at her.

Her hand raised, eyes locked on sight with that same dead look, as if she were looking at an insignificant ant she was about to step on. She extended her fingers, the claws of blood about to pierce straight through her hand.

Except, it didn't. The blood within the claws erupted into a mist before each drop swirled around her. She flipped her palm over, and the misty drops of blood were sucked into her palm like they had never existed.

The vampiric lord fell to his knees while screaming in pain. His smooth, almost jade like skin quickly began to dry up and start cracking from his hand up through his shoulders and across his chest. Even his bright blonde hair started to turn white with age, wrinkles spreading across his face.

One of the strongest creatures in the hierarchy, had not only been defeated by a child, but even deprived of his authority. The other vampires kept their heads lowered at the sight even though they were dumbfounded by the situation that had unfurled. The air of regality he held had disappeared, and nothing but a withered husk of a man was left in her wake.

"That's a *neat* trick." She said with a grin after absorbing the blood of the vampiric lord. The power contained within that blood was powerful. However, she was more surprised at the fact that a sixth-tier lord had resisted her than any mysteries within her blood. After all, vampires were the most hierarchal of all the races.

She had seen many instances throughout history where human slaves and serfs would rebel against their knights and lords when they were dissatisfied. They would wage war with their superiors when desperate or led into a corner. It was a cycle that happened during every age of civilization.

This was, in any case, drastically different from how vampires were. Even if they belonged to different clans, those belonging to the lower class would never rebel against the upper class. It was hard coded in their blood. Even if one didn't know who their opposition was, it would be impossible to for them to succeed once that difference in class was revealed.

There was a stark difference in the power and force between the two. Even if vampires were fully incorporated into human society and embraced their culture and mindset, there was still an irrefutable law that shackled them together.

Lord Halin struggled to raise his head. His chest was rising and falling at a fast pace with quick breaths of air grasping for life. He had visibly gone from a handsome young man to a senior one, barely clinging on to any fragment of life he could. Disbelief crossed his face and was stunned when he saw that not only was she fine, but she was looking down on him with an arrogant gaze after absorbing his blood. There was an unfamiliar emotion that slowly began to move across his aging body. What emotion was it? Fear.

"You drank fae blood. Isn't that right?" she sneered down at him. Her gentleness disappeared at the realization of what they had done.

"..!!!" His eyes widened in more shock as panic immediately took his face.

"And not a regular one... was this a noble? The purity of it. The blasphemy," she continued.

Lord Halin lowered his head, no longer wanting to meet her gaze. Even if she had an absolute level of power, there was no way she could figure that out during their first encounter, right?

"I am not surprised that you would disregard our law. Did all of you partake in this sacrilege, or did you just happen to come across one of their nobles."

Her voice remained calm and monotone with every word she spoke.

Lord Halin kept quiet, unable to answer. I looked over at the young woman as she smiled down at him. Her hand reached down, and a single finger lifted his head up by his chin.

"Confess to me, child of Addison, Lord of Konrad's lineage." She said, her body seeming to glow with a faint purple aura.

His eyes turned blank and glossed over, the light in them disappearing. I watched in shock at the power she exerted with so little effort.

"We started to clear out the eastern side of Camden... and we found an enclave that was... it was transporting a delegation to the capital. Their scent was too good to pass, and we feasted on them..." he murmured to her.

"That blood clouded your senses. If you hadn't consumed them, you would have begged to carry my bags for me." Her tone was direct and nonchalant, almost inconvenienced.

It was as she expected. Even though he was an upper tier Lord, he was completely ignorant of his crime. He was only able to resist her will because of a decently high level of blood purity. That unfortunately didn't change the fact that the fae and vampires had been in a cease fire since the mid-1840s. She shook her head before looking at the others.

I kept my eyes down to the ground as I heard her footsteps move closer to me. She moved with a grace that seemed almost supernatural, her every step a symphony of fluidity and poise. Her attire was both elegant and seductive, embracing the essence of the night with a deep V-necked dress made of rich, velvety fabric, its deep midnight hue accentuating the vivid pink of her hair. Her shortness didn't detract from her smooth, pale legs.

Around her neck, a necklace of blood-red gemstones glittered, emphasizing the mysterious and dangerous allure that surrounded her body. Rings adorned each of her fingers, their designs as intricate and timeless as her own existence.

Her presence was both enchanting and formidable, an enchantress who could captivate with a single glance and yet conceal the unfathomable power that dwelled within her. She was the embodiment of beauty that concealed danger

"Are you Ellie?" her voice was gently and playful. I looked up at her, trying to disguise the panic I felt.

There was an instant knot in my chest as my head lowered back down.

"You look like her. I saw your picture when I was visiting my sister."

"Your sister?" I asked. Who was this child?

"I've never met you. Why would your sister have my picture?"

"Ireena is my older sister. That makes Hayley family, she's like a niece. She could do with relaxing a bit more these days, but that's okay," she cracked a wide smile.

"You're definitely her. You don't smell like her though, you smell like Ireena."

Lord Halin slammed his forehead into the ground and began crying a few yards away. The high-pitched whine from him was a stark contrast from the arrogance he had shown moments earlier.

"Lady Antanasia, I was blind to not recognize your magnificence!" he shouted, taking a full bow, and apologizing as loud as he could.

"Forgive this lowly one for his transgressions!"

His attendants began to panic after hearing their Lord's words and recognizing what kind of situation they were in.

"So, you do recognize me, young one! How lovely. Take this message back to the little Addison for me, will you?" she turned from my side and brought her gaze down onto the group.

"Anything for you, Duchess de Byrne" he kept his head on the pavement of the alley way, refusing to lift his gaze back up to hers.

"Your little aunt is passing through the area touring the sights and I'll be stopping by. I expect a lovely reception on my arrival." She gave a light chuckle as she finished her sentence. For a split second her demeanor shifted again,

"Now scram."

I could hear them scrambling to their feet and running down the alleyway. The echoes of their footsteps alongside the occasionally knocked over trash cans soon gave way to near absolute silence.

My body collapsed on the ground, barely able to sit up. I felt a hand on my shoulder pull me up to a seat. Without thinking, I brought my eyes to her, the golden blue shimmer in them replaced by a beautiful bright crimson. Her smile was gentle, but stern.

"A nightmare of events has unfurled around your existence." She sighed and took another drink from her cup. She smiled at me, noticing my curious stare.

"This? It's warmed blood. Looks like mulled cider but tastes way better."

She handed the cup to me with me with slight head tilt. Not wanting to insult her, I took the cup and had a sip. It was most definitely warm blood and although I wanted nothing more than to throw it all up, it brought such sweet relief across my body. The physical strain across my chest and back was slowly receding, taking any bit of adrenaline with it.

"Anyway, let's get you home! You're probably exhausted, right?" her voice was so gentle that I had forgotten how tired I was. I took a step and came back down onto my knees in front of her.

"I'm sorry. I'm really sorry Lady de Byrne," I had nothing left in me. The energy I had left was quickly leaving my system. I could feel her cold fingers pulling my sleeves up.

She gasped at the sight, and even in this shambled state I could feel her anger.

"I never meant to cause a mess, I just wanted to go home."

"Silence, Ellie. Did Addison do this to you?" there was a darkness to her voice as she looked at the puncture marks up and down my arms. The middle parts of my arms were covered in dark bruise from where they had repeatedly stuck me with needles. There were scars across part of it, and the fact that I still had fresh wounds from earlier didn't help any.

"I never said anything that would bring her danger. I had to keep her safe." I said, feeling the tears returning. The thought of what I had survived, and how I had almost landed back in that situation all over again was more than I could handle right now.

"Sleep, young one. Hayley is lucky to have you." Her hand came across my eyes, wiping away the bloody tears as they came to a close. I felt the stress and anxiety leave my body, not realizing that over a dozen figured had landed on the stone around me. They each came to a knee, their bodies covered in purple and gold cloaks. "Even in this state, your love for her stayed strong. It's been a millennium since I watched a love story unfold."

A tall, well-built man with dark red eyes and long black hair stood up beside her before taking a long, low bow.

"Was your shopping fulfilling?" he kept his head lowered while picking up the body in front of him. "Shall we take her to the car?"

"Yes, Xavier, and I caught more than a good deal." She smiled with a nonchalant chuckle.

"Oh! Kill those four. By my authority as the Duchess of House De'Byrne, their lives are forfeit."

"As you command, my lady." He responded, and with the slightest of gestures and the bodies around him disappeared into the night. I could feel someone lift my body up, and that was all I could remember as I slipped into a rest that had been a long time coming.

The Judgment

REFLECTIONS

"We are the shepherds of the lost, humble servants of the divine. We know not failure, for we are the vessels choses to wield His will. Those who find themselves bitten must be dispatched with the holy rites."
Father Gabriel, Adeptus Oryx, Holy Codex ii

CHAPTER 10

The bumpy road felt almost cathartic to me. Or maybe it was the soft leather seats that took away the painful memories of my captivity. My eyelids were heavy and the bruising across my body was throbbing in pain. There were a few sharp turns that had my head lift for a moment before making a soft "thud" on the window. Did it sting? Yes.

Could I care less? Also yes.

I only peeled my eyes open when I felt the car come to a stop and a hand touch my side.

"Wow! You really were out cold," a cheerful voice came from the seat beside me. I dropped my head over towards her while yawning.

"We're here! I can't wait to rub it in that I found you first!"

Her smile was still bright and gentle, completely at odds with the fact she was an original. She pulled her pink hair back into a high ponytail as the door on her side opened. A gigantic creature of a man held his hand out to help her out of the car. I heard the door on my side click open and a hand with beautifully manicured nails extend towards me.

I took her hand as I saw her face. She couldn't have been much younger than me, but everything from the way she wore her hair down to her heels was immaculate. I was taken aback for a moment at the flawlessness of her skin and the gentleness of her touch. Her nails were an almond shape with black to red glitter covering the tips. I was embarrassed at the thought of how bad mine were. The last manicure I had was, well, a long time ago. I almost pulled away from her hand when I realized my fingers were caked with dirt and blood. She helped me up and out of the car and for the first time I was able to see where Hayley had spent so much of their time.

The estate stood proudly, its multi-story silhouette commanding my attention. An aura of timeless elegance surrounded it, illuminated by the soft radiance of the starlight above. Towering oak trees, centuries-old guardians of the night, embraced the manor, their branches stretching over it like loving arms.

The façade of the manor was a harmonious blend of architectural styles, reminiscent of centuries past. Elaborate stone carvings adorned the entrance, each telling a silent story of the ages. Stained glass windows, aglow with a kaleidoscope of colors, depicted mythical creatures and historic moments from vampire lore.

The entry way up to the doors were lit on each side by raised lanterns that flickered with dancing flames. There was a black and gold chandelier hanging outside the door on the overhang, making the two large doors seem even more regal. I stopped in the middle of the steps and turned around, admiring the fountain and its odd, lonely tree of a centerpiece, as well as the articulately designed landscaping. The grand double doors of rich mahogany swung open, and two figures emerged, the first being a finely groomed gentleman and the other being a woman looking like her evening dinner had been interrupted. I could spot that moment of a glare a mile away.

"Miranda, Conner, it's good to see you again!" Lady De' Byrne hopped out and strolled up and past the two with a wide smile, her fingers clasping behind her head as she entered the building.

"Where's my favorite little animal at?" I heard her say from inside.

I followed the woman who had helped me out of the car towards the front door. The man I remembered. Conner? Maybe? Carl? Whatever it was, he seemed rather relieved that I was here. His smile was gentle and caring. I moved behind the woman I was following when she abruptly stopped.

"Please refrain from doing that," she said while turning around to look at me.

"Do what? I'm just... its... you know, I haven't seen them in so long and I'm really nervous and this entire place looks gigantic and I'm a little overwhelmed," I stuttered with my word while trying to make myself as small as possible.

She put her hands on my shoulders and lightly shook me.

"I've heard your story from Hayley. You both have been waiting for this. All you have to do is take the last few steps and you're home." she said with a caring smile. Her words felt sincere and brought me a bit of relief.

"Thank you. You're right." I lightly laughed to myself. What was I so afraid of? "I'm sorry I'm such a mess, and I missed your name."

"It's Thea," she replied, "and it's my pleasure to meet you Lady Reinhardt"

"Thank you, Thea. Truly." I said.

I looked past her at the two people waiting for me. As I walked up the rest of the marble stairs, I could feel my anxiety building more and more. It had been months since I had emerged as this new being and hundreds of years have gone by. The man looked me over with a smile then motioned to the side for me to enter the manor.

My mouth dropped and I looked around the entryway of the wide open entrance. As I crossed the threshold and entered the main foyer, I was greeted by a soaring, vaulted ceiling adorned with an opulent crystal chandelier that bathed the space in a gentle, shimmering luminescence. A giant winding staircase, marble floors, tons of black. Perfectly Hayley.

"Lady Reinhardt, if you would follow me."

His voice was calm and direct, not a hint of enjoyment could be felt from him. I looked at the rose stitched onto his jacket, recognizing it from the bridge that night so long ago. I looked at him for a moment, thinking about how I should even act here.

"After you." I tried to sound as serious as possible. He nodded his head and twisted around, sliding on the ball of his foot to rotate in one smooth motion.

I followed behind him as he led me through the open foyer and across brightly lit floor. Even the marble beneath my feet seemed to sparkle with starlight. We were guided by the soft, melodic strains of a piano coming from one of the rooms. My eyes moved across everything there was to see.

The pictures, the chandelier, all of it reminded me of the home we had designed together, but never had the chance to build. My pace slowed as I slowly turned around, taking the time to ingest it all. It was almost exact, even the design of the railings was dead on target in their placement. A knot began to well up in my chest at what all of this meant. Had Hayley built our dream home for me? I had obsessed over this for years while we were waiting on all the permits to clear, and it never happened. For the first time since this nightmare had begun, I felt like I had wronged them.

My eyes closed as I sniffed the air, taking in the scent of fresh pine. If it weren't for the million feelings going on inside of me, I may have completely missed it. The entire room was decorated for Yule. Garland made of pine springs lined the foyer, dancing fairy lights covered a giant tree next to the staircase, glistening in their reflection on the marble floor.

I lowered my head in thought, not noticing the various others who had stopped to stare at me. Years of memories came flooding back. The first time we met, our first date. The Christmas markets that we would go to every year. Our wedding night. I had almost forgotten them in my stubbornness. I lifted my head and looked up at the chandelier, only snapping back to it when I felt a hand on my arm. I had stopped in the middle of the foyer, a single stream of red slowly moving down my cheeks.

I wasn't the only one who had been alone. Hayley had lived out here for as long as I had lived in that casket. My pettiness hadn't just cut them, it had cut us. I looked at the man, pulling away from his touch while my eyes ran across every decoration, every picture, every detail as fast as they could.

I had abandoned them.

"Lady Reinhardt," he said, stepping to the side and extending a hand towards a door on the left side of the room. "This way if you will."

"Of course." I tried to choke down the feelings that were all happening at once.

My body went on auto pilot and followed him, my eyes still watching the brightly reflective marble floor while I thought about the years we had missed. What would life had been like if I had accepted it and not been a complete asshole about the entire thing?

Would I have died that night? Would we have been able to make it this far? I remember having a panic attack the morning of our wedding, I was afraid that one day they would fall out of love with me and move on and I'd be left behind. Hayley hadn't, and they had waited literally hundreds of years for me.

He led me through large oak doors and into a wide, open library. There had to have been tens of thousands of books on the walls. The ceiling was vaulted up through both stories of the estate and the bookshelves lined every open area. It was great to see that some things hadn't changed. My eyes stopped as they landed on a set of pictures over the fireplace that decorated the main wall. There was a picture of some woman, and on each side of her were two equally dazzling portraits.

On her left side was a painting of Hayley. It captured everything that I remembered about my wife. The piercing eyes, sharp jaw and flowing colorful hair. They sat on a high wing packed chair lined with black velvet next to the fireplace it was mounted above. Of course, this was painted right here. They really did love their books and from what I could immediately tell, that hadn't gone away.

My head tilted to the side as I looked at the other painting. A beautiful woman sat there. Her gaze was just like Hayley's, but there was a smile on her face. I stepped closer to her picture and couldn't keep myself from asking the question. It looked similar in style to the one that had been there when I was released.

"Who is this?" my voice was soft and quiet, and as I turned to see the man's face, a face now filled with a hint of sadness, and I nearly regretted it.

"If you don't want to answer, it's okay. She looks… *familiar.*"

"Her name is Kamila, the first star. She was an outstanding warrior and Hayley's blood sister. Before I was in service to Lord Reinhardt, I was entrusted to lead one of our operations teams by her majesty Vasiliev and was able to serve with her. Hundreds of years of training went by before I was finally able to lead our brothers and sisters in the war of seven roses."

His voice was calm and straight forward. I watched him as he moved next to me and stared at the painting.

"She was a far better fighter than any of us. She didn't like guards and was often impulsive. She would fight rather than flee, and her dedication to the blade was only passed by her dedication to her maker."

"What happened to her?" I asked, having a bad feeling about where this story was headed.

"Conner left her to die." A sharp voice echoed through the room as a woman entered from the main door.

I looked at his face, recognizing that same level of sadness that I once had. He lowered his gaze from the mantle and stepped away from me.

"Conner was sent to escort a smaller coven that had landed in America. He had a small contingent of our security forces and had been tasked with one simple task. Escort them from the docks to our compound in Hoboken. Kamila set out with him and when shit hit the fan she stayed behind to save his ass at the cost of hers."

I looked over at Conner, watching his head hang in disappointment. He stayed silent while slowly backing up towards the chairs in the middle of the room. As he turned, I glared at the woman who had just entered.

"I'm sure he didn't just leave here there." I quipped in his defense. I didn't know anything about him, but from his body language there had to be more to the story.

"Conner, tell me what happened to Kamila."

My eyes followed Conner as he took a seat, sliding his right leg over his left while leaning his head back into the soft cushioning.

"Miranda is right, it was my fault. I oversaw the recovery and escort mission. You may not know it since you're new to our world, but the territory lines aren't just for us. There are lines that other creatures cannot cross, and there are lines that those who follow religious fanaticism do not cross." He took a deep breath in and sighed it out.

"Kamila hopped in the lead car when we were leaving and joined us. It was a routine pick up so there wasn't anything to worry about, and it wasn't like she hadn't done it before. We drove through the city and down to the docks without any problems at all. Everything was near perfect until we went to leave." Conner paused for a moment, looking at Miranda.

"When our car got to the gate, the anti-vehicle spikes came up, sending two of the three vehicles crashing into the barrier. Ours made it out, but when we slammed on the breaks to check behind us, one of the cars had already been set ablaze. I saw the white cloaks of Cyborea as they opened fire on the cars behind us. One of them turned towards our car. We had six of our kind, me, a guard, and Kamila. The car made it as far as it could go, and I knew we had to abandon it."

The room was silent, and I hadn't heard two other vampires enter the large room. They moved to stand behind Miranda, staying quiet while they listened to Conners story. He gulped down something in his throat and looked straight at me.

"My escort and I pulled them out and we ducked into the first alley way we could find. We were in neutral territory, there was no reason why we should have been attacked. At the end of the alley, we ran straight across the street into another one, trying to move as fast as possible. We had to keep moving. I looked behind us as Kamila stopped so I stopped too. I pushed Jamison forward and told him to keep moving."

"Kamila took my side arm and drew her blade. I tried to argue with her that she had to make it through and keep them safe, but she wouldn't listen. She pulled rank and sent me with them. I made it three more blocks without any issues before I turned around. When I got to the main street, I watched from the shadows as she went toe to toe with Mother Angelica, one of the Priestesses of Cyborea."

"What is Cyborea?" I asked curiously.

"The Order of Cyborea is a fringe branch of the church that specializes in hunting the ungodly" Miranda spoke up from across the room. "If there is any single group of people who are a direct threat to our kind, it is them."

"For once I agree with Miranda. They are well trained, highly motivated, and have absolute belief in their mission to exterminate any and everything that isn't what they deem holy" Conner said with another sigh.

"Only one vampire I know of has ever taken them on and walked away, and she's right up there."

Conner brought his gaze up to the center picture. I looked at her, still wondering who she was. There was sense that she was someone important to me, almost an instinct that caused reverence in her.

"Master Vasiliev, the mistress of the night and head of the Vasiliev household. She is one of the origins, and the maker of both Hayley and Kamila." There was a hint of pride in Miranda's voice as she spoke about the woman in the painting. "As you are sired by Hayley, you are the only second generation in the coven."

"Conner, what happened to Kamila?" I said, turning away from the paintings before walking over and sitting across from him. "Was it the Order of Cyborea?"

He looked at me with a long silent stare. His hands almost seemed to be slightly trembling before he spoke again.

"Mother Angelica was created to execute us. Her entire existence from the time she was born was solely to erase every one of our kind. I watched Kamila take on four of her acolytes and kill all four of them. I stood in the dark of the alley, tucked safely there while hoping she would run my way and we could escape. That was when I heard the bells."

"The bells?" I asked, moving to the edge of my seat.

"Yes, the bells. She has bells hanging on her crazy blue dress, and as she emerged from the darkness, I saw Kamila get serious for the first time. She was carefree at heart and was always cracking a joke even though she was a top tier warrior. We all admired her. She dropped the side arms and drew the saber from her waist, pointing it at the other woman. There were lines of silver and blue crosses decorating the bottom of her long white cloak, and what looked like Latin around the end of each sleeve. I watched her draw two long, thin knives from her belt, and without dropping her smile she moved at a speed I thought only our kind was capable of."

"I froze there. I could have helped, I could have stepped in, but I was honestly *terrified* of the woman she was fighting. At no time did she drop that creepy grin, but it was her eyes that frightened me the most. They were an unnatural shade of blue, and it almost felt like they were glowing." Conner stopped for a moment as he recounted watching the two of them go at it.

"Kamila was slowly losing ground and even as they exchanged blows, I stayed there frozen. It wasn't until she turned in my direction and yelled at me to run did, I snap out of it. She had known I was there the entire time, and I had done nothing. I kept my eyes glued on the battle, not knowing that it was about to be over. That priestess bitch fainted a high strike but instead dropped her blade and drew a glowing paper talisman that she threw at Kamila. They were too close for her to dodge and the second it hit her I closed my eyes. Her scream was something I will never forget." Conner paused again and looked down at his hands.

"When I opened my eyes, she was on her knees in front of the Priestess and there were several more of them. There was a yellow glow that shined through the black smoke that was coming from beneath the paper talismans. I could smell her skin burning even from there. "

I reclined back in the chair, thinking about the young man that fought with Abeo at the lab. His jacket had the same blue crosses decorating the edging and a giant gold cross across his back. Could he have been one of these acolytes? I missed the opportunity to ask him anything since I was a little bit out of it, and Abeo snapped his neck.

"What are those talismans? Are they dangerous to us? Like… that sounds crazy that something like that exists" There was so much for me to wrap my head around and I felt that every question I asked was a stupid one.

Miranda walked over and stood beside us, blocking my view of Hayley's picture. It was a small action on her part that greatly disrupted my comfort in being there. For some reason, knowing they were watching over me from even a painting made me feel a little bit safer.

"They are cloth talismans blessed by a bishop and soaked in holy water. That way when they hit you, they stick to you. It's an archaic weapon designed to inflict as much pain as possible while rendering us immobile." Miranda said perturbingly.

"Consider yourself lucky that you've never felt one of them."

She rolled up her left sleeve, revealing a long black burn mark in her skin. I couldn't take my eyes from the scarring that should have healed long ago.

"They stick to your skin and burn it off. It's the most agonizing pain I've ever experienced." Her words sharp and direct as she spoke to me. "It's meant to negate our regeneration. For those of more diluted blood, it will burn them to ash in minutes."

"Diluted blood? Like vampires that are way down the line?" Was she talking about Taj and the guys from Old Lanc?

"Yes, those creatures who are barely able to survive, but lack any strength in their blood. They're easy pickings for the acolytes, let alone a Priestess."

"How did you survive that?" I was curious how someone who looked as combative as her made it out of an altercation with just that wound. Then again, I had no idea what else she had been through.

Miranda took an exasperated breath and shook her head. I didn't care if I was inconveniencing her at this point, especially with how rude she had been to Conner. I would make this as painfully uncomfortable and irritating as I could.

"I got into it with an acolyte outside of our territory. It was my mistake, and my last one at that." She said while crossing her arms. "Go ahead Conner, finish your story so this one knows the truth."

Conner looked sadly at her, but I could tell that he was hiding a little bit of rage behind his eyes. I hated watching her goad him, but I was really interested in the rest of his story.

"Fine. I watched the priestess carve her up in the street, remove her heart and burn the rest to ashes. Because she was a high-ranking member of our kind, they keep our hearts for their collection to ensure we are never brought back."

He leaned his head back and looked up at the ceiling for a moment.

"Hold on, so she could still be alive out there?" I felt a knot form in my chest at the thought of never dying. It wasn't like living, but to be there and never able to truly die was horrifying.

"Yes, and that's the worst part" Miranda said.

"Conner left her to eternal suffering where she will be unable to meet the long rest. He was a coward, and it was his job to bring you back here safely. You see how well that went. See that silver rose? It used to be red. He was one of the top dogs and now he's down here doing cleanup duty."

"Miranda!" he yelled, standing up for the first time since his story began.

"Yes, Conner?" she said with a smirk. "Or did you not tell her that it was you who was assigned to bring her back here to start with. If you hadn't hired humans to do it, Lady Reinhardt would have been here months ago, and we never would have had any of these problems with Addison."

I turned my head sharply as Conner drew his fangs with a sharp hiss. It looked like he had finally had enough of her constantly reminding him of his failures.

"Put those things away, you know you've never beaten me and that's not going to change because you're trying to defend your honor in front of the new girl."

She stepped over to me and extended her hand down to help me up.

"Besides, I was sent to retrieve her for Master." Miranda's voice carried with it the tone of victory. She had achieved what she wanted.

"What do you mean? I was supposed to-" Conner barely got half of his sentence out before Miranda cut him off.

"You've done enough, take the night off, or go for a walk or something, whatever it is, it isn't my concern." Miranda said looking at me.

"And you, let's go. They waited long enough for you to make it here."

"Of...um.. of course." I kept looking at Conner as I walked past him, following Miranda out through the door. There was a look of conflicting emotions on his face.

As we walked into the main foyer again, we turned and moved through a hallway beneath the stairs. Somewhere in the middle of it Miranda came to a halt, turning to the side at a statue of an angel with only one wing. She stepped up to it, placing her index finger on the round ruby gemstone that hung from its neck. I watched her intently as the wall behind us slid open to reveal a well-lit staircase.

"Step aside." Miranda said sharply. I felt like she really didn't like me, and I wasn't able to entirely put my finger on it. What I did know was to never trust anyone who took you in a dark basement. She stepped by me and into the passageway before turning her head back

"Come along now."

"What did I do to you?"

"Excuse me?"

"You. Obviously, you're upset with me for something, and I would at least like to know what that is."

"You're overthinking it. Let's go." She said calmly.

I shook off the hesitation and followed. Hayley had sent her to escort me and there was no reason for me to be overly nervous. It had been so long already that the more we walked, the more that nervousness grew. There were round orbs of light placed every ten feet or so that covered the stone passageway in pale light.

We kept walking for what felt like an hour. I knew I was in my head and making up a story about it. All I could think about was our first meeting. Would Hayley be happy to see me? Would they resent me for waiting so long? Or for not coming out earlier? Would they have fallen out of love with me? I had so many thoughts running through my head that I hadn't paid attention to how far we had gone. I lifted my head and looked past Miranda at the group of cloaked people that stood at the end of the hallway. There were doors on each side with giant padlocks on them.

That same feeling of panic began to build again. I was doing a lot of panicking lately, and before my anxiety had a chance to warn me to run, Miranda stopped and turned around to face me. The four others moved to the sides of her, two of them continuing forward towards me.

"You really have caused me a headache Elaine. I spent a full century licking the shoes of the butcher to get a shot at a single drop of her blood, and all I got was a secretary chair." Miranda's tone had completely changed. While it hadn't been remarkably friendly before, the hostility it now carried set off every warning signal I had.

I moved backwards as they grabbed me, pulling me back around to face her. She smiled at me as she moved forward, bringing her hands up to the sides of my face.

"You had it all handed to you, but really you should have died two hundred years ago. The humans that released you should have dropped you out in the sunlight and this could have all been avoided." She released an over exaggerated sigh, then lifted her hand swiftly before bringing it across my face with a loud **thwack**.

"But you couldn't do that, could you. You had to make my life difficult. You couldn't die when I sent those fanatic zealots after you. You couldn't die when we let the wolves know where you were. You just... couldn't die."

My mind was racing as I tried to figure out what she was talking about, but before I had a chance to ask Miranda grabbed me by the shoulders and squeezed hard enough that it felt like my collarbone would snap under her grip.

"What are you talking about?!" I winced through the pain.

She smiled with a malicious gleam in her eye and said, "I could have been the one by Hayley's side. I earned it. You did what, get lucky with who you married? Well, those days are over now; time for me to take what is rightfully mine."

I wanted to scream at her, tell her how wrong she was, but all I could manage was an angry "Shut up!"

Miranda seemed unaffected by my outburst as she dropped my shoulders and stepped back, motioning for her minions to drag me along with them as they began walking towards one of the doors. The large metal lock was removed, and I flailed in their arms enough for another one to grab my feet and lift me off the ground.

"Like they ever would have looked in the direction of someone like you. I've got a few hours before I have to deliver you to Mother Surissa. She is looking forward to meeting you finally. She never said I had to turn you over in one piece"

"SHUT UP!" I screamed in her face, my eyes widening in anger. "You don't know a single thing about Hayley. I gave them everything and I never stopped lov—!"

A sharper *SMACK* echoed through the hallway.

She wouldn't let me finish that sentence, her hand coming straight across my face again and before my head could turn one of the men behind me dug his fingers through my hair to hold my face steady. My vision was blurry as I tried to make sense of my surroundings. I quickly realized that all around me, there were six different figures, each one wearing some kind of strange armor under their cloaks. It was obvious that they weren't here to help me—they wanted to get rid of me. How had this happened.

My wrists and ankles burned as they clamped glowing cuffs lined with barely visible symbols around them. I could feel the searing pain move through my arms and legs, and I let out a cry of anguish. I had no idea what these cuffs were or what they were meant to do, but whatever it was, it was painful.

As the seconds ticked by, my confidence began to evaporate until all that was left was a hollow fear within me. The side of my faced was burning yet I managed to hold back any tears. I glared up at Miranda, the rage in my stomach intensifying, the taste of iron already filling my mouth.

Think, Elle, THINK.

Miranda seemed to sense this and smiled smugly; her arms crossed.

"You. Know. NOTHING!" She spat, her voice rising with each word. Her arm shot up and came down with a loud smack - connecting with my cheek. Again.

I felt the sting through my entire face. I wouldn't give her the satisfaction of a single tear, no matter how painful it was. I glared at her, letting the rage start to build in my stomach. Fight or flight, Elaine. Your life is literally on the line right now.

SMACK

"Nothing left to say? Nothing at all?" she cackled, dropping her head back and sending her arms out. She stood up, lifting her leg before driving it straight into my stomach. The pain from her boot sent a shock of my body, making me want to throw up. I felt like she was towering over me, her petite figure gradually taking on the shape of a monster before me.

"You think you can outrun your fate? Well, I'm here to tell you that you can't!" She screamed, her words ricocheting off the walls of the room with a sickening urgency. And then, without warning, she stepped back, balled up her right fist, and drove it straight into my stomach. I fell forward from the impact, the air knocked out of my lungs.

Miranda stepped away from me, satisfied with the shock that had been inflicted. My vision was swimming, it felt like my stomach was on fire and my mind was racing. I looked up at her in with a rebellious look in my eye. *Not yet, Elaine.*

"It's okay," she said calmly, "When Surissa gets you delivered on a silver platter, I'm sure your heart will end up locked in the archives next to Kamila's. It will be even more tasty than when Conner's unit was ambushed by the Cyborea."

I felt a chill down my spine as I tried to process her words. Her head lowered down right in front of mine. I could feel her breath on my face as she lifted my chin up and stared straight into my eyes. It was her. The entire time.

She was the reason everything had been stacked against me.

"And all Hayley will know is that you ran away, that you couldn't do it anymore… and I'll be here to pick up the pieces and earn my place at her side." She smiled gleefully before standing up and turning away from me. Her arms went out to the side, and she shook herself out before beginning to walk forward.

"With you gone and no one left, I'll be all she has left, and I'll be there to comfort her when you run away, never to return."

Miranda's laugh echoed back down the darkened corridor. I closed my eyes, hoping for a miracle. I had made it so far and was so close to being reunited with Hayley.

The hopelessness of the situation sunk down into the pit of my belly and I lowered my head in defeat. I didn't want to be locked away again, or worse, actually die this time around. I had survived being locked up, captured, experimented on, and now I made it right to the finish line for nothing.

A single tear streamed down my face, and in that moment, I had to think of something. I was running out of hope and if I didn't do something soon, I was never getting out of here. I knew I had to focus, so I closed my eyes and began thinking, trying not to resign myself to this.

Click.

I opened my eyes to darkness. Any light that had been dancing across the walls before was gone and the door at the end of the hallway had closed.

"ha… ha… ha ha haahahaha…."

The eerie laughter floated on the air that moved through the hallway, making it difficult to place its source. I closed my eyes again, trying to focus on the source of the sound.

Click.

Hayley's voice echoed through the hallways, and I felt a wave of relief wash over me. They were here with me, and I wasn't alone anymore. I lifted my head slightly to look at Miranda, who had stepped away from me at the sound of Hayley's voice. The guards had moved away, hesitant to draw their weapons as their backs hit the walls.

"Master Reinhardt?" she said hesitantly.

"Step away, Miranda," they said firmly, and she complied without saying a word. The lights had come on brighter than before, and it illuminated Hayley standing in the doorway. Their bright red eyes were stained from the rage that currently overtook them, obviously as affected by this situation as much as I was. Strange tattoos that I had never seen before swirled across their hands like carefully designed gloves.

I tried to muster a smile for them but failed miserably. Instead, my face crumpled in sadness and tears began streaming down my cheeks once again.

"Elaine…" Hayley blurred across the room, the shadows almost moving out of their way without hesitation and wrapped their arms around me tightly. As they pulled me into their embrace and held me close to their chest, all of the fear and stress melted out of me, and I allowed everything to come out. All of the pain was there on display.

I watched their eyes move to the chains that bound me to the floor and wall. Their heartbeat slowed down, and their breath grew heavy. There was no way they could get them off of me without damaging themselves.

They held me in their arms, rubbing their hands through my hair while I cried, until Hayley managed to whisper something in my ear.

"I'm here. No one will ever hurt you again." The assurance in their voice was enough for me to believe that everything would turn out just fine because they were here with me now.

"You…" Their voice was crisp and sharp. Their body was shaking with rage, every pulse of it moving into me.

"Master! This isn't what it looks like, this person is trying to trick you! They aren't real! It's all a lie!"

I watched as their hand moved slowly toward my face, their fingers brushing lightly against my cheek. I shuddered at their touch, my body tensing at the thought of what might come next.

"Every scratch, every piece of hair missing, every bruise or bump you have inflicted," they whispered. "I will pay for with your flesh."

My stomach tightened with fear as their voice echoed in the

hollow prison chamber, not fear for me, but for the seven of them. Every part of my body was frozen in place, unable to turn away or look away from the figure that now stood before me. I held my breath, not knowing what might happen next. The black swirls on their hand expanded into shadows tinged with blood, slowly taking shape into black armored gauntlets that felt like an endless abyss of night had formed. Was that Hayley's midnight brand?

A cacophony of metallic echoes filled the dimly lit chamber as Miranda's vampire guards hastily unsheathed their weapons, their eyes wide with shock and fear.

They had been caught red-handed torturing me. The harder I fought to get out of these chains, the worse I could feel the pain moving up my body. The chains that sizzled across my skin glowed a little bit brighter as they turned a sickly purple, their ethereal aura illuminating the deep pain etched across my face.

"The Keys!" Hayley roared, their voice reverberating off the walls with thunderous authority. The guards exchanged nervous glances, their hands trembling on the hilts of their swords. It was evident that they knew the severity of their mistake - betraying their leader was a crime punishable by death.

"Move aside, Hayley," hissed Miranda from the side of the room, her presence barely noticeable as she tried to escape. Her hair was slick with sweat, and her red eyes darted between Hayley and I, calculating the odds of her survival.

"This isn't what it looks like. I can explain everything."

"What it looks like?" Hayley snarled, incredulous at her audacity. "That is my wife you have chained down. Like an animal. "

"Elaine should have known better than to come here," Miranda yelled back. "She should have died last year when those humans fucked up leaving her outside in the sun. This never would have happened!"

"Enough!" bellowed Hayley, their roar filling the room. They could no longer stomach the vile words and deeds of these traitorous guards. I knew their rage threatened to consume them, to transform them into something darker and more powerful. But despite that anger, they had an outlet right in front of them. I had never seen them this mad before.

As if sensing Hayley's emotions, three of the six guards lunged forward, their blades raised high. In a blur of motion, Hayley's gauntlets hardened more, the edges flattening into sharp blades, their surface shimmering like obsidian. The guards' futile strikes met only the impenetrable armor of their transformed fists.

"Is this what you truly desire?" Hayley asked, their voice barely audible over the clash of metal and my cries of pain from the chains. "To die for Miranda?"

"You don't understand!!" one of the guards spat, his face contorted with rage. He and the others continued their assault, but Hayley deflected each blow effortlessly, their gauntlets like an extension of her own flesh and blood. "You betrayed us when you chose her over your people!"

As Hayley fought, I watched every graceful movement they made. It was an artform born of fury, and this room was their canvas. I could feel their pain as if it were my own.

"Please…Hayley… hurry" I whimpered, tears streaming down my face as my body trembled from the torment. My eyes locked onto Hayley's, begging for release from the pain. The sound of blades slicing through the air was louder than any thunder and more frightening than any lightning strike. No matter how hard I tried to shut my eyes, the sight of the guards' blades gleaming against the flickering torches stuck in my mind like a painting.

"Enough." Hayley's voice was a growl, a promise of swift retribution. With a final sweep of their gauntlets, she sent the last of her attackers crashing into the stone walls, their weapons clattering to the floor. Of the original three, only one was in any shape to even stand up.

"Let her go," she commanded, her voice shaking with fury and desperation. "And accept your punishment."

The remaining guards hesitated, their eyes flicking between Hayley's menacing form and my fragile figure. In that moment, they knew they were witnessing the full breadth of the Butcher's wrath and devotion to their wife, and they quivered beneath the weight of it all. The panic driven woman that had been furiously searching for someone had disappeared, and what stood before them was a conqueror among their kind.

The Butcher of Fort Mill. The Conqueror of Whitehall. The Hero of Partenkirchen. The Vampire Commander who ended the War of the Father. There were so many names, so many titles.

And all of them were on display.

The remaining guards exchanged wary glances before lunging at Hayley with renewed determination, their faces twisted with a mix of fear and desperation. They knew that they had crossed a line, and now the only way to survive was to fight through Hayley and escape.

"Your love for her will be your downfall," Miranda snarled as one of the guards swung his blade at Hayley's head.

Hayley dodged the blow effortlessly and retaliated with a powerful punch from her gauntleted hand, sending him crashing into the ceiling, his ribs shattering from the impact.

"You are wrong," they hissed, red eyes burning with conviction. "It is my source of strength."

As Hayley engaged in the fierce battle, Miranda slipped unnoticed from the shadows, her gaze locked on me. The treacherous vampire had been sabotaging Hayley for the past year in hopes of taking my place by her side. She harbored an intense jealousy towards the woman who held Hayley's heart and was determined to eliminate me once and for all.

"Look what your precious Hayley has done to me," Miranda whispered venomously into my ear while pressing a dagger against my throat. "She's too blinded by her love to see the truth. You're a liability. A weakness "

"Miranda, stop this madness!" Conner pleaded from the doorway as he arrived. His eyes widened with horror as he stepped forward, hands outstretched. "Killing Elaine won't change anything!"

"Stay out of it, Conner!" Miranda snapped, tightening her grip on the dagger. "This doesn't concern you."

"Please... don't..." I gasped; my voice barely audible as I struggled against the magical chains that continued to pull my strength away. I could barely keep my eyes open.

Hayley was a force to be reckoned with. Their movements were a graceful blur, their stance one of determination and strength that had been carefully forged over centuries of conquest and warfare. They had already taken down four of the guards and wasn't done yet. Meanwhile, the remaining guards were trying their best to contain them, their swords clashing against her shadow-plated gauntlets as they were relentlessly pursued by the woman they had sworn allegiance to.

The guards could sense that something was amiss but couldn't afford to let their attention waver or risk exposing themselves to a fatal blow. Hayley was too quick for them, her reflexes honed from years of a punishing training regime. They twisted their body, catching one of the guard's blades within their obsidian fingertips. A quick flex of their muscular arms and the sword shattered, the other gauntlet coming up as it latched onto his face and smashed his skull into the stony wall behind him. The room reverberated with a dull thud, the sound of metal colliding with stone. The guard sank to the ground, unmoving.

Hayley didn't pause, instead turning her attention to the final two guards who had backed themselves into a corner. They picked one, and he could only watch in terror as this indomitable woman advanced towards him, their eyes blazing through the darkness. He had no chance of escape or victory, his eyes wide with fear as he held his sword in a trembling hand.

"Your fight is with me, not her!" Hayley roared at the guards. "Leave her alone!"

"Then let us go!" one guard shouted back; his eyes wide with terror as he desperately tried to fend off Hayley's onslaught. Every strike became faster, stronger, more damaging to them.

"Never," she spat, their heart pounding with adrenaline and fear for my safety.

In that moment, Hayley knew what they had to do. Their blood exploded throughout their body, and they blurred through the shadows of the room. When they reappeared, they stood there, a head of black matted hair wrapped around their blackened fingertips. Haley would not allow their love to be used against them any longer. With that final surge of strength, she had cleanly relieved him of his head. The flickering torchlight cast dancing shadows across the prison walls, painting a haunting tapestry of a blood sprayed nightmare.

The final guard turned to run, a blade swiping across his neck from Conner. He kicked the body to the side before his head hit the ground, and with a simple nod, Hayley turned to face me again.

"Elaine, hold on!" Hayley cried, her voice tinged with desperation as they sprinted towards her me, hoping against hope that they could save her from Miranda's deadly grasp.

Hayley's footsteps thundered against the cold stone floor as they closed the distance between herself and Miranda. My heart raced, threatening to burst from my chest, but I refused to let fear take control.

"Let her go, Miranda," Hayley growled, her black gauntlets shimmering with an ominous aura.

"Or what?" Miranda sneered, pressing the dagger closer to my throat. I could feel the thin blade slice through the delicate skin on my neck.

"You'll kill me? Just like you've killed so many others?"

"Stop it!" I wheezed, my breath coming in shallow gasps as the magical chains continued to sap my strength. "Hayley, don't listen to her!"

"Elaine, my love, I won't let her hurt you," Hayley vowed, their eyes never leaving Miranda. They took a slow, measured breath, allowing their thoughts to drift back to their first date – the tenderness of my touch, the warmth of my smile. It was that love and that connection, which gave them the resolve to see this through.

"Miranda, you've always wanted to know how I could do it. How I so easily buried our kind." Hayley's voice was low and controlled, each word carefully chosen. "I am not a hero that fights for justice, for what is right. I'm not a villain that wanted power and control. Everything I built was for her. Everything."

"You're a fool, Hayley." Miranda spat, her grip on the dagger tightening. "You've always been a fool."

"Perhaps," Hayley conceded, her gaze unwavering. "But I know one thing for certain: your jealousy and desire for power have consumed you, and you've betrayed everything you once stood for. I, however, will show you what vengeance looks like. You want me to be the villain in your story? So be it... "

"Enough of this!" Miranda snarled, pulling me closer. "If you want to save her, then let me walk out that door."

"Never going to happen." Hayley's voice was barely a whisper, their gauntlets pulsing with dark energy. I could feel the coldness of them from here.

"You've already lost." I looked at Hayley with a smile, then bit my lip and slammed my head backwards. I could feel the connection with her nose as she dug the knife into my neck. I felt my eyes close, confident in knowing they wouldn't make it in time. A smile crossed my face, and I hoped the last thing they saw of me would be my smile.

Hayley lunged forward, moving with supernatural speed, and seized Miranda's wrist, pulling it away before the blade went all the way in. The force of her grip crushed her bones, forcing the dagger to clatter to the ground. I crumpled to my knees, finally free from Miranda's grasp. Blood poured down my neck, adding to the horrible state I was in.

"Elaine, I love you," Hayley whispered, her heart aching as she watched her wife struggle for breath. She turned back to Miranda, the rage building within her like a storm. "And for that reason, I will never allow someone like you to harm her again. Every vampire who dares to touch you will seek their eternal rest. "

I watched their fingertips wrap around the sides of her head, Hayley's palm crossing Miranda's face. Miranda screamed at the pressure that they were inflicting, and right before her skull began to buckle under the pressure Hayley struck, driving her other hand straight into her chest and through her assistants back. A spray of warm blood, Miranda's blood, covered the front of my body. They released Miranda's lifeless body, allowing it to slump to the ground with a sickening thud next to me. I stared at her in disbelief, as if I had just witnessed a miracle.

"How?" I whispered, the bloody tears streaming down my face as I tried to comprehend what had just happened. The last minute was a blur, and there were bodies everywhere.

"It *doesn't* matter," Hayley said quietly. "All that matters is that you're safe."

They pulled me close and breathed in the scent of my hair, savoring every moment of our embrace.

"Admiring a hero is easy," Hayley murmured, her gaze locked on Miranda's lifeless form. "But understanding a villain… that requires acknowledging the darkness that stares back at us. I'll make your next wedding ring out of her bones as a reminder to anyone that thinks about touching you."

"Let's go *home*, Elaine," they said softly, offering a hand to help me rise. Conner rushed to my side; his hands covered in blood from searching the bodies for the keys. He unlocked the shackles, revealing the charred skin underneath. Conner tried to help me up, my body recoiling in remnant of panic and fear.

I was barely able to stand before I fell to my knees, my breath going heavy as I opened my eyes. The floor was slick, and I lifted my hands up to my face to stare at them. There was warm blood on my fingertips that forced me to sit back on my heels in my own form of shock. It was everywhere. I didn't know who's body it came from, or how it was still warm. But it covered me, every drop of the red a strain on the room around me.

Hayley's long, armored fingers balled into a fist before Miranda's body was kicked to the side. The force of it hitting the wall was apparent from the number of cracking bones that resulted from the impact. I looked around the figure in front of me and at the two closest people that were on the ground, their heads completely removed from their bodies. I stared at them for a moment, watching wave after wave of fresh blood creep across the floor.

"Elle… Ellie. Babe." Their voice was quiet, and without questioning anything my body jerked forward as I wrapped my arms around them. The tears poured across my face and down onto their clothes. I felt both of their arms come down around me, and I felt our breaths slowly syncing together. For what felt like an eternity, we stood there, holding each other tightly, until all of the stress and the sadness started to fade away.

"It's okay.. we're okay.. we're together now…"

Hayley lifted me up after prying me from the ground. Fortunately for them, they knew I was a clingy hugger and I immediately wrapped myself around them again. Their arms, albeit cold, brought warmth to my chest. After everything that had happened those hundreds of years ago, I was home again.

"I'm sorry Hayley. I'm so, so, so sorry" I murmured and cried through the tears. One of their hands came behind my legs as they scooped me up.

"I'll never leave you again. I'm so sorry."

"Quiet, you've been through enough." Hayley whispered in my ear.

"None of it matters anymore. You're home."

Hayley rubbed the back of my head while I cried in their arms. I had been on the run and trying to figure an entire world out by myself. They leaned back away from me, bringing their lips down onto mine. It was the first time we had kissed since twenty twenty-one. I felt my body melting into theirs, my arms reaching up to wrap around their shoulders. They didn't pull back for several breaths, and when they did it was just for another breath, and they did it again.

I had dreamed of kissing them for what seemed like a million times while I was locked away. I took a step back and looked at them. They were wearing all black, with a deep gray overcoat that ended right above their shiny oxblood boots.

"You left me there." I snapped at them over the tears. The frustration I felt at going through, in my mind, every horrible thing possible was enough to bring me to more tears.

"I was locked up in the dark. By myself. It was so, so long. Like forever long."

"Babe, I would never leave you there. I sent people to bring you to me, and they failed." They looked to the side, right at Miranda's body, then sat me back down.

"I had someone close to me sabotaging me every step of the way. I never stopped looking for you."

"You stopped coming to see me. I was trapped there alone for so long," I said while trying to keep it together. I felt the tears coming on again as I stepped towards them, throwing both of my fists into their chest.

"I thought you had abandoned me and didn't love me anymore and you found something or someone else and moved on and I was just going to-"

Their hand covered my mouth, cutting me off. I stared straight at them while everything between us was silent. Their eyes were soft and filled with sadness. I could feel in my bones that they had missed me just as much.

"Look." Hayley said, lifting their armored hand up in front of me. The shiny black gauntlet disappeared in a rush of smoke, the tattoos reforming on their hands. In the center of their ring finger was a single silvery band with glistening rubies. It was their wedding ring, right where I had put it. They had never taken it off. I kept my eyes on it while staring at the ring intently, immediately thinking about where mine had gone.

"I'm sorry... Addison took my rings when he had me on the table." I said with a low, sad voice. I remembered crying as he pried them off my finger weeks ago. If I ever had the chance to get them back, I would.

"Then I'll just have to propose all over again, my love." Hayley said, bringing her hand up to the side of my face as she wiped away the thin stream of blood-filled tears.

"And this time, it is forever."

Cough.

We both looked over to the side at Miranda's body. There was a deep, dark wound in the side of her chest where blood was continuing to slowly pulse out. A thin stream of the red liquid leaked from the corner of her mouth, her eyes gazing up at the two of us. She coughed again, choking on her own blood.

"Conner."

He moved from somewhere behind me before coming to a knee next to Hayley. I had to tell him everything.

"Yes, Lord Reinhardt" he said, looking over at Miranda.

"Clean this mess up. If she's still breathing in the morning, hang her outside." Hayley said, turning towards me. Their body dipped down, scooping me up off my feet again.

"I want everyone to know what happens when you touch my wife."

The Lovers

REFLECTIONS

"The darkness runs deeper than we ever could have imagined.
Rumors will drift among us, whispers in the nightly wind. It is up to
you to follow your conviction. Tread carefully, Acolyte. These
whispers are their weapon."
Father Gabriel, Adeptus Oryx, Holy Codex ii

CHAPTER 11

I opened my eyes and looked up at the ceiling. The rose gold ceiling tiles were all in order, except for one that was turned ninety degrees. How that single out of place thing managed to get my attention reminded me of how obsessive I was about clean straight lines in our home. A light, carefree yawn pushed its way through my pale pink lips as I pulled the sheets tighter up around my body and rolled over.

Sunlight was seeping its way in through the blinds, bright reds and oranges dancing across the walls to let me know the sun was finally setting. I blinked a few times while getting my bearings before looking around the room. Another yawn broke the silence while I stretched completely out, taking up as much space as I could in the oversized bed. As my head rolled to the side, my eyes wandered curiously around the room. There was a candle lit on the table that sat between a pair of blue velvet chairs. It smelled of sandalwood and rose, my favorite. I immediately knew it was their doing.

Knock. *Knock.*

"Lady Reinhardt, have you awoken?" a soft, light voice floated from a crack in the door. I smiled at the gentleness that it carried. But Lady? Hayley had always joked with me that I was some medieval lady in a past life. What irony that I would become one through the nobility of the night.

"Good morning." I replied with a smile while sitting up. Sighing, I looked down at my arms only to notice that the bruises were almost gone. My nails were almost back to normal although I wouldn't complain about a manicure right now. There were still tiny specks of dark red from where I had been stabbed with needles. Goosebumps slowly started to creep down my arms as I thought about it, and for a moment I had to hold back a panic attack.

"I'm happy to see you awake, Lady Reinhardt." A young woman said as she strolled quickly across the room to the curtains. The sun between them was splashed with orange and purple waves, a perfect sunset in my book. I watched her throw open the blinds, her small frame holding far more strength than expected at first look.

"You're probably starving, right?" she said with a smile.

"Well, I wouldn't say I'm starving" I said. My body, however, betrayed me with a loud rumble from my stomach. I groaned while falling backwards into the blankets with a groan.

"Yes. Food. Where's Hayley?" I was a bit concerned since she wasn't here when I woke up. I tried to not look concerned and wanted to come off like I had some idea of, well, anything really.

"My apologies, Lord Reinhardt wanted to stay but they had a few things to take care of. You've been asleep for thirteen days." she said apologetically.

"WHAT!?!" I screamed and vaulted out of the bed. Thirteen days? No wonder I looked like a complete mess. I paced by the side of the bed in a panic. "Clothes, where are my clothes? And I'm sorry, who are you?"

I had been rather rude to her. I didn't even stop to ask her name. She didn't look like a housekeeper. Even that was rude of me to assume.

"Please breathe and have a seat. I'll explain everything," she replied as I fell back down onto the bed. My adrenaline was already kicking back up again. "My name is Jules, and I'm your assistant. Your clothes were, by all accounts, a disaster so we discarded them.

Lord Reinhardt dropped off new clothes which you can find in the closet."

She looked at me up and down for a moment before coming and reaching her hand out towards me.

"Now, I'm sure you would like a hot shower and some fresh clothes. Let me assist you, Lady Reinhardt" she sounded sincere, and her smile was without a flicker of hostility. I looked at her hand for a moment before finally taking it, smiling back at her as she helped me out of the bed. She wore a pair of black capris, bright green flats, and a loose blouse that had a black bow folded neatly at the top. I was hesitant to accept any help and had quite a few trust issues right now.

"I appreciate the help, but I don't need an escort. Does Hayley think I need a bodyguard or something?" I forced a lighthearted laugh as I walked towards the large armoire.

"You mistake my presence, Lady Reinhardt." She bowed slightly, her tone changing as she continued. "I serve your maker, Master Ireena Vasiliev, the crimson countess. She assigned me to you."

Her tone carried with it obvious pride. I, however, had no idea who my maker was. I thought it was Hayley. Wanting to get my facts straight, I pulled the large wooden doors open to look inside at what clothes Hayley had brought me.

"Lady Ireena? I've never heard of her." I pulled a sundress and cardigan out of the oversized armoire. Its main bar was filled with sundresses, gowns, and casual wear dresses. They knew my style perfectly. "Hayley left me her blood, they're the one that turned me."

Jules stood there while watching me with a smile. Although her gaze had changed, her tone stayed light yet direct.

"You are brand new to our kind, and it's rather unfortunate that you weren't delivered here. Lady Ireena came here just for you. I kind of felt bad for Lord Reinhardt, but what can you do?" she said with a lighthearted shrug. "Hayley took a gift that-"

"That's enough, Julia."

A voice that carried with it a cold, deep iciness that sent a shiver up my spine filled the space between us. I looked at the door while Jules dropped to a knee. There was a woman I had never seen in person before standing in the doorway, and behind her, Hayley. They looked at me with a gentle smile, tears starting to form.

"Were you going to sleep all month, child"

"I'm sorry, I was just... tired? I don't know, when you go through as much trauma as I just did, I'm surprise it wasn't longer." I snapped into business mode and tried to defend myself. The woman was ethereally beautiful.

She wore a silver dress with black embroidery down the middle of it, with barely anything covering her chest. By all accounts, she was one of the most beautiful people I had ever seen in existence. A beauty that you only read about but isn't really real. Her facial features looked Slavic in nature, and there was something about her presence that felt warm, but suffocating.

"Trauma, my dear sweet child. You should have tried surviving through the first crusade." She floated over to me, and without even knowing what happened my body went down to a knee. I recognized her voice

"Hayley, this is your wife? I am honestly surprised, not what I expected at all."

She looked me over several times before I felt arms around me, picking me up. I looked at Hayley, wrapping my arms around her.

"A love that lasted through death, rebirth, and the last few months. Hayley, you made a mistake, and she fought for you. To come back to you." She looked over at me.

"You fought hard, you survived, and you made it back. That much tenacity, you must be of my blood."

I held Hayley in my arms while smiling at Lady Ireena. Hayley whispered in my ear, gently pulling my hair back.

"This is our master, the Crimson Countess of the blood court, and our maker." They said, taking my hand in theirs before bowing. "We greet you, master, blood of our blood and lord of night."

"Enough with the flattery. Make sure she is properly dressed. We will not be returning to Vienna for her ceremony." Ireena said, looking at me again with a smile.

"I have called for a gathering of the Crimson Court. They can come to me this time."

I had little time to ask questions before she turned and left. I looked at Hayley, barely having a moment to breathe before she plowed into me. Her arms wrapped around me, and her lips met mine again. I pulled away, skeptical of everything again. I had been through so much; how could I be sure any of this was real?

"How do I know this is real. What if I'm strapped in that lab still and you're just poking around in my head?" Hayley stopped her approach and looked at me, partly in anxiety and shock.

"Love, it's me. Really." She replied hesitantly. I could tell there was some pain in her eyes as I questioned her.

"Okay, where was our first date?" I asked, crossing my arms. I could still feel a sharp pain in my shoulder from where that werewolf had broken it.

"Our first date was the zoo. We went to see the opening of the bat exhibit that evening and did a late-night dinner in Georgetown." Hayley replied. Everything she said was accurate.

"What is my phone number?" I wanted to increase the difficulty of the questions a bit. There would only be one person alive that had that information, and Hayley had to know it.

She walked over to a small desk near the window and picked up a pen. I watched her, carefully as she scribbled something down and walked over to me. She extended her hand, giving me a piece of paper that had numbers all over it.

"You said it was bad security practice to say your phone number out loud, so I wrote it down for you."

I looked at the numbers on the paper, a perfect match to what they had been. Even her sarcasm at something I used to say was dead on. There was no way this could be made up.

"Hayley… it's really you…" The tears began to fall again as I ran over to her, leaping into her chest.

"No shit, who else would I be?" she laughed, catching me before she put me back down.

"Now, go get a proper shower, we will catch up after. Julia, please take care of her for me."

"You're not staying here?" I asked, upset that I might be away from her for more than twenty minutes.

She looked at Jules, then back to my sad face again. The longer she stared, the sadder I tried to look. I wasn't very good at it since all I had been was sad, so intentionally trying to when I was honestly exploding with happiness inside was difficult. Hayley wrapped her arms around me and planted a soft kiss on my forehead.

"If I stay here, who will make you breakfast? I want to do it myself, your first proper one."

"Fair. I'll come and join you as soon as I'm done."

I looked at Jules with a smile and strolled into the large bathroom. The walls were painted black with a silver flower pattern running across them. There was a giant porcelain bathtub, but I ignored it and stepped towards the shower. While half of it was beautiful stonework, the other half of it was smoked glass. Two showerheads were built into the ceiling, just the way I liked it.

I stood before the glass shower door, hesitating. In the last two centuries I had only felt the warmth of water cascading over my skin once. The memory of my last real shower in our home still lingered in my mind, a relic of a time long gone. I would never forget it, as we would regularly shower together.

My reflection in the bathroom mirror was something of a mess. I could barely tell that part of me was still there, staring back at me. Hayley had often referred to me as a timeless beauty, my chocolate-black hair cascading down my neck back, my almost porcelain skin translucent in the bright bathroom light. I smiled at myself, hoping, yearning, wishing for everything to be over. But beneath the surface, I carried the weight of centuries, each year adding to my loneliness and detachment from humanity. I didn't know the first thing about the world, other than the simple fact that it was just as barbaric as it had been.

With a sigh, I turned the crystal doorknob, and the room was bathed in the soft glow of electric lights. I gazed at the modern shower, with its sleek glass enclosure and numerous knobs. The sight was both fascinating and intimidating. How had things changed so much in my absence?

I took a deep breath and stepped into the shower's giant entrance, my fingers trembling as I adjusted the water temperature. The rush of water against my skin felt almost foreign yet oddly comforting. It reminded me of the rain I had frequently danced in as a mortal, a simple pleasure I had long forgotten.

Jules stepped into the shower behind me, helping me to slowly remove my gown. I would have been fine letting it fall to the floor in a cascade of fabric, but she quickly caught it and hung it up on a hook next to the door. The light reflected from the mirror and I could see through the misty glass a reflection that showed scars and faint bruises, remnants of battles and close calls I had experienced over the last week.

I reached for the bar of soap; its scent unfamiliar but pleasing. As I lathered it between my hands, I closed my eyes and allowed the sensation of the soap on my skin to wash away some of my emotional scars. I scrubbed, not just to cleanse my body but to cleanse my soul.

The damage I had done to people I barely knew, the frustration I gave to a master I didn't know I had, and the worry I gave to Hayley, were far too much to bear.

The water continued to pour over me, a cleansing torrent that seemed to wash away the weight of time. I lingered in the shower, savoring every moment, every drop that fell across my body. It was a simple act, but it brought me closer to the world I had once been a part of.

A streak of watered-down red came down my face, leaving dots of bright red on the tile beneath me. Jules stepped out of the bathroom, giving me a few minutes to myself while I cried tears of both frustration and happiness. The overwhelming sense of freedom I felt right now was enough to exhaust me all over again. I grabbed a bottle of white liquid and squeezed it straight onto my head. How much did I use? I didn't care.

I scrubbed my hands through my hair for several minutes, rinsed, and then did it all over again. After washing it four times, I shook it out, running my hands through what finally felt like a clean head. Even as the water started to turn cold, I cranked it all the way to the highest heat setting it would go and stood there letting the water move across my body.

As I emerged from the shower, Jules was there and ready to wrap me in a fluffy towel. In some small way, I almost felt reborn. I had experienced a moment of vulnerability and renewal, a reminder of my humanity that had long been buried beneath the veneer of immortality.

I knew that my existence as a vampire would continue, and my path would remain one of shadows and solitude with a few select people. But for a brief moment, in the warm embrace of the shower, I had found a connection to my past and the simple pleasures of being human again.

"Please follow me, Lady Reinhardt." Jules said as she opened the bathroom door. I followed her over to a dressing table that had various brushes and bottles on it. There was an oval mirror hung on the wall behind it, covering most of the table's space. I sat down the moment she pulled the chair out, slumping down in it.

"Straighten your back." She quipped, causing me to sit straight up. A light throb came from my shoulder, my head dropping to the side while I tried to stretch it out.

I watched her pick up a brush and step behind me. The familiar feeling of someone pulling something through my hair felt amazing, and painful at the same time. There had been cakes knots of blood that had to be cut out, and after the long shower, I could start taking care of it again. She would grab a section of my hair and rapidly brush small areas, working from the bottom up.

The more I looked at my reflection, the more upset I was at having short hair. It hadn't been this short since my parents abandoned me at an all-girls boarding school.

"Jules, tell me your story. What led you to serving our-"

"Yours." She said, cutting me off.

"Sorry, my master." I finished awkwardly.

"I have been in the service of Lady Vasiliev since the seventeenth century. I had only been turned for twenty or so years and was still coming in and out with my family. I had a daughter I would check in on, a husband that grew old and blind, and grandchildren that I wished to protect.

During those cold and eerie nights, I was careless and was discovered. Religious zealots roamed the land, fervently hunting down those they believed to be creatures of the devil. Among their targets were our kind, the vampires who walked the night, creatures of the darkness who had long held a secret existence. They weren't actually looking for us, but a local wolf pack and I was just a bonus."

Jules moved to the other side, parting my hair, and starting on another section of it.

"I had alluded hunters for as long as I could. When they discovered me, I ran at full speed from the village. I had no formal master, he abandoned me after turning me and left me to learn myself. The strength of our blood was something that I had never unlocked. So, I ran."

"What happened? Did you run into her?"

"Not exactly. I was hunted until I could run no more, and I cried out for help. Lady Ireena sensed me. Following the sound, she discovered me, barely more than a fledgling, cowering in the shadows. I was trembling and terrified more than anything."

"You're really five hundred years old? I really am a child." I laughed lightheartedly.

"Yes, you are."

"RUDE." I huffed, crossing my arms in protest.

"Quit moving. The distant chants of the zealots drew nearer, their torches flickering in the darkness of the forest. I was panicking and without hesitation, she extended a hand to me and said- "Quiet your fear, young one. I shall protect you." The zealots, fueled by religious fervor and ignorance, charged from the underbrush with crosses and wooden stakes in hand. There were almost fifteen men. I watched Lady Vasiliev's eyes turn bright red, and she tore into them with a swift and deadly grace that I had never witnessed before."

I watched Jules reflection smile in the mirror as she continued her story.

"She moved like a shadow, her movements too swift for them to follow. The zealots were no match for her supernatural strength and agility..."

Jules took a deep breath and sighed out.

"She took pity on me and brought me with her. I became one of her attendants, then one of her guards. After Hayley was turned, I was charged with being her attendant, and when you returned,"

"You got handed off to me." I said snarkily.

"I'm sorry."

"Don't apologize, it is my honor to accept the orders of the lady of house Vasiliev. She's famous, you know. And she trusts me to take care of you, and Hayley trusts me to take care of you. I'm sorry I wasn't there to get you earlier."

I let my shoulders relax and slid down in the chair. Jules pulled my hair sharply, forcing me to jerk back up.

She stepped around me, examining her work carefully. While I appreciated her attention to detail, I felt it unnecessary to spend so much time on just my hair. She turned and walked over to another cabinet, pulled out what I assumed was some form of hair dryer, and returned. It didn't have a cord, so I assumed it had some sort of battery inside. I had never seen a wireless hair dryer before and was honestly fascinated by it.

"Are you incapable of sitting still?" she said, her voice maintaining that sternness. She clicked a button on it and hot air blew out of the flat end. She brushed through my hair, drying it as she went. The entire process only took a few minutes, and not only did I look like a normal human being again, but it felt like I had a blowout. I smiled in the mirror, enjoying looking a little more at myself.

"Do you know which dress you will wear for breakfast?" Jules asked.

I turned my head excitedly towards the closet. I had real clothes that were mine again. While I would miss that oversized sweater, I knew I could replace it.

"Can I wear one for breakfast, then another one after?"

"That seems wasteful, but of course. You can wear whatever you want."

My body moved faster than I expected it to as I launched myself over to the closet again. I already knew which one I was going to wear for breakfast and had been thinking about it while in the shower. I ripped the doors open and dove into the soft clothes that hung up inside, pulling out a knee length black dress, a navy cardigan with white accents and a pair of ankle boots.

"Take your time getting dressed, I'll be outside when you are… um… ready." Jules stepped over to the door and looked at me. Her gaze looked, odd. That's when I realized my robe was completely open. I snatched it shut, my cheeks turning red with embarrassment.

She stepped out of the room, and I fell onto the giant bed again. I laid there for several moments, laughing at the awkwardness before I closed my eyes and rolled myself up. "Clothes." I said, trying to take myself seriously. All the stress of the last few weeks felt like it melted away.

I walked over to a long, cherry oak dresser that was topped with a black and red lace runner. A bowl held a new pair of ruby earrings, a matching necklace, and a small jar of jewelry cleaner. I looked at my where my wedding ring used to be, and sadness slowly welled up inside me. I hadn't taken it off a single time after we were married. Not even to clean it.

I felt resentment towards myself for not taking better care of it. For getting captured all together. For losing it. Everything that had happened to me, all of it felt like I had done something to deserve it. Had I not been stubborn, we could have been together for the last two hundred years, but I had to be spiteful.

I opened the top drawer and pulled out a matching set of vermillion colored lace underwear. At least lace never went out of fashion. Sliding them comfortably across my cold skin, I pulled them up around my waist with a smile. Much better, I thought to myself.

My stomach growled as I slipped the dress over my head and pulled it down across my waist. I lifted my hair up and out the back of it, shaking my head out and letting it fall over the cardigan I slid up my arms. I took another look in the mirror, admiring myself for a moment.

"There you are."

The sound of my stomach growing in frustration at me wasting time took over.

"Alright, alright…Let's get some breakfast."

I hopped over to the bedroom door, a robe hanging on the back of it with two letters embroidered into the collar. A bright white E.R. that overlapped in a fancy script I was unfamiliar with stood out against the black color of the robe. I ran my fingers across it with a relieving sigh. Hayley really did take care of everything for me, and that same feeling of disappointment in myself returned. I looked down the robe, bringing my gaze to a pair of leather Birkenstocks next to the door.

Chocolate brown with rose gold buckles, just like they always had been. They were the same ones that I had got on our second date after they told me I needed new shoes. We used to joke about my tiger stripes in the summer, dark brown tan lines that I would get on my feet from being in the sun too long. After the first few weeks of summer, those familiar tan strips from the sandals would be there and stay there until at least mid-winter. While I was sad at the thought of never getting a tan again, at least I didn't have to worry about skin cancer.

Now that I was fully clothed and ready to go, I stepped outside my bedroom and into the large hall. A soft reading chair was across from the door, currently playing host to Jules who had a book in her hands. Without even looking at me, Jules raised an eyebrow as if I had inconvenienced her by taking longer to properly prepare myself than she had expected.

"Well, are you finally ready to eat?" she said without looking at me.

"Yes. Would you mind showing me where-" I barely made it through a sentence before she cut me off. Maybe I was actually frustrating her at this point.

"Of course, you've never been here before so I wouldn't expect you to know where anything is." Jules stood up, closing her book with a tight snap. Her tone was direct and without any inflection of emotion.

"Forgive me for asking, but did I do something to irritate you?" I wondered when in the last hour I had slighted her. Maybe I had and hadn't noticed. Either way, if there was going to be any bad blood between us, I'd prefer to remediate it now rather than later.

"Honestly, no. I prefer promptness and this estate is efficiently run. While we are fully accepting of your presence here, Lady Reinhardt, there are a few things that you are unaware of. Disrupting that can be a challenge for some, myself included. That is all. I would never over-step the boundary of my master and feel any ill feelings towards her progeny."

"I'll try to be better, sorry." I said honestly. Thinking back, Hayley was always the one of us that was on time. There had been many dinners and events where I had joked about being on lesbian time and was always five minutes late. The ability to be on time for something, well, anything seemed to elude me.

"Very well, forgiven. Now, let's not keep Lord Reinhardt waiting."

She turned and walked past me, heading down a stone corridor. There were paintings every few feet, and the stonework on the floor was beautifully inlaid even though it was covered with a long black carpet. As we approached the end of the hallway it opened into a large, expansive room that finally looked familiar to me. The main doors were almost thirty feet below, across from the stairs. A smile formed across my face, and I hurried down the stairs behind her, taking a different look at anything that caught my eye every other step.

The chandeliers glowed with soft flickering light that cast the perfect number of dancing shadows across the grand foyer. I twirled on the last step, hopping down onto my feet with happiness. My head leaned back as far as it could go while I gazed up at the dangling swaying crystals that hung in streamers above. I stopped as we walked under them in another circle so that I could take an extra moment to enjoy the tiny rainbows flickering across their surface with each movement.

We walked down a much wider opening underneath the steps that was lined with bookcases on both sides. Every inch of the shelves was covered with stacks of books that looked as if they hadn't been moved in years. I half expected some of them to be covered in dust, but there wasn't a single piece of it to be found. Part of me wanted to pick one up off the shelf but I wasn't sure if this was a display, or a functional library that Hayley used. Their method of madness when it came to organizing their library was something that I was not about to mess up.

We had a heated debate over book organization long ago, and while I preferred them to be alphabetical, they had declared that the only way was to do it by content type and that anything other than that was blasphemy to the book gods.

"Here you are, Lady Reinhardt." Jules said as she stopped, pulling a door open. I looked through it, the room almost forty feet long with a large fireplace at the end. The ceiling went up two floors, and paintings dotted the walls between even more stacks of neatly lined books.

Hayley sat at the table, our master Ireena taking the seat at the head of the table in an oversized black chair covered in leather. Her fingers moved quickly on the table, each one of them making a crisp tap. I sped up, walking swiftly over and taking a seat across from Hayley. Before I could get there, a gentleman who I had originally thought was a statue stepped forward and pulled the seat out for me.

"Thank you, my apologies on taking so long." I sat down and he helped me adjust the chair.

"Do you feel better?" Lady Ireena asked, looking over to the side with a gentle nod. Three people I didn't recognize stepped forward, pouring fresh blood from decanters into the wine glasses on the table. I was honestly curious what breakfast, or meals in general, would be like. The thought of biting someone every time we fed made my stomach curl up into my body.

I held the wine glass that was handed to me, the smooth red liquid inside sloshing side to side. "I do, I feel…"

"Dead?" she said.

"Pardon?"

"Like the dead. Please tell me you weren't about to say something like 'human again'. The frailty of those creatures has never ceased to amaze me." A woman handed her a glass filled almost all the way to the top.

"Drink, you have been malnourished and mistreated. We have a long night ahead of us." She looked over at Hayley with a smile, bringing a white cloth napkin up to pat her lips. The red bloodstain on it and how casually she just drank it almost made me nauseous.

"Did you complete your task?"

Hayley nodded and lifted the glass to her lips. I could hear her sipping the blood as I looked at mine. For some reason, I couldn't bring my eyes away from it and I stared into the red as it circled my glass again and again.

"Elaine." Ireena said sharply.

"It is unbecoming to play with your food. Drink."

I could feel both her and Hayley watching me. I kept my eyes on it, then slowly closed them. I stood at the threshold of an irrevocable decision, one that I actually had the choice to make. Moonlight spilled in through the sheer curtains, casting a silver glow across the table that made the red seem to glow.

A faint scream echoed inside of me and I could smell that man's fear in the glass. My heartbeat quickened, the room turning to silence that was broken only by the breathing of one of the servants.

Drinking blood had always been such a romantically intimate thing to do in the movies, but here, it was just a glass of human wine. I traced the curve of the glass with a feather light touch, letting my lips hover above the rim as I inhaled the smell of it. I tried not to let the nausea take over. Lady Ireena sat there, staring at me while I danced around drinking it. Just the smell was enough to make my chest pound, my fangs slowly emerging as I lifted the glass to my lips and crossed over.

"Child. Drink." An order, and without having time to think about it my lips hit the cool crystal glass. The first drop pulled out the hunger from my core, and the rest felt like a flood that had covered my body.

A feeling of ecstasy sent a shiver down my body, my fingers lifting the glass even higher while I leaned back in my chair. The leather seat felt cool across my back, and I found I was unable to restrain myself in any way, the blood quickly moving from the glass to my mouth. I sat the empty glass down with a satisfied exhale, pulling a napkin up to my lips.

"Was that so bad?" Ireena asked with a smirk.

"No, master. It was not." I wanted to lie, but something inside of me kept me from yelling out about it. The thick iron taste, the way it hit my stomach, all of it would have made me sick if I had another option.

"Antanasia was kind enough to tell me what shape you were in on arrival. In response to the atrocious treatment of my third daughter, I have called for the Crimson Court to convene." She held her glass out, and within moments it was refilled.

"What does that mean?" I asked, Hayley snickering under her breath, smiling at me.

"Each of the family heads across the continent will convene. Tonight, you will meet my brothers and sisters, an event that is only ever done during an emergency or major happening. You will wear something nicer than that, as it is your first presentation to the Crimson Court and the Ebon Conclave."

She sipped her second glass slowly, almost seeming to enjoy each drop of the red liquid.

"If you are finished, run upstairs and change. I'd recommend wearing something, well, functional."

"Functional?"

"*Yes.*" She replied. Each of her responses seemed to be direct and without waste. I could tell she wasn't the kind of person who enjoyed small talk, but after being alive for so long, maybe they had grown tired of it. If it had been me, I'd like to think I would enjoy conversation more than anything else.

I looked at Hayley curiously.

"Leggings and boots. This is not a time for you to wear your stupid Birkenstocks. I know you hate hiking but think of it more like happy hour. You always loved to get dressed up for that." They smiled at me, finishing their second glass of blood.

"Oh… Okay, I can manage that much." I tried to respond cheerfully despite feeling like I was a third wheel. Hayley had been serving Ireena for over two hundred years, and that relationship was probably way deeper than ours had been.

I had no choice but to attend to that request. I slid my chair back, one of the attendants grabbing it halfway and helping to slide it the rest of the way. It felt like there was nothing I was allowed to do on my own right now, despite how nice it felt to have someone assist me again.

"I'll go change, and I won't keep you waiting this time." I said, mildly stomping towards the door.

"Your wife seems to be in a lovely mood today." Lady Ireena said, sipping her wine while reading.

"She's not… really like that." I heard Hayley respond. I stood outside the dining room with my arms crossed, and Jules next to me.

"Let's get you changed."

I followed her upstairs with a childish huff, not wanting to go out and do anything right now. As I stood before the gilded mirror in my brightly lit bedroom, I sighed in resignation. I had to change into something more suitable for whatever this occasion was, which meant forsaking my beloved Birkenstocks. I had waited literal centuries for another pair. I stomped over and shuffled through the closet, a sea of flowing black- and gemstone-colored dresses, before my gaze landed on an outfit that had been gathering dust in the corner: a pair of sleek leggings, a crisp white blouse, and a pair of elegant flats.

"These will have to do."

I eyed the leggings with distaste. They looked uncomfortable and confining compared to my usual loose-fitting gowns.

"This better be worth it," she muttered to herself.

Grumbling, I peeled off the dress that I had barely had any time in, hanging it on the nearby rack. The leggings slipped on with surprising ease, and I was forced to admit that they did wonders for my figure. The blouse buttoned up neatly, highlighting my pale skin and dark brown hair. As I stared at her reflection in the mirror, the shoes lay in wait at her feet, gleaming like obsidian daggers that made me cringe.

My fingers hesitated above the shoes, which were sleek and pointed, worlds away from anything I ever would have worn outside of the board room. Reluctantly, she slid her feet into them, wincing as the unfamiliar sensation of heels lifted me up an inch. I practiced a few hesitant steps, my face contorted in discomfort. Finally, I took a pass at the mirror, pulled a jacket out of the closet and folded it over my arm before departing with Jules once again.

The tower

REFLECTIONS

"Hunt by day. Do not believe you carry the strength to battle a vampire under the moonlight. Fighting after sundown is reserved for arrogant fools. Do not believe yourself all powerful when fighting the demons of the old world"
Father Gabriel, Adeptus Oryx, Holy Codex ii

When we stepped outside, four black SUV's were lined up and waiting for us. I stood next to Hayley behind Lady Ireena, waiting for the doors of the cars to open. Ireena moved to the second one while Hayley pulled me towards the one behind it. Halfway down the marble steps a familiar voice rang out from the car Ireena was headed to.

"Elllllleee!" the pink haired vampire yelled. I could remember her, but part of it was really fuzzy. I looked at Hayley, watching them bow their head.

"Lady Antanasia, it is a pleasure to see you as always." Their hand crossed their chest as they lowered into a bow.

"Relax Hayley, I asked you to call me Auntie!" she seemed to pout. "Just because Ireena is a stickler for formality doesn't mean I have to be too."

"Get back in the car." Ireena said abruptly to her. I watched Lady Antanasia stick her tongue out at Ireena then crawled back into the car. Ireena looked at the two of us, nodded, then stepped into the darkness of the backseat.

A vampire I had never seen before closed the door and locked eyes with me. Their suit was wrapped in a formal cloak that held a single white rose on it. Whatever that look was for didn't bother me. I had a habit of rubbing people the wrong way and that seemed to be the only thing I had done since arriving here.

Sitting down in the backseat with Hayley, I finally relaxed, laying my head down on her shoulder.

"So... wanna tell me where we're going?" I asked curiously, running my hand up her thigh. It had been so long since we had done something as simple as sit next to each other.

Hayley grabbed my hand, holding it in their own. I smiled down at their finger, looking at the wedding band that was still there.

"My love, we are heading to the Ebon Conclave Chamber. It was originally the continental seat for our kind but was moved to Manhattan eighty years ago. This assembly hall is but one that serves as the hallowed ground where the lords and ladies who govern our kind congregate to deliberate upon matters of global importance for our society."

I sighed, thinking about it for a moment while the car started moving. "So, it's like a vampire congress?"

"Not really. You are going to enjoy it though. The Ebon Conclave is a breathtaking architectural masterpiece, a fusion of modern Gothic and Baroque styles. Massive, obsidian-black stone pillars soar upwards to meet a vaulted ceiling adorned with these beautiful, blood-red stained-glass windows that filter soft, eerie moonlight into the hall. I know how much you enjoy architecture, and this will blow your beautiful little mind."

I smiled and laughed as Hayley continued.

"Tell me more, love."

"Of course," they replied softly.

"The chamber is designed to resemble an inverted cathedral, with its grandeur symbolizing the power and authority of the Crimson Court, the night lords who rule our kind."

I closed my eyes, still tasting the blood from breakfast. No matter how many times I brushed my teeth, the taste wouldn't leave my lips. Being this close to Hayley helped me to relax as the car moved towards its destination in the city. Even the hum of the engine was slowly blending all of the background noise into a single sound that calmed my nerves. The vibration of the car, the warmth of the seat, all of it had helped me to settle into coziness that I had forgotten.

"We're here." Hayley said, rocking my head up. I had nearly fallen asleep on the ride over here and it would probably take me a few minutes to shake it off. The convoy had pulled off the road and into what appeared to be a hotel valet. One of the drivers came over and whispered something in Hayley's ear.

"Yes, bring it upstairs."

Grey stone pillars held up the large awning that protected people from whatever weather was happening. The door was pulled open by one of the doormen, a short, slender human with grey eyes. He kept his gaze low and didn't make eye contact with either of us as we stepped out of the car together. Lady Isabella and Lady Antanasia were already walking through the main door, glass windows sliding out of their way with a clean woosh. I followed Hayley as they fell in line behind the two. Even from back here, an excited Antanasia filled the air with her fluttery voice.

We stepped into the lobby, a perfect representation of modern luxury. A woman in a business suit quickly approached our master, then disappeared back to the desk as quickly as possible. Ireena turned to face the two of us.

"The others are upstairs already. This is good." Lady Ireena said with a smile. There was a hint of darkness in her eyes that sent a shiver down my spine. I couldn't exactly put my finger on it, but it was most definitely there. She turned around and we went to the elevator, a set of large golden doors being held open by a gentleman in a black suit with a grey tie. He was almost a foot taller than me, and his partially grey hair made me smile. The thought of never having to deal with my hair going old and white was a satisfying one. The four of us stepped in, and as the doors closed, she pressed her index and middle fingers onto a piece of glass. A square of light lit up around her fingerprint and the elevator jerked upwards.

There was a floor counter with a little red arrow above the doors that moved one by one as we passed each floor. I expected the elevator to slow down at the fourteenth floor, but it instead moved past it for almost another minute. Hayley could feel my curiosity and leaned over to me.

"There are twelve floors of normal hotel, and the eight floors above that belong to us. You can only access them if you're one of our kind. I'll have your biometrics recorded later."

"Thanks, but I'm not sure I'll be here that often." I replied to them with a smile.

"I disagree, you will probably be here with me." They smiled back. The elevator finally came to a stop, the doors opening to reveal a breathtaking view.

The interior exuded opulence and extravagance. Dark, velvet draperies fell freely from the walls, and glistening candelabras hang from ornate, wrought-iron chains, casting flickering shadows that dance across the marble floors. Elaborate tapestries depicting the rich history of vampire-kind adorned the walls, each thread imbued with the memories of generations past. I tried to keep my jaw from dropping from the sheer beauty in the artwork, let alone the architecture. Hayley had been correct; I was absolutely in love.

I stepped out behind them, immediately slowly my pace so I could take in everything that I saw. There were so many details that really brought the place together, every piece of this giant room was thoughtfully designed in an elegance that I had never experienced before.

Two rows of desks stood on each side of the room, some of them raised so their occupant could work while standing and the others traditionally built. I followed closely next to Hayley as we continued forward. There were almost twenty vampires in this room doing work, their red eyes meeting mine when we passed by. I tried to lower my breath and not make any noise at all, trying to think of a way to make myself invisible.

"That's impossible now, relax." I heard in my head. It was quickly followed by a snickering Lady Antanasia a few feet in front of me. We stepped through a large set of double doors and into a smaller room by comparison.

This room was spread out, thirteen large stone chairs with a velvet cushion sat in a circle together surrounding a raised platform that was almost forty feet wide. An immense, obsidian throne dominated one end of the chamber, where the highest-ranking vampire lord presides over meetings. I looked at that one curiously.

"That is where the lord of our kind sits. From the beginning of our time, there has been a truce between each of the originals, that no single member of the tribe of darkness and Crimson Court will ever rise above another. Whether it is this chair or the one in our homeland, it remains empty." Hayley explained.

"Where is our homeland?" I asked.

"Transylvania." She said, keeping a straight face.

"Wait. Really?" I stopped, shocked.

"No. you really thought it though didn't you." Hayley laughed at me and gave me a hug.

"I missed you so much. Come on, our seats are over there, behind our masters."

Hayley took my hand and pulled me towards two seats that were behind one of the large marble ones.

"Hayley Reinhardt, it has been a minute."

My eyes were drawn to a figure of captivating allure. This woman, an ancient vampire of timeless beauty, moved gracefully across the opulent, obsidian floor of the gathering, her silver hair cascading in a waterfall of sparkles that looked like it had captured the moonlight, her figure draped in a tight, lace dress that accentuated her ethereal allure. Her nose was sharp and her eyes gentle, the red almost blending into the softness of her skin, unlike Ireena. As she approached, I could see the detailing on her dress, and the little crystals and gemstones that had been embroidered into them.

"Countess Elisabeta, it is a pleasure to see you again." Hayley crossed an arm across their chest and bowed.

"It is our fortune to see you."

"You never failed at flattery, child. Who is this delightful treat?" She stepped by Hayley and moved as close to me as she possibly could. I didn't realize how much shorter than me she was until she was standing in front of me. Her arms lifted and she planted her hands on my shoulders, looking me over.

"Hayley, is this the illusive wife we have heard so much about?"

"Yes, this is my wife, Elaine." Hayley replied.

"Elaine, how lovely it is to meet you. I heard through the chattering that Ireena had an accidental child, and we were all curious about it. It's been so long since there had been any worthy drama among us."

"It is my pleasure to be here. This is a lot to take in. Forgive me for being forward, but all of you are ancient, why would you have any drama?" I asked curiously.

"My dear, sweet child. Sometimes drama is the only thing we have. Maybe one day Hayley will let me borrow you for a weekend." I watched Hayley's cheeks turn a pale shade of rose. Was she embarrassed?"

"Countess, it would be my honor to join you for a weekend." I replied, trying to get on her good side. Especially if that would help Hayley.

"Yes! Perfect!" she turned around and faced a man who looked eerily similar to her. Almost like, a copy without breasts. He even wore a lacy top underneath a floor length French vest.

"Paole! I win! That will be five thousand, thank you very much." She turned around, her finger coming up under my chin. The sharpness of her nail sent a quick shiver down my spine and I felt like she was lifting me up with a single motion. She lowered my head down to meet hers

"I look forward to your visit." She smiled, planting her lips on my cheek in front of Hayley.

"Done!" she hopped up, her smile widening enough for me to see her fangs. She patted Hayley on the head, a cringe forming in their cheek. I tried not to laugh at her while she kept a straight face, I knew that was one of the few things they absolutely hated more than anything in the world. I watched her walk across the floor, float up onto the raised platform, and stroll off to talk to others. Every one of her movements was perfect, entrancing.

"Are you crazy?" Hayley asked, pinching me.

"What do you mean? She seemed nice."

"She is, but that's part of her bloodline. She can whisper sweet pleasures, while her brother Duke Paole can weave the darkest of nightmares. They aren't physically the strongest, but to anyone with a weak mind, they're deadly."

"But I didn't feel anything, wouldn't I have known?"

"She didn't *have* to do anything, and you offered yourself up to her."

"I'm not sure I follow."

"BABE. SHE was the drama. An entire scandal. She discarded her husband after almost two thousand years, and she took a different direction."

"Wait. Wait. Wait. Are you saying that she—"

"Yes. She developed a wonderful love for her own kind, her own companions."

"And there isn't really anything wrong with that, is there love?" I said, wrapping my arms around her neck.

"We're the same, right?"

"No. she built her own harem of devoted admirers. Human, vampire, whatever in between."

"Are you talking about Lady Nelo?" a bright voice chimed in.

"Lady Antanasia, apologies for the gossip, I was catching Elaine up on the originals."

"It's quite all right. Even I must admit she always had a flair for the dramatic." She said, swirling a long pink lock in her fingertips.

"Dramatic, yes. All of her admirers are said to be the most alluring and talented of our kind. She collects them, and those inside consider it to be the most, well, exclusive of clubs to be a part of."

"That sounds like something I would want to avoid."

"Indeed, child. But that's what makes it all the more captivating. The underworld is abuzz with gossip and even though it's been a decade, everyone in the city wants to be a part of. And you just got invited."

"You heard that?"

"I heard you agree, so good luck!" Lady De'Byrne looked over to another man who had just finished pouring himself a glass of blood wine.

"Excuse me, I'll catch up after the gathering."

We both bowed to her as she moved off. Hayley took me by the arm and pulled me close to her. There was a long, velvet covered table lined with bottles against the wall with a young man behind it.

"Let's get a drink before this gets kicked off." I strolled over to the table beside them but said nothing when they asked the man to pour our drinks.

At the end of the makeshift bar were two figures, one the twin of Nelo, and the other looked to be an eastern European aristocrat. I kept my head lowered while Hayley spoke to the waiter. It was impressive to me that a vampire wearing a lace bodysuit was able to stand there without wavering to the large man in front of him.

"This land, Konrad, has been in our family for centuries. It is a symbol of our lineage, our dominion over the Balkans. And now, you come to me with news that we've lost a portion of it to those accursed werewolves." His demeanor was like a knife ready to slice through anyone who stood before him.

Konrad, his expression a mix of anger and frustration, countered Paole's accusation.

"Paole, you know I did not give it up willingly. The werewolves have grown stronger, and their numbers have multiplied. We were outnumbered, and there was no choice but to retreat. I gave the order to Kellen and Guy."

"*Retreat?* Konrad, for an ancient of your stature, I *would* have expected a better strategy. We cannot afford to lose any more territory to the mongrels." He said, his voice dripping with thick sarcasm.

I observed the exchange with a sense of unease. Paole and Konrad were known for their fiery disagreements, but this dispute seemed to strike at the heart of their family's heritage.

"The losses can be reclaimed. We will strike back when the time is right, and we shall regain what is rightfully ours." Konrad was adamant about the result, as if it had already come to pass.

"And in the meantime, the werewolves will consider this a victory, an affront to our dominance. We must act swiftly and decisively, or they will encroach further. Your mistake has a direct effect on my land. Every step you take back is one more that they take as a species. Three thousand years and you still haven't learned that."

"Do not dare chastise me, Paole. It's been four hundred years since you picked up a sword."

"I don't need a blade."

"Simmer down you two, we're getting started." Nelo seemed to appear out of nowhere, her presence lightening their mood.

"Go back to your whores, Nelo." Konrad said sharply as he turned and walked away. I took the crystal glass that Hayley handed me. The blood inside was lightly chilled. I took a giant drink of it, then another.

"Are they always like that?" I asked.

"Pretty much. Some of their personalities have never changed, and for others, they just grew over time. Let's take our seat"

I shook my head and followed as close to Hayley as I could. There were five of the chairs already filled with a vampire in their seat. The air within the Ebon Conclave Chamber was heavy with a sense of ancient authority and foreboding. The whispers of centuries-old secrets seem to linger in the shadows, and an eerie silence blankets the room before discussions commence. The scent of rare, aged blood wine wafts through the air, served in crystal goblets by younger vampires, an essential ritual that precedes the deliberations.

Lady Ireena took her seat, the room going quiet. She lifted her glass to her lips and began to speak in a language I couldn't quite recognize.

"Chem la ordin tribunalul purpurio cand intram in Enclava Ebon."

Her words were crisp and clear, and I couldn't take my eyes off the others sitting as her equal. A man sitting across from her covered in a silver and black jacket made of French brocade raised his glass.

"Chem la ordin tribunalul purpurio cand intram in Enclava Ebon."

The man and woman that looked strikingly similar to each other across to our right repeated it, finally in a language I could understand.

"We call to order the Crimson Court of the Ebon Enclave."

I looked at Lady Antanasia, hoping she could hear my thoughts of confusion. In perfect timing, my hopes were answered.

"Before the assembly begins, vampire lords and ladies engage in an intricate and solemn ritual, known as the *"Veil of Sanguine Secrecy,"* which cloaks the chamber in an impenetrable shroud of supernatural darkness, ensuring that their discussions remain hidden from prying eyes and mortal interference. The gathering is marked by a formal procession, with each participant taking their place with graceful, measured steps."

I watched Lady Antanasia, unable to take my eyes off of her. Hayley smiled at me, observing the two of us having a conversation without words. I'd nod occasionally as she explained the entire process and history of the chamber to me. Finally, Lady Antanasia spoke.

"Je rappelle le tribunal cramoisi à l'ordre alors que nous entrons dans l'Enclave d'Ébène."

French? I hadn't taken her to be French of all things. I thought that each of them was from Romania or the Balkans. I'd been wrong before though.

Lady Ireena stood up after each of them took a drink from their crystal goblets. She locked her eyes on the blonde gentleman across the space.

"Forgive me for calling my siblings to meet without much warning. I am humbled and honored by your willingness to come together. This Sacred Assembly Hall, the Ebon Conclave Chamber, is a place where we come together to protect our ancient heritage and ensure the survival of our species in a world where shadows and secrets reign supreme."

Several of the vampires applauded my master at her words. Lady Ireena stopped speaking and turned to face the other man. I recognized in the darkness behind him, were three vampires who were sitting in the shadows of the room. Finally, after another moment of silence he stood up and took a step forward.

"My sister, if you wish for us to play games and figure out why you have summoned us to this sacred space, you are mistaken. Get to the point."

"Very well, dear brother. I want you to execute Addison."

His eyes turned red, the crystal glass shattering in his hand.

"You dare ask me to send my firstborn to eternal sleep, over some bitch your daughter created."

"I agree with Duke Konrad, our children are worth far more than their offspring are." The elegant silver haired vampire chimed in. He had been arguing with the Duke minutes ago, but now seemed to agree with him.

"Shut up Paole, this does not concern you." Lady Ireena snapped back.

Ireena turned in a circle, looking at each of them. Hayley reached over from their seat and took my hand in theirs, squeezing it.

"You must be truly foolish, brother. Elaine Reinhardt is not sired from Hayley. She is sired from me." I looked at Hayley, a soft, venomous smile forming across their lips. The room broke out in commotion, the five Lords and Ladies arguing and yelling at each other in near unison. Ireena raised her right arm, the room moving to silence.

"Addison, I charge you with the abduction of one of our children, experimenting on our kind, torturing your cousin, and malicious intent towards a rival family. For eight months, I felt every cry that she had, every pain that she went through. I could sense her rage, her frustration, her anguish as you cut and carved up my daughter. By the codex that we each signed in blood, as is my right, I call upon his execution."

"Addison was unaware of this; you cannot hold him responsible for this mistake!" Konrad tried to defend him, as best he could.

"Elaine is my daughter, and she was returned to be not only in near pieces, but without recourse. I will not allow your wild dogs to lay a finger on my daughters. You can handle it, or we will."

"Ireena!" Konrad scowled back at her.

"You overstep your place."

"Can everyone settle down for a moment?" A soft, feminine voice floated across the room. I would have thought it was Antanasia had I not noticed her. The countess from earlier spoke up. I watched the woman gently lean back in her chair, slowly sipping from her glass. An attendant stood next to her with a smile, refilling it every time she lowered it.

I watched her eyes shine red for a brief moment as she gazed across the room, then return to blue.

"Do you want to insert yourself into this quarrel, Nelo?"

"Of course, I do not, sister Ireena. But we have a process for this, do we not?" Countess Nelo replied sternly.

"We do. Addison Bolton, will you accept a blood duel from Hayley?" I could see Addison cringe in frustration, and Konrad looked furious.

"Forgive me, master. I will not be fighting Addison." Hayley said, standing and dropping to a knee. The room went quiet at the outburst from her.

"Master. This is a fight that Elaine should do. Let her return every cut, every lost drop of blood, every piece of hair that he took from her."

Ireena smiled and looked at me. Hayley had surprised me, and I was completely caught off guard. Without hesitating, I shook my head in confirmation. A wild laugh broke the air, breaking the silence that hung over the sacred room. It was unrestrained and echoed for several moments that frustrated me. I knew that laugh.

Addison stepped forward from behind the chair of his master with a smile. Konrad shot his progeny a glare then sat down.

"Countess Ireena, I will be more than happy to accept a Blood Duel with your daughter Elaine. She doesn't even have a brand yet. Forgive me if you end up losing another daughter." Addison said, crossing an arm across his chest and bowing to her.

"Quiet, child." Konrad snapped at him.

"While this may be an easy duel for you, do not disrespect my sister. I may not be able to save you here if she were to become enraged."

Konrad turned his eyes to his sister and smiled.

"You have yourself a duel. We stand in front of the rulers of the night, where blood matters above all things. The result of this duel will purge this unwanted bad blood from our ranks."

"So it shall be." Nelo, Paole and Antanasia all echoed in unison. Isabella returned to her seat, smiling at me. I stepped over next to her, lowering my head.

"I felt your flame, I felt your rage. I could hear you wishing that someone would come and rescue you. Now, you have the opportunity to seize your own standing here. Let my brothers and sisters know that you are of my blood. Put him down."

I kept my head lowered until a soft hand touched my chin and lifted me up.

"You bow before me, and before no man. Show me why Hayley waited for you."

"Yes, master." I replied, a ball of excitement and anxiety both welling up inside me. Hayley grabbed my arm, kissing me on the cheek.

"I have something for you." They said with a smile. A cloaked vampire stepped forward with a long piece of velvet covering a slender object in his hands. He took a knee, holding it up to them. I could tell Hayley was happy by how quick they jerked the covering off. It fell to the side, my eyes widening as I looked at the long, thin blade.

"This is Dawnbreaker, the sword I stole from the church. It's tasted the blood of many of our kind, and his. Let it have its fill."

"Thank you, my love." I said as they handed me the blade, the handle of it poking out from a thin leather casing. The hilt of the ancient sword was a masterpiece of craftsmanship, a testament to the skill and artistry of its long-forgotten creators inside the Church. It bore the weight of history and the aura of countless battles, and it was a work of art that transcended time itself. I stared at it, remembering the witches that helped make these blades solely to destroy anything that the church deemed unholy. Anything, including the one's who created it.

Carved from the finest materials, the hilt was a combination of ornate beauty and functional design. Its core was a solid, polished piece of dark hardwood, worn smooth by years of hands gripping it in combat. This wood, perhaps oak or ebony, had aged to a rich, deep brown, and it bore the faint markings of ancient runes and symbols etched into its surface, hinting at the sword's mystical nature.

I ran my eyes across it in sheer admiration. Stories of these blades had been told to me before, but to see one in person, and even get the chance to wield it, was exhilarating. I recognized it from the vision Annabella had shared with me weeks ago.

Did Hayley know where these came from? I was afraid to bring it up, for fear that it would incite more violence against their coven. The cross guard, a sturdy and protective piece of metal, curved gently outward from the hilt, creating a graceful and flowing design. It was adorned with intricate patterns of filigree, reminiscent of vines and leaves, and these delicate details contrasted with the hilt's overall robustness.

The metal, likely forged from steel or even a rare alloy, had not succumbed to rust despite the passage of countless years. I wondered if there was some sort of religious magic that was keeping it in such pristine shape. There was no way a sword of this quality wasn't properly taken care of.

At the base of the hilt, where it met the blade, a pommel of considerable weight added balance and heft to the sword. This pommel was a work of art in itself, sculpted into the likeness of an angel. Sat in its eyes were two precious gemstones even though its wings were dulled with age

The grip, meticulously wrapped in supple, aged leather or possibly exotic skin, bore the marks of countless hands that had held it over the decades. It retained a comfortable texture, molded to fit the contours of a warrior's hands. Even for me, it felt comfortable. I could tell a craftsman had poured their heart into this blade. It bounced between my hands, and I squeezed it several times with a smile.

I had dabbled with leather work in college and although I had truly failed at making anything worthwhile, I knew what level of mastery you would have to achieve to create something this beautiful. What made this hilt truly extraordinary, however, was the presence of intricate gemstones and crystals embedded within it.

These precious stones glimmered in a mesmerizing array of colors, casting an ethereal glow in the dimmest of light. I knew these gems were enchanted, offering protection, power, or some other supernatural boon to the sword's wielder. I wondered which one of those poor souls had been sacrificed to this blade.

The hilt of this ancient sword was not just a functional component but a work of art, a relic that had transcended time, and a symbol of the sword's storied history and mysterious powers. It was a true testament to the skill and dedication of those who had crafted it, an heirloom of an age long past. How many people had the church used this blade to kill? How many innocent people had fallen at their hands?

I wondered how many battles this blade had seen, and how many of our kind had fallen to it. Whether guilty or not, this sword was a weapon of destruction, and it was an absolute honor to carry it. I lifted it up, not taking it out of its hilt and turned to walk towards the raised platform in the middle.

Addison was standing in front of his maker and slowly unbuttoning his shirt. He tossed it off the platform, pulling two curved knives from their resting place on his belt. I watched him roll his head in a circle, not even looking at me. He was disregarding everything about me.

I stepped up onto the platform with a deep exhale. The eyes of the royalty here felt suffocating, but I was far more nervous about disappointing Hayley. He cocked his head to the side while twirling the two blades between his fingertips.

"Sorry about this, Reinhart, looks like I'll be taking her from you again." Addison said with a laugh, bringing one of the blades up to his mouth. He wasn't even looking at or acknowledging that I was here. The anticipation in the room was palpable as the vampire court watched with rapt attention. The vampire stepped forward; his knives poised for the deadly dance that was about to begin.

"Prepare yourself, Elaine. I will make this quick." He hissed, mockingly. It felt dirty to have him say my name in front of Hayley.

I refused to waste any word on him, instead sliding my left foot behind me and taking a defensive stance. Dawnbreaker was pulled from its sheath, a sky-blue light gently glowing across its surface.

"I hope you're ready for one more kill, Dawnbreaker.." I invoked the sword's name, calling out to it in my mind with a voice that carried the weight of my now immortal existence.

"Take whatever you need from me." I offered my own essence, the cold, dark power of a vampire, in exchange for the sword's cooperation. I could feel something coming from this blade and I knew it wasn't just a normal sword. I had guessed that the forbidden ritual the church done was a little more complicated than what I had seen. They really had sealed souls inside these weapons.

I looked over to Hayley, wondering if they ever saw this blade as more than just a weapon. Someone had died to make this thing.

This duel was not just about my own fate; it was a symbol of my own standing within the Crimson Court. I was the youngest member of the royal children and their current expectation of me was little to none. As the first clash of steel rang out, the atmosphere in the hall became electric. I spoke to the sword, my voice a reflection of the genuine respect and appreciation I held for its unique nature.

"I need you." I whispered under my breath while parrying his second set of strikes. It was difficult to remain steady and dodge his follow up strikes. I tried to reason with the blade as I felt its' presence. There was definitely still something in it. I needed it to cooperate with me, and fast. I emphasized the shared power that we could harness together if it trusted me.

I could feel whatever soul was bound to this sword hesitate, for it had been bound to a purpose opposite to my own. It had served the forces of light, but it was now confronted with the proposition of aligning with an immortal creature of the night. And maybe, just maybe, it had been forgotten.

"I'm *going to die* without you." I said as I brought the sword up to parry another of his strikes. A blade came across my forearm, and I jerked back, moving in long strides away from him.

Addison moved with the fluid grace of a seasoned warrior, his twin knives a deadly extension of his will. I was barely able to parry his initial strike with Dawnbreaker, the sword's holy aura repelling him with a burst of radiant light. I was caught off guard by his speed, and even more so by his desire to end this battle right from the start.

Gasps of awe and surprise rippled through the court, much to the dismay of Duke Konrad. My heartbeat finally settled and the familiarity of holding a blade slowly started to return. It was a bit heavier than the one I had been trained on, but the basics were still the same.

"I see you and acknowledge you." I said the blade as I raised it to my lips. I slid it carefully across my lower lip, drawing my blood as a payment. "I need you now."

Addison's eyes burned with a fiery rage at being embarrassed in our first clash. The dark black in his eyes disappeared and turned to bright red, his muscles bulging as tattoos across his chest and back glowed, his heartrate climbing as it pumped the blood faster and faster through his body. A darker red color flooded his eyes, his muscles growing a little bit larger with every step that madman took towards me. He flipped the dagger in his left hand to a downward position and charged at me again. Addison's speed and agility were formidable, but a light glow began to emanate from the blade of Dawnbreaker. Had it awoken in my hands and finally responded?

The feeling of being armed this time around kept me from panicking. I lunged forward, the tip of the blade moving past his body but before he could strike, I pulled my arm back and slashed, drawing it in a beautiful, curved arc across his body. My weight twirled upwards, my own body floating like a dance with a twist that brought it around again.

He stepped forward, trying to get inside my range with the blade but I bounced backwards, my eyes turning their own shade of bright crimson. I could remember the way I felt when I had walked into the wolves' lair, and although I wasn't quite sure how much strength I could tap into, I knew it was better than nothing. *"Please give me more"* I begged the sword again, hoping that it would throw me a bone here.

The blade jerked back to my side, slashing down towards his left side as soon as he was within range. The grand hall echoed with the symphony of clashing steel, and the scent of vampire blood hung heavy in the air as minor wounds were inflicted. Every time he got close enough to me to strike, I would take a half step away, letting him draw a bit of blood but not do anything seriously damaging.

This was the moment I had been waiting for, the culmination of my patience and preparation. With each swing of my sword, I sought to strike a balance between precision and power. Dawnbreaker's blade sang with a melodious hum, a testament to its divine origins, regardless of the unholy process to forge it. Addison, though formidable, could not escape the overwhelming aura of the holy weapon and every time it cut his skin, a black burn mark would appear that refused to heal. I pressed the advantage and started moving towards him, my footwork a blurry dance of light faints and shifts, the blades tip striking, fainting, stabbing, slashing all in random to keep him on his toes as I started to drive him back. Every time his dagger met the blade, I would reverse its direction and thrust, picking apart little pieces of him.

"Hayley, that sword *never* glowed for you."

"Correct, I've only seen it do that for the church."

"She isn't a priest, is she?" Ireena chuckled, watching the fight.

"She hates the church more than me."

I bounced across the floor, barely able to dodge as I watched my wife and maker converse curiously at the side. My goal was in sight, and I overstepped in both confidence and space, giving Addison the much-needed room to counter me. One of his blades found its way into my forearm, and the other across my thigh. Pain shot across my arm as he drove the blade clean and straight, the tip puncturing through my skin with a spray of bright red. Dawnbreaker echoed with a clang as it hit the floor and slid out of my grasp. In that critical moment, he had managed to disarm me.

I had committed the first sin of swordsmanship.

The collective gasp from the court was deafening. My heart sank, but I refused to surrender. I drove my leg backwards and reset my stance while forcefully pulling my arm off of his blade, blood dripping from my right arm and leg. Addison didn't want to give me time to recover and pushed his way forwards to me. I took a few skips backwards, intentionally going slower than I was really able to. He lunged towards my already bleeding leg again, cleanly leaving a smooth curve of red across my thigh. He was predictable, continuing to strike for the already wounded leg.

I leaned away from it just enough to keep him from going down to the bone, and he knew it. He may have outclassed me in strength but there was no way he could outclass me in speed. This time around, I didn't have a bullet in my leg. My body moved without thinking, an instinct taking over that sent me diving to the side. I rolled up to my feet and darted to the side, keeping the clockwise circle of movement around him.

Addison pivoted and slashed, trying again to catch me with a strike that would end the embarrassment he was going through, yet all he met was air. I continued to circle, sliding to the ground where I was able to reach Dawnbreaker. The sword regained its dull glow at my touch, my hand grabbing it on the run.

"I need you to cooperate. *Please.*" I said to it as I continued to circle. Addison leapt up, his body slamming down at mine with a sweeping kick that connected with my arm. I dug in, sliding several feet as I brought the sword up to meet his daggers. Every strike I blocked I would ask the blade for more help.

He slid one of them down towards my knuckles, trying to disarm me once again. I wasn't about to let that happen twice, and I knew he wouldn't give me a chance to recover if I lost the blade. I dropped my elbow down to my hip and thrust, sending the tip of the blade across his cheekbone where it left a line of blood underneath his eye. It almost hummed as the blood across the blade disappeared into it. The sword had gradually yielded to my plea, accepting the exchange of my essence and power for its submission.

"I'll feed you all the blood you want later." I said to it with a smile.

The moment of submission was marked by a shimmering radiance as the sword's artifact soul called out to me in response. For the first time I could feel it in my hands. I felt like the sword, now under my control, had submitted not out of obedience, but out of an acknowledgment of the harmony we could achieve.

The hilt was cold against my palm, and the blade, etched with ancient runes, shimmered with a supernatural light. I knew that this fight would test not only my strength but my skill with this sacred weapon.

Without a word, Addison lunged, his twin knives slashing through the air with furious lethal intent. I parried his attack with a swift, deft movement of my sword, the clash of steel ringing through the air again. Our shadows merged and separated as we danced in a deadly waltz, each movement a calculated response to the other's assault. His daggers were a blur of silver and darkness, his strikes relentless and precise. I countered with the power and reach of my single blade, deflecting his blows with an elegant fluidity that belied the urgency of our battle.

My sword began to move more fluidly, the tip of the blade repointing to his chest every time I was able to parry one of his attacks. I knew this movement. Every twist, every shift was familiar to me. My muscles would shift and contract with every lunge, moving just enough out of the way to counter him. Although my right hand was slowly growing numb from the constant strikes and the strength he had held within them, I was growing more and more comfortable.

I backtracked again, holding firm to my defensive stance while he chased me down, frustrated howls erupting from him every few steps.

"QUIT RUNNING YOU BITCH!" he screamed at me again, my body ducking under a wide swipe that left his side open.

"GET BACK HERE!" My legs came to the ground, turned with a graceful slide, and lifted me up under his arm again, another of his strikes hitting nothing but air. I could feel the tightness in my chest, the initial nervousness finally leaving me as thoughts of ending this battle overcame me.

I could do this.

I could *win* this.

My eyes met his, a crimson hue spreading across them that were just as bright as his own. Another dagger swung a hair away from my neck, my upper body folding backwards and underneath him once again while my footwork danced in front of him. I drilled my left arm up with as much force as I could muster from this angle, connecting my knuckles with the bottom side of his chin. I had watched that strike being performed before and remembered it. My body was moving on its own, cycling through each movement like a carefully practiced dance. The damage, however, disappointed me, my fingers cracking in pain from hitting the mark. At least two of my knuckles were broken from that punch. His body was far harder than I had thought, and I wasn't quite sure if that thick skin was part of his bloodline or not.

Addison took a step backwards in shock, his head hanging backwards in disbelief. I wasn't sure how long it had been since he had last been struck, but I knew who had done it. Hayley cheered me on from the side, quickly getting shushed by our maker. I glanced over at them with a smile, rotating and throwing my fist around towards his throat.

Now that I was inside his striking range, it was more difficult for him to attack and he moved into his own defensive position, his arms coming up to cover his chest and neck.

I looked forward at him, my right leg sliding back where my weight sat. The blade came up, horizontal with the ground as I took a form that felt the most natural, the most practiced. The feeling across my body was unlike anything I had experienced, like I wasn't in control of it. The blade connected with his body again, and although I was unable to break through his thick forearms, I doubled down.

"Eat this one, BASTARD." I screamed at him.

The sword flipped around in my hands, my fingers wrapping around each other as I drove it forward into the thin crease between his arms. While he moved backwards, frustration growing more and more inside of him, his body came to a stop. I pulled the blade to the side, ripping the end of it across his left arm and sending an arc of his blood across the old stone floor. The blade danced across him with every footstep, every slide and shift of my weight. Each flick of my wrist, every thrust of my arm, they all connected with his skin that left burning slices across his body.

Knowing I had him on the run again, my body spun twice, drawing the sword across his arms again and again. On the third rotation, I dipped the sword underneath and lifted, burying it up against his forearms at the hilt. The blue blade hissed, burning his skin with every inch it was drawn against his body. My wrist flicked down with the faint, the handle grip rotating down to the perfect striking position.

"ELLE!" Hayley cried out from the side of the stage, their eyes watching me drive the tip of the sword underneath his collar bone.

His instinct had saved his life, this time. With a sudden burst of supernatural strength, I disarmed one of his daggers, sending it clattering to the ground. The balance of power had shifted, and I seized the opportunity, pressing the tip of the blade even further through him. Every moment it was inside of him the blade would consume his vampiric strength like a parasite. The smell of his burning skin singed my nostrils with a scent that was almost nauseating.

I held the hilt in my left hand, drew my right one back, and punched the blade completely through him. Addison howled in pain, grabbing the blade despite its surface burning his palms. I twisted the sword again, ripping it out and cleanly through his shoulder. A red mist filled the air, the blood spraying upwards as it filled the air. Addison's injured left arm hung off to the side, his eyes now glowing rage.

Before he was able to regroup, I spun, my heel connecting with the outside edge of his right knee. My body felt like it was on fire, more and more of my bloodline coming out as I moved. I didn't know it, but my maker did. My pupils turned as black as hers, reflecting the sparkle of the night in them. A sharp crunch filled the air and his knee snapped, dropping him down to the ground with a howl. I came to a stop, bouncing backwards with a soft, quiet landing a few feet in front of him. A thick, white bone accented with bright pulsating blood stuck out from his leg, his upper body hunched over and barely vertical. I had effectively rendered him immobile and won this fight.

But it wasn't over for me. I wasn't going to allow him the opportunity to recover, let alone do what he had done to me to anyone else. A sharp hiss came from the tip of the blade dragging across the stone flooring.

"Do not DARE!" I could hear Duke Konrad scream at me from his seat, but I tuned it out.

"IREENA!" he howled across the floor at her. She sat there; her arms crossed with a wide smile while staring at me.

"I should have chopped you into pieces when I had the chance," Addison said with a scowl. I could see lines of blood dripping from his body, the same as mine.

In that moment, I felt the fear, the pain, the anger. Nothing was going to satiate the rage I felt inside, nothing other than beheading this monster. He snarled at me; a hiss that revealed his pearly fangs dotted with specks of red from where I had hit his jaw hanging out of his mouth. I would have loved to rip them out in front of his maker.

I lifted up the sword, and with no hesitation, the tip entered his chest. The feeling of it burning through his sternum and entering his heart gave me a flood of relief. Blue flames emerged from his chest, the blade burning through his heart as he screamed. The fire spread across his body, his screams the most beautiful sound I had heard in months. Hayley had taught me to show no mercy to any threat to my life, and this vampire, regardless of his ranking, had not only been a threat to me but had also done me harm. If I didn't do this, I knew Hayley would.

And who knew how many others he may do it to all over again.

Duke Konrad shot up from his seat with a speed that I could barely keep up with. I wasn't sure if he would act or not and didn't have a plan to respond to him. Thankfully, I didn't need one.

"Sit down, brother." Lady Ireena said, landing next to me and between us. The duke landed furiously as two more of the vampires joined her. She stood there; arms crossed.

"The fight was honorable, and your child was just the weaker combatant. May he enjoy his eternal rest."

"She didn't have to kill him!" he barked at her.

"What would you expect?" she laughed, "did you want her to show mercy to the monster that carved her up for almost a year? He dug his own grave; my child just buried him. Simple as that."

"Your audacity has grown, sister."

"So has your temper. I know failure might be rare for you to swallow, brother." Ireena looked over at me, smiled, and gave me a nod.

"Do it."

I ripped the blade from his still burning body and stood victorious with my sword held high, a symbol of my triumph over an adversary who had tested my every limit. His screams died out, leaving a smoking corpse that crumbled into ash beneath me. I twisted my body, kicking the ashes of his body over onto the stone floor.

Hayley's body hit mine, almost tackling me to the ground as they wrapped their arms around me. Ireena turned around to face me, a wide smile crossing her face.

"Well done, daughter." she said sternly, despite smiling. While I felt a bit of disappointment at her lack of excitement, it almost seemed like she had expected this outcome.

Ireena raised her hand, silencing the room.

"Elaine Reinhardt," she announced, her voice brimming with pride, "you have proven your strength, honor, and your connection to our world through this combat. You are worthy of your place among us and have proven you are a member of our court. In the eyes of the Crimson Court, you have earned the right to be my child and the privilege that comes with it."

Wait... earned the right? Is that what she just said? What would have happened had I lost?

A strange cacophony of applause echoed through the chamber, and the adrenaline finally started to run out. The red shimmer receded from my eyes, and I slumped down into Hayley's arms, grimacing in pain. He had left over hundreds of cuts across my body, and it would take a bit of time for them to completely heal.

"Take a break, love" Hayley said, running their hand across my face and pulling hair behind my ear.

"You performed admirably."

"I did it."

"Yes, love, yes you did." They said happily. I had taken back my pride and removed a blemish of time that had been seared into me.

The grand hall was bathed in the eerie light of a thousand flickering candles, casting elongated shadows that seemed to dance in celebration at my victory. I stood at the center of the room, held by Hayley and still catching my breath after the fierce duel that had secured my place among the vampire nobility. It felt surreal- I had killed someone. It wasn't like the wolves before. This had been one of our kind, and right in front of his maker.

As the daughter of the blood countess, it was a momentous occasion, one that came with both immense pride and the weight of expectation. The court had gathered not to witness my triumph but the execution of one of their own, and their expectant eyes bore down upon me, waiting for the affirmation of my newfound status.

But the weight that had pressed upon my shoulders began to lift as two figures approached me. Paole and Nelo, the vampire twins of the nobility, were renowned members of the Crimson Court, known for their striking and elegant presence. With matching hair glowing with moonlight, ethereal beauty, and sapphire eyes that glittered like precious gems, they were an inseparable pair. Their timeless grace and charm had made them legends within the immortal society.

Nelo was the first to reach me, her lips curving into a warm smile. Her voice, a melodious and enticing lilt, carried the court's attention as she spoke.

"Elaine Reinhardt, daughter of the countess, your victory tonight was truly remarkable. You have proven your worth among us, and we welcome you as a child to the Crimson Court. I look forward to spending that weekend with you." She winked and smiled, her brother stepping in front of her.

Paole, standing beside his sister, echoed her sentiments. His voice was a mirror image of Nelo's, a soothing and mesmerizing sound.

"Your prowess with that blade was impressive. We offer our congratulations."

Their words washed over me like a wave of acceptance and

approval. For a moment, the weight of the expectations that had burdened me seemed to melt away. It was as if Paole and Nelo's presence brought not only recognition but also a sense of belonging to this ancient and enigmatic realm.

"Thank you, Count and Countess. Your words mean more to me than I can express. I am honored to be welcomed as one of your children, even if it came at the expense of another one." I replied with a grateful nod.

Paole's eyes twinkled with an almost mischievous glint.

"You have joined us during an exciting time, Elaine. The court is undergoing changes, and your presence will undoubtedly contribute to our future."

Nelo, with a gentle smile, added, "Indeed, the balance of power within our world is shifting, would you mind if I studied that blade of yours?" Paole looked at Hayley, nodding his head in agreement.

"We were wondering if it would accept anyone, as it was far less cooperative with your partner" Nelo looked at the blade curiously, then shrugged.

"Those things have their own personality, at least one of us can use it."

I was more than happy to hand the blade over to them. With the adrenaline wearing off, I hadn't realized that all of the blood Addison had drawn had been consumed by that blade.

I couldn't help but feel a sense of optimism as the vampire twins spoke. The challenges ahead were daunting, but their assurance and support were a reassuring presence in the midst of the ancient and intricate politics of the court. I watched Duke Konrad take his remaining two children and leave with a growl as he murmured something under his breath to Lady Ireena. Antanasia hopped over and punched me in the side of the arm between two long cuts. I almost doubled over in pain from the casual strike.

"Great work!" she chirped happily. It was almost like she was watching a boxing match or something. I had made a powerful enemy today, one that was not only a Duke of the originals, but a warmonger who had survived the front lines of nearly every major global conflict in the last three thousand years. His insight into combat, and his prowess with a blade was nearly unmatched in the court. Avoiding open conflict with him was a high priority.

"Thank you, Lady Antanasia, for everything." I would never forget her saving my life and bringing me home to Hayley.

"It was nothing! Besides, Hayley made a mess and Isabella was fighting with her brother. I was just in the right place at the right time!"

As we continued to converse, I realized that this moment marked not only my acceptance into the Crimson Court but also the beginning of a new chapter in my life. Was I actually eager to embrace the responsibilities and opportunities that lay ahead? If I were guided by the wisdom and grace of Antanasia, Paole and Nelo, then yes.

"Elaina." The originals in front of me stepped away, leaving Lady Ireena standing there staring at the two of us. Hayley held most of my weight and I was slowly reaching the point of exhaustive sleep. My eyes felt heavy, but I bit down on my tongue to keep myself awake and alert, lest I accidentally insult my master.

"You have performed admirably, as expected of one of my daughters. I formally accept you as my blood and will allow you and Hayley to continue your relationship for so long as you both choose to live." Hayley kissed me on the cheek, pressing into a bruise that made me press my face away from hers.

"Ow. Ow. Ow. Ow. Ow." I said, Hayley laughing. "Gentle, love. Forgive me, Master. What would have happened had I lost?

"Take a look, child." She nodded to the side, where Addison's pile of ash was currently laying.

Nelo stepped into the middle of the floor and lifted his hand to the chandelier.

"I call this meeting to close. May we enjoy the favor of the night."

The others nodded in unison and began to disperse. A deep yawn escaped my lips, immediately drawing a yawn from Hayley.

"Don't give that to me, rude!" they said with another deep yawned. I laughed at them for a moment, satisfied with the outcome.

"Can we go home now?"

"Yes. Let's go home."

Lady Ireena looked at us with the first gentle smile I had seen from her. Two other vampires in formal tails stepped up to stand next to her. I watched them interact, unable to hear what they were saying. I held onto Hayley, not wanting to lose her again. We turned to walk away when Ireena halted us.

"Daughters, I will be leaving in two weeks' time to return to my territory. Go home, and I will meet with you when I arrive later."

"Yes, Master" we both said together with a smile.

The Moon
@ CodonaBotta

REFLECTIONS

"The darkness tells of a city in the stars, an eternal land cloaked by unholy power. I have spent forty years hunting the Blood Countess and have survived every encounter. Train hard, strengthen your resolve wield your faith, and you will survive too. We will find the city of stars and burn it to ash."
Father Gabriel
Adeptus Oryx, Holy Codex ii

CHAPTER 13

I laid across the backseat of the large SUV the entire way back to the manor. My entire body was in pain now that the adrenaline from the fight had worn off. As I drifted off to sleep, I found myself drifting through the darkness and into a dream—a dream that was more than a simple flight of fancy. It was a haunting recollection, a vivid memory of a time long past. I was a modern vampire, yet the tendrils of the past gripped me, pulling me back to a history I had once been a part of. I panicked, unable to wake myself.

In my dream, I stood upon a vast battlefield, the air heavy with the metallic scent of blood and the deafening cacophony of war cries and clashing steel. My vision was bathed in the colors of a red moon, a sight I had long forgotten, for as a vampire, I could never bear the touch of daylight. A dark sphere was across its center, casting shadows across the landscape.

My armor gleamed in the searing sun, reflecting a fierce determination that had once driven me. The weight of my sword felt familiar in my hand, a deadly instrument of war that had served me faithfully during a time of barbaric battlefields and holy quests.

Around me, knights in shining armor charged into the fray, their banners adorned with the emblem of the cross, their voices raised in a chorus of fervent prayers. It was the time of the Crusades, a period that had marked the world with its violence and fervor.

I walked forward and found myself standing next to a small pond, horses lined up to take their fill. Was I a mortal knight, bound by honor and duty to fight for a sacred cause? I looked into the water, seeing the reflection of someone else looking back at me. Ireena's gaze met mine, and my heart swelled with the righteous fire that had once fueled my actions. I could feel the days warmth upon my skin, and for the first time in centuries, I felt like I was truly alive here.

As the battle raged around me, I locked eyes with a fellow knight, a friend, and brother-in-arms. His name was Sir Godfrey, another of our kind, and he was as valiant as any knight could be. In my dream, we fought side by side, our swords cleaving through the enemy lines with precision and power.

The dream was a vivid journey into a world that had been left behind centuries ago. It was a time when faith was unwavering, when men and women believed in a higher purpose and were willing to lay down their lives for it. In that moment, something inside of me longed for the simplicity and purity of that era, the clarity of purpose that had driven me.

But as the dream unfolded, I began to realize the price of my immortality. On this battlefield I watched my mortal comrades fall one by one, their lives extinguished by the brutal chaos of war. I survived, but I was changed, tainted by the blood on my hands and the futility of the violence I had witnessed.

As the sun dipped below the horizon, I felt a profound sadness wash over me. The world I had known, the time of the Crusades, had been a harsh and unforgiving one. It was a period defined by violence and intolerance, where the quest for divine justice had often led to unimaginable suffering.

And now, in the modern world, I was a vampire—a creature condemned to a solitary existence in the shadows, forever apart from the world I had once known. The dream was a bittersweet reminder of a time when Ireena had surrounded herself with trusted companions, a time when she had been capable of love and valor.

As I woke from the dream, I found myself in the solitude of the night once more, looking up at the roof of the car. The modern world continued to rush forward, oblivious to the ancient memories that lingered in the recesses of my immortal mind. I really was a vampire, bound to the shadows, and I could only watch as the world evolved around me, carrying with it the weight of history and the echoes of the past. Hayley ran their hand through my hair, my head in their lap.

"There you are. welcome back love." they said, helping me to sit back up.

"I just had the craziest dream. It was like, I can't explain it." I pondered the dream and looked out the window of the car.

"Like you weren't really you?" they replied. "Like they weren't your dreams?"

"Yes. It was weird. I saw my reflection and it wasn't me!" I was worried that I had lost part of myself, and the dream had really freaked me out.

"They aren't your memories, they're our masters." Hayley said softly.

"Now that you have awakened more of your bloodline, what you saw wasn't you. You were able to experience our masters' memories. It happens every once in a while, and is natural. Her experiences are vastly deeper than ours so when you push yourself to the edge part of her blood will slip through and you get a lucky glimpse into her long life."

"Have you seen them before?" I was curious and wanted to know. I had to know. How old was our master? What had she seen in her life-time? How was she even created? What created her? So many questions flew through my mind as I watched the streetlights flash by outside the window.

"Yes, several of them." Hayley's hair flattened itself against the car seat as they gazed thoughtfully at the ceiling.

"Some of them are vague recollections of a world long gone. They could be her memories or dreams... it's difficult to say."

Hayley's voice grew softer, tinged with melancholy.

"They were frequent early on. Images of a shadowy figure in a cloak, her presence haunted me, and I thought they were nightmares until Kamila explained it to me. When I was a young one, they were more frequent as I unlocked my own bloodline."

I nodded; my luminous eyes clouded with uncertainty.

"I saw her as well. I wondered if she's real, if she truly exists or if our minds are playing tricks on us. I'm glad there's an explanation for it"

"There is. We are of her blood, and her experiences have been engrained in every drop. The more you have, over time, the more of her memories and her strength you will be able to unlock." They explained clearly. I had no idea that something like that was even possible.

"Hayley." I said as the car came into the manor circle and slowed to a stop.

"Can you tell me how it happened? And honestly this time." I never knew how our lives got turned upside down. The thought of spending so much time alone, locked up in the dark with nothing but the light of my phone, terrified me.

"Can we wait for this?" they asked, lowering their eyes from me.

"Driver. Leave us." I said rather rudely.

I wanted answers, and to know why we were sitting in the back of a car together centuries later. He stepped out and slammed the door closed behind him. I could see his shadow move across the car before posting up outside the passenger side.

"I want to know the truth."

Hayley sighed, rubbing their forehead with two fingers.

"Fine."

Hayley released an exasperated sigh.

"I went to Blairs dive to get a drink while it was raining. The dimly lit bar was a place I had never imagined myself in., honestly. It was convenient though. The pounding music and the hushed conversations was overwhelming, and I was able to just, sit and reflect on life, one I felt I was never truly part of outside of us. I sipped my drink, trying to blend into the shadows of the corner booth, nursing my solitude and my distaste for the men I was watching. Sleezy, disgusting men hitting on women who were just trying to have a drink and unwind. I hated it."

Hayley took a breath and slid to the side, resting against the door behind them. They reached across, taking my hand in theirs.

"I just sat there, feeling like an outsider in my own world, and a commotion erupted at the far end of the bar. I turned my head just in time to see a man lunging at a strikingly beautiful woman with raven hair, her glowing eyes were the color of rubies. Panic surged through me, and I realized something was *terribly* wrong. Her desperation was palpable, and I couldn't look away. There were several guys attacking her."

"And you couldn't sit by watching men attack a woman, right?" I asked, intently focused on her story.

"Guilty. Without thinking, I sprang into action, propelled by a rush of adrenaline I didn't know I possessed. I intercepted one of them, struggling to restrain him, and inadvertently shoved him into a table. The chaos that ensued was swift, glass shattering and patrons screaming, you know how it is. He was a lot stronger than he looked. I ducked under another one of them and was able to throw him off balance. Something inside me was happy that I was both fighting again and protecting someone. You know how protective I am of you."

I shook my head, listening as I started putting the pieces together.

"I backed into her, saw another guy draw a gun and I threw her to the side. That's when I heard it. The gunshot went through my ribs, and I didn't even feel the pain at first. I was just happy that she wasn't hit. She reminded me so much of you. My body hit the ground, and in the next few moments she had ripped each of them apart." Hayley let out a long, soft sigh and ran their fingers through their hair.

"A human shot you? Why didn't I hear any of that? Wouldn't something like that be breaking news?" I had wondered why they never made it to the rooftop bar to celebrate with us.

"They covered it up. The woman, the one I had saved, stood there with a mix of gratitude and a hint of surprise in her eyes. I could tell when she looked at me. She was different, her presence unmistakably otherworldly. She shared her name with me and extended her hand to help me to my feet. I gave her my name back, taking her hand as the pain coursed through my chest. I was barely able stand at that. When I looked over at them, I saw the black and white bands around their necks. They were from the church."

Hayley smiled, a rare warm one that I had never seen them with anyone outside of us.

"'Thank you, Hayley', she said, her voice like a haunting melody. Despite the pandemonium around us, her name resonated in my mind. Isabella Vasiliev. She was a vampire. A creature of the night, a legend that walked among us. My heart pounded not only from the fight but also from the knowledge of who stood before me. My heart rate tried to go up, but my lungs were slowly drowning me. She smiled gently at me. her eyes pitied me as she took in my dazed and battered appearance.

"You're injured,".

Hayley lifted up the side of their shirt, showing me the scar that was there. It was a small round blemish on their near perfect skin.

"A searing pain shot through my side, and I honestly cried. I hadn't realized that in the struggle, I'd actually been shot. Blood seeped from the wound, mingling with the spilled drinks on the floor. I watched her gaze lock onto my injury, and I couldn't help but feel her scrutiny. I knew what she was when she looked at me. She didn't even need my help at all."

"'I CAN HEAL YOU,' she offered, her voice a beautiful whisper. I was torn. To accept her help meant accepting a connection to a world I barely understood. But the pain was excruciating, and her offer was a lifeline. If I said no, there was no way I would ever get to see you again. I cried more at that thought, only being held up by her. As she leaned in closer, her lips grazing my ear, Isabella spoke with an eerie allure, 'Hayley, I can heal you, save you from this pain, and grant you a new life. All I need is your consent.'

Hayley looked at me, lifting my hand up to their soft lips as they kissed it.

"I didn't have a choice. My heart was racing. I knew this decision I was making would forever alter the course of my existence, and yours. In that moment of vulnerability and desperation, I nodded, my voice barely a whisper. " Please…Save me." That was all I could ask of her. And with a mixture of dread and hope, I felt her cold lips on my neck, the sensation of her fangs sinking into my flesh as she offered me the gift of immortality, and a new life forever intertwined with the aristocracy of the night. The first thing I thought of was how to bring you with me. As an apology and to thank me, she gifted me some of her blood."

I kissed their hand in response. "The blood you locked me up with. It was never meant for me, was it."

"No, I disobeyed my master, and now she is your master as well." Their voice hung heavy with guilt.

"She sent me to Rozenfleur in Austria for years as both a punishment but also to get me acclimated to my new life as fast as possible. That's where I earned my midnight brand."

"Rozenfleur? Sounds like a Swiss all girls school." I joked, trying to lighten the mood a bit.

"More like an all-vampire's military academy. It's where we send all members of our kind who have earned the rank of knight. If they are worthy to protect one of us, they must survive that place."

"And you ended up there?"

"Yes. Master sent me there as a kind of vampire bootcamp to unlock my bloodline as fast as possible. The academy also had a massive library, its shelves brimming with rare tomes and scrolls, their pages filled with arcane spells, ancient rituals, and the chronicles of vampire lore. It was a sanctuary of knowledge and a repository of the secrets of our kind. I spent many long nights in there, reading as much as I could."

"You still have time to read? Don't you have an empire to run?" I joked.

"What do you think I do in my free time? Not like *you* were here to keep me company."

"*Someone* locked me up for two hundred years."

"I don't have an excuse for that. I wanted you to not hate what I had become, and I wanted you to join me." Tears welled in their beautiful eyes, and they vaulted across the back seat of the vehicle, closing the distance and wrapping their arms around me. Their arms were a safe space where I knew I could fall apart when the world was crashing around me. Many nights had been spent in their arms as I cried. My parents' funeral, my dog passing away, my company getting its first investor.

Good, bad, general meltdown for spilling a drink. Hayley had always been there to help me hold the pieces together. We held each other with an intensity that only two beings who had shared lifetimes of love could understand. They lingered in that embrace, feeling the faint heartbeat that was almost absent but not forgotten, and we knew that our love was as immortal as they were.

In that moment, time lost all meaning, and I felt like we were once again united. Our love, forged through centuries of separation, had proven stronger than the march of time itself. And in the arms of each other, I found the eternity we had always sought, a testament to the enduring power of love among the stars. Hayley leaned backwards, bringing their forehead to touch mine. Their lips, full and inviting, captured my gaze as they drew nearer, and the world around us blurred into insignificance.

As their mouth met mine, I felt the warm, velvety touch of their lips, and an indescribable rush of emotions surged within me. The kiss was tender, an affirmation of the love that had endured centuries. Our lips melded together, and the sensation was like an electric spark, a mixture of fire and ice that pulsed through my cold, immortal body.

I bit my tongue, pulling my head away.

"I'm sorry. I have to tell you everything." Hayley looked at me, their forehead scrunching up with concern. "I destroyed the cemetery workers. They were doing construction."

Hayley gave out a light laugh. "I drank all of the Catholics in the bar. Master allowed me to see you again before we left. It's to be expected that you did that, your hunger and desires are so much stronger when you are first turned."

"That's not all."

"Who was it. Who touched you." Their demeanor shifted coldly.

"How could you know that?"

"I know the urges, and I ran the batteries out of my vibrator. I just wanted you."

"And I just wanted my wife. The guys didn't touch me, I promise. Sammy and them were quite helpful, actually." I paused, looking to the side. "But I lost control with one of their partners. A woman."

"One of their wives. You had sex with another vampire."

"Yes…and no. I did and didn't. I'm so so sorry. I couldn't control it, and she said it was better that way than with one of the guys."

"Where is she."

"Absolutely not." I cut Hayley off.

"Elaine." Hayley's tone was sharp. They were rightfully upset. I put my hands against the sides of their face, steading their eyes on me.

"I would never have made it back to you if it wasn't for them. They helped me, and if I hadn't been able to get through those first few days, and at least find a way back, I'd probably have been turned to ash already."

"I am NOT happy about this." I knew they weren't going to take it well. What should I have expected. I wrapped my hands around their cheeks, forcing a smile.

"Love. I'm so, so, sorry. I didn't know what to do or what was happening, and I was terrified and alone and afraid of everything."

"And someone named Sammy got a message to me."

"Sammy is her partner. I owe him. And her. And their friends. They covered up the mess I made, kept me fed and sheltered, and helped me get back to you."

I looked into their eyes, leaning my head up to meet theirs.

"I love you. And only you." Without waiting for any more word, I planted my lips on theirs. It had been far too long. There was a moment of coldness in their kiss, and for a second I thought they wouldn't want me anymore.

They melted into me, leaning completely into my body.

Our tongues danced in a silent exchange, a language of desire and intimacy that transcended words. Each touch and stroke were a testament to our enduring connection, a communion of souls that had spanned the ages. Our mouths moved in unison, each breath stoking the fire within us. My back landed on the door, my head leaving a soft thud on the window as I felt myself losing control. The windows slowly glazed over with a layer of misty residue from our heightened breath.

We pulled away from one another, both gasping for air as we looked into each other's eyes. In that moment, there was nothing in the world but us – no past or future, only an eternity of love and pleasure. I took their face in my hands and kissed Hayley on the forehead tenderly before leaning in for another kiss. We both smiled as we felt the intensity of our connection – a bond that no one could ever come between.

In that moment, I tasted the essence of our shared existence—the warmth of our love, the strength of our bond, and the power of our undying devotion. It was a kiss that affirmed our eternal commitment, a pledge to continue our journey through the endless night together.

"Hayley… we can't do this right now…" I said, lifting my head away from theirs.

"Shut up and enjoy this, Elle." They replied, leaning further into me with another kiss.

With every heartbeat, I felt the echoes of our love reverberate in every kiss. Having Hayley on top of me, sliding me down onto the seat as they climbed over me, sent fire across my body. The weight of our passion hung heavy in the air, as though the very universe held its breath in anticipation. The centuries-long yearning that had consumed us both culminated in this moment, where our hearts beat in unison, our bodies magnetically drawn together.

As Hayley's fingertips grazed my bare skin, a jolt of electricity coursed through my veins, sending shivers down my spine. Her touch was unlike anything I had ever experienced, hauntingly tender yet impossibly intense. Our eyes locked, momentarily suspended in time, as if the world around us had ceased to exist. It was in that instant that

I realized Hayley was not only my lover but my soulmate – a destined connection forged in the crucible of time that had survived the odds of our separation.

Hayley's lips brushed against mine, the softness of their touch akin to a feather's caress. In that single instant, my guarded walls crumbled, unveiling the depth of our desire. As our kiss deepened, a symphony of emotions swirled within me, heights of pleasure mingling with the vulnerability of opening myself completely to them. This had been centuries in the making.

Our bodies entwined and the passion between us intensified, transcending mere physicality. Each touch, each whisper of breath against my skin, carried an unspoken commitment, a declaration of love unbound by societal norms and inhibitions. Lost in a sea of ecstasy, the world became a distant memory, our connection the only beacon guiding us through the abyss of eternity. It had been far too long since we had shared such intimacy together.

Hayley's fiery gaze pierced through me, their eyes a reflection of the depths of our shared love. With every loving gesture, they painted a masterpiece upon my body, illustrating the intricacies of a love so profound that those on the mortal plane could only dream of its existence. Together, we defied convention, shattering the chains that bound us, our love flooding any thoughts of the world around us.

Our tangled limbs, twisted around each other with cold sweat that made our clothes cling to our bodies, ripped as we moved and readjusted. My body felt alive as Hayley's gentle but urgent touch electrified every inch of me. Their fingernails lightly traced up and down my inner thigh, sending shivers all over my skin. I felt their lips moving lower and lower, their soft breath creating an intoxicating mix of warmth and pleasure. I could feel myself growing more and more aroused as they explored and discovered the secrets of my body.

I closed my eyes, savoring every moment as their tongue danced against me with dangerous precision. With each movement I felt myself closer to the edge of something long forgotten yet so deeply desired. My back arched off the seat as their hand moved between my legs, encouraging me on a journey without end.

My hands tangled in her hair while I pressed down onto their head, feeling its silkiness against me. I crossed my ankles behind their body as they lifted me further up, pushing my thighs around either side of their head while devouring me wantonly. I gasped for air as we moved together in an almost choreographed dance of passion that seemed to have no end.

"More, all of it, everything, I want more-" My knees hit the back of the passenger seat; my hands wrapped around Hayley's head while my fingers moved through their hair. Every moment of touch they gave me sent a light moan from my lips that sent me back to our third date, a night I would never forget.

Finally, I felt my body give in to the pleasure as I reached the ultimate peak. Hayley slowly backed away, leaving me breathless and trembling in ecstasy. As I lay there, I could feel my heart pounding, the evidence of our mutual pleasure still wet on my thighs. I opened my eyes, already knowing that I wanted more. Had I known we were rocking the entire vehicle, I may have moved us inside to our bedroom.

We continued, losing track of time and Hayley didn't quit, taking me back to that edge over and over. On the fourth time, my body straightened, and my right foot smashed into the window, shattering it. The sound of glass breaking sent the guards outside the car scrambling around at full alert. Hayley and I held our breath for a moment, and then we laughed at each other. I pulled them up on top of me and curled my arms around them so that I could plant my lips on theirs again, tasting the sweetness of myself on her tongue.

"Let's get you food, and some clean clothes."

"Nothing wrong with *another* shower, just let me get the feeling back in my legs." I smiled at them, letting my body relax in eternal satisfaction. We slid apart from each other while laughing lightheartedly, as if nothing in the world could tear us apart.

We pulled ourselves together and got out of the car to awkward looks from the guards. Some of them looked away from us, ignoring eye contact. I couldn't keep myself from laughing and grabbed Hayley's hand, pulling them around the side and towards the stairs.

Two of the guards were posted at the top of the entrance and pulled the doors open for us. Both looked away awkwardly as I realized they could smell us. I nearly skipped in while holding their hand. Hayley pulled me backwards and scooped me up, carrying me up the spiral staircase and down the hall towards our room. I kept my head buried in their neck, taking little nibbles out of the side of their cold skin.

"Shower?" Hayley suggested, their voice a soft whisper against my ear. I nodded, a small smile playing on my lips when they sat me down. I looked across the room towards where a large opened was cut into the wall. All I could do was assume that it was where the shower was held.

Hand in hand, we walked towards the bathroom, our bodies still humming from our recent lovemaking. The bathroom was a sanctuary, a place where we could be ourselves without any pretense. The warm glow from the overhead lights reflected off the marble tiles, creating a serene ambiance. I had never been in Hayley's bathroom before, and it was beautiful.

A massive, claw-footed bathtub stood at the center of the room, its porcelain surface adorned with delicate floral motifs, and it was so large that it seemed to be a pool of its own. The faucets were ornate, gold-plated fixtures with intricately carved handles. They seemed like relics from a bygone era, and the water flowed from them with a melodious cascade into the deep basin. A series of gilded mirrors framed in intricately detailed frames adorned the walls, reflecting the room's splendor from multiple angles. The mirrors seemed to multiply the sense of space and grandeur, creating a sense of endless elegance.

In one corner of the bathroom, a grand, marble vanity held an array of exquisite toiletries and perfumes, each container a work of art in itself. The mirror above the vanity was framed by sconces, casting a soft, flattering light that accentuated the beauty of anyone who gazed upon their reflection.

The shower was a chamber of its own, enclosed with clear, etched glass panels and adorned with a rain showerhead and multiple body jets. The controls for the water pressure and temperature were exquisitely designed, allowing for a tailored and indulgent bathing experience.

The room was complete with the finest linens, plush towels, and silk robes, all stored in elegantly crafted cabinets and drawers. The overall ambiance was one of sumptuous comfort and refinement. There were black crystals wrapped in golden thread hanging from several places in the shower, most likely a remnant of Hayley's days as a practicing witch before they were turned.

Hayley turned on the shower by touching a piece of glass built into the marble wall, adjusting the temperature to a comfortable warmth. I was excited by the technology and always hoped for something high tech in my bathroom one day. It didn't have to be over complicated; I would be satisfied with listening to music or morning news while I got ready in the mornings. Steam began to fill the room, fogging up the mirror and creating a dreamy atmosphere. They stepped into the shower, the warm water cascading down our bodies, washing away the remnants of our passionate encounter outside I almost felt bad for whoever had to clean up our mess later.

We were both always cold to the touch. But under the warm water, our skin felt almost human-like. I ran my hands over Hayley's body, tracing the curves and lines with a familiarity that only comes from years of intimacy.

They closed their eyes, leaning into my touch. Even though they were a vampire, there was no way they were immune to the pleasures of the flesh. After the amount of tongue work, I had received in the car, I was overly happy to reciprocate here. The warm water, combined with my touch, was a sensory delight for them.

I lowered to my knees, kissing every curve on their body. Every inch of their skin I touched, caressing each part of their body with my mouth. My head slipped slowly down between their legs. My body trembled as I licked my way up their inner legs, savoring the sweet taste of their skin with each playful nibble. Their eyes burned with passion and an intense desire as they gasped with pleasure with every stroke of my tongue. As I looked into their eyes with mine, they clenched around me in a vicious grip, writhing in ecstasy and forcing my head back between their legs. I felt their yearning radiating through every inch of my being.

My fingers moved up their body, caressing every curve on the way. I felt them shudder and moan with pleasure as my touch teased them. My head slipped between their legs, and they gasped in delight. Their soft thighs were like velvet against my skin as I kissed every inch of her. I looked up into their eyes, which were filled with so much desire that it almost took my breath away.

Their legs quivered around me as I explored further, exploring every nook and curve with my tongue until I reached their most sensitive spot. They moaned in pleasure and their hands clutched onto the sides of the shower walls for support as they started to tremble uncontrollably.

I felt their body trembling around me and heard them groaning softly as they came closer to the edge. For a moment, I pulled my tongue back in and stopped, holding them there with nothing, but that feeling of being right there at the precipice.

"Don't you dare," they said breathlessly. I bit down gently on their most sensitive spot and ran my hands along their thighs, feeling them quiver beneath me. I then moved my mouth back up to their neck and kissed them deeply as I teased them with my tongue Hayley grabbed my shoulders, lowering me back down to my knees.

"That's a good girl."

My hands began exploring further while their moans grew louder. They begged for more as I continued to lavish attention onto every inch of them. I explored each area of their body until they were shaking uncontrollably in pleasure, unable to contain it any longer.

Their muscles tightened around me, and I felt Hayley grab my hair, wrapping their hands through it as they shuddered in ecstasy, pushing me deeper into them until finally I felt them release in a powerful wave of pleasure that left us both completely drained yet satisfied. We stayed there for a while afterwards, panting and trying to regain our composure before we finally started to take an actual shower together, letting the warmth of the water wash away all our troubles.

We took turns washing each other, our movements slow and deliberate. There was no rush, no urgency. Just the two of us, in our own little world, enjoying the simple pleasure of a shared shower. Just like we used to. As we rinsed off, I pulled Hayley close, our bodies pressing together under the warm water. They leaned down, capturing my lips in a slow, languid kiss. It was a kiss filled with love, passion, and a promise of forever.

Once they were done, they stepped out of the shower, wrapping themselves in fluffy towel. I stayed in the shower, enjoying the heated rain shower that washed over me. They stood in front of the fogged-up mirror, their reflections blurred and indistinct. But they didn't need a mirror to see themselves. Hayley turned to the open shower door and saw themselves in my eyes, a reflection that captured my love for them.

As we walked back to their bedroom, hand in hand, I knew that we had something special again. I had thought that my love would grow cold and harsh after being locked away for so long. After I had been tortured by Addison for so long. After I had been dead for so long. They had never lost their love, and that was all that mattered. Hayley kissed me again, and backed up, dropping their towel from their back. I let my wet body move over to the bed, dropping right onto the bottom of it. For a quick moment, I watched as their demeanor shifted from carefree to serious and focused.

"Take your time getting dressed, our master would like to meet with you. I'm heading downstairs, join us in a few minutes?"

"Is everything okay?" I asked, wondering if they were in trouble, if I had done something to upset our master.

"She has summoned me." Hayley said casually, planting her lips on mine. They moved across the room and quickly pulled on a pair of leggings and a baggy sweater. I watched closely, taking notice of the nicks and scars that I had never seen on their skin before.

Hayley regarded their maker with an almost reverential awe, recognizing the Countess as a source of wisdom, power, and an embodiment of their immortal heritage. Ireena's age, experience, and the knowledge she possessed were a beacon of guidance for Hayley, and they knew that heeding the summons was a testament to her unwavering devotion. I could understand the respect that they felt for our master, but I didn't really fully grasp it. A summons from their master was a reminder of the inherent power dynamics within their vampire world. The call demanded immediate attention, and Hayley's compliance was not a matter of choice but of necessity.

I stood in the bright ballroom of the manor that was lined with crimson velvet, the walls adorned with ancient tapestries and flickering candles that continued to cast eerie shadows despite the light. Ireena Vasiliev, the enigmatic Blood Countess, my maker, and mentor in the ways of the night, sat before me with her glowing eyes. She was as timeless and regal as the night itself. Every time I was in her presence, I could sense the power held within her existence. Hayley was posted in a black, wingback chair on her right, reflective of her status as well as her duty.

"Elaine," she spoke, her voice a seductive murmur that held centuries of knowledge and power. "You are *far* behind the other children in both power and experience."

I met her gaze, my once deep brown eyes now a softer shade inherited from her, reflecting the intrigue and curiosity that swirled within me.

"What do you mean, my master? What awaits me now?"

"You were lucky against Addison. Luck won't be enough to keep you alive."

I looked over at Hayley who just smiled back at me.

Lady Ireena stood up and approached me, her fingers cold but delicate as she touched my cheek, an intimate gesture that conveyed the depth of her care.

"I am sending you to *Rozenfleur*, the academy of our kind hidden within the heart of the Alps. It is a sacred ground and once there, you will learn the arts and traditions of our kind, hone your abilities, and gain the knowledge you need to navigate the intricacies of the immortal world."

The mention of Rozenfleur sent a shiver of excitement and apprehension down my spine. It was a place shrouded in legend, a sanctuary for vampires, where the secrets of the night were taught, and the heritage of our kind was preserved.

Ireena continued, her voice tinged with a mixture of pride and sadness.

"I just got here though. Hayley and I---"

"Hayley is a soldier. You are not. And this is not a discussion."

I lowered my head, the thought of being away from them for even one day causing my chest to tighten.

"You are my daughter, and you will one day grow into a formidable member of the aristocracy, Elaine, and I believe it's time for you to embrace your true potential just as your wife did before you. *Rozenfleur* will provide you with the tools you need to thrive in our world."

I nodded in understanding, feeling a surge of both gratitude and responsibility. Rozenfleur was both an honor and a challenge, a path I was eager yet nervous to undertake. I just hadn't expected it to be so quick.

"Master, I am ready to follow your guidance... I swear to not disappoint you, my mother or Hayley."

A faint smile touched her lips, and she pulled me into an ice-cold embrace. In her strong, frigid arms, I felt the connection between maker and progeny, the lineage of our kind that extended through the ages. I would have never thought she was one to be a fan of physical contact, and despite her size, she was far stronger than I was. Was this how Hayley had felt? I was caught off guard by the action and looked at Hayley with widened eyes. Their hand rose up to cover their mouth as they held in a laugh.

"Elaine, never forget that you are a Vasiliev, a lineage that holds both power and responsibility. May Rozenfleur guide you and may your journey through the night be filled with wisdom and strength. Hayley will be here when you return."

"How long will I be gone?"

"Until you are ready to return. Some of our kind spend decades there. Others spend a year. What you put into the experience you will have returned ten-fold, so I ask that you not rush so that you may learn and grow." Ireena released me and floated back over to her seat.

"But does that mean I might not see Hayley for that long? I worked really, really hard to get here…"

"And they worked really, really hard to build a place for you two to love each other as your true selves. Even among our kind, there are members of the old guard who look down upon your kind of relationship. If you are to become their true equal, you will have to take these steps forward on *your* own. It is your duty to stand against those who would bring you harm."

I noticed her tone shift sharply, an obvious change in her demeanor accompanying it.

"But, years? That's so long and-"

"It is inconsequential to the eternity you have been given." Ireena cut me off, a flicker or crimson moving through her eyes. "Hayley, does your wife always complain this much?"

"My apologies, master. Yes." Hayley tried to keep a straight face, and I glared at her.

"Rude." I said, tilting my head and looking straight at my wife.

"Elaine Reinhardt, my progeny, by my command, once you depart you will not speak of your relationship to Hayley or I until the day you return here, or Hayley comes to retrieve you. I forbid your use of our bloodline until you earn the title of knight."

I could feel the panic hit me all at once, the anxiety of potentially losing my wife right after I had returned was a cold wave that swept across my body. Hayley leaned over to a man standing next to her, whispering something as he bowed down. I stood there in silence, a thousand thoughts racing through my mind. It felt my entire world was crashing down on me again.

"Master… I…"

"Not. A. Discussion. Hayley was dropped there with the same restrictions. Prove to your wife that you are deserving of her. Prove to me that my daughter did not waste two hundred years for nothing, that every day *you* hurt your wife out of spite was worth forgiving." I could have thrown up on the marble floor in front of her at her words. She was right on all accounts.

"But our bloodline? I can't use any of it? What will I be without that?" I had relied on that power for everything.

"That's the point. You took from me without my permission, and now you must earn the right to use it."

"I had no idea that was your blood."

"That doesn't matter. This isn't punishment for you, it's for Hayley." Hayley's head turned to the side with a quick jerk.

"Master?" Hayley said with an air of concern.

"Quiet. Did you think I wouldn't punish you for this? It's a perfect opportunity for Elaine to show her worth, and for you to get your lovestruck head out of your ass and do your job." She rubbed her forehead and sighed.

"There's now a void in the Americas, courtesy of your wife. It's your job to unite this coast and prepare to become the American seat."

"What about Lady Nell?"

"You know she cares more about who is in her bed than doing her job. She has wanted more freedom and has agreed to give it up and act in an advisory role. You will have the time you need to restructure the eastern seaboard. Victoire and Amile will be joining you to assist."

"Do my cousins believe I need that much assistance? Insulting."

"No. I do. Especially after the disappointment of the last year."

"But master."

Her hand lifted off the arm of her chair, silencing Hayley. "You two were made for each other. I will deal with my brother, and you will deal with absorbing his territory. Now, don't you have something to do?"

Hayley smiled at our master and hopped up to their feet with a wide grin.

"My love, would you join me out on the patio?" Hayley said loudly, walking down and grabbing my hand. I was still panicking when they jerked me to the side. I caught a glimpse of a rare smile cross our master's face as they led me through draped velvet curtains and out onto a large balcony.

Two centuries of longing, of separation, and now my beloved Hayley and I stood together once more, bathed in the soft light of the moon. I was so afraid of losing them again. So afraid of waking up and being back in that coffin again. Their hair shimmered in the night, and their bright red eyes, filled with the warmth of love, held my gaze with an intensity that took my breath away.

I watched, my heart pounding, as Hayley knelt before me, their eyes never leaving mine. In an outstretched hand, Hayley held a velvet box, and within it lay a radiant, centuries-old engagement ring that had witnessed the passage of time as our love had.

"Elaine," they spoke, their voice a melodic whisper, "over two centuries ago, I pledged my love and devotion to you. In all the time we were apart, not a moment went by that I didn't long for your presence. There was a gap in my life, a void that I was unable to fill without you by my side. Now, as we stand together, I want to renew that pledge and propose to you all over again. Elaine Catherine Reinhardt... "

Tears welled in my eyes and my heart swelled with a love that had never waned. The ring, an heirloom of our immortal existence, was a symbol of the unbreakable bond we shared. I looked at it, the giant starburst sapphire surrounded by diamonds. With trembling fingers, they slid it onto my finger, its ancient beauty an embodiment of our enduring love. A halo of glittering stoned wrapped down around the band, glistening in the starlight.

The moonlight cast a gentle glow on us as they continued, "Will you marry me again? Will you be my eternal partner, my beloved, and my heart's desire for all time? Will you spend this eternity with me?"

My voice caught in my throat as I whispered, "Yes, Hayley, a thousand times yes. I will be yours for all of eternity, just as I have always been."

I leapt up off of the ground and wrapped my arms around them again. Kissing them furiously, they held onto me, lifting my feet off the ground as I tried to kiss them as many times as possible to make up for the centuries, we had been apart. I would never be able to get enough of them.

"We will plan a wedding when you return. There are some rules that we have to navigate, but I'll take care of all of that. Master is giving us a week together to get our things in order and make up for lost time and then Lady Antanasia will escort you overseas. I'll keep in touch, so don't go thinking I'm just going to leave you alone somewhere you've never been. I love you. Too much at times, and too much to ever put us through that again."

I grinned. There was a lot of lost time to make up for. And a week wasn't going to be enough.

"Never again, promise?"

"I promise. Forever this time." I looked up at the starry sky above the city, smiling. I had always wanted to go to space as a child, and I found comfort in the night sky.

"How many stars do you think are up there?" Hayley said, wrapping their arm around me while looking up.

"I don't know, I lost track after the first million."

FIRST LOOK

Tears of Starlight

ROZENFLEUR

*J*ules, joined by another assistant, carried my luggage through the halls of our manor. Hayley and I walked slowly, dodging the renovation teams and construction crew that had been called in to repair the damage we had inflicted. The estate held seven guest bedrooms, and six of them were currently going through some form of repairs. Our maker had granted us an extra week, and that had been spent getting lost in each other as we let our bodies catch up from two and a half centuries apart.

I had *zero* interest in going to Rozenfleur, and knowing the car was outside waiting for me I wanted nothing more than to lock myself away and refuse to leave. To refuse a command from my maker. Part of me was afraid to try, but the part of me that had always been a bit rebellious wanted to know how far I could push it with her. Hayley walked me all the way down to the black SUV where Lady Antanasia was already waiting for me.

Hayley wrapped their arms around me and gave me a kiss, a smile forming as their lips broke from mine.

"I know you're anxious. I had trouble adjusting to their rigid way of life, and their instructors are a bit old fashioned."

"I'm not anxious" I lied. "I just don't want to go."

"I'm sorry, love. You have to be able to protect yourself. I can't always be there, and I have to be away for a bit to finish settling the territory you just won us."

Right. The territory I won when I burned Duke Konrad's first born alive in front of him. I knew I'd made an enemy out of my makers brother, a blood grudge that he would never forget.

And grudges lasted a long time when you had eternity at your fingertips.

"I know." I looked away from them, trying not to be sad about having to leave so soon.

"Don't do that, Elle. I know you're upset; I can feel you, remember?" They smiled at me, their hand tucking a piece of hair behind my ear.

"I don't want to leave." I could hear them putting my luggage into the back, the door slamming shut behind me. "Maybe you can talk to Lady Ireena and—"

"Stop. I agree with her. You're a child with a really big sword right now, and the only way you're ever going to learn to use it is there. You need guidance, and despite my hatred of that place, I wouldn't be able to do what I do without it. And I'm not equipped to teach you either."

They stepped by me and opened the back door, then wrapped their arms around me one final time.

"I love you. Your time away is going to be over before you know it, and you'll be right back here. I promise."

"What if.."

"No, Elaine."

My body stiffened as they said my name. There was a coldness to it that I rarely ever heard them speak to me with. They pulled away from me, gave me a kiss and walked back up to the stairs of our home.

"I love you, Elaine. You'll be back soon." They tried to force a smile, but I could tell they knew I wasn't happy about this.

"I love you..." I begrudgingly got in the back seat, Lady Antanasia sitting in the back with a glass of wine waiting for me. Someone outside the car shut the door and I turned my head to the large manor, wondering when, if ever, I would get to see it again.

ACKNOWLEDGMENTS

Meg: You are the most amazing person in the world, my best friend, my source of reason, my rock, and my wife. Without your constant love, support, and cheering, I would never have taken the dive and finished this work. You are my guiding star, the beacon that keeps me moving forward one page at a time. Thank you for taking the time to read, review, and whiteboard this project with me, even when I was more impatient than a child during Yule. There is not enough love in the universe for me to give to you.

Rachel and Chelsey: This book is live because you two wouldn't let me doubt myself. When I said I was not an author, you wouldn't let me accept that I was anything but. And now it's here, and live, and I made it because you both pushed me forward. Thank you – for everything. Every chat, every crazy idea, every bit of insanity that I threw at you. Your feedback and analysis have been a key part of this series, and I can't wait for you to see what's coming next.

Katie: Late night chats, asking when the next chapter will be done, and being in my corner over Covid will never be forgotten. My best friend and sister, there is no one I trust more to have my back than you. You know how grateful I am for all of the adventures past and future our friendship has brought us. You will always be my favorite Jersey Girl and I never would have made it this far without you. You were there for some of the best and worst parts of my life, and I am so thankful for you.

Victoria: When we first talked about bringing art in the style of tarot cards into this world, I knew you would think I was crazy. Instead, you said 'lets do it'. You have captured the magic of each of these characters and places and allowed people to see the same vision that I did. Thank you for everything, and I can't wait to see what we do next.

Ruby Lou: Thank you for giving me first look reactions to scenes. You've been an amazing friend, cheerleader and book nerd that helped Meg drag me through fantasy worlds. Your support and feedback have been indescribably helpful, and I would never have made it this far without you as part of my inner circle.